I0671264

A BSOLUTE
H ORROR

ROB E. NICHOLS

lustwrathgreedenvygluttonypridesloth

absolute horror

copyright 2015
published rob e. nichols and octivium
cover art by rob e. nichols
written by rob e. nichols
edited by rob e. nichols

This novel is dedicated to my wife and daughter.

Krystal and Ana,

Everything I create is because of the person you have helped me become.

You are my muses.

I love you both.

an uncomfortable realization

In the first minute, a sinner woke up with a shiver.

The sinner saw black. The numbing cold caused him physical pain; His joints ached underneath throbbing muscles and strained against his stiff movements. Fresh pain shot through his head. He opened his eyes, expecting hangover pains from the morning sun, but blackness remained. In a blind burst of confusion, he pushed himself onto all fours. He crawled a pace or two on his hands and knees, no more than a lost, broken dog, though lacking the senses of a canine, the unfamiliarity overpowered him.

Smooth tile kissed the sinner's palms. The blindness and pain reminded him of a concussion he suffered in high school.

The sinner had been on the football team. During the last game he ever played, he had been running the ball in for a touchdown. An opposing player tackled him hard, from behind, and with grabby hands. He was hit hard enough that the face mask had been ripped from his helmet in sync with the muscle in his calf ripping from the bone. The concussion and leg injuries healed over time, but his spirit had broken with his body. The thought of taking another violent hit crippled him in a way that even ripping his muscle couldn't. Instead of admitting weakness, he aspired for individual success in a less violent sport: swimming.

Swimming had been a part of the sinner's rehabilitation. The water calmed him. The water cheered with the hushed sound of filters and flow noise. Football pressured a player to please the crowd, the school, the town. Man vs. World. The pool was the antithesis of a football stadium. It pressured a player to please himself. Man vs. Self. Every stroke strengthened his body and his resolve that he was finished with football. His coach, no stranger to football injury, was the only person sincere in both his support and his understanding. Nobody was going to tackle him to hard dirt in the soft water.

These memories flashed behind the sinner's eyes. Every sense struck him with intense realism; each flash was a cell shown through the lens of a clumsy and realistic movie projector. Even the light of these memories had realistic resonance, though the faux illumination of these memory flashes hurt, like bullets shot from the past and picking up speed as they traveled. He cleared his thoughts and switched to more recent memories. From blinding remembrance to cold contemplation, the pain remained.

The sinner remembered mixing codeine prescribed for his nagging back pain with the anti-depressant prescribed after the death of his sister. He washed the pills down with a beer or three, ignoring warning labels to the contrary. In his opinion, warning labels were guidelines for lightweights. Having never woken up in strange place or experiencing such a severe headache, he guess it was time to re-evaluate his opinion. The one thing he could recall was how warm his bed had been, a stark comparison to the crypt-like cold of where he had woken up.

In the second minute, the sinner was approached by fear.

The sinner denied fears advances and focused.

The sinner remembered Sheila. Or was it Shirley?

Whoever the woman from the bar had been, she had fallen asleep as he debated the second codeine pop. He was quick to dismiss her as a suspect for his dilemma. She couldn't have scammed him, and she lacked the strength to lift and move him. Not an ounce of her ninety pounds was muscle. It was unlikely that she could have reached friends with muscle while handcuffed to the bed. She wore the restraints during their wild night of what he passed for love making. She fallen into her deep slumber without a single request to remove them.

Whatever had happened, he should have been able to prevent it. He hadn't been cuffed.

Not him. Never him.

A small echo reverberated; an echo like the first drop of rain on a metal awning. The echo repeated to his left every few seconds. A few drips in, he realized that the sound was moving. The dripping grew closer and louder with each echo, the audible salivation of an invisible monster.

A drop splashed his hand. He jerked it out of the way and trembled. The sound circled behind him and moved to his right.

Curious, he lifted a finger to his lips to flick his tongue at the moisture.

The taste of salt whet the sinner's curiosity. He lived nowhere near a salty body of water. Was it a cave? He couldn't remember if stalactites were salty or if they dripped or if bats had audible orgasms;

the breadth of his cave knowledge was that Batman had one. He didn't need the world's greatest detective to tell him that dripping salt water meant there was an opening somewhere.

In the third minute, the sinner's fear calmed.

Stupid, stupid fear.

The water continued circling the room. On the second lap, water splashed the sinner on the back. He turned onto his ass and scrambled backwards a few feet, sure he looked like a dog scratching away at worms in rewind. Pain screamed with every movement. He whipped his head around, ignoring the pain and desperate for an answer.

Where the fuck am I?

The sinner read an article many years before describing torture methods used throughout history. This reminded him of one of the more brutal methods.

The iron maiden, first used in the nineteenth century, was a torture device that offered release to the lucky. The spikes that lined the door pierced deep into the flesh when closed. If sheer pain or shock didn't leave the victim unconscious, they bled until Death, whistling a tune and swinging a sickle, found them. If the victim was sure of their fate and not lacking in testicular or cervical fortitude, they pushed against the spikes to hasten the process.

The Spanish Inquisition brought torture to a whole new level. Heretics who would not repent the sins that most of them did not commit were burned, prodded, poked, and bled out. Men's penises were sheathed by scalding hot clamps. Heathens were forced to sit in chairs covered with red hot spikes that left permanent scars in unspeakable places. Any combination of metal and heat that caused severe pain and probable cessation of life were invented by the Catholics during those dark ages.

Bloodletting, stoning, beheading, and plethora methods of torture that caused severe pain before death.

To the sinner, water torture topped them all. No pain. No scarification. No heat or metal. A person didn't gain a physical handicap. Death was a seldom offered gift. Damage to the psyche, not death, was the goal, though the pieces of consciousness that made up a man seldom survived the process.

A person would be restrained under a slow drip of ice water. Those with strong will called the bluff and claimed the method ludicrous. Water wasn't a weapon. Water was life! And water claimed life. He had intimate knowledge of that fact, and the knowledge never ceased to haunt him.

The straps would be tightened and the flow would begin. After minutes, depression came knocking.

Thought turned into nonsensical dead weight. Fueled by fatigue, annoyance, and the constant freezing drop, a person started to get cranky and sick to their stomach. Not enough to succumb, but enough to begin considering the different options giving up might offer, if for no other reason than to take their mind off of the drip. A few more minutes, and panic reared above the dark places within their mind, a stealth serpent waiting to strike. Numb and delirious, a person who still possessed the capacity for logic understood how water could destroy what even the mightiest armies couldn't touch.

The more pride and will power a person possessed, the longer they remained the table being kissed by drops of ice water. Those traits, full of valor and envied by most, left their minds and spirits broken. The strong survived as shells of their former selves, driven insane by traits that had once defined them. The weak remained weak. Regret and shame gave them secret solace and left their senses intact.

There were worse fates than guilt. Water torture did not produce martyrs.

The ingenuity of the world's oldest culture was sick, smart, and effective. The sinner was trapped in the evolution of that ingenuity.

In the fourth minute, the sinner began to unravel.

When the dripping became a steady flow, the sinner grew more afraid. The smell of salt in the air stung his nose; the ice water droplets ricocheting off of the ground stung his body.

The sinner had alienated every person he had ever known. He was a penniless creature of envy and shame. Nobody in the world would respond to a ransom note left in his place. That knowledge stung worst of all.

The sinner vowed, upon escape, to never again sleep with Sheila. Or Shirley.

Whatever the fuck her name was.

I'll find whoever did this to me and return the favor seven fold. Fucking bastards!

Delirium advanced forward as each detail of the situation dove head first into the lake of nonsense that filled the room.

Brave thoughts ran through the mind of the sinner until the icy water reached his body. Wherever he was, it was sealed tight. The room would soon be full, and he would drown. It was the one detail that refused to take a plunge.

Knowledge, sense, and rational thought lost potency. A mantra looped, a skipping record playing to the monsters stepping out of the closets of his nightmares.

Water gives life. Water takes life. Water is life.

The sinner was terrified of drowning.

Climbing to his feet with care he began to shuffle forward, with useless eyes and outstretched hands, until he ran into something solid. Pain shot through his fingertips, up through his elbows, and spread through his shoulders. Soreness caused even glancing contact with an object hurt. He dragged his hands along the surface of a wall, caring little about the small stings of pain.

The texture was like solid, sharp stucco. When he put pressure on the wall, the pain in his hands worsened. He shook and wiped his hands on his shirt, hoping the pain was from broken debris, and touched the wall again. The results were the same.

The sinner tried one more time to wipe whatever was causing him pain off of his hands, using his chest instead. Doing the same thing and expecting different results. Insanity defined.

The sinner brought his fingers to his lips. What he tasted was salty, though it wasn't water, and it wasn't cold.

It was the unmistakable rust of warm blood.

Panic had been taking a smoke break since the sinner opened his eyes. The taste of blood was the stubbing of the butt. The realization of blood was the shutting of the screen door. Panic had officially joined the party, bringing along two of his best friends. Irrationality and shaky bladder control.

The sinner shuffled sideways along the wall. New cuts bit into his hands and were ignored. He searched for a door or a lever or a handle with his hands; he searched for an escape. Every few steps, water flowed onto him. He would shiver, shake, and side step the flow.

The sinner hit a wall with his shoulder. He tried not to focus on the stabbing sensation that coupled the bump. He turned ninety degrees and continued along the wall. Logic was still fighting. The water had reached his ankles.

The sinner found another wall, more pain, and made another

turn. He was finding nothing as the water rose faster. At calf level, the sound of faucets was drowned out by the sound of a fire hose. The irony, that the sound indicated his imminent death instead of a warm fire blanket and a sense of renewed life did not escape him.

The strange material on the wall took small pieces of flesh from the sinner's hands. He felt the water rising faster up his legs. Though he welcomed the numbness that took away the pain, he knew that his success in finding an exit would determine how far the numbness would reach.

The water reached the sinner's lower buttocks. Small waves began crashing into his body from the sources of the flow. When the water reached his lower abdomen, he balled his hands into fists and struck the wall, ignoring the jetting pain and screaming "WHY?" to absent ears.

In a moment of clarity, the sinner wondered if he could find the answer on the floor instead of the walls. Cave's had tunnels, after all. He hadn't just appeared in the room. Like a magician submerged in a box of water, he had to find the source of the illusion. The rest would be easy!

Unless the illusion had gone wrong. Not every entrance doubled as an exit.

The sinner breathed deep and plunged beneath the water. The salt licked his fresh scrapes and cuts. He moved his hands along the ground, searching for anything other than the slick surface of the smooth tile. He found nothing and returned to his feet.

Taking another deep breath, the sinner tasted the salt in his mouth. He wondered how long it would be before the water brought him to the ceiling. One man's ceiling was another man's floor. A ceiling could mean a trap door.

The higher the water level, the less of the precious air would remain. If he couldn't find an exit, he would be breathing in the black water that was entombing him, and his struggling would end.

In the fifth minute, the water reached the sinner's chest.

The sinner dove beneath the water once more and let his water trained legs guide him around the floor. His search for an escape grew more frantic.

It had become a nightmarish ritual. The sinner repeated it for as long as each breath let him.

The sinner breathed in deep and dove.

The water level continued to rise.

The sinner resurfaced and braced for footing.

Eventually, his feet no longer touched the floor. Hope had mocked him with each break of the surface. He had nothing to show for the air and time he had wasted.

The sinner dove again and smacked his head against a sharp wall. Even underneath churning water, the distinct dizziness of disorientation took precedence for a few moments, moments where even panic, the uninvited party guest, was quiet. Those few seconds were the happiest he had ever experience.

Panic wouldn't let him relax for long. He was sure that every unsuccessful dive would deliver him to freedom. So close to the wall, the dives brought nothing but fresh cuts. So many more cuts.

One more breath, and one more dive.

As the sinner kicked his legs to resurface, his hand brushed against a metallic object that moved at his touch. The object made a sound he could barely translate under the water. It had a familiar texture, heavy and grooved and rough.

It was freedom. He had found freedom, against all odds. And freedom felt like a chain.

The sinner grabbed for the chain. He caressed the links and loops to confirm his suspicion, ignoring his the pain in his chest warning him surface. He would handle the pain when he was safe and dry. He was willing to sacrifice anything short of his life to pull that chain.

The sinner's lungs screamed for air before he could get a grip. The shock loosened his hands when will power wouldn't let him. The chain was dropped, but not lost. He kicked upward, as straight as possible, so as not to lose bearing of his ray of hope.

Straight up, straight down, pull the plug. A simple plan to end the hopeless ritual.

The moment should have been triumphant. The sinner kicked with all of his strength to escape the surface for that one last breath. The breath promised salvation. His body exploded upward. He found precious air and mild waves. Inches above the surface, his head found the unforgiving ceiling.

The top of the sinner's skull flattened. The bone beneath fragmented into his brain. The skin did not break. From what he could tell, there was no trap door.

The sinner went limp. He no longer felt pain or panic as his body bobbed against the ceiling, so he had that going for him. In time, his body sank towards his unrealized escape path.

The sinner had one final path of thought as the icy water filled his lungs with salty fire. His pitiful life did not flash through his consciousness. His little sister Sarah and her terrible death did.

The sinner was supposed to protect Sarah with his life, as dictated by blood. He had loved and adored her for her grace, humility, and kindness. He also envied her, and that envy turned into selfish apathy. She died because he gave up, and his death would mimic hers because karma came around for everybody in the end. Like the day she died, nobody would be there to save him.

Sarah had died in the sinner's pool while he had slept off a hang-over on the couch. He had not heard her head smack on the diving board or her bloodcurdling scream before she hit the water.

Sarah could have been saved, had he not failed her.

The sinner could not be saved because he had failed himself.

I wonder if Sarah felt this hopelessn. This pain. My God, little sis, I'm so fucking sorry. I should have been there spotting you. I should have saved you! It's over for me. I'll see you soon, little sis! And I'll spend eternity making it up to you. I swear it.

Like most promises the sinner had made in life, the promise was empty and impossible.

In the sixth minute, the sinner died.

The story of the sinner's pain and torment hadn't gone so far as the first letter of the prologue.

Water takes life. Water gives life. Water is life.

In the seventh minute, the sinner woke up with a shiver.

CHAPTER 1

cocaine blues and seeing red

Kyle Thimall took a deep snort and tilted back his head as the cocaine entered his system.

Contrary to what Hollywood movies portrayed, the tilt was not handbook method to prolonging the high. The tilt made certain that little of the precious powder fell from the nose, forever lost and never to be savored.

Starlets and stock brokers were able to wear cocaine mustaches like cheap crochets on prom night. They laughed with the annoying shrieks of the giddy cheerleaders who found excitement in tokens of eventual (and terrible) sex. Kyle was a working stiff. He paid hard-earned money for *every* gram and he intended to relish every gram. Not once had he laughed while snorting, before or after the sniff. In Kyle's world, cocaine had less to do with pleasure, much to do with numbness.

Kyle was a part-time junkie. He snorted when the fares were complete assholes and bad memories filled his thoughts; memories of water and cold skin and of vows cut by the scissors of fate.

The day had been full of daymares. It was their anniversary. Kyle would have kissed her, looked into her eyes, and told her that he loved her despite her crooked nose. She would have slapped him in the shoulder. He would have held her arms above her head with one hand and tickled her with the other, bucking like a bull rider to avoid frantic kicking. Something innocent would turn naughty. They would have made love. Fucked. Whatever the mood dictated. Afterwards, he would have held her. Loved her. As he always did.

As he always would.

Sarah would have smacked his bare ass and demanded pancakes with strawberry jam and butter upon Kyle's return. The smile on his face, a small ember ignited by the memories of Sarah, extinguished once reality reclaimed a hold on his mind.

After one last snort to ensure comfortable numbness, Kyle lowered his head and opened his eyes. He closed the small Glad container where he kept his stuff. Baggies were easy to break.

Cotton padded the container. An indention the size of a large Tic-Tac box, lined with double layer of tin foil, assured safe keeping and no spillage. It was the Berlin fucking wall of cocaine stashes, pre-

Reagan inspired bulldozers and wrecking balls.

A rapping at the window startled him. He tucked the box underneath his seat with attempted subtlety as he looked through the back passenger window. He tried his best to hide his weary and paranoid demeanor with a squint.

A business type with wearing an expensive suit, wire rimmed glasses, and a fresh haircut pulled on the door handle and pointed at his watch to signify his hurry.

Did Don Draper step out of my television? He must be late for a meeting pitching a raunchy billboard add, or to decide who's going to star in the next T.V. movie about premarital sex, sponsored by Mohawk Airlines.

Kyle smiled at the thought and unlocked the rear doors. His high kept jealousy of this man's obvious success at bay. The man didn't look dangerous, which was rare for the neighborhood. He was one of the few cabbies who took fares the area. The profits were worth the risk most of the time. His last fare had stiffed him on a tip. Instead, he let Kyle tip *him* for his protection during the ride with the barrel of a gun and the cash he didn't have locked in the trunk. That guy hadn't looked dangerous either.

Tuesday's. Worst fucking day of the week.

The man had an educated, eloquent voice as he spoke and sat in the back seat. He tossed a modest briefcase to the side as he closed the door.

"Jesus, man, are you driving a cab or are you expecting The Pope? What's with the security?" said the man. He shifted in the seat, looking for a comfortable position while trying not to wrinkle his suit.

"Been robbed one too many times, my good sir, and the locks buy me enough time to see who's going to make me wet my pants. Where you headed?" Kyle asked. He turned the ignition and looked at the man through the rear view.

"17th and Broadway Street. Park in the alley next to Bradbury's Watch Shop, if possible. Playing it incognito. Matters of confidentiality and all that James Bond mumbo-jumbo, you understand. I'll tip well," the man said.

You in the mob or visiting your mistress, my good man?

Kyle was glad his fares couldn't hear his coke riddled judgments. He started the fare counter and pulled out of his parking niche in front of the Shell station. Bradbury's, or Brad's, was a few miles away. He wondered if he could score a juicy story or a decent cut of cocaine out of the lawyer before they reached his destination. Thirty years later and the eighties still weren't over.

After a few moments of silence, the fare broke the silence and asked Kyle if he could light a smoke.

"If you have one to spare," Kyle said.

"Of course. I hope you don't mind Lucky Strikes," the man said.

The fare lit two of the filterless cigarettes and handed one to Kyle while he continued to compare the man to Don Draper in his head.

"Whatever the brand, we end up in an iron lung, no?" Kyle said.

Kyle coughed on the first inhale. He had quit smoking on the regular when he was seventeen, but coke always made him crave nicotine. Every time was like the first time. Embarrassing.

"Too true. A bad habit, but still..." the man said as he inhaled, letting. He let the thought linger, incomplete and thought provoking.

But still.

Kyle could empathize. He took a deep drag of the cigarette, enjoying the nicotine calm coupled with his cocaine jitters. He thought of every "But still..." he had heard during his career as a cab driver and part-time confession booth.

"I shouldn't have hit her so hard, but still..."

"Sure, cheating that client was unethical, but still..."

"I feel bad that he died, but still..."

But still.

The subconscious Doctor Phil; a miniature, balding devil on the shoulder of those unwilling to take responsibility, shooting the words through rational thinking like a bullet of ignorance to the soul. 'But still' didn't ease the pain. The words covered it with a thick coating of lacquer so that pain and guilt offered no struggle while on display.

"I didn't catch your name, sir" Kyle said.

Ten bucks says it will be an alias. Either way, I'll get a payout. Tuesday is looking up!

"I didn't offer it," the man said. He paused to look at Kyle's backseat license, "My name is Lucian, Mr. Thimall. Rob Lucian."

"Pardon me for denying you the usual salutatory handshake, but I should keep at least one hand on the wheel."

Rob Lucian let out a laugh, billowing thick blue smoke with each peak.

"You can make it up to me later," he replied.

"You bet."

Kyle put the window down half way. The filterless cigarettes were filling the car up with more smoke, irritating his eyes.

"So," Lucian asked "why drive a cab?"

"Pardon me?"

Rob Lucian's curiosity was genuine. Kyle wasn't used to being interrogated by his fares. They either sat in silence or treated him as the aforementioned confessional. Actual conversation in a cab was a rare thing. Kyle treated most passengers as he had his high school girlfriends. A lot of head nodding and monosyllabic, mechanical responses in hope for a decent payoff.

"Why cabs? Spics and Arabs drive cabs in this town. Never thought I'd have the guy next store driving me around. To be fair, I'm used to taking a limo."

A common misconception in a town where the lighter skinned were a rich, proud minority.

"This is junkie and serial killer turf, Lucian. Tell me, did you kiss your family goodbye before you left home tonight, Mr. Lucian?" Kyle replied with the spiel he had practiced for that question.

Kyle offered an exaggerated glare in the rear view mirror. After a moment, both men broke out in a fit of laughter.

"You're a funny one, Mr. Thimall. I wish there were more fellows like you at the firm. Preparation H diluted assholes, I tell you. Tighter than a kitten's bung, twice the pucker of a lemon."

A lawyer. That explained his smooth tongue and appreciation for dark humor. Kyle figured him for a defense lawyer. Prosecutors were always too stressed or too righteous to talk, let alone joke, unless they were taking a cell phone call. They had the illusion of honor left.

"Which firm?"

Kyle flicked the remnants of the cigarette out the window as he turned onto 17th Street.

"A private firm. A lot of people have heard of us under various titles. We prefer to stay under the radar to avoid the frivolous cases that most firms eat up like a dog eating dinner scraps. That's why most defense lawyers always look like they've taken a bite of a bad fish sandwich. Blind frivolity in the court room causes indigestion. We're the best, though. Word of mouth is a wonderful fucking thing, Kyle. Remind me to give you a card before we part ways."

"Sure thing. Can you get me off with an insanity plea if they ever find the hookers I have locked up in the trunk?"

The two men laughed again. Kyle enjoyed the laughter. It was a rare commodity.

Lucian flicked his own cigarette out the window before rolling it closed. Kyle was feeling too warm for the weather. He blamed the smoke and rolled up his own window. He wiped sweat from his brow.

"A murderer and a kidnapper, eh? We guarantee six months of house arrest and a pretty blonde parole officer with D cups."

"Where do I sign?" Kyle asked.

He turned onto Broadway, disappointed they had reached Lucian's destination.

"I might be able to work something out. That's Bradbury's right there. Kill the lights when you pull in, please."

Kyle pulled in to the alley way that separated the watch shop from a small hookah bar. Far enough back to keep the cab cloaked from view, but close enough to the street to bolt in a hurry if the need arose. He killed the lights, though he left the car idling.

"Fifteen fifty, Mr. Lucian."

He handed Kyle five one-hundred dollar bills.

"Keep the change, Kyle."

Kyle stared at the crisp bills in his hand and felt the saliva build on his tongue, tasting of nicotine and adrenaline. He could get quality blow with this. Better than the weak stuff in his Glad box. Maybe pay rent on time for the first time in months. He was pretty sure the new Deadpool movie had just come out. Decisions, decisions.

"Holy shit, are you sure, man? This is too much money!" Kyle spoke in an excited whisper

"I promised I'd tip well, and I always keep my promises."

Lucian smiled, but made no move for the door handle.

"You've made great company, Kyle. Mind if I ask you to do me one favor?"

Kyle wavered, his happy thoughts starting to run out of fairy dust.

"Wait. I don't have to go down on you or some sick shit like that, do I? I won't even do that for blow."

Part time junkie or not, Kyle would never let himself get *that* addicted.

"No, no. I'm not in the mood for oral gratification at the moment. I appreciate you entertaining the idea, though. I have a more plutonic proposition for you. Here's another smoke, by the way, and my card as promised."

"Thanks." Kyle managed.

Kyle tucked the bills into his shirt pocket before taking a fresh lit cigarette from Lucian.

Lucian inhaled deep and smiled. Kyle swore he saw his eyes glow in the dark. It was a subtle illumination. He passed it off as the dark playing tricks and took another drag.

Kyle's brow was warmer than it had earlier. He wiped away more sweat and positioned himself to listen to Lucian's proposition, hoping to God his judgment was on point. He wasn't recharged enough to contend with another robbery.

"Do you prefer Kyle or Michael?" Lucian mused.

Kyle's first name wasn't on his cab license. He went by Kyle, his middle name. Nobody alive, save his employer, called him Michael. The first letter was on the license, required by law. Kyle hoped he had underestimated the observation skills of the lawyer in his back seat. More curious than scared, Kyle turned the card in his hand and looked at it.

"Quick question, if I may," Kyle asked, not waiting for affirmation, "but how the hell do you know my first name? I can't recall saying it."

"Oh, I know a lot about you, Kyle. An awful lot. We both do."

Lucian's eyes glowed with prominence. Kyle didn't notice as he struggled to read the card in the low lighting.

"Both?" Kyle asked.

HELL INC.

-YOURS, SATAN

The words caught in Kyle's throat as he read the simple black text on the cream colored business card.

"What the fuck is this, dude?" Kyle said, looking up at his fare with agitation.

Lucian offered a wicked grin, letting smoke slip through the cracks of his perfect white smile.

"Please, please, Kyle. My friends call me Lucifer," Lucian said.

There was nothing subtle or possible about the blood red neon that shone from Lucian's head, as if on cue for maximum impact.

Kyle's eyes were open too wide to miss the glow again.

CHAPTER 2

giving the devil his due

"What kind of sick joke is this?" Kyle said, lacking conviction.

"Oh, I could show you a parlor trick or two, though the whole crimson stare tends to do the trick. I could snap my fingers and your dead wife giving you what you thought I wanted from you in exchange for the generous tip. Head wound, maggots, dead eyes and decay. It would be an interesting blowjob, to say the least. All teeth."

Lucifer curled his lips back, exposing his teeth like Jim Carrey as Fire Marshal Bill. He alternated pushing his tongue to the inside of one cheek and snapping at wisps of smoke to visualize the point.

Kyle's stomach clenched at the thought of his departed wife being mentioned with such disgust. The visual aid made it painful. The very image described had haunted his nightmares for more nights than he wished to recall. Excluding the inappropriate fellatio, the Romero-esque way "Lucifer" had described her was on point. His knowledge was enough of a "parlor trick" to turn Kyle into a scared, awestruck believer.

Lucifer, understanding the silence as understanding, kept pushing buttons.

"I know how many animals you abused when you were young; how many times you masturbated to questionable porn; how many times you thought about killing your step-father when you were a teenager to the precise number with methods and reference material. Stoned or sober, you can tell a liar like you can count the times you've cried yourself to sleep this month."

Lucifer moved forward, grasping the back of Kyle's seat and leaning close to his ear. His breath was like fire on Kyle's neck.

"You know I'm not lying."

Kyle turned and looked at the man. Kyle sensed subtle imperfections beyond his chiseled features. Whatever the flaws were, they made Kyle uncomfortable and powerless. The man hid them with expert craftsmanship.

Despite Kyle's first judgments, the man looked dangerous. More tricks? Was it fear caused by presentation?

Kyle doubted it. Lucifer's hands, close enough for Kyle to see details, were tanned red. Nothing ostentatious. A very light hue, like a mild sunburn before peeling.

Kyle's eyes moved to Lucifer's face. He was beaming. His eyes were literally shining with the truth.

This man, whatever else he was, was not lying.

"Fine. You're the ever loving devil. But what the hell do you want from me? My soul? My servitude? I'm a rotted out shell of a man. I'm fucking worthless! Until this moment, I had given up belief that you or the big guy up stairs existed."

Lucifer inhaled and relaxed back into his seat, looking at the ceiling and blowing smoke rings as he talked.

"He hates being called that. Every time somebody calls him that, He thinks He's being compared to Buddha. God may be a colossal pain in my ass, but he's nowhere near rotund. If I can say one thing about mine eternal adversary, He stays in impeccable shape. Celestial management and absolute power is great for the core."

The temperature in the cab had become impossible. Sweat dripped from Kyle's brow. He had planned on repairing the broken air conditioner in the Spring. He was enjoying his white Christmas. It was colder than an Eskimo's naughty bits outside, but he might as well have been inside the Eskimo's oven for the good the cold was doing him now.

Lucifer sat in silence as Kyle removed two layers of shirts. Kyle was focusing on the temperature to distract himself from the scope of the truth. Lucifer turned up the heat with every layer Kyle removed, loving the slow burn.

God damn, it's blistering!

"Best not blaspheme, even in thoughts. It's true what they say. That self-righteous bastard is always listening. Heed the words of Voltaire, kid. Now's not the time to be making enemies, and He'll be the last enemy you want at this point. He has a stake in this as well, Kyle."

Lucifer pulled two more Lucky Strikes out of his pocket and put them both in his mouth. He snapped his finger and a small flame erupted from the tip of his thumb. He lit the two cigarettes and handed one to Kyle. Kyle took the smoke with a trembling hand and placed it between dry, pursed lips.

Lucifer had tired of simple smoke rings. He began blowing elaborate shapes in the smoke. Simple circles turned into oblongs, and then into visages of screaming faces, before dissipating.

"I said no parlor tricks, but what's the point of power if you can't show off on occasion?"

The front passenger window exploded inward at Kyle, and a skinny red tiger without fur leapt through it, aiming for Kyle's throat. Kyle felt the sting of the glass. The roar the beast let out made him dizzy. He put his hands up, prepared to slap fight the demon cat before it dragged him into oblivion. The whole time, the devil laughed in the back seat.

There was no pain. There was no dragging. Kyle relaxed his arms and looked toward the damage to find the window intact. It had been an illusion.

The devil had not stopped laughing.

"You see? Power is fun!"

Kyle was speechless. He wanted this proposal to end. He wanted Lucifer and his pants wetting illusions out of his cab. He wanted to wake the fuck up.

"You said," Kyle said. He finished half of the cigarette in a drag.

"You said that God had stake in this. Stake in what? Are you trying to open a competitive taxi company? I'm not the guy you want running shop."

Lucifer remained silent for a moment, gathering his thoughts, before answering.

"I'm not here to give you a job, Kyle. I'm here to rewrite Job." Lucifer said, and his eyes sparkled with menace.

"Job? You came up short on that bet, correct? I'm not the best gambler, myself." Kyle said.

"Well, yes. There were unforeseeable circumstances involved in that little wager that I don't wish to reminisce. In essence, yes. I lost." Lucifer didn't look happy admitting defeat, but his smile remained, strong as adamantium.

"What about him?" Kyle asked.

"Since that wager, I've questioned why the righteous little tick never spoke ill of God. His land, his animals, his servants; destroyed. His sons were killed in ways that Nazi war criminals would consider overkill! I have references, I asked them all in the forties! Job was turned into a poor, worthless monster. Yet his faith in God persisted. It bugged me that so much ill could be done to one man without reaction. Humanity is weak! Sons among your kind kill their fathers for less! The unfairness baffled me! I can understand losing to God, but losing due to foul play is how I win. I call shenanigans."

"Job had bad luck and kept a smile. Good for him. Rare breed."

Lucifer ignored him.

"I came up with a sure fire way to test man's allegiance. I'm willing to bet old white would have trouble getting the same results out of someone closer to my plane of existence. Someone who lacks the proper faith. Someone broken and battered before the wager even begins! Someone who has become a poor, worthless monster without His help. Someone like you, Kyle." Lucifer's gaze pierced Kyle's very being.

"Your *plane* of existence? I don't worship you *or* Him. Whatever faith I had died with my wife."

"Yes. What is my job, if not to tempt mortals away from faith that the King of Kingdoms exists? For every strong, pure human, there are thousands with wavering faith. Thousands more treat faith like a bad joke. You have justifiable qualms with God. You were a good person until the moment your better half died. I'm willing to bet that if someone in Job's shoes had lived a life like yours, they would have failed with flair."

Kyle blocked the sorrow nipping at him again after hearing Lucifer speak of his dead wife.

"Please don't talk about Sarah anymore. I don't like the way I feel when you bring her up."

"Are you worried she's with me, now that you know I exist?"

Lucifer propped his elbows on the seat back and stared at Kyle with mischief.

"You're worried that I can taste her flesh when I want it? Scared that I have done things to your wife that you would give your soul to prevent? That she has done things to me that that you would give your soul if she'd do them to you?"

Kyle trembled in his emotional storm. Lucifer laughed loud and leaned back into the seat.

"You are perfect, my boy! Such hate! It makes me hard! Alas, your wife does not burn in my fires. She was a good soul. You used to be a good soul too, Kyle. Before the drugs, the violence, and the sin. All to spite Mr. Almighty because he had different plans for your one and only. I'm proud. You are the perfect candidate. Your soul is filthy."

Lucifer paused to put the cigarette out on his palm. He plucked

Kyle's out of his mouth and did the same. Both butts turned to ash and fell the floor.

The desecration of his wife's memory and Lucifer's crazy story was becoming too much for him to handle. Kyle prayed for a return to monotony as he reached under the steering column for the 9mm he had purchased to protect himself and the cab. He didn't intend to use it, and had a habit of forgetting it was there when the robberies, such as the one earlier in the evening, were quick. This "proposition" was taking time. His adrenaline had worn out. His brain had burned away. He hoped the gun would scare Lucifer off while knowing damn well that it wouldn't.

Kyle heard a deep sigh from the back seat as he reached. He realized that the holster was empty. Lucifer was clicking his tongue and twirling the gun around his finger in the same fashion a basketball coach's twirls his whistle.

"Missing something, pilgrim?" Lucifer said. His John Wayne impression was perfect.

Lucifer stopped the twirling and let the clip loose into his hand, clicking his tongue again at what he found.

"And no bullets, at that. Maybe I was too quick to convey my pride in you, my boy"

Kyle never intended to hurt anyone with the gun, so he had never purchased bullets. He figured that the sight of a barrel would be enough to send any man running. It had always been enough to part him with his money. He didn't regret the decision, knowing how little good it would have done.

He wasn't dealing with a man.

"Guns; the pinnacle of human invention. Far superior to flaming swords and arrows. Wish I had thought of it first, to be honest! My stock has risen ten-fold since these babies came out. Ten-fold more after Boondock Saints got popular."

Lucifer pointed the gun at Kyle so quick that Kyle jumped in surprise.

"Freeze, motherfucker!" Lucifer screamed, this time impersonating Samuel L. Jackson.

"No, not the impressions. I mean, why me?" Kyle interrupted.

"I know. I just like fucking with you. I've been pretty clear, Kyle. You've thrown your life away and filled the gaps in your heart with hate. You are my handicap."

Lucifer grabbed the last two Lucky Strikes out of the pack and crumpled it in his fist. More ash fell to the floor of the cab. He put them both in his mouth and inhaled deep on the dry sticks. They both ignited, to Lucifer's glee and Kyle's indifference. He was over the parlor tricks.

Lucifer handed one to Kyle, not frustrated with Kyle's lack of amusement.

"So?" Lucifer asked.

"So what?"

"Do you want the details? The deal? The game?"

"Do I have a choice?" Kyle asked, knowing the answer.

"He says so, like He always does. If you say no you will end up living this pitiful excuse for a life a hell of a lot longer than you intend too. I can guarantee that not a moment of it will be enjoyable. Suicide won't do you any good. It didn't work after Sarah died and I won't let it work until you've gone so far passed insane that all the butterfly nets and Vicodin in the world won't offer you an ounce of respite."

Kyle's eyes grew wet with tears. He asked Rob Lucian to stop besmirching the name of his beloved.

"Aww, now don't cry, Teddy Bear! If you succeed, you can let go of worry forever! Hell, you might even get to see Sarah again. People still enjoy that happy ending bullshit, right?"

"I'm listening," Kyle said. He bowed his head, thinking that his words would betray him.

The prospect of seeing Sarah again opened a small rabbit hole of hope inside of Kyle that had long shut him out of Wonderland. The promise, slim and full of lie as it most likely was, it was more of an opportunity than he had ever expected.

"Splendid, my boy!"

Lucifer clapped his hands with frivolity. The cigarette bobbed in his mouth.

"So onto the semantics! Job was tested on his own will and convictions alone. He lost everything and still prospered. Your test will be more difficult. Your test involves influences the will of other people. Seven others, be exact. You'd better be up to snuff on your tale weaving, though, because so far you are boring me to death! You have nothing to lose but this pitiful cab and a shitty apartment. The challenges you face will be more obscure than the poor old Shepherd's."

"Seven?" Kyle asked.

"Quite the lucky number, no? One for each of my children! The deadly sins. You must seek out and find a person who embodies each of my little friends. Wrath, greed, envy, gluttony, pride, sloth, and lust. When you find them, you will be charged with, how do you say, showing them the light."

Lucifer put his hands together in false prayer, and a bright light formed a halo around his head. The light filled the cab. The red color of his skin looked far brighter to Kyle underneath the halo. Lucifer continued, his words flowing out as powerful and glib as a televangelist.

"They won't change easy, my brother! Oh no, but both of us will know if their paths have turned true. You won't know *when* you'll meet them, *who* they are, or *where* to find them. It's your job to figure that happy shit out yourself. But if you succeed, my son! Oh boy, if you succeed, and that key word will be determined by "his Highness" and myself, what with our clairvoyance and otherworldly greatness, in saving these seven souls, then trumpets and choirs of angels will welcome you to God's own side! Peace be the fuck with you, you will be praised and loved and rewarded! Amen!"

Lucifer lowered his hands, his voice returning to normal, the mock halo fizzling to nothingness.
"More than we can say for old Job's reward of "I am the Lord" and a cold shoulder, no?" Lucifer said with nonchalance.

"And if I lose?" Kyle asked.

There was no humor or happiness in the laugh Lucifer let out as he leaned forward for a third time. Another halo appeared over his head, but one of negative light. It was black and broken. It made everything dark and gritty, and Kyle was able to just make out those imperfections he sensed at the beginning of this conversation. They were evil. They were terrifying features. If Kyle could see the extent of them, he would rip the eyes out of his skull with his bare hands and be grateful for escaping the halo's darkness.

Hot icicles raced down Kyle's spine.

"You will be mine if you fail, Kyle. Always and forever, you will be MINE!"

LUST

Lust is my marrow

An unfulfilled core; absence

I desire you

CHAPTER 3

satan, lord of the palindrome

"You have seven days, Kyle. Seven sins, seven souls, and seven days. Three sevens to round out a pleasant, holy number. God's little stamp mark on a tasking most unholy. After that, I will drink your soul like cheap merlot and eat your heart like overcooked strip steak. Bite…"

Lucifer lifted his own right hand to his mouth and bit the pinky off with a crunch. Blood poured from the wound onto Lucifer's lap and Kyle's backseat. Crimson spittle splash Kyle in the face. He wanted to wipe it away, but he couldn't move.

"…after bite…"

Lucifer bit off the ring finger, small bronze ring and all. Blood splashed the roof and the seat. Kyle tasted bile on the back of his tongue, but he was unable to turn his head.

"…after bite!"

Lucifer skipped his middle finger, instead going for the pointer. The crunch was unbearable. More spittle hit Kyle on the lips and Kyle tasted putrid death; he tasted hate and war and rape and disease; he tasted the four horsemen. He tasted sin. Lucifer stared at him with those glowing eyes and that blood drenched smile. The two remaining fingers answered every prayer or wish Kyle had ever asked of God, Satan, or any other celestial creature in ear shot.

Fuck you.

"When I'm done, there will be time for the naughty stuff, Mr. Thimall." Lucifer teased.

His hand turned to flame. Seconds later, he stretched the fingers of a fully formed hand before Kyle's eyes. There was no blood on Lucifer's mouth and pants, but the blood on the back seat and roof remained. Perhaps to let Kyle know that while the injury was easy to fix, it had not been an illusion.

"I'll do it again and again, for eternity. Pure agony, Kyle. Trust me when I say I feel your pain, my boy. You aren't even worth eating with a side of Chianti and fava beans."

Lucifer needed to work on his Anthony Hopkins. That stupid thought, that the Devil had a shitty Hannibal Lector impression, helped Kyle digest the vulgar display. Kyle lifted the cigarette to his lips, ignorant to the inch long ash that rested at the end of the filter, or of the transformation into a lit cigarette, thanks to Lucifer, as he took a drag. Lucifer's showboating overloaded his senses.

"How can I trust you?" Kyle asked. He avoided Lucifer's eye for fear of another demonstration. "I mean, this could be a ploy to have me doing your dirty work and not even realize it. You're supposed to be the father of lies."

Lucifer smirked.

"You didn't tell me you were an expert on what my history, my boy! When lying benefits me, I lie. In this case, the truth is more horrifying, so I choose honesty. That's the wonder of discarding the rule book. I only follow rules set by a handshake.

"This deal is bigger than you, Kyle. Somebody had to do it! Like a Pokémon being thrown into Freddy Krueger's nightmare world, I choose you! Do you require something more personal to entice you? A little positive incentive from Daddy Diablo. I can give you motivation to succeed, though I'm certain it will hinder you further. A demonstration not of my power or intentions, but of possibility!"

"Well, when you put it that way, how the hell can I resist?"

"You pick up quick, Kyle! There may be hope for you yet! Before you ask, yes. That was a lie. Now for the bonus features. Do you want to see what happened to Brandon?" Lucifer questioned, stroking his chin.

Kyle forgot his trepidation in a moment of lucid fury. For the third time tonight, his tremble worsened. The anger took over every feature, as if Lucifer had o shit on Sarah's grave instead of invoking a single name. When he repeated the name, his voice resonated with such ancient hate that even Lucifer gave an empathetic nod. Almost.

"Brandon."

"Yes, Brandon. Sarah's big brother. The scum bag who slept off a hangover on a couch when he was supposed to be spotting her. The man who let your wife, his very own sister, die at the hands of his negligence and festering apathy. The man responsible for our palaver."

Kyle could no longer lock the painful thoughts away. Sarah had been graceful in the water. Kyle used to joke that he half expected her to turn into a mermaid if she swam the ocean. Kyle was only afraid the wrong half would become a fish, but his worries were for naught. Sarah abhorred salt water. She was afraid of drowning in the undertows.

Fucking irony.

Kyle missed the way Sarah used to glance at him as she climbed out of the pool. She was mischievous with her seductions. She would walk across the patio, pretending to dry her hair, before soaking him with a flick of the long brunette locks.

This always ended up in play fighting, kissing and biting, and on one occasion, a very uncomfortable UPS delivery driver. He would confess to her that he'd always wanted to be with a mermaid after sex. His love for her renewed every single time they shared that moment. Or any moment.

Brandon took it away by way of his inability and inaction. Three lives lost to the bottle and the pills.

Brandon knew that Sarah took risks with her diving tricks. She wanted the kind of medal that the world celebrated. She wanted Olympic gold. Brandon was there when Kyle couldn't be. Just in case.

Brandon had failed as a brother and a man, and Kyle had forever lost his soul mate. When Kyle heard of Brandon's OD a few weeks earlier, he was not remorseful.

A wild night of bondage, drink and pills led him to a peaceful death while he slept. The woman handcuffed to his bed might have died as a product of his addiction if the neighbors hadn't heard her screams.

Kyle wished he could have watched Brandon take his final breath. He would never get the sick closure of the wronged. The closure every person who lost a loved one to fate's middle finger. It was personal demon, this closure. Like most of Lucifer's creations, it was an illusion meant for destruction.

Kyle hoped his hell was as agonizing as the one Lucifer described. As agonizing or worse.

"Would you like me to show you?" Lucifer said, looking giddy.

Kyle thought long and hard. The choice wasn't hard to make, but knowing that this last display would damn his own soul caused hesitation. A high probability of eternity in agony for one glimpse of Brandon burning?

Kyle nodded a forlorn and decisive yes

"Take my hand."

Kyle did. With a snap of Lucifer's restored fingers, they were gone. The vacant cab idled behind Bradbury's on 17th and Broadway.

if this is hell, what's with all the water

Nausea tugged at Kyle's gut. Sight, sound, and smell ceased to work for the ten second period it took them to reach their destination. For a moment, the only thing that existed in the world was that terrible nausea. And then, they arrived.

Lucifer and Kyle stood on an observation platform. They overlooked a rotting, wet cell. Something solid and transparent separated the prison below from where they stood.

The pit looked alien. The walls were devoid of color and covered with a plethora of tiny black barbs. Kyle saw no point of entrance. A link of chain, like a dead iron snake, grew out of the floor in the middle of the room.

Kyle heard a scream from behind him and turned to face a latched, wooden door stained with rust and viscous splatter that had long hardened into paint. His heart moved fast and hard, trying to escape his chest while it could still take the input.

Red and black tile covered the floor of the observation deck. A rope hung from the ceiling. Next to Lucifer stood a bearded man clad in a long black cloak. His skin was pale, and his cheeks sunk deep into his face. Dark holes replaced his eyes. In those bottomless black pits, Kyle saw a universe of horror he wasn't meant to understand.

"Pay no attention to the screams behind the door. They are debts being paid by the unclean," the man said, voice raspy and weathered by the steams of his position.

"Are we in..."

"Hell," Lucifer finished. "Yes, this is my place. We get new carpeting on Thursday. A bit warm, but I can't get anybody down here to fix the damn thermostat. We seem to be off of the normal route."

Lucifer chuckled at his own wit while Kyle gulped. His mouth was dry. Kyle turned his attention back to the cell. A shape stirred in the far corner of the room. Lucifer coughed a suggestion by clearing the back of his throat. The bearded man pulled on the rope. Kyle heard the rusty squeal of turning gears in the distance. Water began to dribble from four holes positioned around the top of the room. As they dripped, the man popped up with a start. Kyle recognized Brandon's face, even in the shadows.

Kyle's hatred welled up again. Deeper, more violent than tired.

Either Hell had intensified the feelings, or he had suspended belief enough to let the levies of hate leak, like the water from the walls, back into him after so much time worrying about the longer lasting emotions. Depression. Sorrow. Love, or the forever lack thereof.

Brandon searched the walls for an exit, his head whipping around like Stevie Wonder in a torture porn. He made it around the room one time before the water reached his upper thighs. The water began to flow faster. Kyle saw him punch the wall and back away before submerging. His figure could be seen moving beneath the water. Every so often, he would resurface, take a deep breath, and take another dive.

Kyle guessed that Brandon was looking for the chain cemented into the floor. The morbid cruelty stroked his hatred. Brandon found no door, so he was looking for a different way out. He thought the chain was connected to something more than the floor.

The corners of Kyle's lips upturned. The whites of his teeth showed and illuminated this executioner's witness room, much as Lucifer's eyes had in the cab. He never would have noticed. His eyes saw Brandon's Hell through the goggles of vengeance.

The water neared the top of the room after a few minutes. The bubbles stopped rising to the surface. Kyle thought Brandon had drowned. Anticlimactic disappointment begin to well up until Brandon burst upward through the froth and slammed his head into the transparent ceiling. His body went limp as he fell back into the water.

A dark red cloud blossomed outward from Brandon's point of decent. The water grew still. The water drained from the room faster than it had filled it. Brandon floated to the surface as the water reached the halfway point. His lifeless body circled the water in a stiff dance until his corpse settled very near the spot on the floor it rested when the display began.

Before Kyle's eyes, Brandon woke up with a violent shiver. Kyle grasped the genius and horror of the punishment. Brandon's hell was perfect. To spend eternity reaching for hope only to drown in the same manner Sarah had at the peak of hope.

The punishment beyond anything he could have imagined. He'd spent every day since Sarah's death trying, but minds driven by vengeance lacked creativity. Pity tried to sneak in, but Kyle pushed it aside while guilt was locked out of the equation.

Kyle understood that Lucifer was showing him more than a

sampling of Hell's wrath. Brandon was an enticement. His torture was a warning.

Kyle knew, by the wide smile and joyous eyes that painted Lucifer's expression, that what the devil planned for him if he failed would be unimaginable. Indescribable. As Lucifer himself had said, pure agony. His thoughts proved that minds driven by fear had no trouble creating.

Behind him, Lucifer stood motionless. He had set the best possible bait for the only fish that would satisfy his hunger. He was all but dreaming of battering his catch for the deep fryer.

All he had to do was wait for the bite.

but can you levitate

Another snap, another tug, and the two were back in the alley standing next to the cab. Kyle leaned back against the trunk, feeling defeated, as Lucifer spoke.

"Are you motivated, motivated, downright dedicated?"

"You're a sick fuck." Kyle couldn't manage much else.

"Amateur insult as that was, I appreciate the compliment. A couple of things before you begin. First things first." Lucifer reached into the pocket of his suit jacket, his tongue half out with concentration as he searched, before pulling out an elegant black watch and tossing it to Kyle. "You must wear that. Putting it on means signing the contract."

Kyle glared at Lucifer and sighed. The moment Kyle strapped the watch to his wrist, the face turned a dark maroon color and let off a subtle glow.

Instead of twelve numbers circling the face, there were seven. Each of the numbers were roman numerals carved into a transparent red stone. Words stretched from the center of the watch to the numbers. They were the names of the seven deadly sins. Twenty-three minuscule lines separated each number from the next. One hand graced the face, pointing north to the number seven. A decorative centerpiece bore a simple cross, with the old joke at Jesus's expense "INRI" written across the top. The center of the cross was decorated with a pentacle.

How appropriate.

"The seven digits each represent one day, and each of the small lines between them represents one hour. Finish before that hand circles back to the seven, and you become proud owner of this beautiful, useless time piece. Not to mention a guaranteed spot beyond the gates. Fail and that time piece becomes your ball and chain."

The words hit Kyle like dirt from a shovel into his grave. The watch tightened around Kyle's wrist, bearable but uncomfortable.

"Seven days to absolve seven sins," Kyle mused. "I'm the wrong fucking guy for this job."

"Same as that watch, I will be counting each and every second on it. Each of those digits represent a sin and a day of the week. Each time a soul is set back on a proper path, the corresponding number and word will illuminate. All seven numbers must glow by the end of day seven, or else…" Lucifer ended by gesturing his thumb across his throat.

"Where do I start? A bar? A whore house?"

"Quick to judge those who love drink and sex as sinners, Mr. Cokehead?"

The decision weighed more than the watch. Kyle tried not to panic. Lucifer had shown him what a man with nothing left could lose. Everything else.

"Ah, yes. You made a mistake by accepting the terms and conditions without scrolling through the details. Some details may have been useful! I can be a fair creature when the mood strikes me. Watching you wander around aimless for a week would be dreadfully anti-climactic, even if I do win. I got bored watching Moses. All of us did."

"Gee, thanks," Kyle muttered.

"I didn't choose this alley at random. The one thing I have to give you is directions to the first sinner. Follow the alley that way," Lucifer pointed away from the nose of the cab, "You'll come to a staircase with a green rail. You can't miss it. There is a big sign that says The Green Rail above the door if you do. Down those stairs, amongst the scum, you'll find sinner number one. Don't forget that. I fucking hate poetry. I spent a lot of time on that rhyme."

"And *that* rhyme?"

"Coincidence. Make a plan before a-knocking. They have a small armory and tend to be trigger happy when it comes to strange faces."

Lucifer smiled as Kyles face fell.

"Sounds like quite a party. Should I dress like Emmit fucking Kelley and make machine gun balloon animals?"

"Oh, I hope you lose. The one liners alone are worth owning your soul! Keep that sense of humor and I might ease the torture on Tuesdays!"

"I fucking hate Tuesdays," Kyle said.

"If you end up in Hell, Tuesday will be your new favorite day of the week. Already sounds like an upgrade, if you ask me. You'll lose that chipper demeanor lest you lose your head during this little epic of yours."

"So which sin will this person represent?" Kyle asked.

"I said this was an EPIC, Kyle, and you have been chosen because you have faith, no more!"

"From poetry to riddles?"

"More like poetry to rock and roll, Kyle. Point is, you want it all but you can't have it. That's all you get for free. I won't risk losing my new play toy. My only job now is to make sure you fail, snookum."

Lucifer spoke the last words in a high pitched, motherly voice and pinched Kyle's cheek playfully. Kyle turned his head to escape the pinch. Lucifer's fingers were like fresh coals. Kyle's hand shot to his face, fearing the sting of a burn.

"Anything else, oh Dark Lord?" Kyle asked. The spite in his voice was weak.

"Sassy! It's nice of you to try to get used to the words so far in advance. A real go getter! I believe it's time to say adieu, monsieur! So long, fair well, auf wiedersehen and goodbye!"

Lucifer turned his back and began walking toward the street.

"Oh, and Kyle, one last thing." Lucifer said. His voice boomed off of the walls of the alley. He stopped, but didn't turn.

"Yes?"

Lucifer cocked his head to the side and looked over his shoulder at Kyle with an eye that glowed red. "I'll see you in hell."

Lucifer laughed and began to walk again. His form faded into evanescence before disappearing into the night. Lucifer's cold laugh took longer to dissipate from the alley than his person.

"Had to go with the ballsy exit line, didn't you asshole? Well here's mine! I'll see you in...in..." Kyle screamed at nothing.

The single light that shone in the alley exploded in a ball of flame, spraying Kyle with sparks and debris. Kyle dropped to his knees and covered his head with his hands. He stayed that way for a long time, letting reality catch up to him after his tryst with the devil.

Reality sucked the big pickle. Kyle filled the silent alley with the sad laughter of a man about to break. It was the only way he could handle reality without losing it all together.

Reality: Kyle Thimall was alone.

Reality: Kyle would be dead within the week.

Reality: Kyle Thimall was screwed.

Reality: two out of three wasn't always bad, but it was never good.

it's never sunny in killadelphia

Stakes were high as Jonas McMillan turned the third card in the flop. The Green Rail pub had been doing well as of late. The plastic chips they played with offered the winner a cool five grand instead of the usual bottle of Aristocrat Rum and carton of Camel Crush cigarettes.

Jonas held pocket kings, clubs and hearts. His palm itched something fierce, but he made sure to hide anything but vague disappointment.

When the third card flipped turned out to be another king, Jonas maintained his calm. He covered any possible tell, good or bad, with a swallow of black stuff (what the Irish called Guinness). It worked like a charm, though he couldn't remember the end of most poker games.

Jonas wore many masks and was practiced at hiding secrets from his closest confidants and loved ones. It was worst with his daughter Judith. He hid her from the world with a stone cold stoicism that rivaled the British Royal Guard. His poker face was his most comfortable mask. The drink cover was a J.I.C. trick. Just In Case.

Ian Levesque, Jonas' antithesis, always gave himself away by rubbing the underside of his chin and glancing around the table with his good eye. The left one, marble instead of glass, didn't move much. It was the only unnerving feature of an otherwise unimposing individual.

Ian always expected the other players to give away a tell. He only looked when he gave a shit about his hand. Ian's search for a break always left him broke.

James, the smiling crooked fox of the gang, threw in chips to start the betting. Three ten-dollar chips and a motion towards Molly to continue were the only compliments to his never fading smile. Sociopaths didn't need a poker face. Win or lose, James always got something valuable from a game of poker. Information. Good favor. One more step towards power.

Molly Levesque was the only female at the poker table, and the only person that any of them knew, in life or poker, whose poker beat Jonas'. Disappointment, glee, sadness, anger; these emotions never betrayed her true demeanor unless she gave them permission. If Jonas could best the Royal Guard, Molly could have won a staring contest with a still life painting in the Louvre. She threw her chips on top of the pile, both calling and raising the pot, without saying a word. A nod to Jonas indicated his turn.

A king, a queen, and a ten lie on the table. All high cards. Short of pocket aces, Jonas felt comfortable that his pocket kings would get him the pot, if he played them the way he played the world. He called her "bluff" and raised the bet.

"Oh, God damn me."

Ian, of course. His exasperated blasphemy signaled the end of his hand. Ian threw his cards across the table and took a swig from the bottle of Jameson's nestled amongst the chips in the center of the table. This was their method of folding. Ian was drunk by the sixth hand.

James and Molly both called. James turned over the fourth card. A three. Nothing special or helpful to anyone. There were too many high cards on the table to take much stock in a bullshit low card. James threw in a fifty chip, for no reason other than to screw with the table. He sipped his own drink, his smile not disappearing even as he swallowed. Unlike the rest of them, James held a pomegranate and vodka concoction that was far from Irish and far from straight. Nobody gave a damn where James took it, so long as he did so after taking out the trash.

Molly called, a monolith of tragic beauty. Jonas also called. James' little traps were not worth worrying about. Jonas maintained confidence in his hand. James bet high to see who would be comfortable enough to bet even higher. Good poker player, but his nonchalance left him on the losing end more often than not. Nobody bets high in the middle of the flop for no good reason. Though when James did win, he won big.

Tension filled the room as Jonas flipped the final card. Ian tapped on the table with the fingers of his left hand and on the floor with his feet. His A.D.D. would not let him enjoy his remaining money.

Jonas's daughter, Judith, sat across the room brushing her hair and watching Guys and Dolls. She lost interest in poker nights around the age she realized where most of the money they played with came from, but she always paid attention to the conversation. Half of poker was learning secrets. Judith, far from the table, never spilled a thing and never had to look anybody in the eye. In her own way, her poker face was the best. She never lost.

Like James, Judith collected the valuable information shared around the whiskey soaked poker table. Unlike James and his hunger

for power, poker night was the only time she got anything from her
father other than smothering paranoia. Daddy often tried to save her
in his own misguided way. If her father knew half of the things she
had done to survive in her life, his paranoia would have put him into
cardiac arrest before her eighteenth birthday.

In Jonas' fairytale world, Judith was a virgin who had never
touched the drink or smoked the reefer. She preferred tequila, hated
blondes, and had an open minded sexual appetite. Jonas kept her
hidden from his world. She wore her blindfold without on that she
had poked small holes in it, just big enough to see the important
things. Jonas' own blindfold was his naïve faith in her, and Judith took
advantage of it often

"Stop that damn tapping, Ian, before I shove my Ritalin up
your nose! I'm watching something over here!" Judith yelled over her
shoulder.

"Sorry, doll." Ian said.
He folded his hands in his lap, though he continued the rhythm with
his legs, moving them up and down without letting his heels hit the
floor. Transparent as a lock-less glass door, and just as generous to
those who didn't throw unwarranted stones.

Judith continued to comb her hair as Marlon Brando gave a
clinic on how to woo a lass with style and class.

The fifth card was another queen. Jonas drank, same as always,
to hide his glee. A full house was always good luck for anybody not
named John Stamos. Most of the cards on the table were diamonds, but
he didn't care. El Deguello, carpe diem, and damn the man!

James threw ten chips on top of the pile. Molly called and
rose to forty. Jonas, drink out of his hand, took off his poker mask
and smiled a wide toothed grin. He pushed the rest of his chips into
the center of the table and leaned back in his chair, taking a shot of
Jameson's for himself in celebration.

"All in," he said, smug.

When Molly let down her own guard and smiled, Jonas' own
smile shriveled.

Ian snorted brief laughter before Jonas went from dumbfound
to angry. It was rare that Ian laughed at one of the other three. He
never allowed himself more than the quick, snorted chuckle.

The small, sexy gap in Molly's otherwise perfect teeth never
preceded a happy moment for most men. Molly showed them that

the term *balls to the wall* usually involved her staple gun. For Jonas' disloyal clientele, that staple gun was painfully literal.

James, sensing the oncoming storm, folded his cards, folded to hide his bluff. He sipped his Pomtini and waited for the fireworks.

When Molly wanted to be dramatic, she could have impressed Daniel Day Lewis. She pushed most of her chips into the center of the table, saving a handful to throw into the pile, one by one. Each plink of a chipped punched Jonas' confidence. She had covered all of Jonas' chips with her own, a sly bit of symbolism that Jonas hoped went unnoticed. She leaned back in her chair with her hands behind her head, pushing her breasts in his direction as her eyes glimmered.

Jonas couldn't be mad at Molly. He knew the consolation prize.

"You first, boss" she cooed. Her confidence was seductive.

Jonas sighed and flipped his cards. Two kings of his own, one in the river, and two queens. Ian clapped for a moment, stopping when nobody else joined.

"A full house? Not a bad hand, Mr. Saget. I would have stayed in to!"

"Oh, quit your badgering and show me the damn cards, Molly!" Jonas said with amusement.

Molly's smile broadened as she flipped them, like the chips, one by one onto the chip pile. An ace and a jack of diamonds. To match the queen, king, and ten of diamonds resting on the table.

Royal fucking flush.

"Holy shit, Molly!" Ian exclaimed, clapping again.

"Diamonds are a girl's best friend, bitches." she responded.

"Touché," said James.

"Yeah, you flogged me there, Molly. Pardon the pun."

She leaned over and rubbed his shoulder. "Just wait until bedtime, boss," she teased.

"Oh, come off it you nasty little love birds! I've still got a hand or two left in these chips." James exclaimed. The good sportsmanship disappointed him, but he hid it with a smile.

"Well then, shall we remedy that? I'll see you upstairs later, Jonas." Molly leaned over and kissed him on the cheek, melting him. "I'll finish him off quick so I can finish you off whenever the fuck I want."

"Children's ears!" Judith screamed from the living room.

Molly surprised him with the poker hand. Jonas was a man who hated surprises. Loathed them. Molly never failed to make him smile or blush with hers. In business and life, he had found it a pleasant rarity to meet someone that you trusted with both your life and your love. Judith and Molly were the only two who had earned the privilege of both.

The stranger who entered the basement loft seconds later, interrupting their sacred night of gambling and drink, was neither trusted nor loved. If Jonas had known what surprises the man had in store for them, he would have shot him dead on the spot.

a scared white guy walks into a bar..

Kyle hoped to find nothing green or with a rail beyond the graffiti covered wall of the alley. He was a macabre Dorothy following the yellow brick road, knowing that the Emerald City was populated with rapists and murderers but powerless to stop himself from ringing the doorbell.

The green rail existed. Even the building was painted a dark shade of green. Welcome to OZ, motherfucker. The light above the door shone like a beacon of his eventual damnation. At least he had found confirmation on his sanity.

The smells and sounds of the bar leaked into the alley. Liquor, vomit, and Johnny Cash songs. Alcoholics on pension and college students on vacation. It smelled like vomit. He cupped his hand over his mouth and nose as he made his way down the cement stairs.

Kyle hated vomit. The night Sarah died had been a deluge of vomit and tears. The reason he chose coke over liquor was to avoid the taste. Tears would flow. Vomit could be avoided.

Kyle didn't know what to expect inside the door at the foot of the green rail. Lucifer had told him that the first sinner held residence there. Would it be an underground hostel run by a luscious, man-crazy Madame? A room of torture that Jigsaw would salivate over? A meth lab run by a middle aged cancer patient?

He scolded himself for binge watching Netflix during his free time.

The normalcy of the situation within surprised breath he had not realized he was holding out of his lungs.

The tenants were playing poker. The average hair color was auburn-red and they had light complexions. Smoke billowed from the cigar of the largest man at the table. At the far side of the room, a pretty young girl sat on a couch underneath a blanket. She combed her hair while a movie with over-the-top singing played. Something classic and romantic.

One man finished downing a drink of Jameson's from the bottle before looking Kyle's direction. Everybody in the room interrogated Kyle with suspicious eyes.

Great. I ruined family game night.

Kyle sensed a once jovial atmosphere speeding towards hostility. It was as if the king's favorite jester had been executed, and he was expected to fill the coxcomb or meet the guillotine.

Kyle gulped as the larger man stood, arms hooked into his suspenders. He was balding, but strong in both presence and muscle.

"Who the fuck are you?" said the man.

Definitely ruined game night. I'm about to be Mr. Body.

"Kyle Thimall. I was told to save one of you," Kyle stuttered. Kyle gulped. The already quiet room grew eerie with silence. Except for Sinatra. From the T.V. screen he sounded happy. Cocky even. Asshole.

"Save one of us, eh? From what? We haven't had enough liquor to be threatened by a man who couldn't break the leg off a frog!" the bald man responded.

"Want me to take care of him, boss?" asked the anxious, scrawny looking man who had downed the Jameson's. The woman at the poker table stared at him. She pulled out a butterfly knife, flipped it open, and began to maneuver it back and forth in her hands. She was not a fan of discretion or hospitality. Each clink and whoosh of the knife screamed skill and agility. If she wanted Kyle to bleed, he would.

Kyle caught her glancing at crotch as she played with the knife. He stepped backward a foot and clasped his hands together in front of his zipper.

"No need, Ian. If this lad knew who I was, nobody short o' the Devil, himself could have talked him into coming here. 'Sides, he looks as if he'll wet himself, soon enough, the way Molly's fondling her stinger."

"Funny thing is," Kyle choked out, his eyes never leaving the knife, "that's exactly who sent me."

Their suspicious eyes became annoyed, confused, or both. Kyle stood still for a long while, feeling exposed even as his hands covered his crotch.

The bald man eased his face and laughed with heart. His hand braced the back of a chair for balance. Ian joined in, but nobody else did. The other man at the table looked at Kyle with silent disdain. Molly continued playing with the knife. The young girl played ignorant.

Kyle let a small whimper of uncomfortable laughter escape his throat as the bald man began to walk towards him. Kyle tightened up as he patted him hard on the back and led him towards the poker table. He let himself be lead, though his eyes followed the hypnotic movements of the blade.

"That's the funniest God damned thing I've heard in a long while, son. Devil sent you to save one of us, did he? Someone here destined for hell?"

"Yes, sir."

"Guess your pecker is going to fall off, after all, eh Ian? Enough with the "sir" shit. Name is Jonas."

Jonas offered a hand, which Kyle shook.

"Pleased."

"Shall I get more of the black stuff?" said the sallow man at the poker table.

"Aye, James. This should make for an interesting conversation. I don't want it to be tainted with sobriety. Judith, come say hi, won't you?"

"Dad, do I have to meet every damn wino and junkie who visits you for a fix? I thought you didn't mix business with pleasure." She never looked away from the television.

"Crazy he may be, but he doesn't smell of liquor, his eyes are clear, and he is no associate of mine. Just come say hello, will you? Take a break from that golden era shit."

"Fine, but I'm not hugging him! Last time you made me do that, the bastard groped me!"

"If if our friend Kyle suffers the same affliction, I'll have Molly kindly separate him from what makes him a man."

"And then I'll separate him from what makes him alive." Molly said.

Molly made sure Kyle didn't miss the gap in her teeth when she smiled.

"I wouldn't dream of it," Kyle whispered.

Kyle showed no expression as Judith moved the blanket from her lap and walked towards him. Jonas was fairly well built, but had a scarred and battle worn face that it would be hard for most to appreciate. An Irish Danny Trejo. Ian was a skinny, horse mouthed twig of a man with a creepy glass eye. Molly, though well-endowed and lovely, had the presence of a wild animal. James was tubby, wore a hair piece, and was a well-practiced curmudgeon.

Judith was stunning and had an aura of confidence. Regardless of the company she kept, she made his stomach flip. Her eyes shone emerald green. Her light, strawberry blond hair shimmered in the low lamplight, giving the illusion of a halo. Her lips were a soft red, her skin flawless. She wore a tank top and pajama pants, obviously not caring and looking great for that very reason. His eyes scanned her body for a moment that felt like an eternity to him. His subconscious was narrating every painful detail of her in a manner reserved for young adult novels about sexy time with vampires. He was quick to affix his eyes onto her own.

Noticing so many details was a big deal. He had noticed little since Sarah's death, least of all other women. It was strange.

As she moved closer, Kyle noticed the three small, dark dots that formed a crude triangle on her inner arm. Underneath her radiance, her face looked sleep deprived. Her movements were defensive; as if she was afraid Kyle would grab her and add to her collection of bruises as easily as he would shake her hand.

Kyle recognized the look. He saw it in his mirror most mornings. A stirring intuition placed Judith as the sinner he was meant to save.

"Taking it in, lad?"

Jonas's voice and demeanor lacked humor. Kyle's drifting thoughts had left into the space of air where Judith's breasts held residence. Judith looked amused.

"What?" said Kyle. He was shaken. "I'm sorry. It's been a long night and I must have spaced out."

Something hard pressed into Kyle's lower spine. He had no doubt what that something was.

"You'd better join us back here on Terra Firma as fast as you can before I turn you into a fucking jelly fish."

Jonas leaned closer, whispering threats on whiskey breath into Kyle's ear.

"Ya hear me, boy?"

Kyle nodded and looked side long at Jonas as Judith flashed him a sly smile. She made no attempt to lower her eyes to keep from laughing. She shook his hand and gave a sarcastic curtsy before heading back to the couch, laughing and giving him an ass wiggle he only saw through peripherals.

How quick a gesture and good lighting could change a snap judgment.

Kyle locked his gaze on Jonas, who remained flustered.

"Well then. Join us for a few drinks. Tell us all about this Devil who sent you. Entertain me! Molly, clear off the poker table. Let's play a game of asshole and see how long it takes our new friend to meet the toilet! James? Where's the bloody dark stuff?"

Jonas screamed as he slipped a Beretta back into the holster under his arm. Only then did Kyle realize his mistake in observation.

Jonas wasn't wearing suspenders. Jonas was wearing holsters.

On the first day, Kyle Thimall tasted life after years of wishing he was dead.

It tasted like vomit.

PRIDE

Pride is my power

You serve me purposefully

I am unrivalled

only a sinner can call another sinner 'sinner'

Four hours later, the basement apartment bore no evidence of the poker game. The grunts, moans, and culmination of Jonas and Molly's lovemaking ceased. Nobody snored. Kyle lie awake, unable to quiet his inner monologue in the silence. He habitually pointed a fan at himself while he slept.

The free flowing alcohol, coupled with Kyle's insistence to tell his story, turned him into a novelty. Eventually Kyle's anxiety subsided and their lips loosened. The drinks helped him maintain composure, especially when he caught Judith giving him subtle smiles and winks throughout the evening. Too drunk to drive, he accepted the couch as a bed after Judith retired to her bedroom. Her fruity perfume lingered on the cushions, as responsible for his insomnia as the silence.

Judith's face prevented him from reaching his REM cycle. Her effect on him overwhelmed and confused him. His thoughts went back and forth between the distant flirting and the bridge three miles down the road (and if Jonas kept a stock of quick dry cement on hand).

The MacMillan's exemplified modern mobsters: a small, connected family who hid their crimes in plain sight. The Green Rail was a legitimate business and their main source of income. The four managed the business with little outside help. They specialized in favors. If somebody knew the right way to ask, The MacMillan's did their best to fulfill their client's needs for the moderate fee. Sometimes the clients kept their end of the deal and profit was embezzled by all. Other clients defied Jonas, underestimating him or overestimating themselves. All of them learned that small time didn't mean small temper. Kyle didn't have to strike a deal with Jonas to figure that out. His deal was with the devil and he had still learned the lesson fast.

They stole when necessary, traded drugs when profitable, and spent the rest of the time running the pub. Jonas kept guns on his person, pressed against his ribcage underneath a crisp suit jacket. He didn't have a Dirty Harry complex, as he explained to Kyle. Guns detracted the drunks and scumbags better than a middle finger or slamming a door. More important to Jonas, it deterred anybody from doing unfavorable things to his daughter.

Jonas kept Judith under close watch. Five months prior, she started sneaking out. Jonas hinted that more than one fellow would never piss in a straight line again for the sins they introduced to Judith.

Every detail wove a tapestry of pain through a smiling mouth and pained eyes. Kyle understood the purpose of the stories. Beneath the flamboyant gestures and cinema quality narrative, they were warnings, not entertainment.

Touch my daughter, and I'll have Molly touch you with her butterfly knife.

Every syllable bounced from his mouth with perfect annunciation.

Jonas loved his family and friends, but his severe over protection of Judith caused unrest amongst them. A grown woman leaving the nest and being hunted down her father's orders took time away from The Rail, which meant money from their collective pockets.

The bruises and needle marks started showing after her first escape. Judith blamed them on clumsiness. Debris in the alley. Tripping while running. Other less than believable excuses. For a man who made his living not buying into bullshit, he devoured what his daughter served him and asked for seconds. So long as she was safe and so long there was somebody else to punish in Judith's stead, Jonas was complacent.

Jonas shot a boyfriend of Judith's after catching the two kissing on the couch where Kyle lie restless. Jonas returned home from meeting early and neither he nor his Beretta liked what they saw. He couldn't handle anybody defiling her or her loving anyone as much as her dear old dad. He couldn't handle Judith becoming a woman. Jonas put the boy in the hospital. Judith would never have guessed Jonas would react with such paranoid violence before that night.

The boy never spoke to Judith again. Angry and confused, she ran away. She exacted revenge on her father by indulging in various men, women, and drugs. When she returned home, her attitude towards her father changed.

It was too late to apologize, though Jonas often tried. Discussion of her absence was taboo, but he knew what she did on her revenge trips. When Jonas told Kyle how many families were without sons and daughters because of their interactions with Judith, Kyle realized that Jonas swallowed Judith's lies after he punished others for the truth.

Jonas backed off only after Molly, in a rare moment of non-sexual role reversal, informed Jonas that his violence was becoming an obsession, hurting business, and running off clients.

Judith loved her father in the maternal sense, but she could not forgive him as a man. Jonas confessed that truth before taking a shot, motioning Kyle to do the same, the barrel of his gun a baton leading the story of poor Jonas.

Jonas feigned ignorance and always wore a smile around her, pretending to give her freedom. The short leash drove the wedge deeper between them.

According to the watch, six hours had passed. He would let the piss flow when he had six hours left. He knew time would be short once an opportunity presented itself, and preparation was vital.

Kyle ran scenarios through his sobering mind. He had nursed a single beer the entire night, while the rest of them drank pints like water. The night cap of tequila left him dizzy. To fall asleep, he counted out half-assed ideas like sheep.

Violence and restraint were not options. He needed to earn her trust. Any other means would defile the purpose.

He hoped that she woke up early. He had no idea what to say to sell her on the story. Maybe she would humor him to spite Jonas. Even if he was convincing, he feared he would fuck up the actual saving her part.

The more he tried to fit the puzzle pieces into a coherent image, the bigger the puzzle got. There were no borders. A jumbled mess of center pieces, as confusing apart as they were as a picture. He wished he had taken a couple of more shots of tequila and passed out like the rest of them. Scheming was best left to a rested mind.

A hand clamped over his mouth. He struggled, waiting for the feel of metal and the pop of a gun, until Judith's peaked her head over his forehead, her eyes boring into his. Her finger rested on her lips, asking for a silence that her eyes warned was important.

Kyle raised his arms in surrender and relaxed as she removed her hand. He scooted up into a sitting position, hitting his head on the side table. He covered his mouth before the hiss of pain could escape. Judith did the same, holding back a chuckle. Judith covered her legs with Kyle's blanket as she joined him on the couch. She sat close to him, and sat as if she were by herself. He hoped her comfort meant interest. The double entendre dancing through his awakened senses caused him to dart his head around to make sure nobody was coming.

Jokes about farmer's daughters and watermelons being stuck up unmentionable places ran through his head. His eyes fixed onto hers and he forgot why he had been afraid.

She was a strange comfort, and he was still speechless.

"Don't worry. They sleep like the dead." she whispered.

Her demeanor had softened. If Jonas was an honest man, Kyle had misread her innocence upon first impression. That didn't make her a bad person. She was a survivor trying to play the cards she had been dealt.

If Kyle had met Judith when he was younger, he would have been the one in the wheelchair. She was magnetic. Unlike her lost love, he wouldn't have let a bullet keep him away. He would have risked Jonas' guns until they ended the spell she had cast, beyond if possible. Judith wouldn't leave his head, even while she sat in front of him. He hoped Sarah wasn't disappointed.

As Kyle was too distracted thinking of Judith to pay attention to her, she leaned forward and kissed him on the mouth. He succumbed long enough to be drunk in her and pulled away before it became an addiction. His will power surprised and frustrated him.

Judith found it impressive, though she didn't let that show. She had not stopped thinking of Kyle, either, though for more practical reasons.

"What are you doing?" Kyle whispered.

"What your eyes said you wanted me to do. Don't you want me to? Don't you want *me*?"

Judith opened the top of her robe, exposing the tops of her breasts. Awkward as she felt, she forced confidence out through every pheromone laden pore.

Her flesh begged Kyle to dive in. He could swear her nipples were trying to poke through her shirt and give him sad eyes. This was that moment that men waited for their entire lives to write about to Penthouse forums. Kyle wanted to rip his hair out in the tension.

"Jesus, Judith, I can't do that," he said.

Kyle reached forward and closed the top of her robe. He retracted his hands before a slip of the hand left him groping her and losing himself in the turbulent self-control storming through him. He knew he'd be unable to return.

She leaned sideways into the couch, looking confused and relieved.

"Why not? Isn't that what guys like you want? Are you afraid of my daddy or something? I saw you looking at me earlier. I think you're cute enough. Cut the chivalry and let's fuck."

The bluntness in her voice turned him on in a primal way, though her words sounded more a formality than a proposition. A practiced speech, a test of character, nothing more. Giving in to his primal temptations meant failing the test and the entire reason he was here altogether.

One glance at the watch on his wrist brought back the unspeakable sufferings that Brandon would face for eternity. It reminded him that his own hell would far surpass his dead brother in law's. Nobody was worth such pain. Except for Sarah. She was worth being shat out by Beelzebub himself.

He would not let himself admit that Judith was also an exception, and he would not take advantage of Judith, least of all when her own soul was at stake.

Judith followed his glance towards the wristwatch. She grabbed his wrist and pulled it to her face. The soft, red glow cascaded over her features in a psychedelic manner of a Sam Raimi horror movie where someone finds a brutal effigy left by the killer and the screen bleeds red with a scream.

"What's this?" Judith asked.

"Oh," stammered Kyle, his spastic thoughts broken. "It's a relic, I guess."

"What's it for?" she asked.

She moved her gaze from the watch and looked him in the eyes, all traces of seduction gone. Her innocent, curious tone shattered the image of the sexual vixen that she had portrayed. Kyle was grateful for the small favor.

This was the real Judith.

"The "devil" gave it to me to keep track of the seven souls and the seven day period and all that. If I fail, it becomes my symbol of his ownership. Great gift, no?"

"Oh, please," Judith said. She rolled her eyes at both his explanation and his cheesy use of finger quotes.

"They might have pretended to believe you when they were drunk last night, but I'm sure they think you're crazy. As original as whatever story you told may be, the chances that the devil sent you to save one of them are as likely as my dad letting me go on the Dating Game. Not 'effin very, Mr."

Her use of finger quotes was more grammatically correct than
Kyle's. Nerd smitten: the most dangerous kind.

"I know how crazy your family thinks I am, but I wasn't lying. I
wish I had been. Nobody else here has that lost look in their eye. None
of them think they are doing anything wrong, so they can't repent.
They are beyond saving, but I think I'm here for..."

"What? For me?" Judith laughed. "Look, I said I'd fuck you, so
you can drop the Prince Wesley act. I'm flattered that you want to save
me and that you think I'm soooo lovely."
She batted her eyelashes and fanned herself with a hand.

"Thank you for thinking enough to want to save me from such
hell bent wickedry. Unkept promises and fairy tales are for seven year
olds. I don't know if your stalling is awkward foreplay or performance
anxiety. Just fuck me or don't already so I can get sleep, ok?"

This was also the real Judith. Looking for something real to
hold on to and disappointed at every turn. She believed that Kyle was
playing a sick game. It explained why she played her hand first. Men
were putty in the hands of sexy women. It was something tangible that
she could grasp.
Or maybe she feared trusting him. Feared that she was close to
attaining the freedom she had stolen but never owned.

It was Kyle's turn to vent a frustrated monologue.

"Look, you do something to me that I'm finding harder to
believe than meeting Lucifer in an alley behind a watch shop, ok?
You're gorgeous. I haven't been able to get you out of my head since I
met you, and I've seen some unbelievable shit in the past few hours.
Look me in the eye. You know I'm not lying. I'm an addict and a
manic depressive cab driver who was visited by the devil tonight.
I was told I had seven days to save seven sinners, lest I become the
Dark Lord's fuck toy. I'm scared sober, shitless, and my sanity aside,
I couldn't imagine this story on acid, let alone the Splenda diluted
cocaine I snorted before I met him. I need to do something before I do
go insane. You're the only one who wants help more than you need it.
That's what I want to do, Judith. Help you, save you, and save myself.
If I'm not dreaming and I fuck this up, I don't foresee an eternity of
mixing martini's for Satan while he plays poker with his buddies. I'm
beyond scared. I don't think either of us can understand why I can't get
you out of my head with so much shit being thrown at me, but I know
you can understand what it's like to be scared."

Kyle let his body go slack on the couch, exhaustion hitting him too late to do much good.

Judith stared at him for a long while, her eyes scanning his face and eyes, trying to catch the lie he promised didn't exist. Her eyes grew more and more quizzical with each passing glance. After a few moments, she moved her hand from his wrist to his hand. He had not noticed she had been holding it the entire time until she did. The trail her fingernails traced left goose bumps.

"Fine." Judith said.

"Fine, what?"

"I believe you. I was reading your pulse, and I was raised around liars. You're telling the truth."

"Reading my pulse?" Kyle said, dumbfound.

"Little trick I was taught as a girl. Takes a long time to get a knack for it and most people can't. That Criss Angel guy can do it. You know him? The magician? You're telling the truth. If what you're promising gets me away from this place, thanks to the devil, naiveté, or a ride to a cheap motel for the sex you claim you don't want, then I'd like to help you save me. If you take me with you, I will repay the favor with my help and my everlasting gratitude."

"Take you with me? I don't know how I'm supposed to save you, but Jonas won't let me live long enough to carry that little mission out if he finds the two of us missing."

"Oh, come on, Mr. Hero. He'll be asleep for half the day. We'll be close to the state line by the time he decides what he wants for lunch! Trust me, I know. Having me around gives you at least a fraction of legitimacy. You *will* need that. Not everyone will be susceptible to the idea. I can play fanatic. Presentation is key and your monologue won't work for everybody."

"Well..."

"Please? I have doubts." Judith pleaded.

"You'd be insane not to," Kyle interjected.

"To be fair, most cults start out like this. I'm willing to drink the Kool-Aid because *you* have no doubts. I need to get away from my dad for once without sex, drugs, and revenge being the motivators. Those paths always lead me back to the door at the bottom of that stupid green rail. This place is a mausoleum, haunted by ghosts he won't let die and evils he's destined to commit."

"I had no idea." Kyle lied.

"Oh, come off it. I know you saw the track marks and the bruises. I heard him telling you his stories. I know he told you what he did to Mitch. He was my first love. My first everything." Judith said.

Tears welled in her ducts but did not fall. She was used to hiding her tears.

"Jonas paralyzed him because he was greedy and afraid of losing me. Mitch, for all the love he promised, wheeled away without even thank you note. I didn't care that his body was crippled. I loved him. But he cared plenty that my family was crippled, mentally and spiritually. The only two men I've ever loved broke my heart within a week, Kyle. The second Jonas pulled the trigger, he lost me and I lost my innocence."

"That isn't helping my decision, Judith. I don't like hospitals. Or triggers, for that matter." Kyle said.

Judith continued speaking over him, as if this dialogue was more about understanding demons than convincing truths. Kyle and Judith both knew she was going with him. This was pre-quest speed dating to unload the heavy baggage. A Final Fantasy, indeed.

"I don't want to spite my father, Kyle. I want to be free of him. I'm sick of sleeping around just to make myself feel better about hating him! I'm twenty-two, dammit! If you want to save me, then let me come with you. Let me rely on myself instead of scapegoating with drugs and flesh. Give me the strength to do that, Kyle, and I will owe you my soul."

Her grip on his hand tightened. As her pleading eyes bored thanks into his, those welling tears began to fall. Her walls had crumbled. She had intended to play a game with him and had won in a way she didn't expect: she found hope.

Judith kept reminding Kyle of Sarah, or more accurately of how he felt around Sarah. Even if he failed, and even if this was a vivid hallucination, he would take her. He would do everything in his power to save her. He would die for her.

"Ok. You can come."

Her expression was as warming as her lips were plutonic. She kissed him, her calm lips exciting what his conscience could not ignore. His decision gave instant rewards. She broke off the kiss and embraced him, whispering "thank you" into his ear until he, willpower running on fumes, pulled away.

"We'd better get dressed, be quiet, and be gone. I'm fine with the number of holes I have in my body. More might be detrimental to my body-building aspirations."

She laughed the tears away, thankful for what Kyle passed off as humor. A flicker of illumination drew her eyes back to Kyle. The watch began to glow a bright hue of blue. The number three and the word next to it were now brightly illuminated. The word, the color of the sky on a cloudless day, was visible even from Judith's vantage point.

LUST

Judith put her hand to her head, falling back to the couch. Kyle reached for her, but Judith pushed his hands away. She turned her gaze to meet Kyle's. He saw that they were glowing the same color as Lucifer's had.

The red glow transformed into a blue mist as it streamed from her eyes. It floated before Judith, long enough for her to reach a finger into the cloud. Once her finger touched the mist, the cloud, as if being sucked, was drawn into Kyle's watch. The face let off one final flash, this time a bright white, before returning to its original state. The word LUST remained lit.

"What the hell was that, Kyle?" Judith said with mouth wide in awe.

"An answer, I hope. At the very least an idea for an artsy perfume commercial," Kyle replied.

The illumination silenced her inhibitions.

"You *were* telling the truth, Kyle. I'm fucking free! I took a chance and it paid off!" Judith's words trailed off into pleasant contemplation.

Kyle smiled at her.

"I told you I was here to save you."

"Until you finish whatever you are doing, I am your girl. I will help you in any way I can, though I will never be able to thank you enough."

Judith embraced Kyle again, and the whispered gratitude returned. He welcomed each whisper of thanks, enjoying her closeness and the pressure of her body against his. Judith's positivity rubbed off on him. Through the strange cloud, her presence, or knowing that he didn't have to sacrifice a thing he had promised to save her, he felt something that he hadn't in years.

Kyle Thimall felt hope.

CHAPTER 9

high gas prices and holy gun licenses

The taxi sputtered to a stop. Kyle cursed himself for forgetting to gas up after Bradburry's, though forgotten responsibilities could be forgiven after adding "survive" to the top of his short term goal list.

Kyle and Judith had planned to follow the alley parallel to 17th street. Three miles away, 17th street dead ended onto Lowell avenue, which they could follow left or right until they thought of a better plan.

The blinking E on Kyle's fuel meter ended that plan quick, fast, and in a hurry. Kyle wondered if he might have saved the taxi's soul by making a quick stop at the gas station. The cab, certain as heathens were stoned, envied any vehicle that ran on more than the dried fumes it was choking down.

There was a gas station at the intersection, but they were in a questionable part of the city. Kyle wasn't sure if they could make it the last mile without a mugging, a raping, a beating, or a nightmarish combination of the three.

Judith had knocked a vase over, by clumsy accident, in their hurry to flee the basement. Her father and his three stooges were on their way to kill him and bring her, kicking and screaming, back to that hell hole beneath The Green Rail. That was the assumption they were operating on, anyway.

Denying Judith her short lived salvation would be their mission. Denying Kyle the freedom to further take in oxygen would be their reward.

The coke is right below you, Kyle.
He ignored the weak voice of his addiction, needing to stay clear headed.

Staying in the taxi guaranteed an unhappy ending. Abandoning it shifted the odds to highly likely.

"There is an Exxon at the end of the alley. If we start walking now, we can make it back before the lights on the car die."

"Do you have a weapon to protect your fair maiden?" Judith batted her eyelashes at him.

"There's a tire thumper in the trunk next to the gas can."

"How very gritty."

"The most advanced gangland weaponry for you, m'lady."

"Shall we then?" Judith said as she exited the cab.

Kyle left pulled the keys out of the ignition and pressed a button on the dash to turn on a pair of lights he had installed on the grill. They weren't very bright, but dim light was better than none at all.

Kyle popped the trunk and pulled out his tire thumper, a wooden Louisville slugger about half the length and twice the thickness of the normal baseball bat, and a 2 gallon gas can. After a reach under the bumper, the little magnetic box that held his spare key disappeared into his pocket. Most criminals knew of the little magnetic hiding place. If they wanted the car, they would need to work for it.

The tinny echo of the slamming trunk made Kyle uneasy. He handed Judith the gas can and grabbed her free hand with his. His head bobbed side to side like a hungry snake as he searched for signs of danger.

"Maybe we should move over to the street, you know? This alley creeps me out. It might be worth trying to find a ride." Kyle said. He tightened his grip on the tire thumper.

"You don't think the first person who sees you hailing them down with a baseball bat and a pretty girl holding a gas can might get the wrong idea? Do you think you'll need to use that, Kyle?" Judith said, motioning at the bat.

"If we don't, it will be a damned miracle. I don't think Senior Diablo included any of those in the contract. At least it's a Tuesday. As much as I hate them, Tuesday's are like the Sabbath to gang bangers."

"Why is that, oh Historian of the Hood?"

"I dunno. Tupac, Tuesday, it must be an alliterative mourning thing."

A blank stare and a sigh said it all.

"That was a terrible joke..."

"It's hard to be funny when you're broke down in crack town, Judith," Kyle said.

By terror's ever present cue, a loud crashing sound, followed by the familiar song of a car alarm, startled them.

"What the..." they both chimed in unison, snapping their heads to look behind them.

Behind them, a couple of men had thrown a brick through the back passenger window of the taxi. The pair noticed Judith and Kyle at about the same time Judith and Kyle noticed them. They took off in the direction they were walking and began chase.

"Is that little bat going to help, Kyle?"

The building fear in her voice chilled him.

"If they don't have a..."

Again, with Oscar worthy timing, a bullet whizzed into the large dumpster to the left of Judith and ricocheted into the alley wall.

"...gun." Kyle finished, frozen.

Judith, used to guns and the loud sounds that froze men dead, grabbed his wrist and screamed, "Run!" The sounds of the footsteps grew louder. Judith turned down the first alley she spotted.

"Come back, little girl!" one of the men shouted, his faint voice growing in volume with each syllable.

The graffiti and condemned doors multiplied the farther they ran. Kyle's breathe was growing shallow as a charlie horse whinnied a violent objection in his ribs. He decided to remember the pain as motivation to give up smoking.

Damn the devil and his Lucky Strikes.

The shouts and footsteps echoed louder as the two men turned into the alley. Two more gunshots rang out. One bullet zipped by Kyle's face. One hit his tire thumper and split the tip.

Judith was the first to spot the bright street lights that she hoped indicated people. Before she could voice the discovery, her shoe met a pot hole. Still hand in hand, they spilled to the asphalt. Judith scraped her palms after dropping the gas can to catch herself. The knees of her jeans tore like soggy pancakes. Kyle managed falling into an old, rusty shopping cart, puncturing his left arm on a renegade piece of metal.

Great, he thought wryly. *Now I need a fucking tetanus shot to boot.*

The men with the iron lungs approached while Kyle and Judith attempted to make their sore bodies work again. They were close enough so that Kyle could manage no consolation. Gun owner or not, everybody was a coward with a gun pointed at them. Judith crawled to him and accepted his open arms. Blood flowed from the puncture wound in his tricep, soaking the sleeve of her shirt. She grabbed his arm and pulled him close as the shadows of their two predators fell over their battered forms.

The two thugs laughed. They breathed like Olympic runners after a walk to the mailbox. The gun man spoke as he tucked the weapon into his pants.

"Two for one, Jesse! Our lucky night! After we're through with the little bitch, we can show this little pendejo why the chase is only half the fun."

"I hope you brought condoms, Mark, because that little whore looks nasty. Probably caught something from your brother."

"Shut the fuck up." said Mark

Judith buried her head into the crook of Kyle's arm, her bravery exhausted.

Kyle's prediction had come to fruition. The thugs were going to mug them, rape them, and kill them. He was a man who knew that the only thing he knew was jack shit, but when he was right, he hated it. Alone, he'd have begged for mercy. Blown them both for the chance to survive. Never for drugs, but for survival? He was sure he could find a happy place.

Kyle might have even welcomed the bullet to cease his depressing inability to keep up this devil's chore. With Judith next to him injured and scared, that choice was truncated. He had vowed to protect and save her, and he would die trying, if need be.

Kyle took a deep breath and found his inner courage. His expression melted into a scowl as his fist tightened around the thumper. He opened his mouth, tough words dancing on the tip of his tongue, but he never got to speak them.

A powerful voice to their left spoke them for him.

"How can I help you gentleman today?" said the man, He wore a black robe. While the white around his neck symbolized his priesthood, the shotgun in his hands symbolized something from a darker side of faith. Kyle summed him up with one internal thought.

One-Hundred Percent, ordained badass.

Somewhere, Bruce Campbell tossed in his sleep with the subconscious hope that he would get to play lead in this holy man's biopic.

He loosened his grip on the tire thumper, sighing with relief and holding on to Judith.

"Stay out of this, Padre." goaded Jesse, raising his hand to his waistline.

"Or what? You'll pop me with that little pea-shooter you have tucked in your jeans? Not very smart of you to lay down your weapon without knowing what lies ahead, is it?"

Jesse reached for his gun as the priest spoke to him, but the cocking of the shotgun froze him, much as he had frozen Kyle minutes before.

"I'll say this once, and I'll say it nice and slow, as I'm sure you failed out of high school. Leave these two, and my church, and go rape and pillage on your own turf. These are God's grounds, and I'll not have you violate them."

"Ok, Father. You win. Just don't...." Mark started, before dashing to his right, straight towards Kyle and Judith.

The priest's gaze followed Mark, giving Jesse the opportunity to reach for his gun and shoot. The bullet missed the priest by a foot and a half. The priest turned back towards Jesse with unflinching calm pulled the trigger of his own weapon.

Nothing more than a stump and a spray of blood remained where Jesse's gun-toting hand had once been. Small pellet holes littered his arm. He screamed in agony and dropped to his knees.

"Close up pot-shots are a bitch." the priest said.

As Mark turned his attention towards his injured compadre, Kyle swung the thumper with what strength he could muster, striking Mark in the side of his shin. Mark screamed obscenities and hobbled over to his friend. He hoisted him up, supporting him on his shoulders.

"What the fuck, father?" Mark screamed in hysterics. "What happened to turning the other cheek?"

"I'm not that kind of priest," was his sly reply, followed by a second cocking of the shotgun.

Ordained Badass.

"Fuck this!" Mark mustered.

Mark dragged his wailing friend down the alley way with haste, realizing that God's chicken coop was off limits to foxes like him and Jesse.

"Remember! Jesus saves! And I just took your ass to church!"

The priest laughed with mock malevolence as he fired his remaining shell into the air. The gangsters both crouched, covering their heads, before jumping up and retreating at a faster pace. Kyle loosened his grip on the thumper, dropping it to the street. He fell backwards, staring skyward and giving his heart a chance to slow. He was satisfied to have helped in a small way. Judith stared at the priest in awe. Leon slung the shotgun over his shoulder like a baseball bat and helped Kyle up with his free hand. Kyle, in turn helped Judith to her feet. She latched on to Kyle again, exhausted shock overpowering her senses, weary of the priest and his weapon.

The priest offered her a sweet smile and a friendly nod of his head.

"Fear not, my child. My name is Father Leon Grebowski. And I believe you've just been saved."

CHAPTER 10

if chins could kill

Father Leon accommodated Kyle and Judith to the best of his ability. The back door belonged to St. Christopher's Church. Leon led them up a set of hidden stairs, impressing Kyle with the sliding access to his loft apartment. The one window in the apartment was stained glass of blues and yellows. It overlooked the church interior, coloring the pews and walls with psycadelic hues.

Leon nursed and dressed their wounds. He gave them what food and drink. He offered them spare workout clothes while the machine removed bloody reminders of the attack. They put on the sweat pants and t-shirts, baggy and worn, with humble thanks.

Ever the gracious host, Leon also offered them his own room to sleep. Ignoring the "too good to be true" voice in his head, Kyle gave in to his exhaustion and accepted. They had been through too much to end the evening with arguments of insistence.

Kyle had saved one soul in less than a day. Judith had escaped her father's iron grip. The two needed to sleep away the stress and adrenaline wear. Leon insisted that Kyle sleep on a cot. Judith, having resorted to a childlike state, clung to Kyle's injured arm. She wanted as little distance between her ticket to salvation as possible. Kyle remained in control of his faculties for her sake more than his own.

The danger was at bay for the moment. The full weight of what had almost happened hit Judith, who usually controlled any situation outside of The Green Rail. Her strength character had been crippled.

Judith relaxed about sleeping arrangement when Leon agreed to let Kyle set the cot next to her bed, in case she wanted to find his hand in the night. Sins of the flesh didn't worry Leon. Having slept in close quarters with far more people, Leon knew that two people sleeping in a twin bed left both restless and sore by morning. Tossing and turning in such proximity had a way of staving off REM's angels.

Judith was snoring moments after her head touched the pillow. Kyle, though exhausted, was too wired to sleep. Leon made tea spiked with orange liquor for the two to share, admitting it helped his frequent rendezvous with insomnia. Kyle was grateful for the Leon's ailment. He and Judith would be dead otherwise. As a bonus, if anybody could help him decipher the confusing theology of his situation it would be a priest. Meeting Leon was a sign, or fate was manipulative beyond Kyle's comprehension.

Kyle chose his first words from the chaotic incoherence in his head as he sipped the tea.

"Father, I have to ask you something."

"Please, my son. I've seen your blood. It's just Leon."

"Leon, then. Do you, well…do you…"

"Lay it on the table, Kyle. I'm sure I've heard far more illogical and you do look troubled."

"Ask and you shall receive. Tonight, I was visited by Lucifer. He proposed a wager between him and God that places me in the middle of a fantastical grudge bet?"

"You mean like Job?" Leon asked, humoring Kyle.

"Like Job, except I'm batting top of the ninth with two strikes and a blindfold. He gave me this watch…"

Kyle lifted his watch so the face was visible underneath the lamp light. The expression on Leon's face changed from modest interest to near shock so fast that Kyle was sure Leon knew something. Leon knew something.

Leon grabbed Kyle's wrist and pulled it close, causing Kyle to wince. His arm was still sore from the shopping cart tumble.

"Sorry," Leon muttered, not loosening his grip. "Where did you get this? This shouldn't exist, Kyle. This is dark."

"I told you. Lucifer gave it to me. It counts down the seven souls that I have seven days to save. Each soul represents a different sin."

Leon fingered the glowing three, throwing a brief glance at Judith.

"It looks like you've already saved one," he said.

"True, but Judith was practice mode. I had guidance with her."

Leon hushed Kyle with a hand over his mouth. Leon's excitement was a good thing, but Kyle's tongue pressed against Leon's hand as it covered his mouth. It tasted like sweat and gunpowder. Kyle let Leon examine the watch and breathed through his nose. He didn't want to taste the hand of a man forbidden from knowing a woman.

"Wait here. I have something you need to see," Leon said.

Kyle, who had started to drift off during the watch examination, snapped awake.

Kyle heard Leon's footfalls, light and quick, putter down the hallway. The sound of a drawer being opened, followed by rustling, was the Doppler middle point before Leon returned clutching a thin leather bound book. It looked beaten and weathered. Leon handled it with little care for its condition as he fumbled through the pages.

"What is that?" Kyle couldn't help but inquire.

Leon answered as he flipped through the book.

"A book of religious myths. Parables, horror stories, and fables billed as firsthand accounts, written around the same time as the Bible. At least according to the theologians who don't find it a load of bunk. Word of mouth stories involving demons and other like-minded monsters."

Leon stopped talking, answering his sudden silence by spinning the book towards Kyle and dropping it into his lap. Leon reached down, Kyle's eyes following, and rested his finger on a sketch amongst a sea of tiny, foreign writing. The sketch looked like Kyle's watch.

"Is that a sun dial?" Kyle asked.

"A sun dial that matches the design of your watch."

"Nice to know I got the upgrade plan for free," Kyle said.

"I got this book from an old friend as a gag gift during my entry into the priesthood. He asked me if the myths of a myth were a fact. I told him that the only difference between the two was an eye witness or proof. I guess in the case of your watch, he was correct."

"This is a drawing of a sun dial. Nothing more. For all I know, the devil knew I would find you and made the watch to match. He is one hell of a game designer."

Kyle rubbed the bridge of his nose, strangeness making him tired. He knew he was over thinking the situation, but he also knew he had to be somewhat paranoid about what the devil would or would not do for a win.

"Maybe so, but the sun dial is real. It has been documented. At the end of the nineteenth century, a farmhand found it underneath a pig troth on an unimportant farm in Europe. An entire village of people saw it, so you can imagine the fables created to explain its existence. Until this moment, I believed it was what this book claimed it to be. An archaic collectible with an interesting back story. Maybe a hoax planted by a bored mason. A myth."

Leon spoke fast, as if the watch might disappear if he showed anything but the up most excitement about this discovery.

"So this has happened before?" Kyle said.

Kyle remembered Lucifer calling him the second. He had thought Lucifer meant Job. Lying about mundane details offered no benefit, but the important details were lost amongst the words. He was starting to hate himself for not asking questions.

"Not exactly," explained Leon. "As far as the stories in this book go, I can tell you the similarities. Make what you will of them."

Kyle listened, enjoying the exuberance in Leon's voice. It was a good hour for stories. Kyle understood why people would gather to watch a warm, charismatic sermon from Leon. He had a way of making even the darkest news comforting.

"Job had his life decimated. God still won the bet. Story told. According to this, a quarter of a century later, Lucifer called foul play. He claimed that God's omniscience invalidated the bet. Too many rules spoil the game. God must have cheated and hidden it in layers shrouded in secrecy."

"God is infallible and good, right?" Kyle asked.

"Lucifer's point exactly. If God could be proven as a cheat or to have evil in him, Lucifer could use it as leverage. Sure, evil runs rampant, but to have proof that the being that man places such perceptions of perfection in is not so? Guilt of sin would have crumbled."

"Good point, but if God makes the rules, isn't it a bit like Nixon? When I do it, it isn't illegal?"

"Job's faith was at the level of unshakeable that he believed that very thing. Of course Job didn't denounced God. He was committed long before the bet began. Whatever happened was God's will, whatever God willed was ultimately good, so his suffering must have been a blessing. He had no reason to believe God would fail him. He believed that heaven was waiting no matter what ill came his way. Job was willing to suffer anything. God ignored Lucifer's wailing, knowing that the Devil had picked Job out himself. Lucifer became quite the accuser.

He claimed that God had planted an Angel on earth as Job to play a part and assure victory for Heaven, that God went so far as to offer the real Job a place at his side as the ultimate smack in the face, that God had created an alternate reality filled with soulless lumps of creation just to keep the Devil busy and away from mankind."

"Not a bad idea, that last one," Kyle said.

"The earliest form of special effects, Kyle. Lucifer demanded a second wager. Instead of testing a faithful man's piousy, they would test a man with waning or absent faith by dangling the truth in front of his eyes and seeing how well he coped. The man would have to save a soul for each sins. Lucifer would play as many foul tricks as he felt necessary with no interference whatsoever from God. God would have to swear an oath of passivity that bound both Him and His angels.

Lucifer's chosen one was committed to an oath he couldn't break once sworn. In turn, the devil was barred from making any physical contact. This man would count become an unholy faithless avenger. Before you make the comment, yes that would be a pretty bad ass name for a band."

"I wasn't going to say that at all!" Kyle lied.

"No tool of Satan could hurt the holy during the bet, meaning the only way Satan could interfere would be to give free will to a bunch of demon's and hope that one of them felt charitable. Even he isn't that stupid. There are other vague details involving God and why, exactly, the Devil was so anxious to declare the bet when he did. The story is over the top. The meat of the story is easier to regurgitate than the details."

Leon's eyes twinkled as he looked at Kyle for a reaction.

"That sounds like a confusing movie plot, and now I can't shake the feeling that David Lynch is directing my life. So it's the same bet, even if the handshake took a couple millennia. Why now, if this myth is so damned old?"

"Well, God never acknowledged the wager. Adamant as Lucifer was, God cast him out for a reason and had no desire to interact with him outside of business that mattered. Lucifer was denied leverage. When He says no, there's no use in asking for a retrial. He felt no need to play any further games, and the sun dial Lucifer had constructed for the wager was cast aside, his challenge ignored. There must be something very important happening we're not privy too. Unimportant and forgotten details might answer why God has accepted."

"Any clues at all?" Kyle asked.

He hoped he could get a bit of an answer to the ever popular "Why me?" question, but Leon looked at the floor as if embarrassed.

"God is bored? God wants to shake up this planet ant farm? God wants to reverse the growth of Atheism? To be honest, I don't think I can help you anymore, Kyle. I want to, but I've given you what I can," Leon explained, saddened.

"I'm just asking for information, Leon. This may be a stupid cosmic chess game, but I'm still a pawn. Unlike Job, I don't have much faith that it will all end up ok. God is a king, sitting back and waiting. The devil is doing a good job playing the queen."

"As a wise prophet once said, a queen's just a pawn with a lot of fancy moves."

Kyle spared a glance toward the room where Judith slept.

"It doesn't matter. She says she's with me until the end and she is stubborn. Two souls are at stake. There has to be something I can do." Kyle added with raised volume.

Leon hushed him with a quite exhale through closed teeth and a sullen stare.

"You may still stay the night, but when you two wake up tomorrow, after breakfast of course, you two have to continue this path alone. I have much sin in my own soul. The two of you winding up at my back door and showing me this watch has opened my troubled eyes, and I weep for my discretions. They are numerous and heavy. I'm no good to you."

Leon lifted his head, tears falling down his cheeks. Leon had changed in the hour since they had met. The tears left streaks down his dry face. Kyle was frustrated and speechless.

"What I did tonight was not a judgment call I had a right to make. It was God's. Until fate brought us all together, my faith had been dissolving to the point of cessation."

"You stopped believing in the God you preach about?" Kyle asked, dumbfounded.

"All but the positive message, I'm sad to say."

"Then why continue as a priest?"

"My job helped people. It's the whole reason I joined priesthood. I lacked faith, but others did not. Others needed to be embraced and loved by God. I felt that I could do the good for them that I rarely saw God do. I could listen to unheard voices and answer unheard prayers. In place of an unseen God, I would be their God. This watch, Kyle. "

Leon glanced down at it, trying to be strong in the face of his own confession.

"And you. I see now that, despite our disagreements, God is alive and well. It is no longer my place to carry on a mummer's farce. It never was. Only to show those in need how to find him. Now, if you'll excuse me, my son."

Leon stood up and walked towards his chamber door. Kyle wasn't sure, but he swore the tears on the priests face had taken on a red hue.

"Fath...Leon? Where are you going?"

Leon turned and offered what smile he could.

"I have much to discuss with God, my son. It's time we two talked heart to heart. For the first time in a long while."

"You aren't going to do anything drastic, are you Leon? You're face to face will be spiritual, right? I've seen enough blood for one night."

Leon smiled. He shook his head at Kyle's concern and motioned for him to sleep.

"No, no, Kyle. Didn't you hear me? I'm not that kind of priest. Now rest. You and Judith have long days ahead."

"You may not be able to help me much, Leon, but if there's anything I can do, I guess it's kind of my job to help at the moment."

"You already have, Kyle. More than you know. More than I can repay you for. Rest, please."

There was a flicker of light in the hall as Leon flicked a switch. The red of his tears must have been heat or blood pressure, though Kyle swore he saw a misting of purple haloing the priest's head in the space of time that the light bulb blinked out.

The door closed. Again, Kyle thought he would never rest. So much information, so many unanswered questions. Leon said Kyle had helped, though he had done nothing but listen. He wondered if Leon might not be someone to stick around and try to save. Leon had been more generous and kind than most of the good people Kyle knew.

Kyle took Leon's advice and laid down his head for rest, all the while wondering what sin the priest could be guilty of. A bright, violet light from the watch hurt his tired eyes. Kyle squinted to read the display, but his eyes were drawn to the black of the door Leon had closed.

In the space level with where Kyle saw the violet mist halo, the air was moving towards him. The violet mist grew in size and density, all the while traveling in Kyle's direction. As Judith had earlier, once he was able, Kyle touched the mist. It was sucked into the watch,

The dot and number four were now illuminated, the sin written across the display now visible.

PRIDE

Kyle hugged the pillow and took Judith's sleeping hand. She made a small noise, but remained still and asleep.

For all the obscurity, a question had been answered. Leon couldn't help Kyle because of his sin. Something led Kyle and Judith to that back door so that he could inspire the priest give a long overdue confession. If fate left a possible murderer and rapist without a hand, she was alright by Kyle.

Kyle's mind cleared, as if the purple mist in his watch was a spoonful of extra strength cold medicine. He was asleep within seconds.

In a separate room, Leon sat still. The purple mist that flowed from his eyes and the red illumination left him peaceful. He knew he could do nothing to help Kyle, just as he knew that Kyle had added another save to his collection. He was grateful.

Something else happened to Leon as sin poured from his soul. A premonition, a prophecy, a vision-whatever it was called, played in his mind as clear as a newly formed memory.

Leon had seen himself on crucifix, bleeding out and burning. His hands bore holes without nails. Nothing held him to the cross. He was suspended by an unseen or unknown force. And he was in agony.

A flash of dark, and Leon saw why no nails or ropes held him. A winged red beast, horned and red and as tall as the crucifix, stood behind it, holding Leon up by the armpits. Leon's hands were pierced by the wide horns of the demon, thus the holes. Though the vision was mostly visual, he heard one thing echo into the depths of the dark place where fear rested.

Cold, deep, evil laughter.

Leon sat, knowing that though Kyle would sleep, he would not.

His vision burned shades of red.

He was deaf to all but the laughter.

For the first time in a decade, Father Leon Grebowski dropped to his knees and prayed.

it's raining snakes and frogs

Jonas threw the empty bottle of gin across the room, shattering an antique mirror that once belonged to his mother. She would have forgiven his hereditary temper. His lapse in judgment and intelligence would have her rolling in her grave from disappointment.

"None of you heard her leave? Not a single, drunken one of you?" Jonas huffed at a silenced room.

"Well, I heard something fall when I got up to piss. I thought you were still awake, cos I heard voices that sounded like you and Judith, so I didn't think anything of it," Ian said.

Jonas flew across the room with the agility of a man half his age. Ian's back was against the far wall, a gun to the temple of his head, before the simpleton understood that Jonas was even angry with him. Ian's eyes moved from Jonas' grimace to the gun held to his head and back again. He wasn't worried about being hurt, or even dying. Knowing he upset Jonas was torture.

Molly had never seen Jonas so furious. She saw him take care of that Mitch boy, and had seen the glimmer of enjoyment in his eyes. Now all his eyes bore was rage. She would step in if he gave any impression of following through with a bullet. She listened for the gun to cock in silence. Her lover's hands would not be stained at the fault of an insane, theo-babbling cabby.

At least not with her brother's blood.

"Jonas," James started, arrogance in check.

Jonas ignored him.

"You know how she gets, you silly fuck!" Jonas spit into Ian's face. "How many motherfuckers have we had to bury in cement over her? How many since her mother died? You know good and well how I feel about her kanoodling with scum. There's no reason you shouldn't have checked that noise out with a stranger in our living room! She lives to spite us all! Your job is to pay attention!"

"I lost a lot last night, Jonas. I was too drunk to move. If you had told me to stop drinking, I would have. I swear!" Ian pleaded in a whisper.

Jonas, having vented his frustrations with words and shaking, loosened his grip on Ian's shirt collar, understanding that Ian was right. Ian had the ears and the instinct where brains failed him. Jonas insisted on a party and let down their collective guard. He couldn't blame Ian for taking orders. He let go of Ian's shirt and placed his hands to his temples, rubbing.

"Forgive me, Ian. I am not myself today," Jonas apologized.

Ian shook his head, forgiveness given without question. Molly's posture eased. James noticed, and he grinned at the sight of it. They were crumbling and he was loving it.

Jonas's eyes moved towards the front door, where a short time ago, his little girl walked away from him. Possibly forever.

For the sake of Judith's safety and his reputation, he would rectify the situation.

"I should have realized that she'd try it with him, too. Try to take my little girl away, eh cabbie?" he said, as if Kyle stood in front of him.

He slipped the gun back into the holster under his arm, though it was a while before he removed his hand.

"Try to save her, will he? Well, he'd better hope the devil gave him a guardian angel with that fucking watch, because he'll be meeting him early if I have my two bets right."

"I never trusted him from the first," said James. "I just thought he was trying to get us to sympathize and offer him a bed or drugs. Street urchins are rarely convincing. We are all to blame for not spotting it. No reason in focusing on that. Let's get the little prick."

The group offered opinions and methods of how to take care of Kyle. Calm overcame Jonas as the ideas grew in violence. For the briefest moment, he thought that, instead of a ridiculous man hunt that would drive a bigger wedge between him and Judith, he would do nothing.

Nothing at all.

He was a man of good judgment. Despite waking up to find his daughter gone, and despite the opinions of lunacy directed towards Kyle, he couldn't deny his first impression that Kyle was a trustworthy person. Whatever prompted the facade about the devil, he saw the purpose in Kyle's eyes.

Judith was unhappy. Though she was ignorant to the fact, Jonas had known every tryst she had partaken in over the past months. Every single one of them had been quick to disappear into the silent witness protection program that criminals were masters of instituting. She slept around as a way to gain silent power over him, but he wore the smile and treated her like a princess. He exacted his own revenge and vented his own frustrations on the very cretins she turned towards to spite him. Molly and her butterfly knife were indispensable for their help and discretion.

Judith didn't know that Jonas had always known. The deceit was blanketed in false smiles and cold shoulders. The house of cards was close to crumbling, and his decision would either be the final hammer or a new coating of cement on the foundation.

There was the off chance that Kyle was being honest. His words were strange, but he believed them. Nothing about Kyle leaned towards insanity. Nervous, and a tad boring, but not insane. The insane had no qualms about hiding their problems, because they didn't know they were crazy.

Kyle had seemed far too on edge to even think about sex. Jonas had squashed whatever lingering spark of friskiness he might have had with the same threat he used on all men who came into his home to do business.

In that moment, he almost decided to grant Judith the freedom she so desired. She would learn, and she would return. Maybe his mercy would rekindle the relationship they had shared before her mother died. It would lessen the stress around the bar, and within the family.

James was quick to extinguish these thoughts with his always blunt insight, returning Jonas to his senses.

"Boss, I didn't want to say anything to further upset you this morning, but I've been thinking."

"Yes, James?" Jonas said.

He removed his hand from his gun and listened, in the moment for the first time since waking.

"There was a crash this morning, right? The place was a mess when we woke up, more so than the usual poker mess. Over a grand is missing from the safe, and..."

"What?" Jonas screamed.

"Look, he saw your pieces, right?"

"Of course he did! I made sure to shove one of 'em into his face before he got too comfortable. Showing him who was boss. How the hell is that much cash missing?"

James, not wanting Jonas to focus on the money, ignored the

question. The pieces had to be set just right.

James was building his own house of cards.

"Then where's your other gun? You've only got one."

Jonas had been in the middle of strapping his guns on this morning when Ian's cry from down the hall started this whole ordeal. He had only put one gun on. He hadn't thought to go back for the second amidst the confusion. Jonas understood where James was going with the thought and walked back towards his bedroom with heavy, carpet muted steps.

"No need to be paranoid, James. I just lost track of myself this morning and forgot to put it..."

He stopped cold. The strap hung over the back of the chair in front of his desk, but his berretta was absent from the holster.

"What the fuck is this?" he yelled, storming into the living room.

"A hunch, if I may?" James said.

"Oh for Mary's sake, what James?"

"Well, if I'm right, he was a damned good actor. He knew who you were, Boss. I mean, our little side business is word of mouth, but maybe he was looking for someone who wasn't deep in the crime syndicate to swindle. Show up with a crazy ass story, hit the right funny bones while maintaining an aura of nearly pissing himself, drink far less than us. Bam!" James clapped his hands, thriving on the drama. "When we pass out, he steals your gun, forces Judith to crack your safe, and then..."

"Kidnapping." Jonas finished.

His quiet fury far more intimidating than the boisterous counterpart he had been displaying. Molly walked to where her boots sat in the hallway. James was manipulative, and the story sounded shaky, but James pulled strings like an expert puppeteer. She laced each boot up, slipping a sharp buck knife into the sheath of the left boot, just in case.

"Perhaps the vase falling was her final attempt to warn us?" James contemplated aloud.

"Aww, I screwed up! I screwed up bad!" Ian cried out, lacing his own boots in mirror of his sister.

What pissed Jonas off the worst was that he had let this stranger come into his home, against obvious discomfort from the rest of them. He shared his drink. He gave his trust and respect. He was going to offer the man a job, breaking one of his few rules. Kyle had entered The Rail like a spider and Jonas felt the sticky webbing of guilt suffocate him. It was a mistake he would never make again.

Kyle hadn't come to save any of them. He had come to kidnap Judith! Take her, have his way with her, and discard her like the rest of the scum! Not in his life. Jonas hadn't let the men Judith chose walk the earth for long. He promised himself that the theatrical bastard who chose Judith would never see another Christmas.

Jonas would find his little girl, and he would never let her away from him again. She would hate it, but he was her father. He would find a way to convince her to heed him.

Father knows best.

"I'll grab the necessities," James said.

"Yeah. You do that, James. Good thinking," Jonas said.

"Anything for you, boss," James replied.

"Molly? Grab your stinger. We've got a throat to slit."

"Already ready, love," Molly said.

"Ian? Grab your supplies. We're going to make that motherfucker feel every second of pain that my poor heart has felt since my Veronica left me, ten-fold. He'll wish for death before we've finished on his legs."

"Aye, Boss!" said Ian.

Ian rushed, happy to do anything that might put him back in the positive graces of Jonas. Jonas placed blame on Kyle. Little else distracted him.

"I'm going to get my coat and my spare piece. Thank you for showing me the light, James."

James dropped a bag he was packing as Jonas walked to him and held out his hand. James offered his own, and Jonas grasped it between both of his own. He caught James' gaze with a stern, respectful eye.

"I was moments away from allowing this transgression to pass. You're a true friend and you shall get the first cut," Jonas promised.

Jonas walked towards his own bedroom, angry wearing him out with each step. James reached a hand into his coat to fondle the butt of the berretta tucked away in the deep liner pocket. He smiled in a place where nobody else could see it. The cards were holding up as he'd planned.

James, the only real actor in Jonas's presence, was getting his shot at the director's chair.

"With pleasure," he whispered, packing more torture tools and spare cash into the bag.

James couldn't see Molly staring at him from behind, unsure of James's sudden change in disposition. She had seen the smile, and James only smiled when he got something he wanted.

Wondering why the situation felt off, and knowing that James was at partial fault for it, she twirled her butterfly knife to calm her mind. Her own unspoken reservations would not change Jonas's mind. She knew her man better than to defy him when he entered battle mode, and she was certain what his orders were going to be.

The family was going to wage war on Kyle Thimall.

not safe for work

Mark and Jesse stood by, tired and anxious, as the two police officers examined the taxi cab. Jesse's arm hung in a sling. Blood seeped through the bandages. Not enough to cause worry, but enough so that Mark tried like hell to avoid looking at it. He wished that Jesse would have taken the doctor's advice and gone home to rest. The police would have allowed it. Mark would still be at their beck and call until they saw fit. Drugged up Jesse could let a nugget of truth slip, and the two of them needed to stick to their lie. Jesse had been stern, even under the effects of heavy pain killers, wanting to ensure justice was dealt to the man who took his hand.

The drugs they had given Jesse were nothing short of orgasmic. Numbing his entire body, he felt like he was floating on a cloud. Much better than the crap they gave his uncle for arthritis. Though he felt the cloud, there was no fog to blur his vision. Surpassing Mark's discomfort level, he dry heaved each time he looked down at the bandaged appendage, dreading the day when the bandages would be rendered unneeded.

Jesse's girlfriend had always loved the magic he would work with his fingers. He could have her bucking and writhing, begging for more, with nimble fingers and the flick of a wrist. Thanks to the whores his uncle had gotten him for his fourteenth birthday, he knew how to please a woman in bed if nowhere else. He didn't think, without the complimentary hand, that she would be too keen on the idea of a good ole' fashioned wristing. She was kinky, as he didn't take them any other way. The kind of women you could pay to partake in such activities were not the kind of women he enjoyed sleeping with. He counted down the hours until he could take another pill. Half dazed, in silence, he stood staring at an uninteresting pile of trash.

Enjoying his cloud, creating his own fog.

Mark was clear-headed, which meant he was nervous. The cops glanced at them even as they investigated, always looking suspicious. Mark was lucky that Jesse had been the one who got shot. Jesse's family had money and connections. Jesse's family were also good people. Had they known a fraction of the crimes he had committed with Mark, they would disown him faster than an Amish lesbian.

They couldn't call in a favor to have the priest silenced. The police had shown up to take a statement while Jesse's arm was being worked on. Mark had expected cops. The wound had been inflicted with a gun. They weren't going after the crazy bastard alone. Mark wasn't keen on turning the stump look into a fashion statement.

Mark lied to the cops, hoping they would take care of what he couldn't. It would be the word of a priest against the word of two low life criminals, but Jesse was the one missing his hand. Legal vengeance was the best way to end up clean.

Mark doubted the cops would arrest a priest, but their presence would put him on edge. A man on edge was a defenseless man. When the dishes were clean, Mark and Jesse would get revenge.

The cops drove them around in the cruiser, trying to make sense of Mark's story. The pigs had made him feel uneasy. He had done nothing wrong that night but fuck with a couple of scared little turf-raiders. He was never going to rape or kill them like he had claimed, but his life was about maintaining control over turf and drastic gestures were necessary. Fear was enough for Mark. He never stepped beyond that boundary of reaction unless necessary.

The cops were a part of the equation. Mark needed to stick to the lie, ride out the questions, and get Jesse home so they could get sleep.

"You sure this is the right cab?" said the younger cop.

"Fuck, we told you it was, man!" Jesse said, frustrated. "We saw them walking away from the thing and tried to catch up to them to help, but that crazy padre blew off my fucking hand!"

Jesse held up his bloody, bandaged arm towards the rookie, as if he couldn't see it.

"It's the medicine, officer. I apologize," said Mark. To Jesse, he added, "Cool it, man. Let me do the talking, ok? You're high as fuck."

"You fucking cool it, hombre! You can fuck your girl with both hands. You can cup your hand so the soup from your spoon doesn't burn your dick!"

"I think we have something here, Officer Wilkins" said the rookie, removing a small Glad container from beneath the driver seat.

Hank Wilkins, the man in charge, met the rookie by the driver side door and took the Glad box from him. The rookie watched Hank remove the lid, careful not to spill the contents. Wilkins knew it was cocaine before he licked his finger and dipped it into the powder. The little tastes of evil he allowed himself made suffering the pedestal of a good cop tolerable.

It tasted like sweetened baby powder. Whoever the cab owner was, he had a poor taste for drugs or a lack of funds to finance an expensive habit. Hanks opinion always was and always had been if you're going to do wrong, do it right. Disappointing. He locked the lid back in place and held the box in the crook of his arm.

Hank peered over at Mark and Jesse, who both leaned on the back of the cab, an idea fluttered through his mind. He hadn't come as far as he did in the force without a good pair of brains. The only reason that Hank hadn't accepted a promotion due to his unorthodox and effective police skills was because of the desk job that defined it. He liked to smell the filth up close and personal. He relished being the man who made a deserving criminal scream. Every ounce of their blood for an ounce of his adrenaline. It was a fair trade. He had been through gallons. Sure, he had arrested an innocent or two in his time, but innocence was rare.

These two men were not innocent. Wilkins could smell the sin on them, as clear as the wet rot of the trash pile the doped one kept staring at in between hoots and hollers. He could have let them go free. He was responding to a report of violence against them, not by them. Once they had talked to this gun toting super-priest, there would be no reason to keep them. As luck does when it favored the unworthy, Hank was sure Jesse and Mark deserved the violence wrecked on them, if not instigated it entirely.

Plans ran through Hank's mind. He had looked up their records, as was his way, to check the validity of their claim. See if they had any enemies they may have been trying to use the police as tools to get revenge. He found countless charges of robbery, assault, grand theft auto, and a plethora of other petty crimes decorated their files like badges of the scum they were. Mark had even been tried, at one point, for statutory rape.

All charges dropped, without fail, in every instance. It didn't take much digging to find that the one without the hand had friends in high places. Thusly, justice was a stranger to him. That was fine with Hank. He would introduce them soon enough. He wanted the two scumbags to think twice the next time they had an itch to do something stupid enough to lose a hand.

If there was a next time.

"Stand by, rookie. I might need you. Keep your lids peeled and pay attention. I'm about to school you in the fine art of taking out the garbage."

The rookie shifted to his relaxed leg and nodded in affirmation. He had heard stories from the boys at the precinct about Officer Wilkins and his strange law enforcement techniques. The man never played good cop, bad cop. He played lone cop. His interrogations were always successful. He had been responsible for bringing down a few of the city's top criminals. His methods stretched the belt of the law, but he faced little repercussion due to the drop in crime and positive publicity he generated. People were more positive towards police now-a-days, though he wasn't so sure how they'd react if they heard the darker stories.

The rookie was going to get a close up seat and learn from the best. He wouldn't dare turn down the offer. Nothing, not he details of the stories he had heard or the hushed conclusions spoken with fear and awe, terrified him like Hank's "look".

The look was Wilkins' weapon when bullets or batons were unnecessary. It was a look he could use freely on scum and comrade alike when he wanted the Jenga tower to fall in exactly the right way. His way. The look left good men feeling like they had been caught using their parents good washcloths to clean up after masturbating. To anyone else, the look meant that a bad guy was about to get a bad beating.

Wilkins claimed fear was a weakness. The look dared the opposition to call him a coward with an honest tongue. He thirsted for the challenge the way a fighting dog on a leash thirsts for blood before a fight.

It was a look the rookie never wanted directed at him, least of all due to defiance.

Wilkins' hand always hovered over his gun. He exuded a strong desire to use it. Desire was the wrong word. Desperation fit better, but to admit it was to question Wilkins' sanity. And against instinct, the rookie couldn't believe that the root of his learning tree was rotted by insanity.

The rookie, not a religious man, prayed to whatever held him steady that he would never have to use his weapon in the line of duty. Most good cops admit to doing the same thing when talking to boards of professionals or elementary school classrooms. He didn't think those words had every escaped Officer Wilkins' lips, nor entered his thought process as anything other than white noise. If nothing else, Wilkins was honest. He was brutal, and brutal got results.

All things considered, he was damned happy that Wilkins was on his side. And anyway, these were the two guys they were supposed to be helping. Sure, they were of questionable character, and Wilkins had been fairly cold to them since picking them up from the hospital. Wilkins wanted to scare information out of them. Make sure their stories held strong.

The rookie, praying to his steady self, put on the face of a stoic professional, ready and willing to learn.

Officer Wilkins lit a cigarette and walked towards Mark and Jesse. His free hand still on the butt of his gun, as if by cautious accident (or so it appeared to anybody who took notice). Though his hand and his gun were close friends. His hand never found its way to his holster by accident.

"So boys. We seem to have an issue here," he said in a nonchalant voice.

"You're telling me! We've been riding around with you guys for over an hour and you still won't take us to that damned church!" Mark said.
His anger was veiled with an unearned sheen of confidence, hatred of the law seeping through his every word.

"Well, you said that this cab belonged to a gentleman involved in the altercation, and we had to investigate the scene before moving on, sir. In all fairness, we found the first."

"That little bastard doesn't matter! We were trying to help his ass and he led us straight into an ambush!"

"Well, the broken back window and the brick in the back seat speak volumes against that statement. As scared as a cabbie may be of a mugger, that goes twice as hard for the men who loan them their cabs. No, this man didn't break his own window, friend. But that's not the problem I'm talking about, Mr. Handy. The problem I so diligently speak are the drugs."

"Man, the only drugs we have are prescription," Mark said, confused.

"No, no, silly boy. We found cocaine in the front seat of the cab. Quite a bit of cocaine, to be honest."

Hank pulled the box out from under his arm with his gun hand and held it out towards Mark. Mark backed away, aghast.

"That doesn't concern us, man. The little shit probably led us back there to rob us for more drug money, you know? That would explain that crazy priest with the shotgun!"

Or the drugs were the reason you broke the window in the first place, and the two people you were chasing were damn lucky to get away. If they got away. The rookie wondered if his thoughts were in line with Wilkins'. He was starting to see the scope of the situation. Wilkins was good.

The rookie thought that within a few minutes, the men would be cuffed in their cruiser, their bluff exposed, an important lesson learned. Justice served.

Within five minutes, the rookie would know that Hank Wilkins didn't serve justice.

He delivered wrath.

"Well now, it *does* concern you, Mr. Handy. I mean..." Hank tossed the box hard at Mark before finishing his sentence. Mark caught it, surprised, looking at the cop in confusion. "…your fingerprints are all over it," Wilkins finished.

Mark realized the dirty trick that had just been played on him. He admonished himself mentally for falling for it. His nerves had failed him. Fucking cops.

Hank Wilkins put the cigarette to his lips and bit the filter lightly with his teeth to hold it in place. Drawing his gun, smoke pouring from his nostrils, he pointed it, point black, at the span of forehead above Mark's wide eyes. Mark turned to Jesse for help, but Jesse was in a daze, still looking at the pile of garbage down the alley way.

"What the fuck is this, you dirty ass pig? You're supposed to be helping us! I thought you were the good guy!"

The rookie was sure this situation wouldn't turn out well. Mark had committed an unforgiveable blasphemy in comparing Officer Wilkins to a pig. He remained silent as Wilkins slowly stepped toward Mark, the look in Wilkins' eyes smiling in a way his mouth never could.

"To quote the great Bruce Campbell, Mr. Handy, 'Good? Bad? I'm the guy with the gun'. Now, if you would kindly kiss the ground and put your hands behind your back, this sure would run a lot smoother."

As soon as the gun had been drawn, the rookie reached for his own, as per protocol. Wilkins turned the look to him, whispering three words between puffs of smoke.

"Don't you dare."

The smoke billowing around Wilkins' head gave him the look of a god. Or a demon. The rookie knew in his heart that the latter choice was more accurate. His assumptions about the situation turned as suspect as Wilkins' hero status.

"Fuck that, pig!" Mark shouted.

He threw the Glad container against the alley wall, spilling the contents onto the pavement. A cloud of cocaine fell like a light flurry of snow on to the ground. Jesse turned his attention towards it, transfixed, oblivious to what was happening.

"Oh, now see what you've gone and done?" Wilkins said, the muzzle of his gun close to kissing Mark's defiant lips." You've destroyed my evidence. Now that wasn't very nice of you. Not at all."

The sound of the butt of Hank's fun smashing into Mark's jaw sounded like a thick plastic cup being stepped on in a narrow hallway. The sound echoed down the alley. Mark screamed and held his cheek with both hands, denied the silence of a tougher man. The scream brought Jesse out of his spell. Seeing what was happening, he began to turn and run clumsily away from the cab. Hank aimed his gun and shot the ground inches from Jesse's feet, causing him to stumble and fall onto his injured arm. Jesse's own screams soon joined in the chorus. The rookie looked on, horrified.

"Cuff that crippled bastard," Hank said, the blood lust in his eyes unmistakable. He looked changed. Not right in the head. And the rookie swore he saw Officer Wilkins' eyes glint or something, though it must have just been a reflection from the window on the cab.

"All due respect, sir," the rookie began.

Hanks head whipped towards him, his rage turning his face bright red.

"I said fucking cuff him, rook, or you'll join the both of them in agony!"

The rookie quelled hesitance and obliged, knowing with all of his being that Wilkins would make good on his promise if pushed.

Wilkins turned his attention back towards Mark as he holstered his gun. Mark had fallen to his knees, and scooted away from Hank as his one visible eye looked on in disbelief and terror. Seeing the demon in the smoke closer than the rookie had, Mark removed his hands, heavy pants replacing his screams. He attempted to stand and run, hoping that his sobriety would carry him farther than Jesse had gone, knowing the chances of escape were small but there. Officer Wilkins tripped his feet from under him. Mark continued to scoot back, the only motion of retreat he had left, as blood flowed from a gash in his temple. His cheek had turned dark purple, and his eye was blood shot.

His good eye focused on Wilkins' hip, toward the weapon that he was sure would end him the second the demon cop was sick of cat and mouse. Wilkins, seeing this, chuckled through a cloud of smoke.

"Your ass isn't worth a bullet," said Wilkins.

Instead, he reached for the opposite hip, unsheathing his asp and whipping it downwards to extend it. He prodded and poked at Mark with the ball end until he backed into the alley wall. Nowhere left to turn.

"You're fucking crazy!" he screamed.

Had Mark known those would be his last great words of defiance, he might have thought of something more poignant and offensive. Or maybe he would have made things right with the maker he was moments from meeting.

"Well, semantics are a hell of a thing, aren't they?" Wilkins said.

He reared his asp back like a golf club and swung it with forceful follow through. It connected with the underside of Mark's jaw. A spray of blood and broken teeth decorated the pavement like a macabre Pollock painting. Wilkins raised his hands above his head in celebration.

"Tiger gets a hole in one! That'll shut you up," Hank said.

He removed his cigarette from his lips, flicking the excess ash off as he kneeled. Looking over Mark's destroyed face for something else to destroy, he settled on burning it into Mark's neck. Wilkins put little pressure behind the cigarette, letting the burning sensation rise above the pain throughout the rest of Mark's head. After the cigarette ember was spent, Wilkins tossed it to the side and spat into Mark's gaping mouth. He stood up, controlled and imposing, and grinned.

"Now for the fun stuff."

Yards away, Jesse and the rookie watched as the asp cut through the air, striking Mark again and again with meaty thuds.

Whoosh. Bap. Scream. Repeat.

Mark was a human piñata to Officer Wilkins' sugar rush. Soon, the screams and whimpers died away, leaving only the meaty thud of metal meeting flesh.

Hank stopped the beating long after Mark slipped into the coma that carried him to death's door. He was satisfied. Blood had spattered his face, and the grin he wore reminded the rookie of a tiger he had seen feeding at the zoo when he was a child. That memory bred, like he was sure this one would, terrible nightmares. The rookie promised himself that if he survived the day, he would put in for a partner transfer. Maybe a precinct transfer.

Wilkins closed his asp and re-sheathed it the way a man might put away his wallet after paying for a pack of smokes. He regarded his uniform in disgust, whining like an exasperated birthday girl. It was a strange sound coming from a man who had beaten someone to death for the simple reason that he could.

"Oh, hell! You stained my uniform! I just got this pressed yesterday, you fuck," Hank said, kicking Mark hard in the ribs. The dull crack of splintering bone made the rookie nauseous.

Mark's corpse fell sideways. Hank lit another cigarette and looked back at the rookie.

"Put that piece of shit in the back of the cruiser. You'll realize how necessary that was one day, Rook, but for now, let me handle the paperwork. I have no qualms with tending to you in a similar hands-on way, if need be."

The rookie didn't question him. Would never question him, even in his own mind could it be helped. He helped Jesse into the back of the cruiser, silent tears streaming down his face.

"Unit 91 to headquarters, over," Hank spoke into the receiver on his shoulder.

"Yes, Hank?" responded a kind, feminine voice.

"Yea, we need an ambulance to 17th and Broadway, the alley near Bradbury's. "

"Are you ok, sweet thing?" her concern was far more genuine than his response.

"Just fine, Marie. A couple of gang bangers gave us a bad tip and tried to start a fight. One of them grabbed for my damn gun and fired off a round, but I wrestled it back from him. We've got his friend in custody over here, but he put up a hell of a fight and I had to pull the asp. Warn whoever you send that the view isn't pretty. We need one of those Dexter types."

"10-4, Hank. Are you hurt?"

"No, Marie. I'm fine. A little mad he made me work him over, but fine."

"I'm so sorry, Hank."

"All in a day's work, Marie. All in a day's work."

If Wilkins was feigning remorse, which the rookie was sure he was, he couldn't tell. Wilkins had taken on the character of good cop, his lust for wrath sated.

Neither the rookie nor the two people peeking around the corner down the alley way saw Hank's eyes glimmered red as he pulled out a handkerchief to wipe his face.

Reaching into the back of the taxi cab, Hank slipped the taxi license out from the plastic holster on the back of the seat.

"Hello, Mr. Thimall. Boy, I can't wait to meet you," he whispered to himself, smoke billowing from his nostrils.

The bloodshed had just begun.

On the second day, a demon was born.

the cliche, the macguffin, and bacon

When his eyes opened, Kyle's first thought was of how rejuvenating his dreamless slumber had been. After two years of sleeping with nightmares, living in one had cured his REM cycle. Maybe the lack of nightmares was a reward for making use of his mind. No screams or splashing or bloodied pools. Simple, elegant darkness. Whatever the reason, it was a blessing, and an apt one after sleeping in a church.

He hoped for an encore.

Kyle squeezed the air where Judith's hand had last been and found blankets. He sat up too fast and the room spun. For a moment, he thought he hadn't woken up after all. He was still in the nightmare. He scolded himself for sleepy nonsense.

Something terrible had happened the day before, and something worse was happening to Judith while his brain caught up. How could he sleep while she was awake, becoming a victim of Kyle's inner darkness?

Kyle relaxed once the dizziness dissipated and he could see through the morning grumps and the sleep in his eyes. His panic quelled, he shook off sleep and the haunting thought of Judith in harm's way. Judith had woken up earlier than he had, and the only thing that made him uncomfortable, underneath it all, was that her hand had not been close enough to hold when his eyes had opened.

Nonsensical as it might have been.

The rich aroma of coffee, bacon, and English muffins filled his nose now that his mind was clear enough to process it. Kyle breathed deep and held his head back. The snort was more pleasurable than any cocaine. It had been ages since he had eaten a breakfast not cooked at the Waffle House. His rumbling stomach admonished him for this fact and reminded him that he should get to the source of it with haste before it really did turn out to be a nightmare.

Kyle gave his face a light slap to get the blood flowing as he stood. He checked the watch for the time. The weight of looking at the watch gave away to guilt. Nine more hours had passed on the watch, the large hand on the face creeping towards the number two. He had saved two souls, and it hadn't even been a full day yet. He doubted that the other five would be easy. He had lucked out on finding the priest. Maybe the priest had found him.

Dusk was an hour away. Evening travel meant stealth and a plethora of sinners to choose from.

Kyle considered removing the watch. He didn't see why he should have to wear it, so long as he did was he was supposed to and kept it close. The thing was fucking heavy, and the weight was more than mental or spiritual.

Kyle examined the watch band as he paced the room. There was no way to remove it. The band was solid and metal. It was more of a shackle than a time piece; it weighed his soul down low enough for his future master to take a taste whenever he needed a reminder as to why he wanted it in the first place.

It was a dreadful notion.

Kyle walked towards breakfast, not sure if it could be called such when he would be eating it past supper time. He had been raised on breakfast for dinner, and he'd still never figured that riddle out. He followed the scent to doorway that led to a modest kitchen.

A stove. A fridge. A table.

Breakfast.

Father Leon and Judith both looked towards him as he appeared in the doorway, startled out of a conversation. Judith offered a coy smile and looked down at her coffee, blushing. Father Leon hid his own smile with his hand. Kyle didn't understand why until he looked down at himself. He had disrobed during the night and had been too loopy to realize it. All he had on were a pair of blue plaid pajama pants, socks, and certain morning friend that a guy couldn't put to sleep without a good piss or a quick meeting with Rosie Palm.

Kyle turned around, red in the face, and began walk back towards the room, but Leon stopped him.

"Don't worry about it, Kyle. You're still wearing pants, right? Join us."

Kyle was thankful for the laughter. Embarrassment had remedied his problem with haste.

Judith was all smiles, a complete transformation from the scared girl he had fallen asleep next to, hand in hand, the night before. Nor was she the vixen who had propositioned him in the middle of the night when they had first met. She was something that she had been deep down all along, but had never been able to project to the world until the moment she Kyle (and little Kyle) greeted them at Leon's breakfast table. She was far from her father and her dignity was intact.

She was a normal girl. Amazing what a few hours could do to a personality.

A plate with bacon, eggs, and an English muffin, sat at his table place. A pot of coffee called from the middle of the table, the smell of the dark brew singing to him, waking him better than any alarm clock could. Kyle poured himself a cup and drank deep. It was as Goldilocks preferred her porridge; not too hot and not too cold. It was just right. He poured another cup, set it beside the plate, and devoured the best meal he had ever eaten.

As Kyle ate, they made small talk. He had forgotten positive human interaction. Judith wasn't the only one who was changing in short order. He felt needed. Liked, even. The hardship ahead was worth a conversation with real people. Good people, at that. Sudden friendship was strange to him, but considering what they had been through, their company was comfortable.

Kyle had locked himself away in dark thoughts for too long. The Devil had shown him the light by forcing him back onto the world. He recognized possible irony in that, but could never be sure thanks to Alanis Morissette. Her legacy was a song that would forever confuse the common man on what irony really was.

The conversation stayed light until Judith excused herself for a shower. Kyle and Leon sat in silence as Kyle finished the food on his plate. As soon as the first sound of water hitting the shower floor reverberated into the kitchen, Leon placed his elbows on the table and leaned towards Kyle. That excited look on his face screamed importance.

Kyle listened.

"You know, she's not as strong as she makes out to be. At least not emotionally. Her strengths are the reason she's alive, Kyle, but most of them were thrust upon her. Too young and too many."

"I know," said Kyle, remembering how she embraced him last night in the alley, death breathing down their necks.

"We had a long talk while you slept. You need to know something that she won't tell you. Not out loud, anyway. You can take it as you will, but you will have to deal with it eventually."

"Isn't that unethical, Leon? To divulge the details of a private conversation?"

"It wasn't a confession, Kyle. I think she told me so that I could tell you for her. Transparency isn't high on her list of personal skills."

"Okay, then," Kyle said through a sip of his third cup.

"She needs you."

"I know she does. That's why I saved her."

"This means more to her than your conquest, Kyle. To you, she's one person off of your checklist."

"That now how I think," Kyle started. Leon hushed him.

"But it's the truth. You can't tell me you don't feel at least a little better knowing you've made progress."

Kyle couldn't. Not without lying to himself and the priest.

"You might have found someone else who fit the bill. Who knows if there are seven specific people or a slew of them who fall into the proper scope? You said the devil led you to that green rail, and the green rail led you to Judith, and I'm surprised, to be frank, that you found anything other than death in that basement."

"I hadn't thought about that at all. I was so wrapped up in the fantasy that I wasn't worrying about the hells I could stroll in the real world."

"And yet you did stroll into hell, Kyle. Judith's hell. Without you, she'd still be stuck. Nothing more than an Irish Rapunzel in a basement where, joke on her, nobody can see her hair fall. She's spent a long time using sex as a means to hold power over her father. Deep down, her hurting has been lacquered over and ignored, but the breaking never stops underneath any layer of protection. It was love she wanted, not power. Love and affection that stemmed from somewhere other than his longing for her mother to still be alive."

"He does seem more preoccupied with his own desires than keeping her happy."

Kyle remembered the Berretta on his spine and shuddered.

"She put up a facade of sarcasm and strength and defiance for a long time, but all she wanted was her daddy. When he stopped being there for her, she started running. Trying to find someone with enough balls to cut her free from the ball and chain. She never learned how to do that in the traditional sense. Sex was how she found it, as sex was what brought the man she loved to her level of passion and what took him away before she embraced it. Out of anger, her mission for Prince Charming became a mission to spite her father. Every prince was a frog, disgusting mirrors of her father and her lost innocence."

"She told you all of this?"

"In a roundabout way. You surprised her by denying her. She thought you were afraid of her dad. When she realized that you were holding back because of her, to help her, she found in you a companionship that was alien to her. She doesn't know you as a person, but that's not the issue. She's used to quick acquaintanceships, most children of broken families are. She already feels close to you. She feels like you are her protector. Her guardian angel. She said she'd never in her life felt safer than she did last night, and if she would have died, she would have done so knowing that someone was trying to save her for her sake and not their own."

"That's heavy stuff, Leon. Real heavy. I'm nothing special. I was trying to protect her, but that's just how I'm built. I'm just as scared as she is. What kind of person wouldn't have done the same for her?"

"Most people would have let her die if it meant they would escape. They would have felt guilty about it, sure, but very few people have the balls to sacrifice the way you were willing to and you know it. Being lost is an advantage."

Leon poured himself a fresh cup, and finished the pot off into Kyle's own cup for him. Kyle nodded in thanks as the priest continued.

"The man who thinks he has all the answers never listens to the questions. Those are the only type of people she knows. They spill out useless, confusing advice. More to appease their own egos than to help. You are, as you say, broken. Just like Judith. Together, you will be able to find peace, impossible as that may seem, because you're both asking the questions. You are both willing to listen for the answers. There are no egos to hinder progress. All you have is each other. As much as she thinks she needs you right now, you need her more. You can't do this alone."

"And when I've failed and spend eternity burning, what then? How can I help her then? I can't fathom failing and Judith losing all hope when things were getting better. Nobody needs the kind of darkness I'm used to."

"That's a hell of a motivator, no? Stop expecting such a negative outcome. There is a purpose to be served in all of this. You aren't the only person who has ever faced darkness. Your ignorance of success will benefit you. Falsities and presumptions won't cloud your judgment. You are holding a paint brush in front of a blank canvas, and with each stroke your nightmares will turn into something beautiful."

"I wish I was optimistic, Leon."

"Just don't be anything but yourself. You have bravery and strength in you. It won't feel like it because you are afraid and you aren't used to it. Fear isn't your enemy, if you can control it. If nothing else, be strong for her. She needs you, even if she doesn't come right out and say it. You're saving her in more ways than that little wrist watch can represent."

The water in the shower stopped flowing. Leon looked back towards the restroom leaning towards Kyle and motioning for Kyle to follow in suit.

"There is one more I'm going to tell you. I told you I couldn't help you because my prideful ways have clouded my soul. I can't trust my own advice, at least not advice on that level of importance. I can't speak for God. I have to let him speak through me. This is all Leon, though. It sounds bleak and none of the stories are consistent, but you need to be prepared."

"What is it? Excitement? Adventure? To avoid copyright infringement in a holy place, I'm fine with boring," Kyle said.

"No. A sacrifice."

"Of course it's a sacrifice," Kyle sighed.

"At the end of this trial, a sacrifice must be offered. Be that a metaphor, a drawing of blood, of spirit, or even a life, I cannot tell you. Like I said, it's inconsistent and vague. Just be prepared to face that particular demon before you succeed."

Kyle leaned back in the chair, not surprised, but not overjoyed at the news.

"I look forward to that. Shit, this story just keeps getting better and better."

Leon took Kyle's hand in a gesture of comfort.

"I pray for you to find peace and a happy ending, Kyle. I will pray for you until these days have passed. I do hope you will return to me once they have so that we may talk under less stressful pretenses. And how I would love to hear the tale!"

"I have a hard time believing in happy endings, Leon. Spoiler alert. Snape kills Dumbledore. Jesus was killed for the sins of mankind. George R.R. Martin kills fucking everyone. People always die with a purpose. A satisfying ending is never a happy ending, at least not in the stories that count for much. All you get is death or a cliff hanger. The healing, the pain, and the time that would make those people find a happily ever after, well, we never get to read those parts of the story.

We never get to read about the aftermath."

"Have faith, if only for this week. You never get to read those parts because you are supposed to imagine what the perfect happy ending for you would be. You can never be disappointed by an ending you wrote in your own head. Like you, I doubt this story will end with smiles, but there will be satisfaction. One day, after you can smile and love again, you will know the honest struggle that becomes happily ever after. Those three words encompass so much. You will get to define them."

Judith walked out of the bathroom in her washed clothes, drying her hair with a blue towel. She looked refreshed and radiant. And lovely. He could not succumb to the spell she was casting.

For both of their sakes.

"Define what?" Judith said, entering the room.

Both men gave her answered her with embarrassed silence. "Oh come on, what are you being so hush hush about?" she said. She slung the towel over the back of a chair and joining them at the table.

"You, of course, my dear," Father Leon said.

"Me? Like, whatever about?" she asked, rolling her eyes and twirling a strand of her hair in her fingers.

"Kyle swore me to secrecy," Leon said.

"I see how it is. Talk about a girl when she isn't around and play coy when she enters the room. I thought I was the one visiting the ladies room!"

"We can tell her, Leon. She can handle it," Kyle said, playing along.

Reaching across the table, he looked Judith square in the eye and took one of her hands in his. Mustering every last bit of sincerity that he could, Kyle spoke in a soft, serious voice. Judith was taken aback by the gesture.

"Judith. I've known you for a day, so this might sound forward and come as a bit of a shock to you." He licked his lower lip for effect. "Judith, Your shower singing is atrocious."

Judith pulled her hand out of Kyles and slugged him in the shoulder.

"Jerk!" she said through laughter.

Kyle and Leon joined in. Kyle reveled in the closeness, reiterating to himself how much he missed good people. His reclusive side was making way for who he used to be. Breakfast at Leon's had done something he had been trying to do with cocaine for two years.

Kyle tried to remember each detail of their morning. He wanted to enjoy the laughter while it lasted and recall it when all that remained were screams. Gut instinct told him that the time for laughter would be taking a few days off.

Perhaps forever, in his case.

Forty-five minutes later, Kyle and Judith looked around the corner of another alley. Their eyes were wide with terror as they watched the horrendous beating that Mark was taking at the hands of Officer Hank Wilkins. Kyle realized, with terrified awe, how apt his instincts had been.

running from the devil

They sprinted until Judith grabbed Kyle by the arm to stop him. She was panting for breath as hard as he was. Grateful as he was for the break, he wanted to get as far away from the cop as possible before they started looking for him.

They had rounded the corner looking for the cab. Instead they caught the end of the beating that ended Mark's life. Regardless of what the man almost did to the two of them, there was no justice in what Mark had endured. Kyle felt dizzy. What would stop the cop from initiating same punishment on him? Was the violence they witnessed an appetizer compared to what Kyle would get?

Kyle's stash powdered the alley wall. Kyle's license was in the back seat with all the information the cop would need to find him. The cop wouldn't bother calling in his plate number. Kyle's smiling face and company address were out in the open.

"Did you see all that blood?" Judith asked.

"I'm not color blind, Judith. Red is a hard color to miss," Kyle replied.

"Watch the bite, Kyle."

"I'm sorry, but that was my cab! Now we're running from the criminals and the law. He can find out anything, Judith. Up to and including my route for the night."

"I'm scared," Judith said, calm and steady. Kyle was just as frightened, but for her sake, he couldn't say it out loud. She shook in his arms, but not in the same way as she had the night before. The situation was familiar. "Do you think he killed that guy?"

"Well, if he's not dead, he won't realize that he's alive for a long, long time." Kyle replied.

"I can't say he didn't deserve it. I mean, if Leon hadn't stepped in, they would have been hauling our bodies out of this alley tonight. Still, that was horrible. That other cop didn't even try to stop him. He was as scared as us!"

"I'm sure he was. That whole scenario drained me. It was just… it felt so…"

"…evil," she finished the thought for him.

"Yeah. Right. Evil."

Kyle put her at arm's length. Comforting each other gave the bad guys more opportunity to find them.

"We need to find a phone. I don't have many friends left, but maybe I can borrow a car from somebody at the taxi company. If we hurry, we might be able to beat that cop to the station."

"I can help us get a car," she said. She perked up as she reached in her pocket. It made a world of difference. "I mean, it will be risky, and probably not too smart."

"We need to minimize risk. We're neck high in shit and stuck on Australia, as it is."

"That was just bad. I hereby veto board game jokes until further notice. Here," she said, throwing him a set of keys.

"What are these?" he said.

He fumbled through the few keys and read the tag on key chain.

"God is Lead", with a picture of Jesus holding a gun. "Nice key chain."

"My dad has a weird thing for religion and weaponry. Those are the keys to the bar. It's my set, so it won't set off alarms. I have a key to my dad's Pinto, but we need to go back to The Green Rail. To be honest, we'd be better off dealing with the psycho police. I can't imagine Jonas' mood. He liked you. The cop will finish you off quicker," she said. Her doubt was audible.

"How reassuring." he said. He handed the keys back to Judith for safe keeping. "You know, I was starting to think this might be easier than I thought. I've saved two people, narrowly escaped death, I have a lovely sidekick. I'm learning how to count my fucking chickens, if nothing else."

"I guess we don't have a choice, do we? At least they can't trace you to me, considering I didn't know you before yesterday."

Kyle nodded in agreement.

The sound of a siren startled them. They ducked behind a dumpster, bunching up as small as they could, until the echoing faded into ambience. Without words, Kyle took her hand, and they started back towards the pub. He hoped that nobody would be left to meet them at The Green Rail. There was a good chance that Jonas was out looking for his daughter by now, but the man had an unorthodox approach to things. God may know what would happen, but Kyle knew less than nothing. He was running on adrenaline and blind instinct.

They walked two streets over, towards a tattoo shop on 15th Kyle knew they could duck into if need be. Then they turned back into the alley ways. Every calamity thus far had taken place in an alley, so it was unfortunate that they were so reliant on them, but staying safe meant staying invisible.

Their slow and meticulous venture back took longer due to increased secrecy. The pedestrians they passed were oblivious to their presence, focusing instead on cell phone screens or the ground ahead of them, save for one. Kyle and Judith were oblivious to the single pair of eyes that bore into their backs, moving behind them in the shadows with more stealth than the pair were practicing and almost as much to lose.

the father..

Fifteen minutes after the MacMillan gang started looking for the keys to the Pinto, Jonas realized Judith held the only set. He'd never made a spare. Even if Judith had taken it, the car was clocking two hundred thousand miles. She couldn't go far in it. He grabbed the keys to the black sedan instead. It was ostentatious, but it would have to do.

Jonas opened the door for Molly. James and Ian climbed into the back seat, arguing about what radio station preference. Jonas wasn't in the mood for bickering. He told the two that their voices, like the radio, would remain silent unless he decided otherwise.

Ian stared down at his own twiddling thumbs. James descended into his own head, fantasizing about the possibility of power that lay before him. Jonas remained single minded with motive. Molly worried, still flipping her knife hither and thither.

Find Judith.

Kill the punk.

Every woman that resembled her in appearance, attire, stature, or body language caused Jonas' heart jumped to his throat, only to free fall back into his chest. It was never her. Every case of mistaken identity was a blow to his sanity. Dry disappointment coated his mouth.

After two hours of searching, Ian's audible stomach grumblings signaled time to stop for breakfast. They were hung over, on edge, and hungry; ignoring their baser needs would do nothing positive.

James watched Jonas break apart with silent glee. Ian and Molly were faithful to the boss. James was faithful to himself. Jonas ran the only private mob practice in the state. Jobs were selected by want instead of necessity, the money was excellent, and the blood shed was minimal enough to remain enjoyable. The only thing stale about the work was that he wasn't the boss. James did whatever it took, for however long it took, to ensure he was in the perfect position to take the boss's chair when he was ready to retire.

Networking, while vital in any walk of life, was secondary to control.

A few years in, Jonas announced his desire to take Judith on vacation, away away from the needles and sex and the hate. He wanted rehabilitate their relationship. Blood turned to alcohol, thinner than water. James would be left the world until they returned. James was written into Jonas' will and appropriate documents as a matter of protocol.

Ian was too simple and Molly didn't want it. Years of dishonest loyalty put the bullet in the gun.

James didn't have to scheme for long. All he had to do was guarantee Jonas' sabbatical became permanent. Suspicion would always be the trump card under Molly's watchful eye, but even she saw Jonas losing it.

Two weeks after the ink on the paperwork dried, and two days before they were to leave on vacation, opportunity knocked in the form of a naïve cabbie named Kyle Thimall. There would be no trail of evidence if there was never a crime. Best case scenario, all of the excitement would cause the old Irish bear's heart to pop like kettle corn. Worst case, Molly would have a reason to be distracted for long enough to give James his chance.

Unable to help himself, James smiled under cover of a cough.

James thanked the devil for sending the kid.

Molly watched his face twitch in the rear view mirror with the subtlety of a specter. For a man with a poker face as good as James', smiling, however incognito, was a terrible play. Molly's gut told her that she would be dumping two bags of trash in the river before all was said and done. Her gut never lied. She wasn't turned off at the notion, at least not in respect to James.

In the front seat, Jonas continued to break down the facts from the paranoia as best he could. He pulled into a small strip mall and parked in front of Gilberto's Mexican food restaurant. He needed to stretch his legs and grab food for the group. The rest of them remained outside to smoke and keep watch. He returned a few minutes later with a bag full of burrito's and pico de gallo.

Jonas let Molly hand out the food while he ate a bean and cheese burrito and contemplated how tough it would be to find Judith if she didn't want to be found. He usually found out where she was after she returned. She never went to the same place twice. She was crafty, patient, and intelligent (she was his daughter, after all) and she knew how to avoid being caught by her father.

Jonas knew that she was reveling in her kidnapping because she knew what it was doing to him. He was sure that Kyle would have no problem finding a road less traveled by Jonas. Judith would make sure of that, and he had proven himself the conversational type.

Jonas hated few things more than he hated liars, and Kyle delivered one hell of a performance. Without James, Molly, and Ian, he was pretty sure he would have taken a swan dive into a lake of asphalt. There was much to be said for loyalty. After they spilled the Kyle's blood, the faithful would be rewarded.

Judith would learn the hard importance of what it meant to be a member of the family. Getting kidnapped was postponing the inevitable.

Jonas needed a sign; he needed guidance to lead him down the right path.

Jonas scanned his surroundings as the burrito spices burned his tongue. Broken down pawn shops, strip clubs, and mom and pop shops where the parents had long suffered death or senility cluttered the underdeveloped part of town they were in. His gaze fell upon the facade of a church across the street. A monument of simple elegance amongst the shit.

Jonas was a religious, though deeply resentful, Irish Catholic. He had not been to church since the death of his wife.

Worse than Kyle's betrayal was God's for taking his wife away. Jonas always come to terms with his suffering as part of the experience; his complaints were petty, all things considered.

Church on Wednesdays and Sundays weren't the same without Veronica's lovely voice singing the hymns. Her lovely figure, a visible silhouette underneath her spring yellow dress, teased what remained of his innocence. Her Sunday best was meant to celebrate, not mourn.

Members of the church stared Veronica down when she first attended. They judged her bright attire and attitude as heresy, unable to separate their wardrobes and lives from the drab blacks and grays. Others took her confidence as inspiration. It took three Sundays before the pews were filled with bright colors and honest smiles. There were only the evanescent remnants of rain clouds to obscure the color. A simple dress brought excitement to an otherwise dull gathering. He always called his wife a saint, but the way she turned a Catholic church into a gathering of Southern Baptists proved it.

Veronica had been his life force. His very soul. Living without her was more of a sin than murder. He would never forgive God for taking away his anchor. Without her, his faith drifted into a sea of doubt before being swallowed by an ocean of apathy. If ever he did pray, it was always to Veronica.

Because of Veronica, he trusted Kyle with blind haste. Kyle had suffered the same loss. Kyle didn't have the benefit of an empire to lean on. Jonas wanted to be that somebody. He saw promise. He saw himself in Kyle. He saw atonement.

Jonas was positive of, and disgusted by, Kyle's fallacy. Kyle kidnapped his daughter to satisfy a selfish need, but he had toyed with Jonas to be cruel.

It saddened Jonas that he could never grieve over Veronica with Judith. He supposed becoming a vicious and reclusive tyrant put a strain on family bonds, but he tried to be a father first.

Jonas finished his burritos with a belch and decided to visit the church. Kyle had talked at length about the devil and God and his quest and purpose. He figured, if nothing else, the walk might clear his mind enough to form a better plan than "hoping for the best". The food had already done wonders for his mood.

Jonas told the gang to hang tight and shop around before crossing the street towards St. Christopher's. Molly and Ian relaxed. James feigned relaxation to hide his frustration. Jonas was finding his wits again, and when Jonas was at his best, almost nothing could stop him.

James walked towards a suit shop a block over, whistling while his mind worked. Ian shifted from foot to foot, wanting to visit a game shop in the strip mall, but unwilling to do so without permission. Molly gave her brother a small smile, letting him know it was alright.

Molly's well trained eyes followed two men. One stayed on Jonas' back, unwilling to let the man that she loved escape her protective gaze while so exposed. The other followed James. The back of his coat shifted in a strange way, as if he had a nub of a tail moving as he walked. James kept his piece on a side strap, so it couldn't be his gun. Molly filed away the information, more proof that something was wrong. As was her duty, she stood guard and watched.

Jonas approached the large oak doors and stopped. He rested a hand on the wooden door and the other on the metal of the handle, trepidation weighing him to the spot.

"Forgive me father, for I have sinned. I will have his head. Even if I spend eternity burning, I will have his fucking head," he said out loud.

Jonas opened the door and walked into the main hall of the church.

There two people present in the great room. The décor was modest, the simple wooden pews worn with worship. The hall was comfortable. Far less black and gray and a little more yellow than most.

A man sat in one of the pews towards the back of the church. A bible and a notebook rested open on his lap. He would read from the bible for a moment, turn to the notebook and scribble down a few words, and repeat the process, little more than a dogmatic automaton. His only acknowledgment of Jonas entering the church was a brief glance upward and an unreturned salutation. Jonas dropped his hand with a shrug, understanding the need to be left alone, and continued down the aisle towards the second occupant.

The priest at the front of the church was arranging candles around the pulpit and staging area. The long white candles wore cheap ribbons and small chips displaying a praying Virgin Mary pasted to the center. He was so engrossed in his work, moving the candles this way and that, as if feng shui and Christianity had merged into a religious decorating practice, that Jonas almost felt bad for interrupting him.

The priest noticed Jonas before he could leave. Placing the candles into a wicker basket at his feet, the priest walked to meet Jonas' outstretched hand. The priest met him with a firm handshake and a confident face, which Jonas respected and appreciated.

"Jonas Macmillan, Father," he said.

"How can I help you today, Jonas? You look distraught, if I may be blunt."

"I think you're being kind. Distraught is a poor word. It sounds too uplifting for how bad the day has been. I haven't been to a church in many years, Father. Not since my wife died. I swore I'd never come back, but I'm out of options."

"Well, they say He's always listening, and God's church is the earth, but I'm thinking you might want to have a chat with someone who speaks less in signs and parables, am I right? That's what priests are, after all. God's translators."

Jonas smiled.

"You're a clever man. How'd a church in this town snag a clever priest? Someone like you might think my problem on the silly side, I'm afraid."

"The only silly problem is a lost pair of clown shoes," the priest said.

Jonas laughed.

"Well, let's see what you think then." Jonas said. He hushed his voice so that the man in the back couldn't overhear him.

"I met a strange man last night. Considering his story and what took place, this seemed like the place to turn."

"Let's go to my office. I'll do my best to listen and offer what advice I can, however silly it may be."

"I'm not the most comfortable in confessional booths, Father. Claustrophobia runs deep in my family."

"Don't worry, Jonas. I'm not that kind of priest, and St. Christopher's is not that kind of church. I wasn't being metaphorical. I have an office in the back, if you are comfortable talking face to face."

"I would be much obliged, Father," Jonas said, relieved to escape the confining confessional.

Claustrophobia aside, Jonas hated the tiny screened rooms. As if God himself sat at his shoulder with a smiting glove ready. Jonas never wanted to be one of the guilty Catholics that the other religions poked at. Confession booths were the only place where he failed to live up to this self-promise. His sins weighed him down more in those rooms than he would ever admit to anybody, even the man behind the screen. He had committed more sins than he wished to recall since his last visit.

"Which way, Father?" he asked.

"Please, please. Call me Leon. Right this way," Leon said. He placed a hand on Jonas' shoulder and led him towards a door in the back of the room, underneath a giant wooden crucifix.

pause for dramatic effect

"You're hiding something," Molly said.

The statement hung in the air with confidence. James understood the lack of upward inflection as an accusation, not a question. Molly never questioned. She was a woman of decisive action. James respected her for it, and knew that there was little Molly could do on instinct to derail the train James had set in motion. But Molly had a knack for following her instincts until she found the truth.

Molly was an ally to be envied and enemy to be feared.

James used the uncomfortable silence to pack away the suit he had purchased in the rear of the car. Fifteen minutes, in and out, was all it took him to find the suit he would wear the moment his reign was official. Black with thin, subtle red pin stripes. Red tie to match. An intimidating ensemble. He would strip over Jonas' fallen corpse and use the boss's lifeless eyes to comb his hair, if privacy permitted.

Molly would not be intimidated. Not now, not later, not ever. If James couldn't bring her around, he'd have to take into account that he'd be running a kingdom with no court. Good help was hard to find.

James lit a cigarette and leaned against the car next to Molly, using his poker face to hide his racing thoughts. If he was to convince her, he had to believe his own lies. He hoped his skill at the latter would birth the former.

"I have no reason to hide anything, Molly. The entire situation is delicate, and I was waiting for the right time to discuss game plan with you," James admitted.

"Then discuss. Trust me when I say I'm curious."

"It's no big deal, really. Watch boy did us a huge favor. Just promise we keep this between us for now."

"I don't make promises, James. I make things happen," Molly said with a glare.

She made sure James was able to see the knife resting in between two knuckles to define what "things happen" defined. James tossed his cigarette to the side, not hiding his frustration.

"Why are you jumping to hostility before you even hear what I have to say? You think Jonas wants the two of us fighting right now?"

"You've been smiling, James. You're a curmudgeon and a snake and I've never seen you smile with sincerity. Since we left the Rail, you haven't been able to stop, even if it only shows in those beady, shit brown eyes of yours. Not a shred of irony or sympathy. You haven't been happy a day in your miserable life, yet here you stand. Happy. If Jonas wasn't so distracted, he'd take your balls for smiling about so much as a precious kitten while Judith is the priority."

"You're being irrational," James said, dismissing her rant.

Molly moved to James' front and flipped her knife open at his thigh as Jonas had the done to Kyle the night before. The difference was that Molly never pulled her knife unless she intended to use it.

"Pissed as I am about little Judith's disappearing act, I am not blinded by grief. If you don't tell me why I have the urge to turn this outing into a burial, you will get to call yourself a queen without irony for the rest of your life," Molly said, hushed and dangerous.

James' poker face fell away. He was afraid, and if he didn't show it, Molly would be more suspicious. Not a hard emotion to convey with her knife pressed to the layer of clothing and flesh above his femoral artery.

"Molly, you know better than most the importance of secrets. I'm just as sick as you are of Jonas obsessing about what his adult daughter does with her free time. You want honesty? Then step out of high and mighty mode for a minute and listen with an open mind."

James flinched as Molly stepped closer to him; sure she was going to keep true to her promise. Instead, she locked eyes with him and reached her free hand underneath his shirt.

"Molly, my dear, you know I don't swing for that particular team," he tried to joke.

"Shut the fuck up, James," she said.

Molly reached around James to find the grip of the Beretta. Pulling it free from James' pants and exposing it to the daylight, James had a moment of clarity. Molly would understand *what* and *how*, but his survival hung on *why*.

"I knew it. That little bastard didn't steal the gun. I doubt he kidnapped her at all. She's off on another one of her party flings, and you're filling the bosses head with bullshit. It's going to give him a heart attack. I don't give a shit about a will, James. Jonas can't leave you the key to my cage. Have you ever seen a lion out of its cage, James? We bite."

The tip of the knife bit into his skin. He felt warm blood trickle down his inner leg. Molly had, in one sentence, sealed her own fate, in

James' mind. She was loyal to only one leader? Then the lioness would be put down with the king. Ian, dumb as he was, would join them.

The prospect of a clean slate seemed more appealing to James as blood stained the pants of his suit. He had to put grandeur out of his mind and give her an answer before the stain became a pool.

"Think, Molly. Everything Judith does turns into a city wide Easter egg hunt. One of these days, Judith isn't going to let herself be found. Jonas will get sloppy, and she'll slip away for good. Can you tell me that you wouldn't let her do it if you could? Jonas can get over grief, but this limbo he keeps pushing us into is going to kill him. We need finality. Judith isn't a bad girl. She deserves to live a life full of mistakes and sorrow, same as everyone. I gave her the wiggle room to get out so we can move the fuck on. I saw an opportunity to ensure this was the last time we had to play hide and seek. Consider this Jonas' silent intervention."

"Not buying it, James. You don't get to make the big decisions. You've shown no initiative to do so. It's unsettling that you picked this morning to do so."

Molly tucked the gun back into James' pants and backed away, flipping her knife closed and hiding it away. James couldn't help the look of relief showing on his face. His logic wasn't great, but it didn't half to be. Now Molly would be pissed at him for taking unwarranted initiative. The fact that Jonas wouldn't see his daughter again by James' own hand was an unexplored notion.

"We're not done, James. You've dug us into this, and you're going to fix it. The second you twitch when I haven't given you the go ahead, I'm throwing you out of the car with a knife in your back. I'll keep my mouth shut to keep Jonas from losing his shit. Wipe the smile of your face and remove the big boy pants. Don't do anything stupid. We have company."

Molly turned her gaze towards the church, and James followed it. A cop car had pulled up in front of the church during their conversation. Two cops were walking toward the front door. One of them walked with concise, stiff movements. The second cop, whose relaxed demeanor marked him as the alpha, stopped half way up the steps and screamed in such surprising volume that even Molly jumped. Ian, who was ready to question the blood on both her knife and James' pants, dropped both his jaw and a bag from the game store.

The police man fell to his knees, convulsing and cursing. They could see his face turning red. His partner watched as they did, still as a statue. Nobody wanted to risk further complications by playing the role of Good Samaritan.

Molly hoped Jonas could keep his cool. He hated cops.

The officer pointed to the door handle as he regained his composure. The younger officer held the door open with his foot, unmoving, a military recruit holding the door for a higher rank. The alpha cop turned his head and spit into a bush before walking through the door.

Ian picked up the bag and followed James and Molly into the sedan to wait for Jonas. They watched at the front door of the church, each performing a silent mental check list in preparation for any complications.

Focused as they were on the façade of the building, none of them could see, through the tinted windows, a light plume of smoke rising from the bush where the cop had spit.

...the son..

Leon's office was simple. A small bookshelf with various religious texts. A desk. The type of wooden table you would find at a bingo hall or a professional wrestling match. A wooden cross. The desk was as barren as the room. A folder, a bible, and a laptop sat atop it; the battered bible looked like a relic from the future compared to the rest of the decor.

Jonas closed the door behind him. A black clock hung on the wall next to the door frame. The clock reminded Jonas of the watch Kyle had been wearing. Jonas struggled to control a fresh surge of anger that tensed his muscles. He made sure that his face was calm and relaxed before facing the priest.

Leon motioned for Jonas to sit, and nodded his head once Jonas did. Jonas took in a shallow breath and spilled his story.

Jonas told Leon about Kyle and his sudden arrival to the Green Rail basement. About the conversation him and Kyle had had that lasted until the sun was not long from waking. His trust of the boy. The kidnapping and stolen goods. The betrayal of such an undeserving trust. With hesitation, he told Leon about Kyle's strange quest. How he had sworn that he was there to save one of them from one thing or another, even as a gun had been staring him in the face. About the seven digits that bore the names of the seven sins next to them. An elegant time piece that, in Jonas' mind, was nothing more than elaborate prop to claim Judith for himself.

Jonas expected a look of speculation from the priest. If Leon owned a phone, Jonas wouldn't have blamed him for calling the cops. The story made Jonas sound insane. Sure, Kyle was the crazy one, but Leon didn't know Kyle. Leon sat still, palms together, fingers to his lips, eyes unreadable.

When Jonas finished his tale, he felt better. The food had helped. Leon's acceptance that Jonas wasn't spouting off a crazy story for kicks gave him hope for guidance, which he needed.

Jonas sat, eyes wide and eager, basking in the small release of tension and waiting for an answer.

Leon sat in silence for a long while, contemplating. He never thought that Kyle and Judith's plight would revisit him within twenty-four hours of leaving his presence. God had other plans for Leon. Leon wasn't sure rather Jonas' arrival would be a blessing in disguise for the pair, or an afternoon of torment for himself.

Leon's silence, misread as deep thought by Jonas, was a struggle. He didn't know how much to tell the man. He knew that Kyle hadn't kidnapped Judith. Judith didn't strike Leon as a woman who would suffer Stockholm syndrome. Their adventure was consensual.

That Leon had met them was proof enough that they had not stolen Jonas' gun. The cat and mouse game he had broken up by taking the paw off of the cat would have been short, sweet, and full of bullets. Leon's memory of the pair would have been nothing more than shots fired in an alley. Not uncommon.

Jonas was far from guiltless. Behind those eager, pleading eyes was a selfish monster of a man. A giant whose golden goose had flown the coop. Kyle was the most recent incarnation of Jack, though far from the first.

Judith had spoken with Leon about her father. Specifics aside, Leon pitied him. Jonas was a man driven to extreme hate due to unyielding love.

Leon didn't want to lie to Jonas. Judith's explicit stories hadn't even filtered through a nightmare yet, and the man responsible was sharing the same air not five feet away. Scared was underplaying his emotional state.

But lying would break his renewed faith. Kyle's service would have been for naught. Like an ex-smoker, one little taste would put him two steps backward from square one. Leon was at peace with God and was not in a hurry for a second lapse in faith on either of their part.

Leon took solace in not knowing where the two were headed. He could tell the truth and not meddle with the plan, whatever it was. Jonas could *not* find Kyle and Judith. Not in the next six days. If Leon were to cause pain to either of them, he had misplaced his new faith. He prayed.

Don't let my words lead this man to blood. Amen.

And as for next week? Well, God help them both. God help them all.

The thoughts, racing through Leon's head within a few seconds, allowed him to take a deep breath and close his eyes.

"They were both here last night. They left a few hours ago," Leon said.

"What? They were here?" Jonas asked.

Jonas didn't wait for an answer.

"Of all the churches in this damn city. My Judith was alright, wasn't she? That bastard didn't hurt her?" he said.

Jonas was concerned. Anger was dormant, for the moment. Leon was thankful.

"Judith was fine. A couple of men attacked them last night. I heard the commotion and was responsive enough to dispatch the two and offer Kyle and Miss Judith whatever help I could afford to give. I gave them food, shelter, and a shoulder. I don't know what was winning between fear and exhaustion when I found them, but the battle was close. They left with smiles on their faces, Jonas."

Leon made sure to emphasize that nugget of truth to press the point home that things might not have been what they seemed to Jonas. Jonas' concern turned to anger as his face contorted into a snarl

"My Judith attacked? I'll kill that son of a bitch for bringing this on her."

Jonas pounded the desk hard with a downward strike of his fist, grunted, and hit the desk with the other fist. A pen fell to the floor. His eyes followed the pen as it rolled across the floor, sucking the malice from him. When the pen stopped rolling, he turned to Leon, hatred in his eyes. Intelligent, scheming hatred.

There would be no saving Kyle. Not from a man with such complicated layers of wrath. If Jonas found Kyle, Kyle would die. And it would be Leon's fault for fueling him. Leon would never know the outcome of Kyle's quest, but the pain in his heart that felt like betrayal would follow him to his death bed.

"Where did they go? Where did he take her?" he demanded.

"I have no clue. They left hours ago, as I said. They left after breakfast. If they had any idea where they were heading, they didn't tell me. Seems to me they were running blind though, Jonas."

Leon picked up the pen, happy to escape Jonas' gaze for even a moment.

"That crazy, kidnapping little fuck."

Jonas cracked his knuckles and stood up to face the door, ready to renew his search. Leon stopped him.

"If I may? You came to a priest, and I should at least give you a shred of input," Leon spoke.

"May what, huh? Try and make me calm? Weave me a tale of

how God has a plan and I must be patient? Give me a fuckin' cracker and an order to stand by?"

Jonas had turned an ugly shade of purple in his fit, but Leon remained level, hoping to appeal to the little piece of Jonas still riddled with concern.

"I think you have Kyle wrong. They acted like best friends, not strangers. There was no hint that she was with him against her will. She had plenty of opportunities to rat him out to myself, call the police, dispatch of him. She told me he was saving her. I think you should consider she is exactly where she needs to be. Weigh out the options of what you are going to do."

Jonas pulled the Beretta out from under his jacket and kicked the chair out from underneath him. He leveled the barrel into the chest of the priest, ending their makeshift confession. This was the second time in Leon's life a gun pointed at him, all within the span of twenty-four hours. Leon shut his mouth and made no gestures to show his fear. He had to be strong and collected to deal with Jonas. Fear was a mighty foe in these situations.

Jonas' eyes were like steel when he spoke.

"Options? This isn't a choice between turkey and ham for Christmas dinner, padre. This is my daughter! Now you listen to me, Leon. He gave up his options the second he took her from me. She's mine! My daughter! He had no right to take my little girl.. I'm going to find them both, I'm going to take her home, and I'm going to kill him. Consider that a pre-paid confession. And if I ever…"

Jonas leaned in close, his voice taking on the intelligent fury his eyes had shown for most of his visit.

"…ever find out that a word you spoke to me was a lie, my little metal friend and I are going to consider you accomplice. Do you understand me, father?"

Leon replied, his voice displaying a strong passive quality he wished the rest of him felt.

"This is a mistake. Shoot if you want, Jonas, but if you follow through with this plan, you can guarantee that you'll lose her forever. Let her be. Let both of them be. Grant her the freedom she so desires. God is watching over the both of them."

Jonas fought not to let the priest's words rekindle the earlier thoughts of granting her that very thing. Realizing he would get nothing more out of the priest, he holstered his gun and turned towards the door, letting anger guide him.

"You know nothing, you simple man. You're wasting my time," he said.

Jonas opened the door and walked into the solid chest of a man on the other side. He was startled into annoyance. Sure, he was a cop. A cop who looked like he had gotten a years worth of sun in the past half an hour. A cop who had a mild case of the twitch fits. A cop who stood between Jonas and his daughter.

The cop smirked at him, enjoying Jonas' building aggravation. Jonas began to reach the point of no return, his fists balling into rocks. The cop stepped to the side and motioned him to pass.

Jonas shoulder checked a second cop, who stood still as a statue behind the red officer, without worry of repercussion. The red cop eyed him until he neared the entrance.

There *was* no repercussion for Jonas, of course. Not within the confines of the church. Jonas would have his punishment when anger gave way to despair.

Officer Wilkins had come to make his own confession. He was there to see the priest.

If Leon thought Jonas was a man layered by centuries of wrath, he was about to meet the raw ore from which wrath had been chiseled.

The rookie remained in the main hall, waiting for his cue, as Wilkins entered the office.

"A cop and a demon walk into a church, and that's just the first guy," Wilkins said under his breath.

It would be the final confession that either man would ever take part in.

GREED

Greed is my conscience

Craving what I cannot have

Hating those who can

...and the holy shit!

That someone plagued by such severe sun stroke functioned at all surprised Leon. The cop's exposed body parts were a deep, uniform red. There was a noticeable shake in his posture. The cop must have had one hell of a pain threshold.

If only you knew, Padre.

"Good day, Mr. Grebowski. I'm Officer Hank Wilkins. I have questions, if you'd be so willing to oblige me."

"Of course, officer. Have a seat."

Officer Wilkins snorted away the offer, seeming distracted.

"No thank you. I prefer be up high, where the action is. I'm a lot less paranoid when I can see what's coming."

Leon shrugged, as if to say fair enough, and took his own seat. He had expected a visit from the police and was little concerned by the upcoming interrogation. He had been well within his rights to protect his property, and had followed legal self-defense procedures.

Officer Wilkins pulled a Moleskin pad and a pen out of his breast pocket. He uncapped the pen and licked the tip.

"My partner will be jumping on in once he ensures our little criminal compadre has left us in his dust. Just a rookie, but boy is he learning a heck of a lot on the job today."

Leon heard the door to his office close before he saw the rookie, Wilkins' large form obscuring it. A young, auburn-haired man in a matching police uniform walked to the side of Wilkins and stood motionless.

The rookie's eyes projected the kind of terror reserved for fanatics claiming to have seen the devil. His gaze traveled over Leon's head.

"You were right. He must have had a hell of a day. He looks like he's in shock," Leon said, unable to hold in worry.

"Yeah, well, had a dispute turn violent on us. He'll be fine. Now, just pay attention, rook. You've learned a lot today, and I assure you it will all come in quite valuable. Don't you forget a thing!" said Wilkins.

"Yes, sir."

Wilkins reacted with little concern to Leon's empathy. Leon guessed the rook had seen his first up close murder victim, or perhaps had fired his weapon for the first time. Leon could imagine the horrors a job as a policeman subjected one to. He felt sympathy for the kid. Wilkins wanted the topic changed, probably to keep the rookie calm. Leon tried to help.

"So," Leon said, "what can I help you with, Officer?"

"Well, I'm pretty sure you know why we're here. I won't blow any gun smoke up your ass. Do you have a permit for the weapon?"

"Of course. I was hoping to go hunt a buck or two before the season ended, but I've lost my appetite for shooting this year, I think."

"Understandable. I know one hundred percent how having to fire a weapon at somebody takes the joy out of having to fire it at all. So what happened? Keep it short and sweet, padre. We have three more visits like this before break."

Leon wiped his forehead with the sleeve of his robe. Though he had set the thermostat to seventy, he was sweating. He prayed it wasn't a cold, though he wouldn't be surprised after such a stressful day.

"Not much to tell. I was in the back of the church and I heard running and commotion through one of the high windows. There was a crash, followed by loud voices. I heard the words rape and murder, and grabbed the shotgun to see what was happening. I'm not the sort of person who plays ignorant. I intended to scare a couple of bullies, nothing more. I saw a couple being held at gunpoint, tried to resolve the situation, and was shot at. I retaliated."

"Not turning the other cheek, eh?" joked Wilkins.

"They asked me the very same thing, Officer," Leon said with a smile. "Not when it comes to firearms. I had already committed myself to resolving the situation. If they had killed me, those poor kids would have soon followed. Rape and murder is never a joke. The two who were armed had moved beyond scaring for laughs. I had no choice. I didn't intend the shot to hit either of them, but I guess God had other plans. Drastic measure, but a measure within my rights, I believe."

"Perfectly, father."

"How's his hand, by the way? Or lack thereof."

"Oh, he's wishing he had just let it be, I can assure you that. They had criminal records, so I took their report with a grain of salt, but I had to get your side. Fair is fair, though rarely earned. Scum as they were, they're both dead."

Leon was startled.

"Dead? Did I…", Leon began.

Wilkins stopped him with a gentle smile, putting the whole of his attention on Leon for the first time.

"No, no. It wasn't your fault in the least, padre. They had a shaky story. We questioned them too hard while looking for a cab they rambled on about. We never found it. When stupid criminals run out of good lies, they get violent. Bad move. You can understand why the rookie is so…"

Officer Wilkins stopped talking, his words morphing into a sudden roar of pain. His writing hand shot to his temple, massaging it with such force that Leon saw the tip of the pen pierce the skin of Wilkins' forehead. There was no mark to show for it.

"Aspirin?" Leon asked, rummaging through his belongings.

"No, no," Wilkins declined, regaining his bearings. "Never touch the stuff. It will pass."

"I've got plenty."

"No, thank you. I mean it."

Leon shut up, not liking the hint of aggression in Wilkins' voice. His eye stung with sweat, and he made a mental note to check the temperature of both the church and himself as soon as Wilkins left.

"All better. Where was I? Those two scum bags?" Wilkins said, as if nothing had happened.

"Sounds right to me, Officer."

"Those two gave us no choice but to use force. Good riddance, I say, but the rook here is taking it pretty hard."

"I can see that," Leon commented, noticing that the panicked look in the rookie's eyes was worsening the longer he stood still.

"Now, one last thing before I leave. I am curious about this couple. A Mr. Thimall and Ms. Judy…" Wilkins appeared to search his notes for the last name.

"McMillan," Leon finished.

Leon wiped fresh beads of sweat from his face and longed for a table fan or a glass of ice water. If he could sit through Jonas' hissy fit, he could tough it out until Wilkins was finished with him.

Oh, I'll be finished with you before you know it, Padre.

"Yes. Judy McMillan. Guess I need to write that one down this time," Officer Wilkins said, and he did.

"They were victims," Leon said.

Wilkins made a clicking noise with his mouth and wagged his

pen towards Leon, as if scolding him.

"Victims in this case, maybe. But Mr. Thimall is far from innocent. We found coke in the vehicle, licensed to him, he abandoned in a restricted alley way. The station has an outstanding warrant for multiple failures to appear in court. I'm not one to judge without..."

Officer Wilkins was cut short by another fit of screams. The pen and pad fell from his hands and shot to his head. For a moment, Leon swore he saw something move beneath the skin of his forehead. Wiping his eyes, he passed it off as sweat from the heat getting into them. Leon stood, concerned that Wilkins was having an aneurysm or a stroke.

"Why are you standing there? There's something wrong with your partner, you fool! You saw violence. You're a cop! Call it while I get him something for the pain!" Leon barked.

"No!" Wilkins screamed.

The sheer volume and power of the scream put Leon on his ass, back in his chair. Through the heat, he felt chills creeping up his neck.

"No," Wilkins repeated. "Just been a long day. Migraine is all. Rook here is in more pain than I am. You better believe it. I must speak with Mr. Thimall. It's been a trying day for all of us, so I'll be as lenient as possible. But the law is the law, Father. You understand."

Officer Wilkins' inflection had changed. Hunger had replaced curiosity. Leon suspected that the rise in heat had nothing to do with a faulty thermostat. The temperature rose with each change of emotion. Leon had never experienced such heat. He looked to the rookie, still as ever. His eyes still screamed of unknown horror Leon didn't want to begin to imagine.

Every ounce of unease and panic Leon had been able to push aside hit him at once.

"I'm not sure where they went, Officer. They left in a rush and without much information. I wish I could help, but I have work to do. God's law is God's law, you understand."

Leon made to stand.

"Stand up, Father, and I'll have my partner shoot you through your God fearing skull."

"Pardon me?" Leon said flabbergasted.

His knees bent somewhere between sitting and standing, his hands gripping tight on the arm rests. More than Wilkins' words were freezing him in place.

"You heard me. So sit the fuck back down. Rookie? Raise it."

Officer Wilkins picked the fallen pen and pad off of the ground, stuffing them into his front pocket. He raised a thumb to his left temple, rubbing it with gentle circles, all the while his eyes bore into Leon's.

Leon could do nothing but stare back into them as an unseen force planted him into the chair. Wilkins had dropped facade to show Leon his true intentions. He never cared about the criminals. He wanted Kyle. Controlling the overwhelming panic was the hardest thing Leon had ever done in his life.

What little of it remained.

The rookie pulled the gun from his holster and raised it level with Leon's head. His movements were mechanical, but the terror in his eyes doubled. The rookie, like himself, was sweating bullets. Wilkins skin let off not even a light sheen of moisture.

From that moment until his last breath was drawn, in the depths of his very soul, Leon Grebowski prayed for salvation.

"What is this?" Leon spoke, raising his hands to express his helplessness.

"Padre, you don't understand how important finding Mr. Thimall is to me. I need him quick, fast, and in a hurry. Your false ignorance is just pissing me off. That shit worked on the little bitch's daddy, but I am motivated by something far less pathetic. I am no fool, and I am not in the mood for arrogance. Where are they?"

"I don't know! I told you that! Who the hell are you, anyway?"

"Shoot," Wilkins said.

The rookie pulled the trigger. The recoil made Leon's ears ring, which distracted him from the fresh pain in his wrist for a good half of a second. Leon screamed in agony and clutched his wrist to his chest, blood flowing onto his skin and robes. Sweat streamed down his face. His breathing became deep and guttural.

"I ask the questions, Leon." Officer Wilkins said.

His voice had lost all semblance of humanity.

"Now, where are they?" Wilkins repeated.

"I don't *know*, you crazy bastard!" Leon screamed.

"You know, you're the second person who's called me that today? I must admit, it has a rather nice ring to it. Perhaps it will be my

new epithet. Hank "Crazy Bastard" Wilkins. Again, Rook."
Wilkins sounded impatient, but there was no doubt he was enjoying himself.

Leon raised his good hand and ducked, instinct driving his defense mechanism. The bullet hit him through the right forearm, higher that where the bullet had struck his left arm. Leon's arms, a sick mix of numbness and excruciating pain, fell to his desk. Blood flowed over the wood, staining the surface with the color that drained from his face.

No tears could fall. He could scream incoherence for the agony coursing through his every nerve.

But he could not cry.

"You're three holes away from stigmata, padre, and we've got four bullets left in the clip. Tell me what you know or join the ranks of every other forgettable martyr who died for their pride. It makes no difference to me," Wilkins said, growing bored.

Leon mustered what saliva he could and spit at Wilkins. The small bit of liquid traveled no further than his desk, where it dissolved into the blood, but he felt the intention was no less powerful.

"Fuck you," Leon grunted, looking Wilkins dead in the eyes, trying to convey anything but the fear and pain he felt.

Wilkins' eyes turned black and opened wide with fury. In that moment, Leon saw what was behind the voice and contorted face; what was in his soul.

Evil.

This was no sunburned man of the law. He was not a man at all. His ice breaking joke hadn't been a joke at all.

"A police officer and a demon walk into a church, and that's jus

the first guy..."

Officer Wilkins was a demon.

"You God damned fool! I should..."

Wilkins couldn't finish the sentence. His scream shook the church. Dropping to his knees, he clutched at his head again. Wilkins pulled at his hair and slammed his fists into his temples, swinging his head back and forth as the scream pouring from his throat changed in depth and tone. The scream caused the glass of the black clock to explode outward, peppering the rookie, still frozen, with small incisions on his face and hands.

The cop writhed in pain, convulsing and shaking on the ground. Leon's vision grew weak with blood loss as the cops screams subsided to deep, heavy breathing.

Wilkins stood up and let out a sigh of relief. Giving his neck a violent crack in both directions, he turned sideways to face Leon. Even as his sight faded, nothing could obscure what Wilkins had become. What little power remained bled out of him, and he shed a tear in each eye.

The last bit of life left in his body streamed down his cheek. He would not escape the church with his life. He hoped he had made enough peace with God to keep him from ever having to see a sight like what stood before him again.

Wilkins' eyes had turned a dark blood red. The veins in his eyes, in his neck, and on his head had turned black and were pulsing beneath the skin. Two lumps had emerged from his temples, four inches in diameter and curving forward out of his skull. Staring the priest down, a wide smile bore his teeth, which had turned blinding white and dripped viscous black saliva. When Wilkins spoke, his voice was a deep harmony to the subsided screams, shaking Leon from his core.

"One more chance, padre. Live or die. I can make the pain go away. I can renew you. Just tell me. Where is he? Where?!"

Rather it was realizing that Wilkins was lying about his promise, or knowing that he was moments from death, Leon grew numb and calm. He would never betray Kyle, Judith, or God. He had the energy for his life's final sermon, which would be heard by a man possessed and the spawn of hell, and then he would die.

But he would do so with grace.

"You are the devil, sir, and I am no Johnny. I will not cater to your ilk. No golden words or threats of hell fire shall tempt me!"

Leon stood, using his elbows for support.

"Make good on your threat and send me home, demon! You cannot judge me, for you are not God!"

Leon grinned and spread his arms wide, as if for a hug.

The demon grinned back. He moved the rookie's arms so that the gun aimed at the priest's heart.

"Maybe not," he said, mocking in his voice. "But I'm the next best thing."

The demon snapped his fingers, and the rookie pulled the trigger. Leon closed his eyes as the bullet drove him into chair and against the wall. He felt nothing as the bullet pierced his chest, ripping through muscle, bone, and the very heart that had already spilled more blood than it could ever hope to replenish. Leon was dead before his body slumped from the chair to the floor.

"Put it away," the demon said to the rookie.

"Yes, sir" he replied, following the order.

"Meet me in the cruiser. And for fucks sake, turn the heater up. Way up."

The rookie nodded and exited the room, the tears streaming down his own face the only indication of his inner horror.

Wilkins stared at the lifeless priest for a few moments as a curious child would stare at piece of road kill. Breathing through his nose, the sound of hawking back whatever mucus and saliva he could muster akin to a kitchen blender, he launched a loogie into the center of Leon's face. As soon as the loogie made contact, the Leon's body burst into flames. The wall behind him blackened. Within seconds, the room was aflame.

"Spit on me..." Wilkins said, turning to leave the room.

Looking out of the office doorway into the ominous main hall of the church, Wilkins put his hands on his hips and inhaled. Though his face contorted to one of disgust after inhalation, a wicked smile crossed his face upon exhaling. Raising his hands above his head, he screamed into the empty room.

"Behold, my demonic chorus! Your debut has come at last!"

Flicking his wrists with practiced flare, the candles that Leon had been setting up around the pulpit not an hour ago lit themselves. The flames, a dark blood red, rose ten feet into the air and emitted a dark black smoke the rose to the roof. Within seconds, darkness obscured the ceiling.

Wilkins dropped his hands to waist level and made his way to the three stairs that led to the aisle between pulpits. He crept along, eyes closed, humming to himself as he moved. The smoke from the ceiling followed behind him as he crept. His wrists moved, conducting music that only he could hear and evils that only he could see. With every step he took past a pew, the bench of worship would burst into fresh red flames.

"The strings, more vibrato!" he sang, flicking his invisible baton to the right.

A painting on the wall, depicting Adam and Eve, burst into flames. It fell from the wall, the flames contorting the complacent faces Eden's only inhabitants to grimaces of torture. The flames jumped to decorative curtains hanging over windowless walls and lit them, the thin material burning in seconds.

A few more steps, and he flicked to the left.

"Now for the percussion! Let me *feel* it! And don't go easy on the cowbell, Mr. Walken!"

An audible blast sounded as the remaining paintings around the room burst outward with flame. Mary, Moses, Joseph, and Jesus reduced to piles of burning wood. Fuel intended to expedite the destruction of the house where so many worshiped their words and memories. The two windows that let sunlight into the room burst inward, spraying glass about the pews.

The demon had now reached the back of the room, eyes still closed, still humming the macabre tune under his breath. Pivoting around, he opened his eyes.

The church filled with dark black smoke. Embers and flames highlighted the impressive destruction. The pictures and curtains had burned to ash. The black smoke was thick enough to block his view of the front of the church. Putting his palms together, as if praying, he spread his hands apart at a calculated pace.
The pulpit and large cross at the head of the room were the only things left untouched by flames.

He pointed his invisible baton at them, saving the best for last.

"The brass! I want you booming!" he sang.

The pulpit exploded into a ball of flame. Burning cinders and ash rained down through the smoke like fireworks.

Wilkins breathed the smoke in deep and pivoted again, facing the church's main door. Jesse and the man who had been taking notes when Jonas walked in both sat propped next to the door. Each had a bullet hole in the middle of their foreheads. Wilkins tilted his head toward them and opened one eye.

"Ah, fans! No need to be shy. Of course I will sign your programs."

Wilkins reached his shirt pocket and took out the notebook and pencil. He signed across the two pages in the middle:

To my two biggest fans. You're fucked. So sorry.

Wilkins tossed the pencil and notebook at corpses and offered them a thumbs up.

"There now. Don't forget to tell your friends! This show is to *die* for!"

Wilkins turned the thumbs up into a finger snap, and two bodies burst into flames. Their hair singed and their skin crackled, much as Leon's was now doing in the office that would become his tomb.

Not turning to look behind him, Wilkins thrust his hands sideways in either direction, mocking crucifixion. Tilting his head backwards, he sang loud enough to overpower the symphony of destruction that surrounded him.

"And the chorus swells!"

With that, the large wooded crucifix at the back of the room lit and fell from its place of glory. Wilkins dropped his hands to his side, the smoke that he had separated as Moses once parted the sea filling back in at the motion, and exited the building.

The demon had gotten what he wanted. A place to dispose evidence and a name he could only receive from the willing. He stuffed his hands into his pockets and walked to the cruiser with a skip in his step, whistling the same macabre tune to the background conflagration of destruction.

On day three, St. Christopher's church burned to the ground

CHAPTER 19

riddles

Kyle and Judith trekked back to the pub as if being followed by crocodiles, zig-zagging the labyrinth of back streets in hopes of throwing off the monsters that followed. With every precious minute that ticked by, Kyle knew that being careless could cause a number of setbacks. Suspicion. Acquisition. Questioning. A bullet with his name on it. Thoughts of misused handcuffs and over utilized pistol whipping turned Kyle's stomach.

Kyle, in a moment of curious idiocy, asked Judith which she thought the worse outcome was: Jonas or the malicious cop with the bad case of bloodlust finding them first.

Judith shrugged, her answer unsettling to them both.

"Jonas wants fear and respect. The verbal torture is the worst part if you can handle a few cuts from Molly. The dying part is quick. That cop didn't do much talking. Blunt force trauma isn't a fun way to go, I would think"

Kyle shuddered at the imagery.

"I'm glad you tagged along, Judith."

"Oh, don't be so dramatic. They'd have to find you first, right?"

Kyle supposed that she had more of a reason to be carefree when danger wasn't looking them in the face. If it was Jonas, she'd be back to the life he had saved her from, but she'd be alive. Kyle doubted the cop was going to care much rather he found Judith or not, as long as he got Kyle.

The cop would soon have access to Kyle's entire life if he wanted. His dealers, his co-workers, his therapist. His blood type and food allergies. The blueprints to his apartment. Fucking Google.

He couldn't tie Judith to Kyle, seeing how they had met less than two days ago. She wasn't the cokehead, after all. He took solace in that fact.

Jonas didn't strike Kyle as a man who would include authority in his vengeance. Judith had mentioned Jonas's abhorrent hatred of the law, due to their lack of justice and general disorder. They were scum without principles to him. Irony, though often depressing, was Kyle's friend for the time being.

Jonas was his own moral authority, unorthodox but efficient. The cop had the law on his side, and played with it loose enough to use it as a jump rope. Either way, if he was caught, he would disappear. Cops and criminals both knew the best rivers to dump their dirty laundry.

With so many hell hounds nipping at his heels, the warm mist from the River Styx clung to his brow. He regretted his penny flicking habit in a moment of black humor, reminding himself to make change for the ferry toll, lest he go from death in a river to eternity stuck on the banks of the river of death.

The cop knew Kyle's face only by photograph. Jonas knew his face by the intimate remembrance of betrayal. They bought a couple of baseball caps from a corner store. The weather was too warm for much facial covering. Judith paid while Kyle waited outside to avoid the security camera behind the cashier.

Judith stepped outside with two hats, smokes, and a gallon of milk.

Kyle understood the cigarettes, and took one from the already opened pack with the unstable fingers of an addict, breaking two of them in half before he managed to light a full stick.

"Milk?" Kyle asked through the slow exhale of a Camel.

"I'm lactose intolerant. I mean, sure, I can eat the stuff. I had a couple bites of Leon's eggs, not wanting to be rude. It's the one thing Jonas never bothered controlling, because for the most part I stay the hell away from it on my own. But in the off chance that Jonas stops here, I don't think he'll care about the customer who bought milk and smokes."

Street smart was all about simple. Kyle would have overthought it. He was never able to grasp the K.I.S.S. concept. Keep It Simple, Stupid. She was a blessing.

Judith tossed the milk into a nearby dumpster on their way back into the alley. Three cigarettes later, Judith told him that the pub was five blocks away. Jonas may or may not have left someone behind just in case, and even the simple minded Ian was good with a gun.

"So stay quiet until we have the car or I take two to the head. Got ya," Kyle said, humor doing little to hide the stress.

"If someone is home, you can take the keys and the cash and leave. Nobody's going to hurt me at the Rail. If there's a trap, I can run interference and bullshit them. Just wait until I get them inside so I can start an argument loud enough to cover the engine noise. I can buy you time," Judith said without conviction.

Kyle couldn't bear letting this new, empowered Judith, far

removed from the Judith he had met in the Green Rail basement, die off without a fight. Sending her back into the cage to further his own purposes felt contradictory. That decision would be the worse of two evils.

Her strength gave him strength. They had both chosen the more difficult path in aid to the other.

As his actions the night before had proven, her discreet lack of strength had the same effect. Even before slipping into a downward spiral, he wouldn't have been so brave in the face of danger at the defense of someone he barely knew. She gave him a more realistic purpose for success. Something real and organic. Though odd, he felt that severing that tie would be failure in itself, stupid oracle watch or no.

Kyle was selfish, but he accepted it. He couldn't muster the strength to let her go. He wouldn't try unless there was absolutely no other choice. Needing her around was a weakness; any superhero worth their cape could empathize. Dragging her into danger, volunteered or not, was selfish.

The honest truth, which he had known since Leon's, was that he *wanted* her with him as much as he *needed* her with him. The selfish truth, he realized once she gave him the option to leave her behind, was that he wanted *her*.

"Not on your life, lady. Just because they won't hurt you doesn't mean you wouldn't be in pain. I'm not going to let you sacrifice this fun freedom of yours just to give me a slight head start. If we can get the car together, great. If we can't, we move to plan B, which in this case means going door to door like a couple of trendy Mormon's and saving whoever the hell we can before someone finds us," Kyle rambled.

"Because that's not a way to attract attention. You sure this isn't an elaborate plot to get in my pants?" Judith said.

Kyle froze, his face twisted into something that mixed the embarrassment of getting caught looking at skin magazines by a parent with the nervous euphoria of going for that first open mouth kiss.

He couldn't twitch of excitement the proposition extracted.

Judith grabbed Kyle by the wrist, yanking him from his dumbfounded stupor and leading them toward the pub.

"I'm fucking with you, Kyle. Tuck it back, ok? Wrong head to be thinking with right now" she said, smiling with giddy relief.

Judith's relieved smile would have made the decision, selfish as it was, worth it if he had seen it. Judith remained in front, leading them to their goal, mutual focus shutting down what most would see as an open invitation to a pants party.

Judith peeked around a corner, looking for clear passage, when a loud siren sent the two into the wall. She squeezed his hand hard enough to turn it white. Paranoia, perhaps, but frivolous risk had been left] at the church. Though it was true that paranoid people browsed conspiracy theory blogs in their mother's basements, ranting about the Russian Area 51 or the grays living in the mountains of Colorado, they also did a pretty good job at staying alive.

The siren, from a fire truck instead of a police car, was followed by that of an ambulance. The sound drowned out before Judith loosened her grip on his hand. Kyle winced as the returning blood shot pins and needles through his hand.

"Sorry!" she whispered.

"I'll need this hand to kung fu more gangsters if need be, Judith. What are you, a pianist?" he joked, shaking his wrist.

"Massage therapy," she smiled. "I've had to kick an ass or two my..."

Something moved, and it was close enough for Kyle to catch the flicker of a shoe disappearing behind a dumpster. Had he glanced in the same direction as Judith, he might have thought leftover paranoia.

The shoe, connected to a leg, provided that "it" was a "who". Paranoia and rationality took a rare moment to discuss the issue. They both reached the same conclusion.

Someone was following them.

Judith, confused as she saw the quizzical look on Kyle's face, didn't protest as he put a finger to his lips and motioned for her to follow. They crept towards the dumpster, her mimicking his every step and trying not to giggle at the Tom and Jerry piano music playing in her head to every tip toe.

Dun...dun...dun...dun....dududududududududun!

They both had been too busy thinking of the dangers that awaited. They never thought someone so adamant about being secretive would have been following them. Jonas and the cop would have no reason to hide.

They had the firepower, and Kyle and Judith were hiding from *them.*

Hoarse breathing echoed from behind the dumpster. The closer they tiptoed to the dumpster, the quicker, and louder, the sound became.

Again, the question was not from where the sound came, but from *whom*. Whoever it was knew they were there, and was afraid of them. At least they were able to control their breathing. The unidentified party sounded like a teenage smoker after a gym class.

Kyle placed a hand behind him, brushing across one of Judith's breasts. He felt none of the satisfaction of second base, but all of the pain as she bent his pinky backwards. Watching his face as he turned, trying not to scream made, Judith want to laugh again. She didn't mind the accident, but wanted to remind Kyle that she could take care of herself. Pain had always been the way she got the attention of boys she liked. Though it was often unconscious, it wasn't always.

Kyle feigned anger and shook the pain from his pinky while he motioned for her to stay put. She agreed with a nod, as her hand was holding back laughter that would deluge the alley if she opened her mouth.

Kyle used his mild aggravation to inspire his best mean face, which was like watching a kitten's first yawn, and counted to three. With about as much grace as a newborn kitten, Kyle pounced around the dumpster to confront their silent stalker.

A moment later, Judith lost the ability to stifle back her laughter, danger be damned as Kyle Thimall opened his mouth and let loose not the roar of a lion, not even the meow of a kitten, but the scream of an eight year old girl.

way too many colloquialisms

Had Kyle screamed after seeing evil bred in the imagination of the devil, Judith would have sympathized. She likely would have joined his high pitched shriek with one of her own. The breathing, scared man that Kyle had tried to surprise was no agent of the devil. Not a zombie, nor a vampire; not even a dwarf in a pointy hat.

The bearded face that cringed up at Kyle around the corner terrified him. The man was toothless, dirty, and had an eye colored white as a fresh glass of milk. Kyle would have been better prepared for any of the aforementioned monsters before he was prepared for the man his imagination had dubbed Ed the Head Eater.

The second the man had offered a sign of sound or movement in reaction, proving that he was no trick of the mind, Kyle lost it.

The movement was a cringe. The sound was "Please don't hurt me!"

Kyle Thimall, in that moment of terrified recognition, almost wet himself.

Judith, laughing to tears and unafraid of the consequences, if Kyle was going to scream like that, fell to her knees. Anybody who saw them would wonder why two crazy people were bothering a hipster. The bearded man, for a few moments, was the most normal of them.

They wouldn't have been wrong, either.

Kyle's scream died into a quiet gasping and he lost breath control. Judith calmed down enough to keep Kyle from hyperventilating, though the occasional chuckle still escaped her throat.

"What the hell was that, Kyle?" she laughed, patting his back like a baby being burped.

"He had a fucking white eye and a scary beard and he looks like that dirty bum from Mulholland Drive and I think I pissed a little and the white fucking eye and he's a demon and..." Kyle yammered.

Judith smacked him across the face mid-sentence, shocking him into silence and proving that sometimes slapstick works.

"Kyle, he has cataracts in that eye. He's not a demon. He's half blind. Hell, he's squeezed far enough into the corner to fit behind the damned dumpster!"

"Please, please don't hurt me, please..." the man repeated in small sobs.

"Hurt you?" Kyle said with the tone of someone who can't take a joke.

"You were the one following us, nightmare man! Were you trying to get us alone and take a nibble off of my scalp? Trying to follow us into the house and steal the good china? You'd be shit out of luck unless the market value of plastic cutlery has skyrocketed in the past two days. Just what were you doing?"

"You're not making any sense. He looks more scared than you do, even if he doesn't scream like a little..."

"Not the time, Judith. He knows what he did in *here*," Kyle said, tapping his temple and glaring at the bearded man.

The bearded man looked to Judith, his fear turning into something more akin to confused wonder. Judith shrugged and put her finger to her own temple, twirling it in the internationally known gesture for insanity.

The bearded man nodded, as if he understood with that simple explanation, and Judith lost it again. The bearded man, sensing no reason to be afraid, joined in with deep, bellowing laughter of his own.

"Oh ha ha. Everyone laugh because of my high soprano. That doesn't change the fact that I've had nightmares about this guy since I was a teenager, and now I find that he's been following us. Earth to Judith, but when the evil-day sends me on an est-quay and shit starts popping out from my ightmares-nay, what am I supposed to think? He's...he's..."

Kyle's words faded into contemplation as he examined the bearded man. Kyle sounded like a small child, but this man looked like one. Curled into a ball, shaking like a kid awaiting the switch or a belt or a fist. Buck's good eye was filled with trepidation. He lacked the sharp canines and general urge to go for Kyle's throat that defined the nightmare-hobo.

He felt guilty. The bearded man just needed a nip, a nap and a meal.

"Oh, hell," Kyle said, giving up reprimand. "I over-reacted. I'm sorry, man."

"I didn't mean nothin' by it. I swear! I won't go rob you or nothing'. I was just curious and I wanted a nickel for a coffee," the bearded man said, sounded a tad rehearsed.

The inherent lie sensor that Lucifer had pointed out was beeping. Kyle could tell that the man wasn't telling the entire truth.

Still, he reached out a hand to help the man to his feet.

The man flinched at first. Sudden movement was never a good thing in his world. Realizing that Kyle meant no harm, he took it and stood to his feet.

He looked awkward and shifted from foot to foot. His eyes never met their own for more than a moment. His hands were deep in his pockets, picking at ghost lint that body bugs had long ago eaten away. Kyle noticed that the man smelled like sweat, old pizza and old spice. Not a whiff of booze whatsoever.

Not a threat, as Judith had pointed out. But not honest, either.

Judith stood up, wiping tears from her eyes with the back of her hand. Kyle felt his stomach flutter as she took his free hand with her own to help him stay relaxed.

"We've had a long night man. I've turned into a paranoid freak and I shouldn't take it out on you. It just isn't the best time to be a stranger following us through an alley."

"Oh. Well I'm sorry, but you can call me Buck, or whatever you want for a buck! See? Now I'm not strange no more!" Buck said.

The man smiled a wide, toothless grin at his own wit. Kyle and Judith couldn't help but do the same.

"I'm Kyle," he said, reaching out his hand to shake.

Buck shook it, the confusion never leaving his features.

"And I'm Judith, Buck-o."

Judith shook Buck's hand with a light squeeze. With the laughter behind her, she grew cautious, remembering her luck so far with strange men in alley's.

Buck looked like every passing second of conversation put him closer to being screwed out of his coat. Judith clutched his hand like a date trying not to lose her way through crowded concert pit. Kyle, a minute removed from the epitome of horror, was at ease.

"You *are* alone, right Buck? You don't have a buddy waiting for you to say the code word before hitting his with a pipe? Or a gun? So help me, if I see another gun before the day ends..." Kyle said, glancing around the alley for an unseen party.

"Oh, no, 'course not. Buck ain't got friends. Just me. Maybe a roach or two," he said.

Buck checked his coat pockets thoroughly, his tongue resting on his upper lip. He produced nothing more than the hands he had been born with.

"Nope, must have gone home to the roach motel. Just me, then. Dad always said guns were for right 'Publicans, and that we men with no home were left for the Left, so we shouldn't use 'em."

"My dad would have shot your dad in the kneecaps," Judith said.

"He got hurt by a gun, and he had metal kneecaps. That's why I don't have no home, because he couldn't afford one with the money from the beer factory," Buck said without sadness.

"Well, shit," Judith said, guilty.

"Oh, don't feel bad, Miss Judith. He hit us when we was little anytime he came home from the beer factory without his free booze. I was taller though, so it didn't hurt much."

"This is getting awkward," Kyle said, turning the last word into two drawn out syllables.

"The beer factory? You mean the Haskins Beer factory? So you're from here, then?"

"Well, yes an' no. Sometimes I stay under the bridge with a nice lady in the city. She give me food and hugs on lil' Buck. I wander, but I was born here if that's what you mean," Buck replied.

The streets, though hard and callous, didn't judge anybody who survived them. Kyle knew as well as Buck did. Street life didn't have to be bad life. One had a tendency to learn. People said told amazing secrets around those they felt under them. Buck was quick to figure things out.

"Hey Buck, have you ever had a job before?" Judith asked.

"Oh no. Can't work. I tried once, down at the docks in The City, but everyone poked fun. I got paid 'neath the table and they always stole my money to go buy ladies at the filth house. Dad said God would take my pecker if he ever caught me with a whore, or I'd have went. Now I just walk around. People are awful nice and I get food. I eat what I find and that's my job."

"I have an idea, Buck," Judith mused.

"Buck had an idear once. Cost me an eye. But the street folks think I'm like that Noserdanus fellow, so I get the good share of the booze for sharing fortunes. Wanna know a secret? I always tell the same one. I learned that from a TV show with a magician, heh! Saw it in a shop winduh."

"Sounds like a job to me, Buck," Kyle said.

Crowd manipulation made for a profitable paycheck. Kyle had once been paid one hundred dollars by a Las Vegas magician, who wore an excess of bling and eyeliner, not to divulge the location of a freshly vanished elephant.

"I promise you won't lose an eye, Buck! Or your pecker," Judith exclaimed.

"Well, I've only got one of each, so that'd be much appreciated, Miss Judy."

Judith kept the truth to herself. Buck could lose far more than an eye. He was an unexpected and welcome trump card. Trickery was an unfair path, but some people worked better when they didn't know how dangerous a job was. Judith knew things about Jonas she hadn't thought to recommend until Buck had found them.

Jonas would never hurt a homeless man. Most of his information came from the homeless, and Jonas had promised to protect them and do what he could to ease their troubles without stealing their dignity. Jonas kept his promises, ass hat that he could be. He took care of Buck and his "street folks".

"Judith, Buck. Never, ever call me Judy. I have a job for you, if you are interested. You're the perfect person for it, but I need you to trust me!"

"Will there be people stealin' my money again?"

"No, Buck. That won't happen. Nobody will know you've earned a nickel. Nobody will pick on you. Not with Kyle still needing a fresh change of underwear."

Judith looked to Kyle for support, though his mind had drifted into a daydream of how many ways the devil could torture his winky, whether he touched a whore or not. Judith elbowed him in the ribs, bringing him back to reality.

"Oh, uhm, what she said. I don't lick anything but ice cream cones, Buck."

Buck snorted.

"Pick, you dolt! Not lick! Who would lick on him?"

"I'm a cab driver, Judith. People are inherent fetishists. Give a guy credit, jeez..." Kyle said, rubbing his ribs.

"So Buck, what do you say?" Judith asked through a smile.

Buck blushed. Pretty girls didn't smile at homeless men. They frowned and held their noses. But smiles couldn't always be trusted, and he remained tentative.

"What do I do, Miss Judith?"

"Well, you know the alleys back here, so you've heard of Jonas, right?"

"Oh, that big mean Irish guy? Yeah, he stops by the car garage sometime to give out wine and find out about people. Buck never tells him much. He looks crazy. In the bad way."

Kyle saw where Judith was heading with her idea and improvised.

"Well, Buck, he's Judith's dad. We're trying to do our very best to hide from him so we can go take care of very important business. There's a big cop who might be following us somewhere. Not the good kind that saves lives. The bad kind that likes to hurt people. We need to get to Judith's car from The Green Rail without anyone spotting us or knowing we were ever even there. We need you to be our eyes, or at least our eye, and our ears. Sort of like a…"

"Bodyguard?" Buck finished for him.

"Sort of," Judith said. "Can you follow us and make sure nobody else is behind us? When we get to The Rail, make sure the coast is clear. We need enough time to get in my car and get out of town."

Buck hesitated.

"All due respect, Buck's not dumb. Jonas hurts people who displease him. If you want to run, he might not hurt you if you're his lil' girl. But Buck? Buck doesn't like pain, and Jonas will be mad, somethin' fierce," Buck said.

"Trust me, I'm in the same boat, brother. You're a blessing right now. He can't hurt you if he doesn't know you're helping. Just be yourself. We'll handle the rest. And we'll pay you. Mucho dinero!" Kyle said.

Kyle fumbled around in his pocket, searching for the c-note Lucifer had given him. Judith beat him to the punch, pulling from her purse not a hundred dollar bill, but an entire roll of them held together with a thick rubber band. She unrolled it and pulled off a few bills, handing them to Buck, who was as wide eyed as Kyle.

"Is this enough for now, Buck?" Judith cooed.

"No, no. This is crime money. I can't take this! I can't!" Buck said, his fixated eyes not matching his voice.

"You can and you will, Buck. Even if you don't help us. Nobody got hurt for this money. I earned it on my own. This wouldn't begin to cover the help you could give to us. I want you to have it."

"Jesus, we can buy reconstructive surgery instead of ball caps with money like that," Kyle said.

Judith hushed him. Kyle obliged.

Buck squinted his eyes for a long while. He looked between Judith and Kyle, not once glancing back toward the stack of bills in Judith's outstretched hand. It looked as though Buck was trying to piece together a riddle, trying push the answer clutching to his tongue off of the ledge, come hell or high water.

The riddles dancing in Buck's head were not as simple as A + B = money in his pocket. Judith and Kyle, cash in hand, were a positive A, but the secrecy that would be exposed and the uncertainty of the situation was weighing on the negative side of B.

His face had turned stoic. His eyes, locked onto them and dancing with intelligence, set off Kyle's internal lie detector for a second time.

The look left Buck's eyes before Kyle could pin point what unsettled him. Buck's face turned soft and simple again. He took the bills from Judith's outreached hand, shoving them deep into his pants pocket.

"Well...ok. Buck'll help. It's the least I could do."

Judith rubber banded the roll and placed it back into her purse. Kyle's eyes followed the cash into her purse, still dumbstruck underneath his understanding of why she had kept it a secret.

"I took it from the safe, ok? It was my little stash that he kept aside for me, lest I ever be allowed to touch it. It's not as if he's hurting for cash with the expensive shit he buys the magnificent "Molly", that knife loving little..." her words faded away into displeased grunts.

"Judith! He's just a boy!" Kyle mustered.

"Buck on duty, m'am! I'll be the best body guard money can buy!"

Buck gave a stiff salute, a business composure replacing timidity.

"You'd better give the best..." Kyle began.

Kyle was interrupted by another one of Judith's sweet puncture wound punches. *Jeez, with a punch like that, who needs an insane, homicidal father to keep the boys away?* He felt guilty for the thought and was glad he kept it to himself.

"Thank you, Buck. We're going to keep going. Stay behind and when I wave my hand at you like this…"

Judith motioned her hand towards herself and Kyle.

"…then come forward and check the area out. You got it?"

"Sure do! I'll keep look for you! That guy said you were mean and would hurt Buck if he was caught."

Bucks words grew muffled, the end of his sentence lowering as he turned to walk away, but Kyle heard them. Buck's hand slapped over his mouth, stopping mid-step and trying to force the spilled words back. He turned around to face Kyle and Judith, wide-eyed. Kyle grew tense, wishing he had listened to his instincts.

Realization filled the tension. Buck knew he had slipped. Buck hadn't been afraid of being followed, but of being caught by those he was sent to follow.

Buck, for all his simplicity, was a spy.

A spy who told they were dangerous. A spy they had just paid five hundred dollars to help them succeed. A spy who may have been paid far more to make sure that they failed.

None of them spoke as they processed the information, unwilling to exacerbate the tension. Buck was the first to crack, his words laced with sobs.

"Oh you both must hate me now! I'm so sorry. Buck's a bad spy. He doesn't deserve to be your guard or anything!"

He began fumbling for the money in his pocket, but Kyle stopped him.

"Keep the damn money, Buck. Consider it payment for telling us who told you to follow us. Was it the cop?"

"A cop? No, Buck don't trust the law. It was a guy in a suit. Looked churched up, but it ain't Sunday. He gave me ten dollars to follow you. Ten! And I thought that was a lot!" Buck said.

"Focus Buck, please. This is important."

"Sorry, sorry. He said I should call if you done something 'spicious, but I don't have a phone. And then he said just whisper my name, and I'll hear you. Gave me the willies, but Buck was hungry."

"What was the name, Buck?" Kyle said, frantic.

"Somethin' easy. Lou. Small, easy to remember. And he had glasses."

Kyle's shoulders slumped. His hand went to his forehead to message his temples.

"Shit," Judith muttered.

"What?" Buck asked.

"Lou. Lucifer. The asshole who told me to wear the watch or he'd make my life hell? He sent a simpleton after us to avoid the complications of intelligence. Guess his damned crystal ball is at the repair shop. Shakespeare must have gone to hell, for Lucifer is playing at one tragic comedy," Kyle said.

"Buck is sorry for lying, Kyle."

"Don't be. Just help us out, Buck. Maybe not whisper any names for a few days? God knows how many of the homeless army he sent to keep an eye on us. And he's not allowed to help."

"Do you want your money back? I don't deserve it. I'm bad." Buck said.

His hands went into his pockets with little enthusiasm, but he held the wad towards Judith, intent on returning it.

"No, Buck," Judith said. "It's yours, I told you. I don't want it. Even if you were hired by the wrong side, you still helped us out!" Judith said.

"Take it back. Buck was bad! I believed a bad man! I could have hurt Mr. Kyle"

Buck pushed the money towards Kyle, instead, hoping for a different reaction. Kyle raised his hands skyward, not touching the bills.

"No harm done. Just keep it. Didn't you see her bag? We are loaded."

"I don't want to," Buck whispered, looking at the ground.

"Well, we're not taking it back, so you'll just have to…" Judith started.

"I don't want the damn money!" Buck shouted into the alley way.

His voice lost any semblance of simple or naïve. Vacant qualities flooded their ears with the scream. His posture had changed. His slumped shoulders and the way his body had been half-turned from them had morphed into a full fronted, square shouldered stand.

A soldier at ease. His goofy smile disappeared. Worry lines filled his brow like so many small canyons. The dirt took on a quality of stage makeup instead of careless hygiene. The awareness and intelligence on his face was no longer strained or forced.

The subtle changes in his eyes were more drastic. Kyle would have sworn Buck spent his thinking time piecing together a puzzle with simple blocks. Buck had been working with an erector set. Every word and movement had been a fallacy, and the ability to hide such knowledge and experience underneath the façade impressed Kyle.

Keyzer Soze would have been proud.

Buck didn't make them wait for an explanation. His true voice was deep, dripping with the charisma of a lounge singer when not altered by forced retardation.

"I'm not feeble. I'm not a coward. My name isn't even Buck, alright? My name is Ken. People throw more money at when you put on the whole Forrest Gump routine, and they'll say and do damn near everything when they think you're an idiot."

"What in the hell? You scare us, make our acquaintance, go on and on when I know you realized this wasn't just a normal busk job, and now we have to reset the clock and do it over again? It's terrible literature, I tell you," Kyle said, trying to control his volume.

"Hey, I didn't lie, alright? Lou did approach me, and he did pay me to follow you. Guess he knew that even if I told anybody else what he told me, they'd believe a distinguished man in Armani over a 'tard any day of the week. In that he was correct."

"He knew you weren't feeble, Buck…I mean Ken. He's not like us! He knew curiosity and greed would drive you to play your role and find out what you could!"

"Impossible. I don't play my role, I live it. There's no way he knew the truth, regardless of who he is. The closest I've come to breaking character in years was knowing you had seen me. If you were as dangerous as he said you were, I'd be dead. Your, uh, scream kicked that notion in the nuts. Hell, until you got eerie on me when brought that Lou guy up, I was ready to take the money and bolt. Five hundred might as well be a million to the poor."

Judith, on the opposite end of impressed than Kyle, somewhere around the livid marker, pushed him hard in the chest.

"So that's what you do, huh? Trick people into giving you pity money by acting like the people who suffer? What kind of sick fuck does that?"

Ken looked her dead in the eye.

"You'd be shocked to know what people in my place do for a beer or a burger from the dollar menu, little girl. Not a damn thing is sacred when it comes to eating. I never once said I kept it to myself. In a world full of charlatans, those with nothing to lose are the worst offenders."

"Then why confess? You waiting to jump us for the rest of the wad so you can live happily ever after in Mexico, building boats like you were Andy freakin' Dufraisne?" Judith said.

"Nice reference," Kyle said, hoping to ease tension.

"Shut up, Kyle!" she retorted.

"No. I'm telling you this because if I'm in bad shape, you two are a week old piece of road kill. I have the lice and the smell, but you? The crap this guy told me sounded like adult Dungeons and Dragons game with one too many shots of vodka laced mountain dew. The look in your eyes when I so much as mentioned the man in glasses would have fooled Freud. You're either crazy, or terrified."

"We'd be crazy not to be terrified," Kyle said

"And I'm about to be damned pissed if you don't get to the point!" Judith said, crossing her arms and tapping her toes on the ground.

"I'm lazy, alright? I do what I do because it's an easy way to make a living and I don't mind sleeping on hard surfaces. Homeless life isn't hard if you have a niche, and I found mine with Buck. You guys are facing hard shit at the moment, no?"

Both shook their heads with the weight of the "shit" they were facing. Even Judith looked somber at the thought.

"I've spent the better part of ten years screwing people out of cash and little else. The easy way. But even I used to be a Boy Scout. Made it to Weblo. That little voice has warned me that if I don't give back to those who are "actually suffering", as you put it, than I might as well book my hand basket to hell in advance. If you need my help, and it doesn't involve cussing me out to make you feel better about yourselves, I can't justify doing it for money. I've spent too long tossing and turning to guilty dreams. A small price to pay for my lackadaisical cash cow. Trust me or don't, either way. I can't keep the cash. Not after seeing that look. Not this time."

Kyle had forgiven Ken during his long winded speech, out of

empathy he assumed. He had spent years making money how he could, not giving a damn about the consequences or being useful afterwards. But Kyle did work hard while making it. It kept his mind off the worst of the depression, if only in momentary spurts.

"So you want to help us to ease your guilt over being a con man? Is that it?" Judith was not as impressed with the monologue.

"I've been up front with you. And don't tell me for a second that little Jonas has a clean enough slate to cast stones in my direction. Maybe you could tell me why the hell you two are walking around alley ways like secret agents with plate sized bruises, talking about Lucifer and secrecy? Forget the cop and your father, you need to be worried about someone calling white coats. Rule number one in the crazy club is you don't talk like you're in the crazy club! What would make you abandon the subtleties of stealth in favor of a baseball cap?"

"We don't have to tell..." Judith started.

"It's ok, Judith. We can tell him." Kyle said.

They sat against the wall of the alley, Kyle holding Judith's hand while telling Ken their version of the truth.

Ken reacted as expected, with disbelief coated by horror and surprise. Kyle looked for subtleties as Ken told the story. The change in his eye that rivaled Buck becoming Ken. A change said Ken believed Kyle. Believed *in* Kyle. A click that signified wanting to be better, wanting to help. A small little glimmer of the eyes Kyle wished he had been aware enough to let happen before this nonsense.

Why had he spent so much time talking with him? His instincts had kept him from running, and quieted his need to express them. Kyle's instincts had taken him in the right direction before, why not this time?

Either Ken was a deterrent, or he was one of the seven.

That little change proved his instincts right. A sign of time not wasted, what precious little of it remained. If Ken denied truths advances, he had done his job as a deterrent. If Ken embraced, Lucifer's plan had backfired. They would gain much needed help and soul in the bag.

Either way, Kyle told the story with haste, knowing that time spent on the mission at hand could afford little frivolity. Any other approach meant wasting his last week on earth on a winless scavenger hunt while Lucifer readied the whips and chains that would lament every day thereafter.

Yes, the devil prepared for Kyle's arrival.

For his eternal servitude.

For his damnation.

And oh, the burning...

the eye approaches

After far too many unsuccessful hours of searching to not permit a bit of down time, Jonas dozed while Molly drove back to The Rail. It was restless sleep that left his mind worse off when he awoke, but Molly had insisted. When Molly told him to rest, he knew that it was advice best taken.

Jonas dreamed in quick flashes, unable to reach REM but able to frighten his psyche. Dreams of his daughter beaten bloody. Raped and tossed aside. Left for dead, the way Jonas had left many a thorn in his side. He felt her slipping farther away in these dreams than while awake. Awake, he was fueled by blind rage. While he slept, her face was so clear to him. So close.

Though the dreams were doing little to put his mind at ease, even a man as inhuman as Jonas couldn't deny the sandman. So Jonas slept. Ian practiced a charlier cut with a deck of cards. Molly drove, knowing that before the day was out. James would need to come clean.

If he didn't, she would gut him clean.

James stared out the window at nothing in particular. The weight of Jonas' gun pressing into his back from the waist of his pants was still comforting, but only because it gave him a few more bullets if things turned south. The comfort of having a tool to take advantage of Jonas's weakness had soured.

James didn't doubt he would overcome the small snag. He would survive the inevitable and hold the kingdom for his self. Darwinism at its most fundamental. If he needed to improvise, in a worst case scenario, he'd steal the kingdom, instead, and leave them all shot to rot. He knew the passwords, the secrets, the ledger locations.

Before weeks end, or night's end, if Molly played her hand too soon, Jonas would be dead. The chance that James could be the one at the end of a muzzle didn't cross his mind. Even if James wound up penniless and poor, like one of Jonas's street informants, Jonas would die. James, by gift or by force, would be on top of the world.

As always the case, the old clichés are apt remembered for a reason. This situation was no exception.

James was half right.

CHAPTER 22

becoming the fool

"That's one hell of a story," Ken said. "My forehead is still sweating from when I met Lou. I'm agnostic, but this gives the pendulum a push. I would never call somebody who told me that story a liar."

"I wish to hell it was a lie," Kyle said.

"Now that, my friend, *is* a lie," Ken accused.

"Pardon me?"

"How is a life or death situation such as this any different from somebody else's? Take away the metaphors and parables, and the only thing you are doing today that you weren't doing a week ago is giving a damn. Every day is a fight for survival. Take it from a guy who spends his life wearing a mask. This is a good thing. Time is short and you lack a blue box to make things easy. Whatever punishment may await you for failure, you're doing something that means something because you woke up. Because of her."

Ken pointed at Judith, who was sitting to Kyle's right. She couldn't hide the blush welling in her cheeks.

"I'm not sure that running for my life and dragging Judith along is something that I needed to wake up. Coffee works just fine."

Ken ignored the joke, responding to the statement.

Ken spoke with intense surety, as if Kyle's story mirrored his own.

"Of course you needed it. You've been running from your life. Now you have something and someone to fight for, a reason to move on. Saving your soul and protecting her are giving you your life back, even if terror hides that fact from you. I think at the end of all of this you'll be happy that it happened. Less so if you become Satan's little errand boy, but anything is better than self-aware non-existence."

"You may be right. Then again, I may be dead. What if this is my hell?"

"I resent that, ass hat," Judith said.

"No, I don't mean you, Judith. If you were a part of my hell, I would question what people are teaching us about being naughty. I remember what I saw Brandon go through, and the similarities are too hard to confuse. Constantly struggling to fight a battle I lost before it began. I'm beyond help, stuck in limbo. Two steps forward, ten steps back, you know? To be fair, you people believe this shit way too quickly," Kyle said.

"Something about you makes it easy to believe, Kyle. Sure, the watch proves it to those you save, but it's nothing more than proof of whatever faith you instill. If you are in hell, at least someone had good taste in the woman you're stuck with for the rest of eternity," said Judith. She flipped her hair back and gave Kyle an exaggerated batting of her eyelashes.

Ken slapped his hands on his knees and stood, sighing the sigh of a man who has made a heavy decision. Kyle and Judith stood from their cross legged positions to join him, wiping off the seats of their pants in the process.

"There once lived a man, a great man, who was thrust onto people who were not ready to receive him. He asked little and gave us joy and hope, and he suffered for it. I don't believe he'd take back a single smile he gave. He was a blip of proof that goodness existed in an era of tumultuous faith. For that faith, he was taken from us, but we remember and love him because he was the example of how we should be. He stood, honest and unwavering, in the face of inhumanity, and he did it with nothing more than his ability to speak, inspire, and cast a few small miracles."

"Jesus?" Judith said.

"No, George Carlin. If you're calling resurrection a small miracle, you aren't as rational as Kyle thinks you are," Ken said, smiling at his own wit.

"And what miracles did Carlin perform, wise guy?" Kyle asked.

"Ever see Bill and Ted's Excellent Adventure?" Ken asked.

"Yes," Judith and Kyle both said in unison.

"Ever see the sequel?"

"No," Kyle said.

"They made a sequel?" Judith asked.

"Make an educated guess as to who wasn't cast for the sequel. Carlin, baby. And it's a fucking miracle that anybody liked the first one."

Ken stood, satisfied with his answer, as the two mulled it over in a few moments of silence.

"Point proven," Kyle said.

They laughed, Ken's laugh fading into another sigh. The sigh of a man realizing the sacrifices he had to make.

"Ok. I don't know what I'm getting into, but something tells me that my busking days just reached critical mass. A story like that makes me feel like a real asshole, you know? I was lifeless by choice. By lethargy! And look how much time I made you waste convincing me? A man who had his life ripped from his chest."

"Your eloquence is getting annoying, Ken," Kyle said. Bitterness built behind his lips, but not towards Ken's comments. Only in how truthful they were. How even through a story somebody could tell how far he had fallen. The story itself detailed what could be seen all over him. Leon had proven that with his own, equally uncomfortable observations.

"You may be my catalyst to move on to something different. Something nine-to-five. Something where I can drink lattes and earn my money by screwing people in a more proper way. Or maybe I can, you know, be productive. That's for later. For now, Indiana Buck is at your service!"

Ken laughed far too loud at his own joke. Nervousness, Judith suspected. Fear, Kyle thought.

It was both, and so much more.

Excitement. Newness. The change in him Kyle had been waiting for. It happened not with a light bulb in the brain or a clearing of the eyes, but with a loud laugh at an unfunny joke that snapped something inside Ken to attention. Though it would be Buck who helped them further their goal, Ken would emerge and leave that mask wherever it fell, if there was emerging to do.

"You two cute kids get moving. I've got your back," Ken said. He patted Kyle on the back and took his hand, shaking it with firm fervor. "Just make sure you to keep an eye ahead."

With that, showing confidence he had thought long lost, Ken reached a finger into his eye and slid the cataract back and forth. The cataract was nothing more than a dull, white contact. Realistic as it looked, it was just one more part of the mask that was Buck. He retracted his finger with a milky wink.

"Thank you," Judith said.

Her faith straddled the fence of uncertainty as it pertained to Ken, who very much reminded her of the Wizard of Oz. She wasn't sure who the man behind the curtain was, but he was no idiot.

"No need to thank me. Karma is telling me to get off my lazy ass and make a difference."

Judith and Kyle continued through the alley way, checking over their shoulders at infrequent intervals for a thumbs up or a wave from Ken. The traveling was much quicker with a watchdog of sorts helping the progress, though the sound of sirens stopped them dead on one other occasion.

Within an hour they reached The Rail.

They peeked around a corner and saw no armed sentries. No knife wielding Irish lass on a permanent PMS trip. No pissed off fathers. Just the green rail leading to the basement, a Pinto, and an empty parking spot.

"We got damn lucky," Kyle said, turning and motioning Ken to catch up.

"Or we're early," Judith said in a grim tone. "They must still be looking. Jonas wouldn't expect you to have the balls to come back."

"One hundred percent brass, baby," Kyle said, lightly knocking on the front of his pants.

"Let me try that," Judith said.

"Wait, but...ooomf!" Kyle choked out as Judith cup checked him.

Ken walked up, knowing the signs of attraction, and smiled. He'd seen it a million times. Kyle and Judith would be just peaches, if they lived long enough to enjoy the cobbler.

"Hmm, more like soggy grapes, but I'll take your word for it. You should have used those brass raisins to fake a ransom note or a threatening Polaroid. Fear comes from the unknown. Jonas thinks I'm dead behind a Men's Warehouse somewhere. I guarantee it." Judith said.

"So we lucked out?" Ken said.

"They aren't here, if that's what you mean. If Molly isn't standing guard by the Pinto, he took them all. James gets bored and distracts himself with his phone. Ian gets paranoid and everything becomes an emergency The only person he would trust to watch for me is the whorish lethal weapon that never leaves his side. But luck? Doubtful. They have the element of rolling up on us whenever they'd like. If this were a movie with a predictable plot line, they'd be back in the next five minutes or so. Suspense, like your dear karma, is a bitch," Judith finished, looking to Ken.

The three exchanged a very uneasy laugh.

"End of the line then, kiddos?" Ken said.

"'Fraid so. Listen, you've helped us a ton. I know following us for an hour doesn't seem like much, but…" Kyle started.

"But you accomplished more than sneaking around an alley way?" Ken finished for him.

"Well, yeah. I mean, I don't want this to turn in to a Final Fantasy sized team of combatants, otherwise I'd ask you to come."

"So after the lies, almost screwing you over and taking your money, telling you that I was basically in a sub-plot with the devil against you, you'd entertain the idea of having me? I wish my ex-wife were as forgiving as you. I'd have eaten less trash this past ten years."

"With all the screwed up things we've dealt with, more people couldn't hurt, Kyle," Judith said, the trust surprising both Kyle and Ken.

"Well, usually it's the more the merrier, but even putting you in the mix makes me uneasy. The more the gorier. Old horror movie credo."

"I'm a big girl, Kyle," Judith said.

"I'm a big girl too, you clod!" Ken said, feigning offense.

Kyle ignored Ken's hand on the hip look of judgment, as if Ken were his mother, disapproving of muddy shoes in the kitchen.

"I'm sure you have both graduated from Judy Bloom novels to the glorious world of Twilight, but I'm the only one who has to do anything. This isn't your boxing ring. Judith is my wing girl, and all, but Ken, are you sure?"

"Birds need two wings to fly, Kyle. I've come this far you know? Turning over the proverbial leaf takes more than a short trip through an alley. Pretending to be feeble is a hell of a lot easier, but I haven't felt this alive in years!"

"You see, Kyle? We could use him!" Judith said.

"What am I supposed to say?" Kyle said, irritated. "Great! We'll steal the car and pick you up and then what? I have no clue! I've been at a loss since day one. My instincts are bipolar lately."

"Best things in life happen when you aren't looking, no? Listen, just get the car and I'll keep a lookout. I can at least help you get away safe if I can't do anything else."

"I'm sorry, man…it's just…" Kyle tried to explain.

"No. Don't apologize. I understand. You opened my eyes to

things I haven't let myself think about in years. As you said to Judith, this is my fight. You were the one to finally ring the bell. And I'm grateful."

For the second, Ken reached a hand out to Kyle. They shook firmly with brotherhood and finality, both sensing that the encounter was meant to be brief.

"Go! I'll watch!" Ken pushed Kyle away.

Kyle and Judith looked both directions down the alley, a couple of grown-up kids trying to cross the pot-hole riddles street to get home. Seeing nothing, they ran to the pinto and crouched by the driver's door. Judith fumbled for the keys.

Not thirty seconds passed before Kyle heard Ken's screaming voice. He didn't need to make out the words to understand what he was yelling.

"Oh shit..." Kyle breathed

"Daddy's home," Judith finished.

Suspense had come to the party a few minutes after they predicted it would. They should have expected a fashionably late entrance.

A few blocks down the alley, a sedan pulled around the corner from the street and headed towards the spot where Judith and Kyle fumbled for the keys to their salvation.

SLOTH

Sloth is my first name

Unmoving and uncaring

I please only me

silent duplicity

Lights off, his own car creeping behind the big black sedan, he smelled everything. The sweat pouring from the rookie's brow in the seat next to him. His idle engine burning oil and gasoline. The anxiety and anger from every dark tinged soul in the sedan. The fear of the two he'd spent the day searching for as they hid like mice from a large new house cat. The overpowering goodness of the man who destiny had fated him to destroy.

The goodness, in particular, was an overpowering smell that burned his sinuses. It was disgusting, like fresh baked cookies, or a Yankee Candle. He made a mental note to burn down a candle shop once he was finished. It was the worst smelling motive for evil he could imagine.

More than the immediate smells of the games key players, he smelled the rain storm that was weeks away, the clouds still holding palaver to decide precipitation and lightning volumes. The bodily fluids spilled across the city from the homeless and the drunk, feeding their inner demons to someday serve him. The dust from the bricks and mortar wearing away from time and erosion. The termites and woods of buildings that would fall long before he did, once he secured his target.

Yes, the smells filled his nostrils and let him see farther than his eyes were able, though he felt that would change soon. His eyes would lead him to satisfaction, and his nose would lead him to slaughter. His hands would lead him to power. His patience would keep his senses in check. Killing was no fun when the victims died quick.

With such a play stirring before him, he knew that a far more potent scent would drive his patience into hibernation.

The father, come home to find the goose who ran away and her perceived captor. A lazy bum still stricken by the arrow of change in the crossfire. A Judas among them all, ready to take the leap. It was a fucking schmorgesborg.

He would wait in the dark for them to spill each other's blood. He would bathe in their carnage. He hoped the avenger, protected by his holy artifact, would be disarmed in the battle. If not, well, there was always the rookie. The unwilling Robin to the Knight of Darkness he had become.

When their hate and fear had reached a boiling point, and the actors were gasping for the breath to deliver their final lines, he would swoop in to finish off whoever remained.

The leftovers. The quest. The feasting.

Dinner and a movie had never excited him until that moment. Black saliva fell from his lips. He let his appetite grow as the second act approached.

Let the pawns do the fighting. I will be a king…neigh… a God amongst them soon enough.

So he sat, waiting for the perfect moment.

And then he would taste their blood.

Intoxicate himself with it.

Wade in it.

Bathe in it.

Destiny's crown hovered above his head, and his red eyes smiled.

Patience. So fucking worth it, in the end.

CHAPTER 24

clean up in alley way three

Ken walked towards The Rail, not trying to hide his presence. That had been the plan, and knowing that five minutes less dialogue would have eliminated the need was frustrating. If he ever got to meet the writer of his life's story, he intended to give him a hard punch to the head for putting such a dramatic sequence.

Judith's hands shook too hard to make use of the keys. She reverted to the Judith that needed Kyle. The Judith who was still the child of an overbearing madman behind her toughness and sensibility. The Judith who would never embrace freedom until there was nobody left to take it from her. The only somebody who *could* approach.

Judith kept slapping Kyle's hand away when he tried to help. Ken reached their position and snatched the keys from her, ignoring her stubborn protests. The Sedan was five hundred feet away, but the headlights were off. Small favors led to big debts, but Kyle would deal with in time

The sedan was half way to its destination.

Ken unlocked the back door shoved the pair of them inside, onto the floor area instead of the actual seat, and whispering for them stay quiet. Ken tossed Judith's purse and keys at their feet and shut the car door.

The Sedan pulled up just as Ken was able to find himself. He put on his face and walked around from behind the Pinto in the stumbling fashion Buck had. Kyle and Judith could see none of this.

Kyle laid flat on the floor of the Pinto, with Judith on top of him. Such a moment would have been intimate in any other circumstance. Giving any of the fucks that intimacy required, neither had experienced it in years.

As for this moment, they gave a damn. They gave more than a damn, to be blunt, though neither was of clear enough mind to know it. Intimacy had no room to blossom amongst the pain of pushing themselves as far into the floor of the car as they could. Discomfort to Kyle, anyway.

Ken knew this would be the performance of a lifetime. One slip up and Jonas would shoot first, ask later, as per his creed. Ken would have a hell of a time talking his way out of visiting Jonas's home, a strict no-no, even without two people in the backseat of the car they intended to steal.

The sedan parked next to the Pinto. Kyle and Judith stiffened, thankful that there was a blanket to cover themselves with. It was a superficial disguise, but it beat exposure.

Unlike the Sedan, the Pinto lacked tinted windows. The Pinto windows were covered in grime and dust. They both hoped Ken would be alright, but Judith's guilt was worse than Kyle's. The details of what Jonas would do to him if things went south ignited vivid memories.

What followed left them bereft of words that, if uttered, would have finished Kyle's journey. Though Ken hinted at playing decoy, they both thought Ken would turn and walk away from The Rail. Another homeless wanderer.

Instead, there were voices. Voices muffled by thick windows, but voices that were audible, weary, and without anger. Confused voices. Heard by those in the Pinto who embraced in a tight hiding space, like a couple waiting out a tornado in a bathtub. Those who dared not let their own voices be heard.

"And who is this guy, eh? Friend of yours, Ian?" It sounded like James.

"I don't know him. Probably a bum. Sure as hell smells like one," Ian said, his high voice was unmistakable.

"Get away from my fucking car, buddy! I'm not in the mood. Go get your beer money elsewhere. Shop is closed for the night," said Jonas.

"Buck need a dollar, though! This is a good place for a dollar, and he can't eat! Buck for buck, please? He work for it. I came all this way!"

Kyle laughed in a silent whisper, finding humor that Ken, with half a grand in his pocket, was trying to scam Judith's family out of a dollar. Judith applauded Ken, realizing that he was doing them a favor.

All they needed was Jonas to forget what they were doing long enough for them to get away. If Ken annoyed them enough without pushing them over the edge, they'd have a window for success.

Hating herself a little, she grasped for and held on tight to that one straw of hope.

"What are you, some kind of man-whore, Buck-O? Adjust your asking price. Inflation is a bitch. And get the fuck away from the boss's place, ya hear?" James fumed.

Ian interjected.

"Oh, come on James. He's a bum. Half our information comes from bums. You know the bosses rule about bums. And information," Molly said, smiling in a way that made James uncomfortable.

"If there's one group of people we don't piss on, it's those who've been pissed on often enough already. Besides, I've heard that buck for Buck line. He's a good guy. Slow upstairs, ya know?" Ian said.

"Slow like you, Ian?" James shouted. "This is the wrong day for this. I'll give him a damn bullet to chew on if he doesn't back the fuck off! Too much weird shit has happened today. Last thing we need is vermin at our stoop."

"You're right, James. Nobody likes a rat," Molly said.

"James, please. This is the alley," Jonas said, weariness overpowering his voice.

"Buck just wanted to eat," Ken said with pleading.

"Just give him ten dollars so he can go in peace. I'm not in the mood for your insufferable yelling. It echoes, James! I have a splitting headache."

Molly wrapped her arm around Jonas and shot James a snarl before walking with him to the stairs. James dug crumpled singles out of his coat and threw them on the ground. Ken dropped to his knees and scrambled for money, throwing in utterances of "Oh Boy!" and "Thanks" for to be extra convincing.

Ian eyed the Pinto for a moment, feeling something off but knowing that the boss would be pissed if he was wrong. He rarely spoke, James often the cause with his cruel wit, but something in him let the words slip before he could shrug them off, as was often the case.

"Hey, Boss. Want me to check the Pinto? Kind of weird that he was hovering around it when we pulled up, you know? I know he's a nutter, but maybe he saw something, I dunno, moving over there?"

Ian's silhouette appeared at the window, darkening Kyle and Judith's hiding spot. His turned back offered no solace as he reached for the door handle. The mechanism unlatching the door from the body could have been a shotgun cocking for all the tension it caused.

"Nobody comes back here except for the homeless, you dolt, and that's because we need them. Super cunt over there has done a good job of giving us privacy, at least," James said.

Molly and Jonas stopped at the head of the stairs. Had she not been concerned about Jonas, she would have given the city another reason to fear her knife, using James as a canvas.

"Ian. There's not a damn thing in that car worth missing. Half of what matters most to me is already gone. If the feeb can figure out how to steal fuzzy dice, all the better for him. I need proper rest, and I need you to cover the police scanner in case you hear anything. James? I love ya, boy, but you call Molly a super cunt again, and I'll let her have at your tongue. Last thing we need is dissension in the ranks."

"Your call, Boss," Ian said, making his way to the stairs.

All the while, Ken sat, arranging the money and listening, knowing that even while discussing him right in front of him, he was invisible to the family.

"Speaking of dissension, you need to talk to Jonas before he regains the energy to make unpleasant decisions. Or before I go ahead and handle business while he's asleep. Idle hands are a son-of-a-bitch to keep limber, James," Molly said.

Jonas gave Molly a sidelong glance of confusion as they descended the staircase. James pounded his fist into the side of the Pinto, which got a jump out of Kyle and Judith, considering they hadn't known he was close enough to do such a thing. James muttered curses under his breath as he walked to join the family, unsure rather or not he wanted to keep building on the web of lies to cover his ass, or throw away the pretenses of honor and innocence and shoot the lot of them with Jonas's gun. He was looking for any reason to hurt someone.

Relief was shared by all when the green door closed for a second time. Kyle didn't think Judith would have appreciated him wetting both of their pants if things had turned ugly. It might have dampened their bond.

Judith turned her head from the sideways position, meeting Kyle's own and giving him a look that said if relief was a dessert, she would outsell cheesecake with it.

Her mind, like his own, had a habit of wandering. Inches apart, face to face, embraced in the dark, they could have been at some make out spot. Lover's Lane. Cupid's Point. Somewhere, anywhere, enjoying a night of bright stars and passion.

Kyle saw her eyes wandering and felt guilty, knowing that her mind was four steps ahead of his while he was lost in her emerald eyes. His stomach moved in a way he thought impossible. He lost his breath for a moment that lasted for one eternal second and had no idea that

Judith felt the same.

They barely knew each other. He was to save her. She was to follow and escape. Was, is. Rules both governed this adventure and ceased to exist. What rules were there to such connections when any moment could mean death? Were such connections even real?

It was an innocent moment, one where the kiss is the joyous finale to endless moments of nervous staring and subtle hinting. The endless moments, thoughts and emotions racing through them in the time it took Buck to pocket the money and walk towards the Pinto, felt like eons.

Judith let out an exhale of breath she didn't know she had been holding.

"Just do it," she said.

As Kyle made to reply, she cut him off with a kiss. A soft meeting of semi parted lips. Kyle wondered if she had been talking to him at all, or trying to encourage herself. Later, she would tell him it was both.

Ken's tapping on the window, giving notice that the coast was clear, went ignored for the length of their kiss. Kyle thought of nothing but her, Judith of nothing but him. Somehow, they found the opportunity to lose themselves in the entirety of what a first kiss was supposed to feel like, with the experience needed for the memory to be worth keeping. It was a completely illogical exchange that neither would find in any other as long as they lived.

Sounds returned. Sanity was slower to approach. Kyle pulled his head back from hers. She bit her lower lip throw a smile and let out a hum of satisfaction, her eyes never opening. Kyle heard Ken's tapping as she enjoyed the moment. He looked over her shoulder to see Ken peering in the window. His eyes squinted, and his grin was wide enough to make his face look half teeth, and held two thumbs up. Ken, who watched little television, found a way to breed Barney Stinson and Quagmire into a living gesture.

The moment was gone.

"Looks like it's time to go," Kyle whispered.

"Looks like it, sugar lips," Judith said. She climbed into the back seat so Kyle could move.

Kyle grabbed the keys from the floor and hopped out of the car, patting Ken on the back as he approached the driver's door.

Ken offered a nod back, jotting a mental note to use the money in his pocket for a hotel room to shower, shave, and land a job doing something. Anything. As soon as he got a good nap and a bite to eat. Adventure made him hungry. Now that he could afford it, he wanted nothing more than a rib eye from the surf and turf restaurant where he busked. He hadn't decided if he would eat before or after he showered and shaved.

All of these realizations and appreciation floating on the wind of change were blown away with tragic suddenness from their respective minds seconds later.

As Kyle looked behind the Pinto to reverse, a cop car with no lights on sped out from the dark, hitting Ken. Ken slammed first into the hood, and then into the windshield, where he bounced and landed sprawled out on the ground.

Unmoving. Completely still. Dead?

Kyle's wide-eyed shock made him look like a surprised anime character. His eyes were huge, and his mouth formed the shape of an O.

The figure who stepped out of the police car didn't offer a single glance towards the man he had hit. He looked at Kyle and Judith, flashing a blackened grin full of sharp teeth.

His face and upper body were dark red. Even in the dark, it was impossible to mistake the hue of half dried blood on his skin. Horns were growing from his temples. What clothes he wore, much like The Incredible Hulk, hung from him in tatters. A gun rested under his left hand as he made his way around the front of the cruiser, hopping over the fallen Ken with the grace of a ballet dancer.

Ken had taken the punishment meant for Kyle. He wanted to vomit.

Kyle tried to push the gas to back the car up, but nothing happened. He assumed the smoke billowing behind the car was from the exhaust, and his momentary panic pushed the fact that he hadn't started the car yet out of his mind. The alley filled with enough smoke for a small forest fire, but it wasn't from the Pinto. Little of it was from the cruiser.

It was coming from the demon thing. What used to be Officer Wilkins exhaled through his nose, letting dark smoke jet out, to cement the fear into Kyle.

Kyle turned the ignition, not wanting his narrow window for escape to shatter.

"Is that the cop?! The one with the asp?" Judith screamed.

Kyle ignored her and stepped on the gas.

The car drove forward a few inches and into the wall, not hard, but enough to shake Kyle and put Judith against the car door.

A loud banging coupled a harsh vibration as the demon thing slammed both fists into the rear of the Pinto. Judith screamed, a high, shrill sound. Her hands flew to her eyes, though the vision burned into her covered retinas. Kyle's own hands would have flown to his own face had he not clamped them onto the steering wheel.

The car shook again, and Kyle saw the grin in the rear view mirror. With a self deprivating grunt, he slammed the shifter in reverse and pushed down on the gas pedal. The car jerked backwards, knocking into the demon beast. There was a loud crash as Kyle pinned the demon between the Pinto's rear end and the door of the cruiser. The sudden scream from the demon's gullet was deep, loud, and caused the back window to crack. Kyle felt no relief as he switched the car into drive and sped toward the open alley way.

He gave a quick glance into the rear mirror and saw the demon standing, hands on his hips, mouth open, head back. He could have been screaming. Or laughing. Kyle didn't care. He wanted the highway and distance.

He thanked Ken out loud, and apologized, though Ken would never hear his words. Though it felt silly, he prayed. Prayed that Ken was dead, and not dying. Hoping he would be spared from whatever hellish torture the demon cop could cause him to endure. Kyle was sure, harsh life or not, that it was quite a lot more than Ken could handle.

On the road again. Judith sat, quiet and still, in the back seat. The laws of the road flew out the window the second Mister Satan shrugged off a vicious car sandwiching. Kyle sped through red lights and pedestrian crossings as if he were being chased by the devil, himself.

Which, of course, he was.

halfway to hell

Hank would have been surprised at how little being sandwiched between two cars hurt. He had seen (and caused) accidents of such brutality that most would have found death, however graphic, merciful. The cliché stepchild of all accident utterances was that the victim died quick, so at least there was no pain. The notion helped the living cope, sure, but every face twisted in agony, regardless of the severity of the injury, spoke in defense of pain.

Yes, Hank would have been surprised to know that, about painless death, he was wrong. But Hank was gone. He had been slipping out of control since before the asp and the alley. What remained didn't resemble the man in any likeness.

Hank would have been surprised, but the demon was not. Surprise, fear, caution, and other inhibiting emotions had been replaced with confidence and knowledge. Knowledge of what he was capable of, and confidence that the world over would know the same before weeks end. Knowledge that nothing could stop him from meeting his ends, and confidence that he would abuse that power as if life were one big grindhouse flick.

Knowledge that Hank had taken his rightful place in Hell, and confidence that Kyle Thimall would soon do the same.

As Kyle sped off, leaving a dented bumper at the demon's feet, he felt his body over for injury. Instinct was always the last to go, outlasting memories that were no longer a part of himself. Instinct proved what knowledge told him all along, and the satisfaction was tremendous.

Not a single piercing or cut or crushing or bruising. Not even a superficial scratch. Not a drop of blood. Not his blood, anyway.

The demon, as he was formerly known, was untouchable. A monster. What once bound him to mortality died with Hank. The body was a shell to root him to earth. Those roots were ferocious in their feeding. Soon, he would be immortal.

For that, he needed Kyle.

The demon laughed, relishing the sound as it echoed off of the alley walls. His hands rested on his hips, his head tilted back, as his laughter bellowed out with a seemingly never-ending supply of oxygen.

"So it begins," the demon said to no one. "Nothing can hurt

me. No one can stop me. Check caution at the door and wear Kevlar arrogance to the party. I sing to myself, what a beautiful world!"

The last words were screamed in a deep sing-song devoid of what most would consider beautiful.

The demon walked to the driver door of the cruiser, hopping once more over the body of Ken as he did so. The door fell off of the cruiser as he opened it and he tossed aside as most would a ball of paper. The door sailed down the alley. A dog whined in the distance, and the demon wondered if he had crushed it on the way to The Green Rail.

He hoped so.

The demon placed his hands on the roof of the car and began to push, expecting the metal to squeal and peel back, giving him more room to sit in his expanding form. Instead, the roof turned a bright yellow red and began to melt. The metal melted into itself for the most part. Hot drops fell into the car and burned holes into the interior. A small glob fell into the rookie's hand, on the passenger arm rest where it had been the entire car ride. The metal sizzled into his skin, blood and burn wafting into the demon's nose, but the rookie could do nothing to express the pain other than cry. The demon controlled him as he controlled Hank's body. Hank was the vessel. The rookie was the weapon.

The demon couldn't touch the holy, but he could command that it be done. He had sacrificed much for the power. Possession was only the beginning. The rookie's eyes were all the demon let him control, and only because the pain in them brought a smile to his face. It was as simple and horrific as that. Now that he could smile and laugh, he wanted to do so often.

After the demon melted a large enough oval in the roof for his head to fit, he sat in the cruiser and slammed his foot into the pedal, steering in the direction Kyle had gone. He didn't turn on the headlights. His night vision was perfect. He didn't even need to start the engine. Like the placid rookie, like Hank's body, the vehicle was a tool at beck and call to his bidding.

The rookie, his nerves in agony from the burn of the metal and the actions he had been forced to commit, swayed like a skinny kid in a mosh pit as the demon drove the car. All he could do was pray the movement didn't crush him before the ride was finished. Hope that a strong turn would throw him from the car and let him sleep. Erase the evils that he had seen. The evils he had been forced to commit.

The rookie wouldn't let himself think about whether or not there would be an encore. He had seen the Prophecy movies. He didn't like entertaining the idea that the demon would resurrect him, again and again until he completed his mission.

"Stand by, Rookie. We've still got a mess to sweep under the carpet, you hear? And if you ask real nice, I might just take the broom to your skull when we're finished. Give you a Kurt Cobain haircut and take a little off the top. End your miserable, weak existence. I gotta tell ya, Rook, I don't envy your Hell one little bit."

Wilkins' voice deepened with every word, overpowering Hank's accent with sounds of hissing and pain.

The rookie's eyes were puffed and red. His tear ducts had been dry for hours. Whatever liquid his body had retained waited in his bladder for a better moment to expel itself. The demon, sensing the rookie's misery, forced him to wet himself.

But only a little. He would leave the rookie with the feeling of a vice grip on his penis, the water behind it pushing against his lower body while the demon blocked it like a dam. Going back and forth, treating the rookie's bladder like a kitchen faucet, would amuse him for a while. If it got boring, the rookie had other plumbing he could fuck with.

Far in the distance, the rookie could make out the tail lights of the Pinto. The demon followed, making no effort to catch up with them. He wanted them away from people. He wanted them all to himself.

Patience.

The demon clicked on the radio and began flipping through stations without removing his hands from the steering wheel.

"How about tunes to pump ourselves up for the fireworks, ehh, Rook?" he said.

The radio knob turned itself, filling the car with static and brief snippets of pop hits, Tejano, and country-western. The demon stopped the radio on a rock station playing Van Halen's "Running with the Devil".

"How apt, hey Rook? How very fucking apt!" the demon exclaimed before joining David Lee Roth on the chorus.

The tone was set. His senses were tuned. His could smell his prey.

Taste them.

The chase was on.

it was a little shark

Jonas saw the tail end of the cruiser disappear around the corner as he ran up the basement stairwell. He'd heard the sound of colliding cars, but paid little attention to the commotion. He was tired, and in no mood to help anybody with his own problems growing by the minute.

Jonas was surprised he had heard a crash at all with the chaotic argument taking place in the basement. James, Molly, and Ian had been tiptoeing around him for most of the day. He was grateful for their consideration and wanted rest before continuing the search. He would get no rest while Molly and James exchanged high volume aggression.

"You think by keeping quiet, nobody will realize what schemes are cooking in that little brain of yours? You're done here! You broke my trust! You have no valid excuse without the trust to back it up!"

Jonas had never seen Molly so red.

"All due respect, Molly, you're being a bitch! You want Jonas to hear the truth? Fine! But you are responsible for the aftermath. You have all the intuition in the world, you psychopath, but you are low on initiative. I did what had to be done!"

Jonas popped two Alka-Seltzer tablets into a glass of water and waited for an explanation. He was beyond caring about the buildup, and at this point Jonas didn't care what James did beyond two truths. Either Molly was right, and she would deal with it, or James was right, and she would deal with him saying so.

Ian, ever loyal and uncomfortable with strife, looked like he wanted to belt James for referring to his sister as a psychopath. Bitch was no new nickname for her, but calling his sister a psychopath after the things she had done for him, after their father, a true psychopath, had met a vicious end by her blade, after she had spent years erasing the damage done and treating her little brother as the son she'd never had, was enough to boil his own anger.

Jonas, knowing these truths, sent Ian outside to find out why there was so much racket. Ian, thankful for the bone, ran with it.

"Jonas, here's the deal," James said.

Jonas, who had begun to tune out their pointless bickering, gave his attention to James, ready to be over and done with the mess.

Ready to sleep.

"I took the gun out of your holster this morning. I don't know what happened to the money…"

"Bullshit!" Molly interrupted.

Jonas settled her with a gentle raising of his hand, his interest piqued, and motioned for James to continue. Molly sat hard enough to shake empty beer bottles from the kitchen table, not happy with being treated like a dog.

"Thank you, Jonas. Like I said, I took the gun. I walked into your room and took it as soon as I was sure they were gone. I'm sick of paying the price for Judith's arrogance. She's a grown ass woman, Jonas. A woman who found another boy toy to manipulate into springing her from home. Either she's going to come home when she's used him up or she isn't. Why waste time and energy hunting them both? I made you think it was kidnapping because it was best for business."

Ian returned, his pale face white and his eyes wide with surprise. He wanted to interrupt James and diffuse the bomb he had lit with news that Judith was outside that very moment. Two things stopped him. Judith wasn't alone, and what kept her company looked as though it would shrug off a mortar shell. Beretta's and butterfly knives were laughable weapons.

He tried slow his racing heart by waiting and breathing.

"So you made me think it was kidnapping," Jonas repeated, exhaustion on hiatus.

"Yes. I wanted you to fear for her. To use that angry energy and give reason a chance to shine. She's a burden, Jonas. I love her, same as we all do, but she's a burden. I hoped you wouldn't find her. I hoped you would grieve and let her go. I hoped that…"

Jonas stood up, cutting James off again, and walked towards the man. He understood James's decision. He understood why Molly had been mad. He understood what needed to be done to right the situation, and approached James with eyes that would be trusted. Eyes that displayed forgiveness.

Eyes that lied to James, as James' had lied to Jonas.

As Jonas reached James, relief washed over his face. Jonas smacked the relief away with a knuckle heavy back hand. His head throbbed, but having a new direction to steer his anger made his stomach feel better.

"You hoped that I would be too scattered to put the puzzle together. You hoped that I would grow weak. You hoped that you could hire a man to take my daughter, my money, and my sanity, just so that you could steal rest without a fight. You hoped you could have the kingdom, and you were too impatient to wait for the King to die before you got the crown."

"No, Jonas! You're wrong!" James cried, his cowardice hid behind a bruised cheek cradled by trembling hands.

Jonas, in one swift motion, pulled his gun out from under his arm and aimed it at James. He may not have been completely right, but he had gotten close enough for James to cower.
Jonas spit at the coward. He was on autopilot, his full trust in Molly's intuition.

Had Ian not spoken up, his words tripping over each other before they could escape his mouth, James' role in the story would have ended.

Jonas sheathed the gun and ran out the door, followed by Molly and Ian, to see for himself whether or not his little girl had come home. He may not have understood most of what Ian had spouted, but he understood that much.

Judith was home in time to spare him a costly carpet cleaning bill.

Jonas saw nothing more than a body and the aftermath of a wreck. There was no Judith. No Kyle. No vengeance. And no Pinto.

Jonas, ignoring the complaints of exhaustion, turned towards his crew. They wore the same expression of surprise. Even Ian, who had seen action in Afghanistan, was in awe over the aftermath.

Jonas spoke with the calm of an active war general, not fazed by the carnage, as it gave him a direction to move.

"James, you will be dealt with later. Pray you can do something useful enough to ease my temper by then. Everyone grab your stuff. It looks like our day isn't through," Jonas said.

The body groaned. Jonas jumped, but his nerve remained. If it had been the first time a dead man had regained consciousness in his presence, he might not have been so brave.

The man held his back as he groaned, using his other hand himself to a standing position. The man turned, and Jonas recognized the mess of scrapes and bruises that was Buck. The bum who had been meandering around the Pinto when they had arrived home. The man who was, even now, distracting Jonas from the miles Kyle and Judith were putting between them.

In other words, the distraction, though Jonas didn't know it.

Jonas, overcome with misplaced guilt for the homeless man whom they had sent away, approached him with a compassionate heart. The more defined the wounds became. The more blood he saw.

Buck (Ken) gave Jonas a sideways glance as Jonas approached him. Jonas offered him a hand, using a big motion to show that he was trying to help, not harm. Buck took his hand, as Ken knew that Buck would never deny the aid of a stranger.

Ken wished the accident had killed him forthright. He didn't like bleeding in the presence of wolves.

Wincing, he stood and took a few hobbled steps, fighting off dizziness with controlled, painful breathing.

"Go get me the first aid kit and a wet towel, James," Jonas said.

"Didn't you just say we had to get on the road?" James said, still dabbing at his bruising cheek for signs of blood from Jonas' backhand.

What the fuck was that? A man is bleeding in my parking lot, my car is missing, and you want to give me lip? Keep turning the other cheek, James. I fucking dare you."

"I didn't mean it like that, Boss..."

"Then shut the hell up! One more peep and I'll keep those liars lips in my back pocket for safe keeping. I'll let Molly have your tongue."

James quieted and retreated to the basement to do as told. He would take Jonas' tongue for even proposing the threat. Sure, they were on to him, even if they didn't have the whole gist of his plan, but the distraction had saved his life.

And he still had Jonas' gun.

"Do you need help?" Jonas asked, turning back to Buck (Ken).

"No. No, I'm fine. Just give me a minute."

"Alright, just take it easy."

Jonas wanted to make sure the man would be alright before leaving. He was antsy with adrenaline. The Alka-Seltzer was doing its job. He had energy. Hope. A second wind. He wanted to get on with it.

"You are her father, aren't you?" Buck (Ken) said.

The words hit Jonas like a cup of ice water. The bum sounded different. He would have blamed it on the accident, but he didn't sound gargled or stupid. His voice rang with clarity, intelligence, and authority. And with a voice like that, the bum had spoken to him like a subordinate.

"What did you say?" Jonas whispered.

Ken knew what was going through his mind. His emotions. He could see right into the intensity. He took a deep breath, ignoring the pain in his ribs, and looked Jonas dead in the eye. Without fear, without disrespect. The second man that day to look at Jonas that way.

"Judith. Is she your daughter? The woman with Kyle."

Jonas snapped. He grabbed Ken by the collar and pushed him backwards, that surge of adrenaline taking over. He slammed Ken into the wall, where he winced with pain but made no sound. He needed to speak, and he needed to stay calm or else Jonas would kill him. He could see that in Jonas' eyes.

James returned with the towel and the first aid kit, his gait slowing as he approached Ian and Molly and took in the scene.

"Looks like he didn't need these, after all," he whispered, tossing the kit to the ground and putting the towel to his face.

"Don't think you can hide from him for too long, James. You got lucky. This isn't going to end well for you," Molly said to him over her shoulder.

"Well we'll just have to wait and see about that, won't we?"

James smiled on the inside and watched, happy that Jonas was taking out his reserve energy on a useless informant.

"She's my daughter, you fuck! Now where is she? And where is he?" Jonas yelled, the last word coating Ken's face with hateful saliva.

"I'm going to tell you something, and I want you to hear me, because her life depends on it," Ken said, calm as he could. "I know what type of person you are, and I know how people like you get when you're pissed, but I'm alive, so I'll make use of it. Can you put me down for five minutes so I can talk?" His face was turning red from Jonas' choking grip.

Jonas dropped Ken without hesitation, and rough enough to let him know that five minutes would be all he'd get. If he'd learned anything from the past ten minutes, it was that thinking time had ended. Jonas needed to listen and act. Jonas backed away, arms folded, and stared holes into Ken.

"Talk," Jonas said.

"Boss, are you sure?" Molly spoke.

Jonas nodded once. His eyes never left Ken.

"I don't understand whatever those two are doing. It might

be psychotic and meaningless. It might be the most important thing in the world. But they believe in what they're doing. Four hours ago I would have out acted anyone with a severe mental handicap for sandwich money. Those two showed me a determination and passion I haven't seen in my life! Someone needed me."

"What the hell does that have to do with anything?" Jonas said.

"I lost faith in people a long time ago. Same as you. I found them lazy and selfish and unwilling to help unless it improved their REM cycle. So I screwed them all. I couldn't beat them, so I joined them. I used every negative bone in my body to play them. To take from the rich and eat like a king. What started as a social spite turned me into what I hated. Those two made me care again. Made me want to help. That dude exudes weird charisma, man. He fixed me. None of what he told you was a lie. I've seen it for myself! I'm saved!"

Ken knew his words were triggering nothing about halfway through the speech, Jonas' unwavering, but he finished strong in spite of himself.

"Well great. A con man conned you into cleaning up your act. Circle of life strikes again. Now the lions are hungry. Molly?" Jonas called.

Molly smiled. She'd been waiting for someone to play with most of the day, and if James' wasn't to be it, she'd have to make due with pretending. Without waiting for a word of instruction, Molly had whipped out a knife and began twirling it in her left hand.

Ken was not happy to see her approaching. Jonas was acting in warm blood. If Ken had the right words to calm him, there was a chance. Molly would kill him with no hesitation, and with no means of escape. Her blood ran icy and cold. Chills ran up Ken's spine, growing colder with each step closer she took. She wouldn't stop until her cold heart felt warmth, and only blood could warm a heart.

In this case, his blood.

"Your tale of self-discovery is boring me. I want to be gone from this alley in two minutes. You have one left," Jonas said through clenched teeth.

"I got hit by that fucking car and woke up long enough to see the devil. No Kyle, no Judith, no white lights for me. Just a big red fucker with horns, laughing before driving off in a cop car. Guys like me spend our lives avoiding too many devilish things, because we know full well we'll meet him when our time comes. Tonight, as I stand here breathing, I could smell Hell through my bloodied nose. My blood turned as cold as your assassins, Jonas. Even she would feel the pain of the cold in that thing's presence. That thing is evil and it's after your little girl. You want to be on the road in a minute and a half? Let's go!"

"Let's?" Molly asked. "And where do you think you're going?"

"What she said, boy. The only thing you've told me is that I've wasted my time with you! You're an expendable distraction. I've already got a liar on the team, and I'll be damned if I'm going to take on another."

Molly inched her way closer, the knife no longer moving in her hand, pointing instead at Ken's chest.

They were going to kill him, and Ken was out of cards. He stepped towards them, stopping himself an inch from the tip of Molly's blade. If he couldn't stop them, he would at least take away their satisfaction.

"Look, if there's anything that girl is not, it's kidnapped! What she is in is danger! They trust me a hair more than they trust you at the moment, but they wouldn't run if they saw me approaching. Otherwise why would I have been helping them sneak up to steal a getaway vehicle from you? Her own father?"

The knife moved to his throat, her free hand behind his neck. Her lips were close enough to his to kiss, and her breath in his mouth before he could finish his sentence. She tasted like cigarettes.

"So you admit your transgression! You're a liar and a thief! Between Kyle and James, three's a fucking crowd, my friend!" Jonas screamed.

"You need me!" Ken screamed.

Ken nicked his throat on the knife as the scream stretched his throat. He saw lust in Molly's eyes. He didn't have much time.

"They trust me enough to let me close enough to distract them. As much as I hate to go behind their backs, she's safer with you than with that monster on her tail! I'll get Kyle and leave, but I'll help you get your daughter first. I can do that much to ease my conscience and make up for my waste of life! That's all I've got, big boss man! Kill me or move it, because you were supposed to be on the road two minutes ago."

Ken fell to his knees, spent. He'd been Buck for over a decade, and had done very little self-expression in that time. The genuine emotion, fear, and excitement had worn him out. After playing Buck, it was like going from puberty to middle-age in the span of an hour.

"Ian, what do you think?" Jonas asked.

Ian, who was happy to be the glorified personal assistant to the real criminals, had not once had someone ask advice of him. He was a man of few words, wishing to please those who had treated him like he existed. As with anything asked of him, he complied with no hesitation.

"I think we keep showing up after the shit hits the fan, which most people might consider lucky. I also think it's a matter of time before the fan sneaks up behind us and we don't have a chance to avoid the same shitty fate."

Ian's answer was simple and honest. He was not wrapped up in the deceit and havoc. His straight forward words sent Jonas' mind back to asking questions. He questioned motive. He questioned explanation. He questioned his own sanity at this point of exhaustion. Killing him would be easy. Trusting him would be the hard part.

"Those two gave me a small chance at purpose," Ken whispered. "I am grateful and indebted to them. Even if I die trying, I'll do whatever I can to help them escape that devil. So help me God."

Ken relaxed and closed his eyes. A blue, glowing mist seeped out of Ken's nostrils, flowing in direction of the cruiser and the Pinto. Behind closed eyelids, his irises shone red, concealed from his interrogators. As for the mist, none present were pure enough to see it, though one sensed it.

Molly licked her lips, her pupils dilating as she fixated on the blood running down Ken's neck.

Ian left for the basement to gather their things, ready to be on the road and done with the events that were tearing the family apart. Unlike the others, Molly feeding her hunger would put him in a worse mood. He had not received the hereditary bloodlust from their father like she had.

James' stomach tightened, the burritos from breakfast to escape from whichever exit was most convenient. Something about Ken, be it his words or the serene look he wore in naïve martyrdom, made him ill. Moments before, James had been ready to face the same fate, all in his quest for power. James, always so sure of himself, had never experienced empathy before that moment.

With the weight of the chase on his mind and the hourglass on empty, Jonas made his decision.

Miles away, as Kyle exited onto the highway, fleeing the demon who chased him like a specter, a light blue glow sucked into the wristwatch, illuminating another word.

For the third time in so many days, the face of the watched pulsed red, begging for the attention of the wearer, as the light blue script turned crimson.

SLOTH

CHAPTER 27

death is a highway

Kyle caught the glow with his peripherals, but paid it no attention, not willing to take his eyes off of the road. Judith climbed to the front, relieving herself from back seat watch had proven fruitless, to read the illuminated word out loud to him.

"Sloth," she said, buckling her seatbelt.

Kyle held his wrist at eye level, shifting his eyes between the road and the face with the rapid motion of actors in lead up to a kissing scene. Each glance burned a letter into his memory.

S. L. O. T. H.

When he read the last letter, he put his hand back to the wheel. A negative of the word hung in the air in front of his eyes like a ghost in the contrasting darkness.

"You think it means Ken?" Judith asked.

"I'm guessing so. I don't understand how leading a man into a head on collision with cop car is an acceptable definition of "saving" him. Makes me wonder what being on the Big M…God's good side wins you, doesn't it?" Kyle said, careful to avoid the blasphemous nickname.

"You didn't get anybody killed," she said.
"Are you…"

"Kyle, watch out!" Judith screamed over him.

Even shocked by the sudden volume change, her warning gave him enough time to swerve around a slow moving mini-van ahead of them. The tires of the Pinto made a grinding sound on the asphalt as Kyle turned the wheel far to the left, far to the right, touching forearms both times, before resting back into a forward position. He had learned the technique in a defensive driving course as a good way to avoid collision, if you had the reflexes.

Kyle, thankful for the sober mind to pull off such a maneuver, reached for the cigarettes in the cup holder the moment they were on a straight path. Judith grabbed the pack from his hands, lighting a cigarette for the both of them, understanding the relief that nicotine brought even the most successful quitter in high stress moments.

Kyle sped up, the cigarette jutting out of his mouth, and drove alongside the van, his middle finger at the ready in lieu of a more gentle salutation.

The driver of the van offered no response. No middle finger. No threatening fist pump. Not even a confused glance at the car that had almost slammed into the rear of it. The driver must have heard the tires grinding. Had Kyle or Judith, who offered her own double birdie, been able to see the driver through the smoke clouding their vision, they would have found it odd.

Instead, Kyle built to, and then exceeded, the speed limit, unaware of the dead eyed obstacle that had almost ended their journey.

The white divider lines in the road blurred into an evanescent solid. He focused on the space in between the lines, relying on tricks of the eye to keep him straight. He had to trust Judith to be the eyes in the back of his head.

"That was close!" Judith said, collapsing into her seat.

She put a hand over her eyes, the other to her mouth with the cigarette, willing her heart to slow.

"Any sign of the cop car?" Kyle asked after ten more miles had fallen to their rear.

She turned, squinting into the dark.

"I don't know. I can't see anything behind us, but it's dark as pitch. If he's back there, he doesn't have a nightlight on, let alone a siren."

"Element of surprise I guess. What makes me so uneasy is the fact that we can't see him. He didn't need lights to take Ken out. But I'd bet my junkie soul he can see us."

"You mean you would if it wasn't being held in escrow by the devil?" Judith said with hopeful humor.

Kyle gave the windshield a cold stare, but could not deny Judith her props.

"Good one," he grumbled.

The traffic was light. Each time they approached a vehicle, none going as slow as the van, Kyle stepped on the gas to pass around them, pushing the Pinto to its limits and ignoring the whine of the engine as it begged for a measly few miles less per hour.

Kyle would have sold his soul for a few more, finding it funny that doing so would make running pretty pointless.

"Ok, we'll drive a couple hundred miles and stop somewhere inconspicuous for food. I'm starving. If he doesn't find us by then, we may have bought time. We can figure out the next step then."

"Can I turn on the radio Kyle? Music helps me relax."

"Sure. No country. Just keep looking for the cop car, ok?"

"Sure thing."

She turned on the radio and pressed the search button, passing static and uninteresting music, until she heard a verse of Dio's *Rainbow in the Dark*. She smiled, pleased with her choice, and positioned herself with her back to the passenger door so that she could maintain a view of their rear. She bobbed her head to the steady rhythm of the song, joining Ronnie James' high pitched vocals with her own parody falsetto.

Kyle wanted to high five her. The girl knew her cheesy metal.

"You know, sweetheart, your car voice isn't much better than your shower voice," he joked.

"Oh really? Then why do you have sweat dripping down your face, huh handsome?"

She sang louder, throwing in exaggerated facial expressions and air guitar to compliment her performance. Kyle used his pointer fingers on the steering wheel like drum sticks. He noticed the sweat once she pointed it out. It was a warm night, and the car was running hot. It felt like the cab had during his conversation with Lucifer, because the heat was caused by the same force, though he didn't yet know that. He said nothing, letting her attribute it to his admiration for her borderline vocal talents, though he felt uneasy about the heat.

Naiveté could be bliss at times.

The song came to an end. The DJ's voice filled the car with a bright, soothing tone not unlike Casey Kasem.

"That was Ronnie James Dio here on 99.1 "The Hard Place", Hell Valley's number one rock station, where the only thing between the rock and The Hard Place is you! Don't forget, kiddo's, that this is your MID-NIGH-RUSH-HOUR!!! All requests from nine to five! While the world's asleep, we will PARTY!"

Kooky sound effects played, sounding like a children's party at the collapse of the Berlin wall.

"Let US be your cup of coffee. Now, we have a special request here from a guy who sounds fired up this evening!"

A fire hydrant sound effect.

"From Big Loose, to Killa Kyle and Ju-Ju, he's looking to shake your nerves...to rattle your brains! Here is Jerry Lee Lewis with..."

Kyle had to use every ounce of self-control he could muster

to keep his surprise from sending them sidelong into a passing semi-truck.

"What the..." he said.

"Coincidence, Kyle. Come on. Ju-Ju?"

Coincidence or not, as the song began, Judith pressed the tuning button again to change the station. Ju-Ju was getting the heebie-jeebies. There would always be other rock stations.

She pressed, punched, and flicked the button to no avail, trying to drown out the descriptive symptoms of shaken nerves and rattled brains. The radio tuner was useless. She couldn't change the station. She leaned back and kicked the face plate of the radio out of fearful frustration. The song continued playing.

"What the hell is wrong with this thing?" she strained out with a scream.

"Did you try turning it off and back on again?" Kyle asked.

The song choice was apt. As the last words of the intro boomed throughout the car, the volume control turned to the highest level and became stuck. The next few seconds of the song were drowned out by the hissing of fire and the crinkling of glass. It sounded like a stick of dynamite going off in a greenhouse.

On a long and lonesome highway, with a semi and a possessed radio for company, the literal great ball of fire collided with the Pinto, leaving Judith and Kyle covered in superficial cuts, supernatural heat, and a whole new set of nightmares.

only the fools die young

The rookie was dying. Color had drained from his face and the outline of his teeth was visible against his cheeks. The forced state of rigor mortis had taken a toll on his nervous system, but the demon had one final job for him.

"Rookie, I'm going to give you a present. You've been such a good lapdog. I think you should experience this power. It is addicting. You'll never forgive, but you'll understand, Rook. You'll understand just fine."

The demon reached over and touched the rookie on the shoulder, his hands free from the steering wheel. A small flame torched through the rookie's shirt and burned into his arm, leaving a smoldering black hole on his upper arm.

The rookie opened his mouth, as if to scream, but it was part of the ploy. An orange glow escaped his mouth, and a tendril of smoke began to flow from his nostrils.

"Wait for it," the demon said, holding his hand over the rookie's chest like a general holding an army at bay.

The radio clicked on in the car, and the demon heard the D.J, sending his message to the inhabitants of the Pinto. The demon possessed the D.J, from miles away, with a thought. The D.J, was his servant, same as the rookie. He would escape with his life, unable to remember as anything beyond a bad dream. The rookie would never forget the fire that followed. It would haunt him long into the grave.

As the song neared the middle if the intro, the demon whispered into the car.

"Now."

The rookie jerked forward in his seat, a scream of pain building into a roar. The glow from his mouth flashed bright and expelled itself from the rookie's face as a large ball of flame. The flame shattered the windshield of the cruiser and sped forward into the night, seeking out a target to feed its destructive nature.

The rookie's mouth remained open, the glow from his mouth bathing the lower part what remained of his face. The lower half of his face and the top half of his uniform had burned black by the ball of fire. His lips were little more than cracked memories, exposing blackened teeth. His tongue smoldered, joining the smoke from his nostrils now being sucked from the car through the space where the windshield once was. The hair on his head was gone. The flash had blinded him.

There was one positive to the pain emanating through him; he was acting as a witness to the horror.

The ball of fire left a trail of illumination behind it as it fled. It was beyond sight within seconds. The car moved faster at the behest of the demon. The demon cracked his back, ignoring the immense pain he felt in his shoulder blades, and turned to the rookie.

"You're time on this earth is done, rookie, and damned if I even know your name. What is it?"

The rookie whimpered for a moment, silenced himself, and let a dry choke escape his throat.

The syllable riddled choke, 'Chghgher', was understood by the demon.

Christopher. His name was Christopher.

"Well, if this shit goes south, it was a pleasure to use you, Christopher. I am…"

The demon pause. Hank was dead. Whatever his name had been when hell fire spawned him eons ago, it had been sacrificed for the chance to rule. A name was more than a definition. It was important.

He had taken a soul, and he had gained the power, but he was nothing without a name.

"What am I, Chris? *Who* am I? I don't want you to reach your final destination without having my name tremble from your lips for the rest of eternity, and but I don't have a name to give you. Your final service shall be to name me. Trust me, it's a fucking honor."

The demon leaned in close to Christopher's face, relishing in the fragrance of barbecued lung and burnt enamel. He breathed the smoke from Christopher's mouth into his own, smacking and licking his lip, not wanting to waste the flavor.

"You are delicious, my boy. So fucking pure. So name me. Tell me what you think when you see me. With all that I've done to you, with all that you've seen me do, GIVE ME A NAME!"

The demon bellowed these last words into Christopher's face as his grew more and more fuzzy. Yes, his clock would soon tick its last tock. His final act in life would be naming a creature with a talent for causing terrible deaths. But if naming the beast set him free, name the beast he would. He was ready for his own terrible death.

What choice did he have?

The rookie was a fan of a band called Hurt. Their first single was about Andrea Yates, the women who drowned her children in a bathtub to protect them from the oncoming rapture. A specific line of the song, delivered with painful, turbulent emotion always sent chills up his spine.

Two choked words, the last lyrics of that very line, came out of his throat, filled with dying embers of hate and conviction. The demon understood both words very well.

Absolute Horror.

"I like it, Christopher. Fine fucking name, indeed."

Christopher whimpered for the last time, feeling the heat of Horror's hand touch his chest.

"Fine lap dog you are, my boy. Now do it again!" Horror screamed.

Another ball of flame ripped from Christopher's mouth, heading in the direction of the first. What was left on his head had burned black. His upper back and skull had burned to the seat, maintaining his seating position for him. His mouth, still glowing, remained open. Christopher, by the hand of mercy, was unconscious.

Unconscious, but alive.

His nightmare was almost over.

Almost.

The smell of burned hair and cooked flesh lingered in the air. Unable to help himself, Horror reached over to Christopher's head and pulled off a cooked ear, tossing it into his mouth. He did not chew, but sucked the few juices left onto his tongue before swallowing it whole.

"Fucking delicious, my boy. Five star hors d'oeuvre, though it lacked in presentation. Now, how about we find guests for the barbecue?"

The cruiser sped up again, reaching the momentum necessary for its final strike.

Flames began trailing the cruiser and burned on the sides of the road, like a demonic Delorian heading towards a bleak future.

The demon hovered his hand above Christopher's chest, focusing his burning gaze ahead, ready to introduce Kyle and Judith to

Absolute Horror.

"Again," Horror whispered, and fire filled the night.

the trappening

Kyle was unable to stop the car from careening left and right. The wheel jerked in a violent manner underneath his sweating palms. The car had come to life, as if Stephen King had picked the setting for this chapter of his adventure, and he hadn't yet reached the character development in his story to make survival necessary or death important. They would die as a footnote.

Control returned without warning. His sweat acted as an adhesive instead of a lubricant, and he was able to pull the car back onto the freeway before it hit a road sign.

He lined up the divider lines in his field of vision again and slammed his foot onto the gas pedal. The engine whine overpowered the radio, drowning out the song. He knew that the song had nothing to do with the fireball. It was just a cruel, spit-in-the-face punch line.

Judith moaned in the passenger seat, little droplets of blood forming where the glass shards had hit her arm. She picked at the shards in silence. She had reached the point where fear became inconvenience.

The whine of the engine and the static on the station harmonized into a song most foreboding. It was the soundtrack to a horror movie that would make even the masked stalker grow uneasy. Jump scares were all about surprise. Consistent, lurking noises were the foundation of true horror. Nobody expects to be scared outside of the silence. The sound in the car kept growing and growing, taunting them. Kyle swore he heard laughter in the static.

Kyle glanced into the rear view and saw an orange light was hurtling towards the back of the car. A car which lacked the glass protection necessary to protect its passengers from the compact conflagration.

Three hundred yards.

Two-seventy five.

Two-fifty.

Behind the orange ball, surrounded by a separate wall of flame, Kyle caught a brief flash of the cruiser before it faded into its shroud of darkness.

The lights were off, of course. He hated being right.

Kyle changed lanes in time for the flaming ball to hurtle past them. The intense heat licked at him as it passed. The ball hurtled forward for a distance before dipping and hitting the rear axle of an truck ahead of them.

The underside of the truck exploded upward, sending tools and bags of manure riding through the air on a small mushroom cloud. The entire bed of the truck fell from the cab. Sparks from the slowing bed and the back end of the cab filled the air like fireworks. The truck pieces slowed enough to avoid before the Pinto reached them, but only just.

Kyle looked into the rear view. He wanted to make sure the driver was alive.

The truck bed was empty. Not a hand on the wheel nor a foot on the pedal. An illusion? A prop?

Judith watched all of it crouched on her knees, gripping the back of the passenger seat and unable to look away from the barrage of wreckage the highway was becoming.

She saw a flicker of orange from somewhere far behind them.

"I think he's about to fire another one, Kyle," Judith said in a flat tone, her words muffled by the back of the car seat.

When there was enough distance between them and the vacant Ford, Kyle flicked off the Pinto's headlights. He knew there was another twenty or so miles of straight away, and any edge was helpful. As long as no cars ahead of them had broken tail lights, things would go peachy.

Do they ever? he thought before the words could escape his lips.

As a bonus, they were coming up on farm roads. If they could find one and exit, they had a slim chance of escape. Or at least respite.

Kyle lacked all of Solo's cockiness about beating the odds, but he also lacked a choice. It was the only practical option.

The static had become the constant. The whine and the radio were entirely drowned out. The static, the whine, and the radio disappeared with the lights. All they could hear was the heavy breathing of the wind. Kyle realized he had been wrong about the silence. The eerie quiet intensified his fear.

"Judith, is there an atlas in here?"

"Yes," she said, opening the glove box behind her without looking, demonstrating unnecessary flexibility in the face of danger.

"Is it detailed enough or just the type with major roads?"

She snickered.

"Kyle, my dad makes a living hiding skeletons in the closet and bodies in the desert. He needs to know every inch of the state, especially this close to the city."

She tossed the map to him, her eyes still facing backward, waiting for the culmination of that orange flicker to reach the car.

Kyle retrieved his cab keys from his pocket, arching his hips upward so that his crotch touched the wheel. He tossed them to her, throwing the atlas back at her, as well.

"Perfect. I need your eyes. Nothing we can do to stop what's behind us. There's a little flashlight on the key chain. Try and find a farm road. We're sixty miles outside of the city. I want to try to lose this bastard."

"Will that work?"

"We don't have another choice, babe," Kyle reiterated his earlier sentiment.

"You know, I've always been strong. Monsters never scared me. People did. But this shit? I feel like a four year old mute girl hiding from the boogey man."

"Maybe because you've seen proof that the boogie man is real."

Judith turned on the flashlight and began turning pages with fervor. She found the page she wanted and scanned the road with her finger, her tongue hanging out over her lip.

Kyle afforded another rear view peek. Silhouetted against the distant remains of the truck, he saw the cruiser. Plums of flame surrounded the vehicle. Everything on either side of the cruiser was left burning as it sped towards them.

One hundred-fifty yards away.

The gap was closing, aim no longer a factor. A point blank fire ball would finish them.

The car would flip. They would die. He would fail.

Fifty yards.

The cruiser hauled ass, and Kyle tried to speed up to no avail. The Pinto had given its last warning. It would go no faster. A sound like crashing waves filled the car. Another orange ball of flame passed the driver window and blew apart an oversized mile marker. A piece of the metal struck the Pinto.

A chuckle came over the radio, breaking the silence.

Did ya really think I'd lose you if you turned off the lights, boy? Come on, now. You can't hide from darkness in the dark!

The cop car, little more than scrap metal on wheels, pulled next to the driver side with ease.

The captain would like to remind you to keep your seat belts buckled in case of unexpected turbulence.

The cop car veered left, smashing into Kyle's side door and jerking the Pinto sideways. The atlas fell from Judith's hands.

"Fuck!" they screamed in unison.

Kyle tried to keep control as Judith picked up the atlas, racing to find her place.

We're sorry about that, passengers! We've hit some rather strong dramatic timing! If you'll please stay calm and give in to relaxation, this will all be over soon. And remember! No smoking while on board! No, there will be plenty of time for that later.

The chuckle.

"Why don't you just blow us off the damn road, you sadistic bastard!" Kyle said, damning dementia and turning his head.

Kyle looked past the rookie, who sat charred in the passenger seat with fire still burning his mouth. He looked past sheer size of the demon, past the red skin, past the dark humor, and into the smirking, malevolent eyes. The walls of fire now surrounded both the cruiser and the Pinto, illuminating those eyes. They were crimson, same as his watch. Same as Lucifer's.

"Where the hell is the road?" she said, oblivious.

"Keep looking," Kyle droned, unable to turn away.

The voice on the radio had paused, giving Kyle time to consider what he had asked. The demon could have been a statue. Kyle, losing this particular game of chicken, turned a full one eighty, looking at Judith with shock induced stoicism.

"Find the road or we're dead, Judith," Kyle said.

The voice returned to the radio. If Kyle had still been looking, he would have seen the demon mouthing the words. It was the voice from the alley way, disguising itself as something somewhat human.

Now, Kyle, my dear boy. I don't want a simple traffic mishap to get all the credit for ending the life of God's last hope! I'd much rather feel your blood running from my lips as you beg "Why me? Oh, Mr. Devil

Man, why meeeeee? The horror! The Absolute Horror!!"

The chuckle. It was irking Kyle's nerves, despite the fear.

"God's last hope? What the hell do you mean?" Kyle screamed, knowing full well that he could have whispered and the demon would have heard him.

Nice little nickname, no? Of course, in moments it won't be relevant, but I like seeing a glimmer of hopeful satisfaction before I tear apart the enemy. Stand by for more turbulence, passengers!

Kyle, not a stranger to the demon's brand of dramatic flair, took advantage of the cue. As soon as the radio returned to silence, Kyle moved his foot to the brake and tapped it. The Pinto jerked backwards. The cruiser swerved towards where the Pinto should have been. Having nothing to hit, the cruiser overcompensated with a violent spin and skidded to a sideways stop in the middle of the road. A roar of rage came from the radio. Kyle slammed on the pedal again, swerving around the cruiser and cursing the Pinto's lack of pickup for wasting what little time he had bought them. He wouldn't allow himself relief, though he did allow a small twinge of satisfaction.

Fine! You want to play smart? I'll play dirty!

The walls of fire that lit the sides of the road, extending along the cruiser's trajectory, extinguished into nothingness in an instant, as if by the flick of a switch.

The darkness had returned.

"Hey! Half a mile up the road! Turn into the field and drive like hell! There's a back road. You might piss off a farmer, but..." Judith paused.

Her gaze set on Kyle's wide eyes looking in the rear view. She turned around to see another fireball, much larger than the three earlier conjurations. The heat was becoming painful It moved with slow grace, though Kyle was sure it was a mind trick due to the sheer size of the thing.

Judith remembered the first time she had watched Star Wars as a child. The ship entering the screen from the top that kept coming, slow and steady and infinite, always left her in awe. You knew it was something evil, but it demanded admiration.

Judith cradled her head in her hands, realizing they had seconds to live. Kyle looked down to her, hating himself for not doing a better job, and swore he heard her mutter something with his name in it. He reached out to touch her, accepting it would be the last human contact he would experience and knowing that his punishment was upon him. He had tried.

Another scream roared from the radio. A scream of pain. Judith shot up in her seat, reacting to a death that hadn't happened. An explosion boomed behind them, but the large fireball had snuffed out.

A semi, one they had passed early on the highway, Kyle realized, had t-boned the stalled cruiser, causing the explosion. The semi skid to a slow halt, the tail end burning and covered in flaming bits of the cruiser.

A low hum overtook the radio. Kyle reached to the volume knob, and it turned without hesitation. A semblance of normality had returned.

"Holy shit!" Judith exclaimed.

"Guess the semi didn't see him without his lights on," Kyle said.

"That was a stroke of luck, Kyle. Damn near divine intervention."

"I'm not allowed that kind of help, remember? If luck is separate from divinity, remind me to thank every one of my lucky stars if we get a chance to sleep again. Guess we can skip the farm road."

She glanced at the atlas again as Kyle flicked on the headlights.

"Grapevine is about thirty miles away."

"That's a relief. We need gas, the car needs a break, and I need new trousers."

"You and me both. I think Depends may be on the shopping list if things like that are to become a regular occurrence."

He sighed.

"What?"

"I think I picked a horrible day to quit snorting cocaine, Judy."

"Don't call me Judy. Or I'll kill you as dead as he tried to!" she threatened.

"Sweetie?"

"Warmer..."

"Sugar tits?"

"You must have been a real charmer in your younger days, buck-o."

Buck's name silenced them. The word SLOTH on his watch didn't mean that Buck was dead, but he was positive that Judith's family weren't giving him the VIP treatment. How many would suffer for his futile mission? Kyle dreaded to contemplate the answer.

"We were almost ghosts, Judith."

"It will be easier without that thing following us. You just wait and see."

They both knew that a setback didn't mean the demon was done chasing them, but Kyle couldn't bring himself to contradict her hope. He didn't ask if she would like to check out the wreckage and answer the question, because he knew the answer she would give.

Kyle turned off the radio and they drove forward in comfortable silence. Judith gave the blaze one last ounce of attention before resting her head on Kyle's shoulder. He leaned own head sideways, resting it against hers.

They travelled that way until Grapevine, each relaxing a little more with every mile of separation.

If they had stopped to check the debris, an unscathed, red hand breaking through the twisted and flaming metal would have answered their question.

The chase wasn't over.

Not by a long shot.

devil - 1   semi truck - 0

There was little left but fire.

So much fire.

The semi-trailer jackknifed, engulfed in flame and sending a distress signal for those who could no longer be helped. A smoke signal of the dead.

The cab of the semi was the only piece of the wreck that offered real insight to the biological damage. The drivers face pressed against the spider-web shattered windshield. The cracks filled with blood. The inner windshield and dashboard were caked with snot and bile and more of the precious red fluid. The sight was reminiscent of an eerie mosaic. Something out of a nightmarish Tim Burton film.

The cruiser was unrecognizable. The remains sat two hundred feet from the wreck. It was folded in half, sandwiching Christopher's arm between the fold like a burnt piece of sandwich meat. The roof resembled an accordion. Investigators would be hard pressed to find proof of windows by searching the debris.

Christopher decorated the pavement and the field beyond the roadsides, a forgotten confetti of tissue and bone. Absolute Horror controlled the tail end of his life, but a tired semi-truck driver, with ignorant mercy, had taken the glory of finishing it from Horror.

Horror admired the carnage that would soon make the strongest of crime scene responders sore from vomiting.

It was beautiful. The fire, the broken glass, the black skid marks, the presence of death on the night wind.

Sure, losing the vehicle was a disadvantage, but his creed of patience withstood this stroke of dumb luck without wavering. He would find another method of travel. Perhaps a fresh innocent to replace Christopher. As much damage as the Pinto had taken, much like Kyle's psyche, it still struggled forward, running like hell. No conjuration or parlor magic could put him closer to Kyle. He'd need a new way to catch the savior and his little whore.

Though he thought himself above pain after being smashed between two vehicles less than an hour before, his back hurt something fierce. The mind games, the projecting, sharing his power in another, and the countless other nuances he had conjured had worn on his adrenaline, though he didn't feel fatigued.

The snake spot, between his shoulder blades, was the epicenter. He had grown to such a size that no amount of reaching or bending allowed him to scratch the itch. He pushed the pain aside, knowing it would pass.

Absolute Horror didn't want to walk. He had become such a terrifying creature that hitchhiking would do him no good. The cars would move too fast to hypnotize a driver, and unless one of them had a death wish, none would stop. Fireballs, walls, and jets would destroy the vehicle he would need. Sure, if anyone came along and saw the wreck they would stop. Police, ambulances, fire trucks, and news reporters were on the way.

Though the key players knew what he had become, he didn't want the world to know about him yet. He had not reached his full potential. He had to be smart. Sure, he could kill them, but a bigger scene meant more questions. His job wasn't to expose the truth, it was to kill the messenger.

The semi helped cover his tracks. It would be considered a horrendous accident, but an accident nonetheless. If he was discovered before he reached his full potential, before God's little savior was destroyed, he would be forced to take action. There was no fun in destruction without the promise of torture He knew he would reign over humanity in due time, an infernal puppeteer with a planet full of marionettes.

Still, the dull moments were no fun. No fun at all.

The inconvenience made his head ache, but it left him with the opportunity to dispose of the final rope holding him from his true potential. For now, he'd let Kyle Thimall run away and recharge his fight and confidence.

First things first.

Horror closed his eyes. Taking deep breaths, he grasped the wrist of his left arm with his oversized right hand and squeezed. Squeezed hard. His throat purred a song of demonic meditation. The pain in his back bit harder, but he blocked the pain away. It was a superficial bang of the knee compared to what he was about to do.

Any mortal cutting blood flow to a body part would be left with skin the color of powder, coupled with pins and needles, until the hold was released. Too tight and too long, like a properly administered tourniquet, and the part would decay and die.

Something that had been decaying inside of Absolute Horror finally died. Hank Wilkins had gone silent when Horror came forward, but a small part of him lingered. A shred of soul and humanity held back Horror's full potential. Where a human hand would turn white, Horror's hand grew smaller, turning from red to pale pink. Turning human. Turning back into the hand of Hank Wilkins.

The purring in his throat stopped, and Horror pulled. Once was all it took. The hand separated from his arm and flew into the wreckage with an arcing flourish. There was no blood. The wound flamed over, cauterizing itself. Horror let out a deep breath and opened his eyes. He was glad to be rid of the tiny voice that spoke a language he would never understand, yet bothered enough of him to require extermination.

The hand would grow back, in time. The hand in the wreck would also grow. It would grow an arm, a chest, a body. It would grow into the discarded shell of Hank Wilkins. It would burn in the fire. It would be tested. It would be identified. It would be reported. Everybody would believe Hank died in a terrible crash, his soul gone to that happy donut shop in the sky. They would be close to the truth. Hank's soul had indeed gone somewhere with fryers.

Mortals only cared for the body, and Horror had given it to them. If they knew the truths of the afterlife, the honest to God truths, the entire race would have killed itself from sterile agoraphobia before it learned to throw a spear.

They had their body count. The numbers would add up. Horror would remain in the shadows a little while longer.

Horror's eyes pierced through the air where a new hand would soon be and settled on the smoldering carcass of the rookie. Of Christopher. Rearing back his powerful leg, he kicked the head from the torso with the force of a punter, sending it crashing into the grill of the semi-truck.

The head, still open mouthed but lacking the destructive glow Horror had bestowed upon him, splattered across the front of the semi like a spilled bowl of porridge. Not too red, not too white. Just the right mix.

A roar parted the smoke in front of his face. Pain drilled through his back. He fell to his knees in front of Christopher's torso and punched through the dead rookie's chest cavity. After a few moments of chesty grunting, the pain subsided.

Horror's hand remained in Christopher's chest, searching for a moment, until he found what he was looking for. He pulled his hand out, the souvenir nearly camouflaged by his massive red fingers.

The rookie's heart.

Horror bit into it. His sharp, black canines ripped through the lifeless tissue like Simon Cowell through a tone deaf super model.

He chewed, trying to find the flavor of the organ. His tongue moved the sinewy chunks from one side of his mouth to the other. Once he registered the taste, he choked in disgust spit the pieces onto the pavement. He threw the heart into the fire, licking the air in disgust as he did, hoping the smoke would rid his buds of the taste.

"Fucking vegetarians. Pussies, every one of them, and still they taste like a dirty asshole," he grumbled to himself.

Horror turned on his heel to take his first step towards his destiny. On the third step, the pain returned, putting him back on his knees. In what would have been his sixth step, he was on all fours, bellowing. The ground shook beneath him. His fist closed, crushing the asphalt to ash by force of his grip.

The spot in the middle of his back exploded outward. Long, bone like protrusions burst from the snake spot, looking more like spiders legs. Bits of blood and flesh dripped from them as they flung outward, curving in odd angles. Audible cracking noises filled his ears. Each one was met with a punch to the ground that left small craters in the highway, until the handless forearm burned with the same pain as his back. He continued to use it on the asphalt, unaware that it was growing back while in the anti-orgasmic throes of pain.

The protrusions solidified, taking on the texture of stone and turning a hearty red color. They matched the hue of his skin. Thin flaps of flesh fell from his bones, like pennants falling from the archway of a drawbridge paying respects to a visiting nation. Curved veins popped up, connecting the loose flesh into a large, thin flaps.

In what would have been his sixtieth step, the pain subsided. The punching stopped. The bone, flesh, and veins of his reformed hand were good as new.

He was whole. He was pure. He was absolutely horrifying.

Though the pain was tremendous, in the moment that would have been his sixty-fifth step, Horror realized he'd never have to walk again. The ragged clothing that clung to his form had fallen from his body in the transformation. He rose to his feet, naked and proud. Clothing was how mortal's hid shame, and he had cast the final link to mortality into the wreckage.

He had proven himself worthy.

He had earned his wings.

He spread them wide and reached back to feel them. They felt like slimy, tough leather. He spotted the silhouette of his wingspan across the pavement, thanks to the light from the flames. They spanned a body and a half each. The light shone red through them, giving a maroon shade to the ground at his feet. They were imperfect, riddled with holes and flaws. But they were a gift.

They were his.

And he would use them as they were intended.

For intimidation.

For destruction.

For his destiny.

They would be the badge of his throne he was sent to earn.

He kicked off of the ground, he flapped them hard a single time, instinct nullifying the need for a "learning how to fly" montage and cheesy Joe Esposito tune. His feet relaxed beneath him, inches from the ground and rising as the wings twitched and fluttered of their own mind, keeping him afloat. His moment of gratification over, his earned reward savored, he flapped his wings with force, rising skyward.

He stopped a hundred feet above the ground, gaining his bearings, eying the visual scent left by Kyle. A minor adjustment, and he was off.

The pause button depressed.

The chase resumed.

The transformation was complete.

Absolute Horror had taken wing.

ENVY

Envy is my blood

Show me a worthier life

And I feel contempt

CHAPTER 31

a clever idiom

The G.P.S. monitor, infuriating thing that was to decipher, led the black sedan past the highway wreckage. James was at the wheel at Jonas' insistence, to keep his hands busy. Molly sat behind him, snoring with steady, troubled snorts. Her closed eyes leveled, unwavering, at the nape of James' neck. Ian sat beside her, dozing on Ken's shoulder, who in turn rested his bandaged head against the darkened window in his own slumber. Jonas had claimed shotgun.

The final stretch of Jonas' road to revenge had begun with overflowing tension. They had wasted a half an hour changing a tire punctured by loose metal from the wreck in the alley, and another forty minutes chasing ghost coordinates while the G.P.S. searched for a signal. All the while, Molly goaded James, looking for an excuse to decrease the passenger load. James, heavy of mind, let her. Whatever scheming dedication filled him had withered under solemnity, though nobody thought to reacquire Jonas' gun amidst the confusion.

The G.P.S. monitor tracked the Pinto via a device under the hood. Jonas had traded the G.P.S. devices to clear the debt of a gambler with a knack for electronics and security software. It was another in a long list of tools that helped him keep tabs on Judith. Until this particular event, he was the only one who knew they existed.

User error caused a delay, but the long straight highway offered little deviation from the path for a Pinto to take advantage of. The sedan's gas tank was full, and it was in better shape than the Pinto. Once they reached the coordinates on the screen, they could end the increasingly poisonous hunt for Judith.

And then there was James, ever the loyal employee and ultimate betrayer. Jonas didn't want to know how long the betrayal festered in James, but he had lost any gold stars earned through loyalty.

Any other day, Jonas would have shot James dead. Daddy missed his little girl. Lucky for James, nothing else mattered.

"What the hell were you thinking James?" Jonas asked, not without rhetoric.

"Can you blame me, Jonas? Having personal motivation doesn't make me a liar. She's an adult, and yet all business comes second to her paternal prison sentence."

"You don't understand. You don't have kids, James."

"You're right. I don't understand, and I don't agree with it. If you were so concerned about her after your wife died, why didn't you stop? I've seen the finances. You could have left it all behind and wanted for nothing until judgment day. Why didn't you quit the business, or retire from management and reap the rewards of ownership? You overextended yourself to the point insanity. All I have is this business, and I'm happy enough with the occasional one night stand to not let a family interfere with that. When she died, you became Judith's family. If you wanted her safe, why did you keep her in the most dangerous situation you possibly could?"

James, not knowing that the very question he asked plagued Jonas, was surprised at his quick response.

"I'm a greedy bastard, James. That's why. I never believed, for one second, that she would turn into her mother. So independent, so full of life. I thought she wanted to follow in my footsteps. Thought she worshipped me like she did when she was a kid. Never once thought she would become a runaway pain in the ass. And because I'm a greedy bastard, even when it did start to happen, I stuck it through because I knew I could fix it. *Knew* I could," Jonas said, happy to speak the words aloud.

"Yeah, well, that worked out well for you, didn't it, Boss?" James replied.

"I don't understand why you didn't just ask, James. I listen when it comes to business. I would have taken your words into consideration. I would have been pissed about it, but I would have listened. Hell, I might have even given you the keys to the kingdom and taken your advice. Until today, you were a son to me."

"Until today, Jonas, I didn't want the keys given to me, because I know you're a greedy bastard. How long would it have been before you came barking for reinstatement by pain of death?"

Jonas remained silent. He knew it wouldn't have been very long. A month, if he found something interesting to occupy his time. Most likely, it would have been half that.

"Honest to God, Jonas, I didn't want your charity. I wanted to kill you. To turn your own gun on you and take the control you've squandered away for years. Nobody would take it back from me, and nobody would dare steal it. I may be a jealous snake, Jonas, but it's because you had options, and you checked every single box, unable to forego one pleasure for another. I just wanted to prosper in this city, which meant going through you. It's all I've ever known. Even so far removed from the politics of the world, I have to kiss babies and shake hands. I'd rather shake the former and spit on the latter."

"You would kill me to run small time crime out of a basement?" Jonas asked.

"I would have killed you to run my own small time crime out of a basement, Jonas. Those two words make a huge difference."

Jonas couldn't fault his logic. Long ago, before family was a word whipped men used while drinking micro-brew, he would have done the same thing. James was jealous of the army Jonas kept, and angry that he lacked the conviction to maintain it.

"Would you kill me, James? Shoot me dead with my own gun, still pressed into your back, comforting you like a pacifier would a baby?"

"Take the damn thing," James said, pulling the gun from the back of his pants and handing it, butt end first, to Jonas.

Jonas took the gun, replacing it in his holster and letting himself enjoy the relief of the weight.

"I just don't care anymore, Jonas. Three hours ago, I was contemplating and scheming. I would have killed you all, even if it left me alone, just to rid myself of the disgust I felt every single time I watched you squander away an opportunity thanks to your fucking daughter. Molly almost took a man's life because you lost your shit. Paranoia and apathy are all you have left. I may not give two shits about people, but our business thrives on lives. You ordered a sloppy kill because you lost yourself. He almost died because you wanted to kill me. We all might die because you want to kill Kyle. I realized tonight that I couldn't have done that. I can't kill without a reason. Even on your orders, there is always a reason. Tonight, it would satisfy nothing. Accomplished nothing. That wasn't the father in you, Jonas. It was the leader. The boss. If that's what power does to a man with a family to keep him grounded, it would destroy me."

Jonas listened to every word, realizing that something in James snapped him out of the treacherous frame of mind. For a dog like James, that was a hell of a thing. Jonas had visited a church looking for a miracle, and James found that miracle thanks to the intervention of a demon.

"You're a criminal. We have to be emotionless, James. It's part of the job. Why would tonight be any different than any other job I've given you? Why would that homeless piece of shit matter more than the druggies and perverts we've taken out?"

James exhaled, feeling as if he'd been holding his breath his entire life. On the wind of that exhale, a green mist flowed from him and out of the cracked window, invisible unless it was being looked for.

His eyes were wide open and focused. He couldn't hide their red illumination in full daylight. Jonas' listened to the words that granted James his salvation with silent condemnation, understanding that in them was the power of truth. The truth as it pertained to both James and Kyle.

"It finally matters because, after tonight, I believe in the devil, Jonas. If the devil exists, I've spent my entire life on the wrong fucking team. If I killed you to take something that would turn me into what you've become? Hell, if anything turns me into what you've become? We'll forever tied at the ankle in Hell's chain gang. We will become the servants that the evil little voice in our heads send us running from, with a master we have no hope of overthrowing. That fucking terrifies me."

James was right. His envy, Jonas' greed, drove them away from suppression in life and towards tortuous servitude in death. The red faded from James' eyes, and he drove on as if he didn't even know what had happened.

But Jonas felt the same terror James expressed with such calm eloquence, and in light of what just transpired, four things became clear to him.

Kyle Thimall, and the priest for that matter, had been telling the truth.

The Devil *did* exist.

Instead of rescuing Judith from Kyle, they were now rescuing the pair of them *from* said Devil.

And last, with clarity that made his soul weep, the realization that thanks to the life he had lived, regardless of what happened by weeks end, he, Jonas McMillan, was fucked.

friends in lower places

Contrary to the small town's name, Grapevine contained no hints of foreign culture or pomposity. The word Chic came to mind when sandwiched between Fried and Ken. The city population, scrawled across a sign out of an ad from the 50's, inviting guests in with "Welcome to Grapevine! Stay too long and you may never leave!" The truth of the statement made Kyle uneasy. If he hadn't seen the proof of Hell's existence, this glorified truck stop would have been his comparison.

Five hours had passed since they had seen tail (and he was sure the red fucker had one) or hide of the demon. He was positive that the welcome sign was meant to be warming, not warning, though he had been tricked by irony enough times in the past four days to silence his hopes.

The grumbling stomachs (of both the two humans and the car) had forced the stop. Hunger outweighed everything, in the end. They had driven for far longer than they had expected to, rehashing a mantra of five more miles any time the goal was reached. Grapevine had become a ghost town, chasing them away with the settled in dust of desertion. They'd been fighting hunger and exhaustion for long enough to be disoriented. He would have failed a sobriety test.

Kyle pulled into a rest stop (an amalgam bar/gas station/diner/ gift shop) on the main strip of the road, waiting to be seduced by relaxation. Kyle was thankful for the size of the town. He was sure they would receive more than one off putting glance, but the parking lot was full to capacity.

It neared midnight. In a town such as Grapevine, that meant options were limited. Everybody in Grapevine was dining, drinking, or causing trouble. With the amount of people about, Kyle assumed it was a night unburdened by the labor of tomorrow. He assumed because he was having trouble remembering what day it was. Adventure affected a person's internal time clock. He looked at the watch as he pumped gas into the Pinto and found another red word.

ENVY

The fourth word confused him. Kyle shrugged it off, deciding to be thankful for the luck. He would give it thought when his stomach was full and his heartbeat normal.

Kyle couldn't be sure if the demon lived, but three letters shifted the odds further from their favor.

G.P.S.

Kyle found the tracking box while checking for damage under the hood. Of course Jonas tracked his cars. In case of theft. In case people like Kyle showed up. Judith was proud that Jonas had been able to keep a secret from her without her using it to her own advantage.

Worrying about being found thanks to G.P.S, was much like being paranoid about an unfaithful spouse. Either it would happen or it wouldn't. Until something did happen, there was no reason to fuss.

"Food first, then we worry," Judith advised.

Kyle topped off the gas tank and drove to the rear of the building, away from the street to diminish visibility. It was a good fit. The Pinto was as dusty and dented as the rest of the vehicles in the lot. Every one appeared to be owned by families who understood, in great detail, the proper acquisition and usage practices of a food stamp.

Kyle shook Judith awake. Her eyes fluttered opened, and she smiled.

"Food, my lady?"

Judith yawned, rubbing her stomach to indicate her hunger, and hugged Kyle.

"That sounds great. Do we get a movie too?" Judith said into his ear.

"Not tonight, I'm afraid. I think a terrible romantic comedy is waiting to play out."

"You're telling me. I'm done with horror for a while."

Kyle, ever the gentleman, opened her door and took her hand. They walked to the side entrance in a comfortable silence. Hand holding implied things, and a hug wasn't an invitation to those implications. Her hand felt good in his, and the returned pressure let him know that she shared his thoughts.

Sarah had been out of his mind for a majority of the week, but the memory of holding her hand flooded Kyle's mind on that short, silent walk. He still loved his wife. The attraction to Judith filled him with guilt. As he walked with Judith, hand and hand, the whisper grew in volume.

The whisper told him to let go of guilt and be happy. That he should give a damn with the remaining time.

Sarah's memory had been the reason he agreed to the damning contract in the first place, but the whisper told him that it had never been about Sarah. Death would keep her from him forever, and he would lose the soul he treated with absent negligence. Staying alive would keep him from her for a while, but his soul would heal. *He* would heal.

Finally.

Kyle opened the side door, and Judith's hand went to his bicep. She held herself close. The music was loud, and smoke poured from the door when they opened it.

They received a glance or two on their way to find a place to sit. The music didn't stop, the bar didn't quiet. They continued playing pool, drinking pints, tapping their toes to the country musician with his acoustic guitar. Three couples danced to the music as if the world was a facade compared to their love. The atmosphere was relaxed.

Strangers or not, they brought something Grapevine saw little of; new faces and new money.

Kyle and Judith walked to a rear table. They wanted line of site of the entrances. Her father might kick doors open at any moment.

Her father, or something far worse.

A young, blonde waitress approached them wearing a beaming smile and pigtails. A pen and pad were at the ready to take their order without a fuss or a falsity. The two couldn't help but react to her infectious smile. Whenever Kyle forgot happiness existed, he met somebody that redefined it. As dark as the adventure was, there were blinding bright spots.

"What can I get you two love birds?" she asked.

"Oh, we're not..." Kyle started.

"Two burgers, two cokes, and as many fries as you can fit on a tray, please."

"Good choice, m'am," the waitress said. "We've got the best fry recipe in the two hundred miles, so we've been told! Don't need ketchup or anything!"

"I believe that, considering the last town we saw looked like the aftermath of a Romero movie," Kyle said.

"Don't be rude!" Judith said, smacking his arm with the hand holding his, bringing it along for the ride. "This is a bar full of guys who consider her a sister. Last thing we need is attention."

"Aww, these guys are big teddy bears," the waitress said. If she noticed the rudeness or Judith's subtle hinting at their problems, she did a good job of hiding it.

"So two burgers, two cokes..."

"Make it four," Judith said.

Kyle looked at her with wonder.

"What?" she said. "I'm hungry. If your poor wittle tummy can't handle it all, I'll make sure we don't waste any."

Kyle sighed with a smile, enjoying her ability to take control.

"And a heap ton of fries?" the waitress finished, that smile never leaving her face.

"And a beer," Judith added.

"Seriously?"

"Why not? You're driving," Judith said.

The waitress winked at Judith before turning to take their order to the kitchen.

"You know, if I didn't know any better, this would feel like a Friday night out after a long work week. First date I've been on in years." Kyle said. He caught himself too late.

"Oh, so we are on a date now, Mister Man? Is it habit to treat your kidnapped sidekicks to meals at such elegant establishments?"

"That's not what I meant. It's weird how you can be so calm and fun after we nearly got blown, in the literal sense, to hell. It's relaxing."

Judith smiled and rested her head on his shoulder, where she could whisper and he could listen without looking awkward.

"Not that this isn't nice, but people remember out of place strangers with stress on their minds, Kyle. The shady depressed couple who keep glancing at the door? It's a subconscious thing to take note of. This place is packed!" Judith waved her arm, sweeping across the sea of happy, drunken joviality.

"If we escape without issue, and curious parties come asking, people will be more likely to inform on a couple of scared loners than a fun couple who buys the bar shots!" Judith said, screaming the last few words. The bar cheered as she lifted an invisible glass to toast. "It's the same reason I bought milk at that corner store. Normalcy. A bite to eat, dancing, and we'll be invisible! No need to rush."

"You make sense, but it will be hard to...wait..." Kyle stopped, wrinkling his brow and denouncing his appreciation of her logic. "Dancing?"

"Oh, I thought you'd never ask!" Judith said, her voice taking on a false southern twang.

She pulled him by the hand towards the dance floor, giving him little time to react.

"But I can't dance!" he whined in weak resistance.

"You think, with my dad, that I went to prom knowing how to do the waltz, Kyle? No. I didn't get to go to prom. So you're *going* to dance with me. And you're *going* to like it. I'm not asking for anything more than to look stupid with me."
Her tone left no room for argument.

"Well, that will be easy if you dance like you sing," he joked.

"Dick!" she laughed, stepping into his arms.

And so they danced. They weren't terrible. They were far from perfect. They were as mediocre as the crowd, exactly as they would have been at the prom Judith never attended. When the songs were slow, they danced close. When they were fast, they shared hooked arms and stomping feet with the rest of the crowd. When they sat down to their meals, both ate with ravenous speed, their last true sustenance from Leon long since depleted. Judith looked disappointed that she didn't have to finish Kyle's meal for him.

After enjoying themselves enough to blend in, they called for the check. They paid the tab and tipped well. Kyle sipped the last of his coke and waited for Judith to come out of the bathroom. A man kicked open the front door of the bar, sending Kyle into a brief state of fear.

We were leaving in five minutes! You couldn't wait? he thought.

The man who entered was not Jonas, any of his flunkies, or the demon. He wore jeans, a cowboy hat, boots, and nothing else. He was tattooed and muscular, and he looked angry.

This time, action in the bar did cease. The man's eyes scanned the bar, his head turning back and forth like a security camera on a swivel. All eyes were on the cowboy while also avoiding his shifting gaze. When they reached Kyle, he knew he was in trouble. The cowboy smiled, hands on his hips, and began taking wide arced steps in Kyle's direction.

"Shit," the waitress said, showing up next to Kyle. The smile she had worn all night turned into a frown.

"Who is that, Cowboy Gaston?" Kyle whispered from the corner of his mouth.

"No, that's my husband Ray," the waitress said, exasperated. "He likes to start fights with the out of towers. Keep Grapevine's reputation tough. You better have a silver tongue, sir. I'd hate to feel guilty later for that tip you gave me."

"Just my luck," Kyle said.
Ray reached his table, grabbed his wife, and kissed her with possessive passion.

"Who's the city boy?" he said, breaking the embrace and sizing up Kyle with no hint of tact.

"Oh, he's just passing through with his girl, baby. He's no trouble!"

"I don't see no girl," Ray said, not bothering to confirm. He bent his head close to Kyle. "Get a good look at my wife while you was just *passin' through*, city boy?"

The sarcasm and blatant use of finger quotes stung. The fists probably hurt worse.

"Not particularly. My own girl is in the restroom. We were just leaving. No trouble needed, right?"

"So you're saying my wife ain't pretty enough to check out?" Ray spit. "Little whore your with is so much better looking than my wife, is that right?"

Judith walked up to the scene and stopped. She knew Kyle was in trouble, and knew she could do nothing to help. She stood with the rest of the bar in silence as the interaction heated.

"I'm saying that there's no reason to look at your wife as anything other than the superb waitress she has been. Pretty or otherwise. I've got my own company to keep. I'd appreciate it if you kept from calling her a whore. Sound good?" Kyle scowled. He didn't want to fight, but after all the running, he was ready to stand up for something.

Judith smiled at Kyle's defense, but knew that if he got hot headed the entire two hours of incognito would be wasted. She slid next to Kyle, taking his arm, ready to take action if necessary.

"Oh!" Ray said, turning to the bar and yelling. "This one has sass, boys! You're a smart ass, ain't you, slick?" Ray stepped to Kyle, their chests inches from touching.

"No, but I'm a coke addict three days clean whose got an ounce less patience than you're demanding. If you want experience on the effects of adrenaline in junkie withdraws, be my guest and take a swing. Cut out the mind games and meet me out back. If you don't, then shut the fuck up and buy yourself a beer, alright chief?"

Kyle held a twenty dollar bill in Ray's face, his eyes never leaving the cowboys.

Ray scowled for a moment longer before breaking. His face turned from vicious to friendly in a transformation worthy of a David Copperfield special. He grabbed the money from Kyle and wrapped an arm around his neck. Judith backed away, looking as confused as Kyle, who remained on the defensive.

"Damn, do I like this kid, Amber! You want one too?" he said, waving the bill at the waitress.

"No sweetheart. I go on break in ten. Meet me at our table, ok?"

"Sure thing, darlin'" he said, and the two beamed at each other. Discomfort became adoration. The kiss he planted on her was gentle and tender, the purpose far more innocent than it had been. Their eyes locked when he told her he loved her, running a hand through her hair. The man that let go of his half hug to kiss his wife disappeared.

Stranger Ray had been an act. He didn't wonder why Amber smiled the way he did anymore. Sure, the clientele and the small town atmosphere was always nice. But that man worshiped her, and she him. And they both knew it. She looked at him with the eyes of love where every day is the first as he walked to the bar to claim his prize.

Then she looked at Kyle with amazement.

"I'm impressed," she said, beaming.

"I am too, Kyle. Way to step up the testosterone!" Judith giggled.

"Most tourists get tough and punched in the jaw before the door he kicks in even closes. Or they get tongue tied and embarrassed out of town before they finish their meals. You must've impressed him. Sure did me!"

"I've been pushed too much not to push back, but I didn't want to fight him." Amber placed a hand gently on his forearm, looking at Kyle with a pleading gratefulness.

"Well thank God for that, Kyle. I'm just glad he won't be getting into a fight tonight. He's been in three this week. There's no way we're going to make that baby if..." Amber paused, her hand moving to her stomach, pain in her eyes. "Well, let's just say he comes home too bruised to cuddle more often than is appropriate."

"It's a power trip then. Like my father." Judith said.

"No. He's got an addiction to fighting. He says it's a drug. It makes him feel alive in a way that only loving me does, but not in the same way. He's done it since he was little, and everyone in this town knows him and respects him as a man enough not to feed his addiction. They don't want to hurt him. He respects them too much to push them into it. Tourists are the only action he gets. And he does win his fair share, but power? No. He usually wins out of tenacity and tolerance. A bloody man is an intimidating thing."

"Addicted to fighting?" Kyle asked. "I've never heard of that."

"It's a masochistic thing," Amber stated.

Her voice was shaky, as if each word determined the fate of peace in the bar. She'd never explained it out loud as Ray had once explained it to her. She wasn't sure how.

"He loves the pain. He's a glutton for punishment. It's a quirk. Pain gets him high in a way that drugs and alcohol just can't. I think he loses on purpose when he does lose, for the little extra rush. The last drop from the needle, you know? It worries me. But I love him."

That love shone in her pain filled eyes. She looked across the room at Ray, chatting with his buddies loud enough for the bar to hear. Ray caught her eye and smiled at her, raising his glass in her direction.

"If it weren't for his best friend, Randall, he'd be in a coma or dead by now. Randall always knows when enough is enough. Nobody messes with Randall."

She pointed towards Ray again, towards a man that came up to the top of Ray's head while sitting. He looked like a body builder, but his face lacked aggression. He watched Ray's antics with the same sadness as Amber, always on alert for when his services would be needed.

"Amber, if I'd have known that, I wouldn't have given him beer money."

"I'm glad you did. No other tourists here tonight. I do worry, but I can rest easy for the evening. He's gotten his fit out of the way.

Excuse me. It's my break time and we've got to try and get Ray Jr. in the oven before shark week!"

Amber walked to the back, embarrassed at how forward her words had been. Ray, noticing her walking to the back door, set down his beer and began to follow, a bray of hands clapping him on the back as he walked.

"Good night," Kyle said after her, his voice too weak to carry over the crowd noise.

"Well that's a hell of a tale," Judith said. "I do hope they get that baby. They look so in love, and maybe it will calm him, ya know?"

"Yeah," Kyle said in a distant tone.

"Well, we ready to hit the road?" she asked.

"Not yet, Judith."

Kyle looked at his watch again, the four lit words a constant reminder that three had yet to glow.

Kyle had grown into his instincts over the course of the week. As much as they wanted to add distance to the space between what followed and where they wanted to end up, there was still a purpose to the chase.

Kyle wasn't sure who number six and seven would be. He wasn't even sure who number four had been. But as Ray and Amber proceeded to their secret rendezvous, Kyle was sure he had found number five.

GLUTTONY

Gluttony feeds me

Sugar coated dreams are constant

I fast for no one

if you bring a knife to a gun fight, you'll lose

"I don't know if it's intuition or the need alleviate the woes of others, but Ray fits the mold. I mean, I don't want cause any problems, but I need to talk to him after her break is done."

Judith sat next to him in the booth they had been standing by, scooting in close.

"Not everyone we meet with a problem is going to be on your watch, Kyle. I know you've still got people to save, and every light on that watch glows because of random chance, but there has been a flow. The person who led you to me sent Ken after us, and Leon fit the mold after an entire day in his church. We've known Ray for five minutes and they make entire reality shows out of guys like him. We're cutting it close and I don't want to lo...I don't want you to fail, ya know? I enjoy your company." she smiled at him.

Kyle rubbed her thumb with his, finishing her thought in his head. He didn't want to lose her, either.

"I just have a feeling. The devil, meeting you, this crazy mission I'm on, random, like you said. There is no chance. We were meant to be here. I feel it in my..."

"Gut, I know, you've mentioned it," she said, exasperated. "Good burgers do that. If you want to do this, I'm with you. Whatever feelings in your gut are prompting this, mine are telling me to leave as fast as we can. I can feel him. He's close."

Kyle didn't ask if she meant Jonas or the demon. Both of their instincts had proven useful, but this was the first time they had clashed. If she wanted to be gone, they would leave once he got verification.

"I'll be back to you as quick as I can, ok? Then we can leave and continue down the path of illuminated confusion."

"You'd better be. You're my protector, remember? I'm going to grab another beer then. I'm still too shaken up for a proper buzz."

She gave him a quick peck on the cheek and made her way to the bar, joining in on the hoots and hollers of the regular patrons.

Ray confused Kyle. How could anybody relish pain? He'd been in pain for the better part of three years, and not an instant of it had been enjoyable. He would give anything to eliminate that pain from his heart. If that meant losing Sarah, he was ready to accept it. The pain would scab over and scar. His broken hearted hemophilia had found a cure.

Her name was Judith.

He understood the difference between physical and emotional pain. That was the reason he couldn't fathom Ray's condition. Choosing to suffer both willingly was a cry for help. It had to be. His life depended on seven of these cries being squelched.

One missed chance could mean more pain and suffering than even ole' Ray would enjoy. It was the first time Kyle had given decisive thought to having to save one of the souls his watch longed for. If they had all relied on decision alone, he'd still be wandering the alley where Lucifer left him without hope or a clue.

Judith returned with her beer, and the two sat and talked while Ray and Amber attempted consummation. They avoided the topics that had plagued them for days and relaxed. The purpose was to pass the time, but it became more about knowing the person they were sharing this strange quest with instead of their strange quest.

It was, in truth, the most pleasurable and successful date either of them had ever been on, outside of Kyle's post marriage dates with Sarah. Before he put a ring on her finger? The anxiety of trying to impress her clouded his enjoyment.

They were the couple in the back, invisible to the room. Neither noticed Amber returning to the floor with a fresh smile and a lustrous sex glow. Ray approached the bar, rambunctious as ever, not needing make excuses for where he had disappeared to.

Ray would fight, Ray would scoff, Ray would joke, but Ray didn't kiss and tell. Behind his charisma, he was a private person. An hour after Ray and Amber had escaped for their lovers frolic, Kyle stood to use the restroom.

Eying the clock as he exited the bathroom, shaking the last bit of water from his hands, he realized that an hour had passed. Kyle passed the booth where Judith sat and pointed towards the clock, then to Ray. Judith looked to the clock with a small expression of shock and pointed towards Amber, who was folding silverware into napkins across the bar.

As Judith walked towards Amber, Kyle approached Ray as he would have an old friend, hoping the gesture of buying him drink still resonated in the area of his mind where bar friends became family.

"Hey Ray," Kyle said.

"Slick!" Ray said, patting him on the back hard enough to bruise. "Thanks for the beer! This is the guy I told you about."

Ray introduced Kyle to his friends, calling him "Slick" and "Ole' Boy" and "Wee Man" even flattering Kyle by claiming he had "balls as big as a Clydesdale's."

"It's time to hang up your damn fightin' hat up for spell, Ray. I'm getting tired of driving your drunk ass to the E.R. every other night. I'm married too!"

Randall, of course.

"Oh, that's why you take me, Randy! To drool over how good your wife's ass looks in her nurse uniform. You can't deny it!" Ray fired back.

"It is a perk I am afforded by law, you masochist, but I can't do more'n look bleeding all over her!"

"What can I say? I'm O-Negative. I need to do my part, as a universal donor."

"Actually, O-Neg can cause bad reactions during transfusions due to antibodies," Kyle said.

Ray and Randall both looked at Kyle with raised eyebrows.

"I dated a hematologist in college," Kyle said with a shrug.

Ray and Randall both nodded and relaxed their faces as if Kyle had just helped them solve a difficult crossword clue.

"Well you taught me something new today, Slick, so what can I do to pay tuition?" Ray said.

"Mind if we talk outside for a minute, Ray? I have to ask you something."

"Oh, I see," Ray said, slamming down his beer glass. "Buy me drinks, get me all liquored up, then you want to take me out back?"

Ray put his hands up to his face like a boxer and started jabbing at the air in front of Kyle.

"Don't think I'm out of fight 'cus I'm a bit dizzy, boy. I'll float like a butterfly and sting like The Police!"

A roar of laughter erupted from Ray's friends.

"You wanna tussel, boy?" Ray said

"No, Ray. I just want your advice. About..." Kyle looked around for something that would buy him a few minutes. His eyes happened across Judith, laughing along to a joke some patron had told Amber. "...women. Relationships. You and Amber look so good together; I thought you could help me before we left."

Ray put his fists down and looped his fingers through his front belt loops, letting out a hearty laugh.

"Oh, your girl's a pretty cookie alright, Slick. Don't blame you for not wanting to act the fool. You want to woo her? You want her to love you like she'll never love another? You want her for always, do ya? Need ole Ray to give you girl advice, hey?" Ray said, batting his eyelashes and making kissing faces all the while.

Kyle smiled and ran a nervous hand through his hair.

"That's exactly it, Ray," he said.

"No prob, bub!"

Ray cupped his hands over his mouth and projected towards his wife.

"I know my way around an undercarriage better'n most, don't I babe?"

"Sure do, baby. Not a man better." Amber said, piling up a tray of empty glasses with Judith's help.

Ray finished his pint of beer in one chug, not spilling or leaving a drop. He put his arm around Kyle, like a father about to bestow upon his son a life lesson of grave importance.

"Be back soon, boys. Gotta school Junior here on how to please the missus!"

The group let out a round of cheers and a banging of glasses as Ray escorted Kyle to the exit door. Judith looked at Kyle as he passed with a look that said "What are you getting yourself into?"

Kyle's return look said "In case I die, you've become the best friend I've ever had. Don't let them cremate me."
By the way her face contorted into a look of false confusion, he was sure she understood.

Ray fumbled a pack of smokes out of his jeans pocket. He pulled two out, lit them, and handed one to Kyle.

"Real men smoke," he said.

Kyle took one without hesitation, still amazed out how good something that killed slowly tasted when death crept so close behind him.

"So tell Papa Ray what's on your mind," Ray said, exhaling.

"Well Ray, there's no way to say this without sounding like an insane person."

Ray bent in close, squinting into Kyle's face.

"You ain't one of them Jehovahs, are you?" he said. "'Cus I ain't buying that bullshit. No sir."

"No, I'm not trying to sell you on religion, Ray. Trust me, that's the last thing I'd try to do this week. But this does involve religion."

"What, she saving herself till marriage? Christian thing to do, Kyle. You can't disrespect that."

"No, no. This isn't about Judith, Ray. It's about you. I think I'm here to help you."

"Save me? Shoot, you see the boys in there? If there comes a day when Ray needs his ass saved, they'll sure as shit put someone underground, if need be, to do it."

He punched Kyle in the opposite shoulder as he slapped earlier with enough force to stress that he didn't need help of any sort. Least of all from Kyle's skinny frame. It took willpower not to rub the area, not that it would help if he did.

"That's just it Ray," he said "There's not a person on this earth you would need saving from. Not a single one who could hurt you permanently. It's not my place, and I'm probably going to earn myself a curb stomp, but you need help. You need to be saved from yourself. Before you get so hurt that you Amber and that little baby you're working on conceiving lose you."

Ray flicked his cigarette to the ground, stepped forward, and stood nose to nose with Kyle before Kyle could register that Ray had moved his arm. Whatever bit of friendship the twenty had bought him had tapped out. It was business time.

"That a threat, boy? You trying to tell me that little old you is gonna take me from my wife? Huh?"

"No, Ray" Kyle said with a bit more force than was helpful. "But you're a glutton for punishment! I heard them talking about the E.R. Amber looked scared when she even thought you'd fight someone tonight. I see the bruises on your ribs. When did you get them? Yesterday? The day before?"

Kyle kept the fact that he'd spoken to Amber quiet. He thought that Ray knowing he'd shared such a personal conversation with his wife would exacerbate the situation.

"They need you around, Ray. And one of these days your buddies will be too drunk, occupied, or fed up with picking you up again, to 'save your ass'. And you'll be dead or crippled and…"

Kyle's speech was interrupted by Ray's left fist connecting to his jaw, knocking him to his tail bone.

"So it's gonna be like that?" Ray said. He rubbed the knuckles of the hand he'd used to punch Kyle.

Kyle pushed himself up to all fours, trying to regain his footing.

"Pity. I thought you were one of the good guys," Ray said, delivering a kick to Kyle's chest and knocking the wind from his lungs.

Ray kneeled to Kyle's level, smacking him on the back of the head as he gasped for breath, the smacks emphasizing the periods on each sentence.

"You're one of those types that stick their noses in dog's asses. I'm surprised I didn't smell it when I walked into the bar! But oh, I smell it now!"

Smack.

"Now you don't have a breath left in you to tell me how to live my life!"

Smack.

"You're doing a great job with yours, getting your ass handed to you by a simple ole' redneck, huh Slick?"

Ray went for another smack, but Kyle had become used to the rhythm and blocked his hand, catching it underneath the crook of his arm. Ray's face lit up.

"Oh, so you are going to fight back! Good, boy! I thought I'd feel guilty for fucking you up tomorrow!"

Ray head butted Kyle so hard in the side of the head that he went black for two seconds. His hands went to his head, leaving Ray's arms free. Kyle moaned as Ray strutted back and forth in front of him, his hands on his hips.

Like a predator, he was playing with his meal.

"Ray," Kyle coughed. "I can't stress the hell I've been through today, so I say this in the hopes that you'll listen."

"I'm through fucking listening!" Ray said.

Ray threw his body into a punt that missed Kyle's head, only because he was able to duck away from it.

"Ray!" screamed Amber, running through the exit.

Judith followed close behind, gasping at what she saw. Kyle used the distraction to get to his feet.

"You stay out of this, babe," Ray said, his eyes not leaving

Kyle. "Someone needs to learn their manners, and I've got a degree in teaching people to mind their manners."

"Kyle, what..." Judith said, running to him.

He held a hand up, stopping her.

"I've got this," he said, his confidence pleading.

Ray took the opportunity to thrust a palm into Kyle's chest, knocking a sigh out of him and the two new spectators.

"Ray!" screamed Amber, running to Ray.

Judith, who wasn't going to let Kyle take a beating from the person he was trying to help, dropped her purse and ran to his side.

"I said butt out, Amber!" Ray said, shoving her out of the way.

In his rage, he underestimated the strength of his shove. Amber flew backwards and into Judith, who grabbed her before both women could fall into a heap. Judith ended up falling instead, the force of the push transferring to her, but Amber was in the most pain. Pain of the heart. Amber crossed her arms across her chest, looking at Ray as if he was a violent, offensive stranger. Contempt replaced love in her eyes.

Lost in the sea of tense emotion, a sound, like a handful of chips being thrown into the poker pile, went unheard.

Ray's features softened. He had hurt the one, potentially two, people who gave his life meaning.

"This is why I don't fight around you, baby. I take care of business outside, you take care of business inside. You don't need to see this! I don't want to ever hurt you!" Ray said, excuse after excuse drooling from his mouth.

His arguments were weak. Guilt weighed his arms to his side.

"But you do hurt me, Ray. Every single time, you hurt me."

A tear fell from her eye, and she turned into Judith, who hugged her close. Ray reached a hand towards Amber, but Kyle used the distraction to tackle Ray to the ground. He wrapped Ray's arm up and over his head, holding his wrist tight, and threw his free arm around Ray's throat. He pulled up with enough force to keep Ray still, but not to hurt him. If Ray struggled, he pulled up on the hold. The struggling ceased every time.

The Cobra Clutch, ladies and gentleman.

He had been called a fool for watching wrestling. Fake, they called it. Pretty boys in slapping ass in their underwear, they goaded. Deep down, all men felt the same about wrestling as they did about breasts. The fake stuff works just as well when done right.

And it was still real to him, dammit.

Ray was quick to lose energy from struggling. Amber and Judith watched, not saying a word. Amber didn't know, but Judith might understand that restraining Ray wasn't the goal. The shove had taken care of that. He had to make Ray listen.

Kyle loosened his grip enough to make Ray comfortable, but held on in case Ray fought back.

"Now listen to me, Ray. You don't know me, and I'm sure at this point you don't trust me as far as you can kick me. Which is five feet, if you remember. But I'm offering you my trust right now in hopes that it will penetrate your thick skull and cause you to reciprocate. We're on the run because I made a deal with the devil. No, that's not a fucking metaphor, Ray. If I don't finish what I've started, I'll burn like Joan of Arc. Am I crazy? Probably. But I need to help you. Five minutes in the same town as you is enough to realize how in love you are with her. I might be dead before weeks end, but at least I know my time limitations. All I'm asking you to do is give up this need for punishment so that your wife can live without the constant burden of waiting for the phone call that informs her you won't ever make her smile again."

"He's right, Ray. I'm afraid. Afraid that you won't be there when I wake up. Every day I worry I won't see you the next," Amber cried.

"Amber," Ray mustered.

"I loved my wife the way Amber loves you, Ray. It's taken me more than three years to recover from her death."

"Kyle, he's going to be okay," Amber said, separating from Judith and walking towards them. "Come to me, baby."

"I'm going to let you go Ray. Please don't..."

Kyle was cut off by the sound of crashing and yelling inside the bar. A very angry, very familiar voice yelled for his daughter, threatening pain if she had been hurt by one of the "scraggly fucks" at the bar.

Judith went white.

"Daddy!" she yelped under her breath.

Randall's deep voice echoed from inside the bar, demanding, not requesting, that people calm the fuck down.

Judith's hands flew to her pockets as Ray stood up, offering Kyle a dirty glare and embracing Amber.

"Shit! The keys!" Judith said.

"What? Where are they?"

"They were in my pocket! Oh, this is bad, Kyle! Molly's probably standing by the Pinto with those knives of hers, anyway! And James, with his guns! I knew this would happen! I knew this guy was a waste of time!" Judith screamed, her posture accusatory.

"Judith, we need to leave. Right this second. Maybe they'll realize we found the GPS and think we hitched, or stole a car. If we don't leave, this entire place will be held accomplice."

His eyes happened upon Ray, and he couldn't help but feel sorry for Amber. Damn the redneck if he ended up too stubborn to listen. Amber would live in constant stress. Their child would know the world's demons too early. He hoped he had gotten through, but he didn't have the time for Ray to turn another sin red.

Ray's eyes bore through Kyle.

A gunshot popped in the bar. Amber's hands flew to her mouth to muffle a scream. Kyle grabbed Judith and pulled her close.

"Take Amber and go, Ray!" Kyle said in an aggravated hush. "These are bad fucking guys, and neither Amber nor you deserve my crossfire. I hope to God your friends can handle themselves."

Kyle's eyes scanned for an escape. Any minute, an ugly Irish face would peek through the back door. Those faces would mean Game Over.

Another gunshot.

Amber buried her face into Ray's naked chest. He wrapped his arms around her, his eyes never leaving Kyle.

They stood, two men with questionable sanity and issues that stretched volumes, holding what they vowed to protect. Pride needed to be cast away before resolution could be reached.

Ray's face softened. He looked at Amber with love. Admiration. Discovery.

Dishes crashed out from the open window ten feet from where they stood.

Another gunshot.

Kyle turned so that his back was to the door, shielding Judith, his head ever on pivot, looking for an escape.

Kyle knew that it wasn't his crazy words or survival instinct that would help Ray, but the need to protect. It was the sight of him shielding a woman Kyle hardly knew, throwing pride and self-preservation to the wind to keep her from danger.

If Ray couldn't give up the sadism to protect his wife and child, Ray would turn into the bad guy. He'd lose what he loved and be the shell Kyle had become; only he'd fill the emptiness with anger. In those moments, Ray made his own sacrifice. Amber's words, Kyle's actions.

Ray would never raise a hand for any reason other than his family's protection. His days of fighting were over. This once, he had chosen to trust. Seeing the pain in Amber's eyes, he had chosen to love.

Ray would never be the reason Amber felt pain again. All it took was a little push.

An orange mist flowed from Ray. Ray's eyes shone red, blending with the orange mist in a mirage of flames. The watch let off a faint glow, as it had in the Green Rail, the church, and the alley, and the mist sucked towards Kyle's watch. The watch grew brighter and brighter before flashing orange the sin which had been rectified.

GLUTTONY

The orange faded into the familiar red glow as Ray's eyes cleared. Ray found the illumination interesting, but blamed it on drink. Kyle found it rewarding, and blamed it on the same.

The fifth check mark on his list had been tallied.

Kyle smiled. He had been right.

Another gunshot wiped the satisfaction from his face.

"Come with us," Ray said.

He grabbed Amber's hand and began leading her away from the back door.

"My truck is back this way. I don't park it in the lot."

Kyle and Judith followed, letting themselves be led. The red watch face was all the proof required to ignite their trust. Within thirty seconds, Ray's blue truck was in sight.

Within two minutes, the truck, with darkened lights, made its way onto a back road and away from the sound of screams and gunshots.

Three minutes later, an angry Irish father kicked in the back door, searching for his daughter and Kyle, furious that he'd had to use gunfire to make his point despite his change of heart.

Four minutes later, Jonas' eyes settled on something familiar on the ground. He picked up the car keys that had fallen out of Judith's pocket and ran his fingers over the keys with sad longing. He turned and re-entered the back door of the bar.

Four and a half minutes after Ray had thrown his old life away, bringing Kyle one step closer to salvation, a demon blew the front door of the bar off of the hinges, killing three people in the process.

Anybody who had thought a few raised voices and intimidation bullets shot into the ceiling were cause for a panic were in for a treat.

Absolute Horror smelled his name on every cringing, crouching patron left in French's combination rest stop, and his stomach screamed for sustenance.

Their fear concentrated sweat would slake his thirst, but the smell of blood bit his nostrils, weakening him with the overwhelming scent of his main course.

God help anybody who stood between him and his meal.

Demons liked to play with their food.

CHAPTER 34

the enemy of my enemy is my dinner

It took fifteen minutes. The only thing left in the bar that didn't resemble the aftermath of a tornado was a single pool table. Absolute Horror walked around the tattered stress reliever, lining up the shots and contemplating rather or not to hit a solid or a stripe.

Not like anybody else was playing. It wasn't a game of one on one or cut throat, where the possibility of his losing hung in the balance until the last ball sunk. The entire table was his. He could sink what he wanted, when he wanted, however irregular the order. Much like this little game he was playing with Kyle, he held the only cue that mattered. Kyle's was as withered as that shriveled pair of baby's balls that somehow kept him a few miles down the road. No matter. He could bide his time and enjoy a relaxing game of solo-pool.

He wanted to let his dinner settle, lest he spoil his dessert.

He lined the cue pool up to hit the six-ball. Time stood still. His breathing ceased. He pulled the cue stick back and forth in crude pantomime. Just before the stick made final contact, one of the gagged men whimpered and struggled. There was no real strength in the effort, but the suddenness of the sound broke Horror's concentration.

The six-ball missed the corner pocket by a fraction of an inch, bouncing off the nipple and smacking idly into the nine-ball. Horror stood up to his full height, two feet taller than Wilkins had been, though to the gagged few it might as well have been twenty. Gripping the handle of the pool cue in one large paw, he whipped his arm sideways with frightening speed, cracking the thin end into the side of Ian's face.

Ian's head whipped sideways in one violent snap, his chin slumping to his chest with the limp groove of a bobble-head. The blood that trickled from the fresh wound would have looked gruesome had the entire bar not already been painted with spatter-o-patron.

Horror turned around with a small sigh and flicked the air with his finger, sending the six-ball into the intended pocket.

"I hate to cheat when it's unnecessary, you little ginger fuck. You'll spend eternity sitting on splintered pool cues for that."
Horror surveyed the room, calming himself for another shot. Five unlucky people were tied to chairs. Two of them were dead. Ian would be soon after the crack shot he had received. Raising his gaze from the

bound, the real horror sprawled the room like a McFarlane landscape.

Thirty people in all. Those who escaped, the inhabitants of Grapevine who would later clean up the slaughter, were lucky in that they would be free of anguish for the evening. Those who were stupid enough to try to fend off the big bad boogie man had been ripped to pieces in a matter of minutes. Blood dripped from most of the bar's surfaces, resembling Carrie's worst nightmare.

PETA would be proud. Not a single pig had been harmed, depending on how one defined the word. Randal, the big bastard, had been a pig in his own way. He was the first to pull a gun. For his troubles, he had been crucified to the jukebox with pool cues, his throat slit with a broken Johnny Cash record. Where his heart used to be was an empty cavity.

Randal, bless his heart, had been a meat eater.

Horror tossed the broken pool cue to the side and walked towards the rack to grab another.

Molly struggled in her chair, fire burning in her eyes. A woman's scorn grew exponentially when that woman was a sister. Horror thought it a pity that he'd have to kill her soon. She had such fight in her! Such pure loathing and evil! She would make the devil's right hand happy; brandishing her knives and using them against the pitiful pious. For now she was tied to a chair like her brother. Like the stranger. Like her enemy. Like her lover.

Horror turned, chalking the new pool cue as he leaned against the wall. The way his wings rested made it look like he was resting on the air. Jonas was sure the illusion was purposeful, just as he was sure it didn't have to be an illusion. Jonas' eyes stayed down. Any escape plan would be as transparent on his face as the glee of a child getting a Christmas puppy. Surrounded by booze and not a drop of liquor to help with his poker face. If the next pool cue touched his head, they would have no chance at all. His obsession, leading to his poorly executed heroism, tied the knots around their wrists. Whatever the outcome, it would be his burden to shoulder.

Because Kyle had been right. If James' red eyes had hinted at that fact, this red horned demon proved it. For all the insanity, the thievery, the kidnapping Jonas had condemned him for, he was guilty of nothing.

Jonas was glad Judith was with Kyle, wherever they were. He seemed to have a knack for evading the bad guy. Her blood was absent from the walls.

"Only because I wanted you first, dear Jonas! Are you so naive as to think I'd let you try to negate the work I've put in? Do you know the glory his head will bring me when I lay it at the feet of my master?"

Jonas' lifted, his eyes meeting the demon's, who leaned against the pool table and twirling the pool cue. Though his mouth remained unbound, unlike the vocal Molly's, he was speechless.
There was no hope, after all.

"Oh don't look surprised! The thoughts of scum like you are easy to hear. Before it was a look in their eyes. The look you're afraid would give something away if you could think of a plan! Or that little twitch that couples a lie in an interrogation room. The one that pushes you from miniscule doubt to torture, if the truth would spill. Now, your every lie, desire, and fear are broadcast on high definition radio, Jonas. To cure what little hope you have, I give you this pill."

Horror walked, or glided for all Jonas could tell, to his chair. He leaned down to Jonas' level, putting his face inches from Jonas'. The burn Jonas felt was akin to changing a freshly burned out light bulb after forgetting it had just been on for half the day.

Sweat dripped.

Jonas was afraid. He tried to stay calm, even as he smelled rancid kill breathing out from between the demon's lips. It smelled like decayed flesh. Be it chicken or human, he wasn't sure. If it tasted the same, as cannibals attest, shouldn't it smell so? If his throat hadn't been closed by fear, he was sure the smell would bring up what little his stomach contained.

"You won't leave this place, Jonas. You will die here. You aren't like the rest of the worthless toss away trash in this room. You deserve a death so much more grand than theirs! To go out like the criminal you are!"

Horror stood back up, turning his back to Jonas and walking back to the pool table to shoot.

"But not without me taking what I can from you first, Jonas. No, you won't die afraid this night. You'll die terrified. You'll die in desperation. You'll die knowing that everything that happens to your lover, your friends, and your daughter was because of you! You and your greed! When you bow at the feet of Satan, your tears will be so fresh!"

Not even the loud crack of the pool balls could snap Jonas from where his thoughts wandered.

His fault? Kyle may not have been a liar, but his presence had set everything in motion! Whoever had begun this game was at fault. He wanted the safety of his daughter, and though guilt was a plague he had long learned to live with, he was sure of his innocence against these accusations.

The demon stopped mid shot, his booming voice rattling the broken glass on the floor as his laugh billowed out.

"Innocent? Innocent?! Your innocence died the day you took up your uncle's mantle peddling wares, weapons, and world altering chemicals to low lifes the real mob wouldn't give credit to. Your wife died with the burden of that guilt on her heart, and your daughter has been tortured by your guilty paranoia since she's been old enough to coo. You think your slate is clean in this matter? That's what makes such sweet justice of your inevitable sacrifice. Kyle may have saved your daughter, Jonas, but it's because of you that she needed saving in the first place."

"You're a fuckin' liar! I would never bring such hell on my little girl!" Jonas spat, his silence broken by fury.

"Locking her up like a prisoner, forcing her to escape to live? Crippling a boyfriend because you feared she'd be happy and leave said prison forever? Forcing her to do your biddings against her will? Turning her into what amounts to a common whore to feel any semblance of love or closeness?"

"You don't know a thing. You don't..." but the fight in his voice gave way to sadness.

He had done those things to protect her! That bastard kid would have ruined her life. Would have left her broken on the street, like a common street rat. Happiness didn't buy clothes and shelter. It didn't feed a belly! He wanted her to run the family business, not scorn it! There was honest work in thievery, so long as the thieves got the shaft end. If she had seen it, she could have loved it. She could have had gone so much farther than Jonas with her brains and beauty. The world was at her very feet, and she ran from it every chance she got. It was her destiny! He wasn't a bad man for being a stern parent, for being overprotective, for loving her too much. But Jonas refused to take the blame because Judith wouldn't...wouldn't...

"Choose the life you wanted for her? The destiny was yours Jonas. Not hers. You held her back until she was broken. Not on the street like a rat, but smothered by blankets and weighed down by feasts that couldn't satiate her. You stole the only thing she ever wanted. Her freedom. Kyle will meet his maker, as you will yours, but he's done nothing but given her that choice. He didn't kidnap her, as you well know. She ran with him, to escape you. Because something greater called her. Because he saved her, as pitiful as that luck stroke was. Your friend James stabbed your trust through the heart to put the fire of fear and anger under your ass. You were ignorant enough in your desperation to miss that until there was nothing you could do but forgive him. He wanted power! A coup de grâce to rid himself of his own smothering blanket! To conquer the empire of worms you'd built for him. Amazing what trust offing a few dead beats can earn a sly cat like our James, no? And because he finds his own fear based salvation, you deny your own rightful instincts and let him be saved. By forgiving him! I've got to tell you, champ, it's fucking pathetic."

The demon finished shooting the last ball in as Jonas contemplated these words, as if acting out the final blow he had dealt him. He'd learned that when a man learned the outcome, the lies became pointless. Of course it was all true.

Knowing he had played a part in doing something good gave Jonas a boost of confidence. The confidence to forgive himself. The confidence to apologize.

The confidence to let himself be saved.

Horror put down the cue and walked towards him, smiling all the while.

"You know, men like you are why things like me go bump in the night. This little quest of his? You're one of the vessels he was supposed to turn from the wicked path. Thankfully he's spent the entire time running from you! I don't care how evil and black your heart is, or how you long for one last hug from your little girl. Without you, his quest is futile. His blood will be the sweetest when I know his soul is destined for my master!"

The demon could not hear the words Jonas was mumbling over his obnoxious laughter. Didn't even know he was talking until he looked down and saw his lips.

"What are you saying?"

Jonas kept mumbling, eyes vacant. The demon took three large strides towards him and lifted him towards his face. Jonas stopped for the briefest of moments to offer a smirk of his own.

"...but deliver us from evil," Jonas finished.

A yellow mist flowed from Jonas' every pore, much stronger than the mist of salvation let off by any of the others. It surrounded him and his captive family like a swarm of bees. Horror swatted at the mist, as if to catch it, and pulled his hands back in shock.

It had hurt.

In that moment, Horror realized he could feel pain, after all.

Horror's eyes grew dark as he sensed the repentance in Jonas. In knowing that he had the smallest fraction of his life left, the demon had made the mistake of gloating his wrong doings to make him suffer. Too long for death. To realize the evils he would be tortured for. That arrogant chiding made Jonas realize that any sin a demon laughed at was one worth apologizing for. With his last breath, even as he admitted to himself his true stake of the blame, he asked forgiveness.

Not from his victims. Not from this demon. Not from God, himself.

"I'm so sorry, Judith. I give my life for you. I love..." Jonas said, his eyes glowing a red that rivaled Horror's own as the yellow mist flowed, with haste, out of a broken window.

The demon snapped the old man's neck with a flick of the wrist before his final word could fall from his lips, but the wind caught in his throat finished the sentence for him in a macabre death rattle of repentance.

"...you," Jonas said, his final words hanging in the air as thick as the mist that had dissipated.

There was no booming laughter or satisfaction in the kill. Horror knew that he had been blocked from Jonas' thoughts because they had been pure. They had saved him. Horror blamed himself for pushing Jonas into salvation.

He wasn't what you would call a "happy camper".

Screams from his gut shattered the remaining windows. Fire billowed from red finger tips to extinguish the mistake. Molly, quiet and still for a number of minutes, shed a single tear and closed her eyes. She would not watch the walls collapse around her. She would not be blinded by the splinters or ash. She would imagine the faces of those she loved. She would embrace the warmth as if it were the closeness of a lover. She would block out the hellish screams with her childhood memories of Irish springs. She would let the fire take her to where her brother and lover would meet her. Far from the pain, and how it hurt now. Far from the...

Her eyes snapped open. The tape was ripped from her mouth.

"What are you doing?" Molly asked, her voice flowing with rage.

"You think I'll let you die that easily, you little cunt? No. You'll live until I want you to die, and not a heartbeat sooner. You're my trump card, you angry little beast. Since Mr. Chivalry decided to repent in his final minutes, you will serve me as I serve my master, or live forever in limbo. Cold and alone. I'll warn you now that forever can be a mighty long time, lass."

"You can't do this, you fucking bastard!" she wailed, beating on his chest, desperate for a knife and knowing it would do no damn lick of good if she had one.

Horror backhanded her across the face. The sound of one hand clapping a cheek was lost amongst the falling debris and screaming flames, but she was out before her head could turn. He slung her over his shoulder and looked down at the dead man with a snarl, knowing one of those lights on that little antique must be glowing.

"Wish you would have just played along, darlin'. Too bad for you. That'll smart!"

It was time to end the game.

Time for revelation.

Time for his just desserts.

The demon pushed himself off of the ground and through the ceiling, taking flight in the direction he was sure they'd go. Which meant he was traveling in the exact direction they were going. Weak, yes. But he couldn't blame Kyle for being predictable.

Absolute Horror had been predicting his victory for days. The human who guaranteed that victory rested on his shoulder. He had made a promise to himself and his master, and he was dead set on making an honest creature of himself.

still a better love story than _ _ _ _ _ _ _ _

The troupe settled into the truck after a quick fill-up at a private gas pump. They ate more than their fill, and the itis hit them both hard. Judith sat in his lap, head dug into his shoulder and legs curled up into his chest. He was happy to let somebody else drive for a while.

Judith's closeness was pleasant, despite her heels digging into his ribs. She was asleep before the engine started. Amber sat in the middle seat, her head against Ray's shoulder, letting off little snores of her own. Ray and Kyle caught each other's eye and smiled, a transaction often denied to even the best of friends. Not twenty minutes earlier, they had been close to obscene violence, and now they were smiling at the angelic faces of the women they loved as they slept.

Kyle was sure he would not rest, but he would relax. Ray drove on, oblivious to Kyle's look of wonder, which he would have found amusing given the circumstances.

Kyle tried to make out the shape of Judith's face beyond smooth of her forehead and the wisps of her hair. Her nose, perfect and straight, glistened in the low light. The vague outline of her lips spoke to him without moving.

Love? Who was he to fall in love with a stranger before the week was out? Hadn't finding Sarah been the whole reason behind this mission? To succeed as best he could for the chance to live beside her in eternity? The best gift the devil could have given him was to break the chains that had held him for so long. To mend his heart and make him whole.

Kyle had accomplished that very thing. No drugs. No cab driving. No soulless existence. The adventure was stressful, but Ken had been right. Kyle was happy it had happened. It brought out a side of Kyle he long thought retired in the mausoleum with memories of Sarah. Purpose had been thrust upon him. Responsibility choked his every thought. He felt no bondage, because the old habits that kept him down and set his soul to misery disappeared the second he saw her.

Judith.

He admitted the attraction to himself. He even admitted that reuniting with Sarah was little more than a prize dangled from a string he would never reach.

But love? What kind of asshole fell in love with so little time to contemplate what it meant? Extreme circumstances brought people together with a passion that years of closeness never could, but love? He had known love once. Unparalleled, unstoppable love.

The love he felt for Judith (though he dissected it, he would not deny it) evoked a different facet of the emotion. Kyle loved Sarah because of how she made him feel. How she accepted his antics with a smile, and one upped them more often than not. Her dedication. Her love for life. She was his world. He worked hard for her love, and winning it had been better than any Olympic gold medal or collegiate prize.

Kyle had not done one iota of work to love Judith. It hit him with the stealth of a head shot. They hadn't spent time courting or discussing their commonalities and dreams with each other. They fit, the good and the bad parts, in a way that decades with the wrong person could never duplicate. They were strangers, but that did not mean he didn't know her. Telling himself otherwise was a lie.

Kyle had done her more selfless good for her than anybody had ever done by need or force, including her father. The strong willed person she had been when they met was part of who she was. Even on that first night, as he listened to Jonas', and then Judith's side of her story, he knew there was someone else within her. Someone who watched Guys and Dolls alone, wishing for a song and dance partner.

She wanted someone to love her. Someone to take care of her in the same way she would take care of them. She would give the world to the man who would return the favor. Kyle had been that man to her since the moment they met without even realizing it.

They knew each other on a more intimate level than him and Sarah ever had. Though he loved Sarah, and always would, their complicated relationship had been multi-tiered. Built through years of labor and sacrifice, as defined by the status quo.

With Judith, the house had been built. The fire burned. The furniture, pristine and lacking plastic wrap to keep it clean, stood waiting. Judith just wanted someone to share that house with.

The part of her that longed for such had woken up when Kyle had made his promise to her. The promise had introduced Kyle to the true Judith. His first impression of her, solidified in that moment, had started a knocking in the back of his mind. The part of him that was able to be that man had been harder to wake up, but he could now hear the knocking loud enough to know it was impatient for a response.

Was it fair of him to claim that first impressions were everything while denying the prospect of love at first sight?

The sleep deprived thoughts, more truthful than any conjured by insight and rest, processed into two thoughts. Those two thoughts summed into one truth.

Kyle loved Judith.

Judith loved him back.

The end game of the mission lost meaning with that understanding. Sarah, God rest her soul, was in a better place. Away from this plane of depression. Judith was here. She needed Kyle. He had told himself that he would die for her, but he had reached the point where he would kill to be with her. The weight of his world was held up not by the chains of depression, his hearts throngs of pain, or the watch strapped to his wrist. The summation of his happiness no longer rested on succeeding.

Instead, it rested in his arms, breathing a soundless wind. Judith's love, real and alive, was what mattered. It held more importance than the will of God, himself.

Kyle would fight on as a testament to the person his deal with Lucifer had made him. He would succeed as a testament to Judith.

In that moment, the option of failure disappeared.

Judith was the only option that mattered; the only option that existed.

Not sixty seconds had lapsed since Ray had put them back on the road. Kyle's sudden epiphany had taken what strength remained and released it through his pores. He wrapped his arms around Judith and he kissed her exposed forehead.

"Maybe I'll have the balls to say this to you when you're awake, if I don't tumble into Hell's pit with the grace of Lear's fool, but I love you Judith." Kyle whispered into her ear, needing to say it out loud before it devoured him. "I think that this has all been for you. I am forever your servant. I will die before I let anything hurt..."

Kyle's words were cut off with a yawn, his yawn with sudden slumber. The sun rose over the horizon, painting the sky with purples and pinks, beauty amidst the chaos. Ray's own arm wrapped around the love of his life, his free hand on the steering wheel, his eyes focused and clear for the first time in his life.

Nobody in the car could see the moisture welling in Judith's closed eyes, the corners of her mouth lifting into a smile. Their connection could not be replicated with centuries of dating and conversation, but he had plenty to learn about her quirks.

How to tell when she was truly asleep, or still on the verge of drifting off, for example.

Kyle would have forever to learn them, so long as he wanted it.

"I love you, too..." Judith whispered, digging her head closer into his chest before sleep took her.

On the fourth day, true love was realized.

every redneck has a bunker

After enough time had passed to render the landscape unrecognizable, Kyle woke up. His neck was sore, his back stiff, but his mind had cleared; he was refreshed. The sun, bright and high in the sky, set the travel time at ten hours or so. Judith slept in his arms, her face buried into his neck. Night drool dried on his clavicle.

Each slumbering exhale Judith let out sent shivers through his body. *Every* part of his body. Familiar with the unpredictable nature of man's morning visitor, he conjured up horrible thoughts from the past few days to quell his own little demon.

"Jesus, Kyle, you'd think that impending doom would be the last thing to bring Mr. Happy to life," he muttered, shifting.
The female laughter from the driver's seat caught him off guard.

Kyle looked over to see Ray fast asleep on Amber's shoulder. Blood rushed to his face, embarrassed at muttering a private comment out loud without confirming his surroundings. He thought Ray was still driving.

"Err..." Kyle stammered.

"Don't worry. If I had someone as lovely as her in my lap, the fate of the world would not be as pressing an issue either!"

"I can't believe you just..."

"I'm married, Kyle. Not invalid. I'm not stupid, either. I saw the way she looked at you when we both thought Ray would be deep frying you in catfish fry and serving you at the next town picnic. I saw the way you looked at her in the booth. Love can't fool the loved."

Kyle smiled, remembering the thoughts he'd had before sleep took him.

"I don't know what's wrong with me. I mean, can love be so quick? I have loved before, the kind that breaks you when it ends. Luck brought me to Sarah, and fate brought me to Judith. It sure wasn't swagger. I don't know shit about women," Kyle said.
Kyle had been through this in his own head, but was hoping for female affirmation. He had realized young that he would never understand women, which lent to his charm. But he always listened for the glimmer of a hint when a female offered it, even if she regurgitated his own inner-advice. He had fallen asleep plagued by questions, and getting them off of his chest was cathartic.

"Love isn't about the constant search and the long winded chase to the altar. Maybe folks like to draw those things out, knowing that if they don't they'll be back at the starting line before the second kiss. But the love I've seen work best? Cupid hit's you hard in the chest and breaks the end off of the arrow, and that kind of spell never fades. Ray swept me off in a matter of minutes. Within months he was my husband. Fools rush in when blinded by ignorance. Marrying to spite parents or to save a relationship is why we have teen moms. But sometimes you just know. When that uncontrolled voice in your head doesn't ask questions and you realize you're talking to yourself, you know. It's a rare occasion when you find that."

"When I used to hear people say that love was enough, I called bullshit. When Sarah died, and I realized how much I depended on her, I understood. Twice in one lifetime? I'm not that lucky. Judith has gotten what she always wanted. Her freedom from the iron grip of her father. Far be it from me to confess my unyielding affections and trap her again. Not when the next two days are filled with uncertainty. What do they say about birds?"

"Corny as the love at first sight thing may be, Kyle, at least I've seen it in action. In real relationships, both birds are always free. They just can't get enough of each other to exercise that freedom."

"So I have to afflict Judith with Stockholm syndrome."

"No, you silly ass. Just be yourself. I think after a mess like what's happened, you both know what the other brings to the equation. Did you ever think that maybe you are Judith's lucky find?"

"Great much I bring to the equation, with the looming threat of oblivion hanging over my head."

Kyle had to blush a second time as Judith's hand reached up and cupped the side of his face. Kyle looked at her, hating that his mouth was working while his brain was still waking up, his eyes wide.

"And I would follow you there in a heartbeat, my bumbling knight. It was you who gave me freedom when you brought me along, and I could have flown away if I wanted to. But you have my wings hidden somewhere tricky, because I don't have the ability or will to fly away from you."

"What are you..."

Judith stopped him with a kiss. Not an innocent kiss, or a kiss in want of something. A kiss of passion. Raw emotion. In the chaos, Kyle lost himself in that kiss. He was too afraid to close his eyes in case he was dreaming. When Judith pulled back from the kiss and opened her own eyes, Kyle's eyes, still wide in surprise, threw her into giggling fits. Kyle half-smiled. Judith smacked him lightly in the face.

"Hey! What was that for?"

"Well, one, to get that stupid look off of your face. I'm not a creature made entirely of breasts. And two," she kissed his lips again. "For making me fall for your goofy ass."

"I did nothing of the sort! You fell of your own volition."

"The unsure, charming, and noble ways you've protected me helped, my bumbling knight."

"With what you've been through, I never would have thought of you as someone who needed protection. At least not when I met you," Kyle admitted.

"You don't know shit about women, do you, Kyle?"

Kyle looked over at Amber and said, "See? See?"

"I hope you made the most out of that kiss. We're here!" Amber said.

Kyle and Judith scanned the barren scenery as they amber drove up a long dirt driveway and parked near a wind worn barn. Red paint chips decorated the base of the barn them. They hadn't been sure where they had been heading, but where they ended up was as practical as a mosh pit. Amber eased their apprehension.

"It's an underground storm shelter and bunker that Ray's granddad built during the nuke threat. Paranoid schizophrenic who brewed his own beer and turned his piss into water. Apocalypse Preparation Specialist, he calls it. That bunker goes down at least a hundred feet. He was an admiral and had connections. The inside of the barn has steel supports and walls and all that fancy blast shelter stuff. The barn facade is so nobody tries to vandalize or mess with it. People around here are closed minded about things that look governmental and scientific and whatnot."

Kyle looked around, seeing desert and shrubbery. They were a long way from the Amber and Ray's quaint home town.

"People around here?"

"The alien freaks, Kyle. The people that come around here searching for pieces of metal with inscriptions, and football shaped skeletons to make their millions and win the Pulitzer. Crazies will do anything to uncover a conspiracy. To them, every discarded toenail clipping is extraterrestrial."

"What good will a bunker do us?" Judith asked.

"What *bad* would a bunker do you?" Amber replied.

"I can't argue with that," Judith said after consideration.

Kyle looked at his watch again. The only word on the watch not illuminated was Wrath. Another ghost deed had cured a sin. Greed was alight. If Amber or Ray had seen the watch glow, they said nothing.

"The locals freak me out as much as whoever might be following us. For whatever good it will do, planning out the next step with blast doors protecting us doesn't sound like a bad idea," Amber said while trying to wake Ray. "You two go inside. There's tons of stuff in there. Dried out food, weapons, supplies, entertainment, and furniture. Ray and I don't need much, but since his granddad wanted to watch the world burn in luxury, we don't want for much either. We never thought we'd visit this old bunker. It's good that we didn't have to wait for a war to use it."

"I wish that was the truth," Kyle whispered.

"Pardon? You say something Kyle?" Amber asked.

"I said I'll try to keep the world from burning around us while we're inside, Amber." Kyle said with a smirk.

"Well, we won't be here to see it. Me and Ray decided to go on up to his grandma's house while you figure things out. It's a half an hour drive, and we always have to see her when we're up this way. Talk about Ray's granddad and such. I have to be honest, Kyle. I don't want to be around when that thing arrives."

Kyle remembered telling the two a condensed version of their adventure on the way to get gas. Even short and lacking in detail, he was able to get the point across that they were in deep shit.

"I don't blame you," said Judith. "You have a kid to worry about, as well as Ray. He's done enough fighting for a lifetime. You two go appreciate each other. I've never seen two strangers so willing to go so far out of their way to help someone. And I've never seen a couple more in love."

"Oh I've seen close, a time or two," Amber said, offering a wink.

It was Judith's turn to blush.

Amber gave up trying to wake her husband.

"Now get in there quick so you don't get burned. The desert sun is a bastard. His grandma's number is by the phone, as well as our cell, if you need us. Just give us time to celebrate life, if you catch my drift. His grandma shouldn't be home another hour, and much like Kyle here, the prospect of hell fire has my loins itchin'.'"

"What?" said Judith, looking at Kyle with a raised eyebrow.

"Ho-ho, a joke, my dear!" Kyle shot Amber a disapproving look. She winked again.

Kyle opened the door and helped Judith to turn on his lap and exit the truck. He moaned with the movement and, realizing what he had done, altered the moan into a sound of pain rather than pleasure.

It had been both.

Kyle grimaced and grabbed his knee with exaggerated pain as Judith looked back at him. He thought the charade worked well enough. He didn't see awkward discomfort on her face, anyway. Kyle hopped into the dirt and turned to close the door.

"More than you both will ever know, I thank you," Kyle said, shaking Amber's hand in one gentle movement.

"No need. In the same way you were chosen, it's nice to think that maybe God had a bigger part in us meeting than we thought was possible. It's nice to have positive words for the old guy, no? Have faith, Kyle. He must have faith in you. You'll need these, by the way," she said, tossing him a pair of keys.

"I only hope I live up to the expectations. I fucking hate pressure. Thanks again. God speed and all that noise."

Kyle closed the door with care, so as not to wake Ray, and walked to where Judith stood waiting for him. He reached out and grabbed her hand, interlacing his fingers in hers. If this was going to be the last couple days of existence before eternal pain and damnation, he'd be a fool to not show her the love he felt. To accept the love she returned. Something special had formed. There was no desire in him to push her away until the fleeting moments of his story ceased.

Some protagonist he made.

At the door, Kyle pushed the keys into the lock. Judith, in an amazing show of strength, turned him around and pushed him against the door. She pressed herself into him, and he felt every inch of her. Her breasts caressed his chest, her nipples tearing at her shirt like puppies yelping for freedom at the pet store. Somebody was paying attention to them and they were damn sure going to make a good show of it. She wrapped one hand around the back of his neck, bringing his mouth to hers.

The kiss turned fervent. Kyle began moving his own hands across her back with frantic need. It was as if he was a virgin who had memorized the Joy of Sex as a preparatory measure. It felt new and right. Judith moved her mouth away and looked at Kyle with a strange intensity. Her eyebrows furrowed, but the eyes themselves were full of adoration.

"Did you mean it?" she asked him. One hand moved to his chest, the other reached behind him.

"Mean what?" Kyle said, lacking eloquence as men were wont to in times of passion.
He felt like a willing rabbit being chased by a sexy greyhound. If she wanted to eat him, it wouldn't be a long race.

"What you said last night. About being my servant. About dancing into hell like a fool. About loving me."

Kyle looked down at her, her hands moving ever closer to their destinations of his belt and the key. He knew the outcomes.

If he said no, or offered a protracted excuse laced with half-truths to protect his memory of his wife, she would kiss him once more. Her hand would move away from his belt, and she would push open the door with a click of the key. Judith would stay beside him as promised, and they would share a bond forever because of the endured hells. But she would never forgive him his transgression. Lying to her when she had heard the intensity in his voice while he thought she slept. He had let go of the past in every way but the one that mattered. This was a pivotal moment and the true goal of their adventure. Not to change the world, or even to save it, but to do both for himself. To let his wounds heal and be happy.

There were many doors in front of him, each representing an equally unsure future. The only door that mattered resulted in Judith wrapping herself around him; the only future that mattered was one with her in it. The door that would give himself to this women with love and a promise and the possibility of a post coital cuddle.

Once Judith had become an option, choice ceased to exist.

"I meant every word of it," he said to her. "Until the day I die, Judith, I am yours."

Judith smiled and unlocked the door while her other hand unhooked Kyle's belt.

"In case that day is today..."

Instead of their skin, restraint burned up in the desert sun. Judith was on him again, kissing him. Loving him. Leaving him no chance. The locking mechanism of the door barely clicked before clothes were flying to the ground.

Then, they were on the ground.

Then, Kyle was inside of her.

Never had she felt so perfect. He fit her in such a way that any slight twitch or penetration hit her in the spot that left her light headed and face melted. She arched her back into each thrust, kissing him as much as her moans would allow him.

Romantic as the moment was, it was primal. Kyle could think in small, uncoordinated phrasing that repeated the same dirty thought in his head; that he had never felt anything so moist, least of all in the middle of a desert. Those thoughts had a tendency to creep up when Kyle let his little brain take charge.

Each kiss tightened his bond to her. They thrust with little miscalculation. Judith came first, followed soon after by Kyle, both crying out and collapsing onto the floor.

Six minutes was all it took. Six minutes of passionate culmination. Six minutes of ecstasy.

Six minutes of Heaven.

They panted. They kissed. Judith lit them both a cigarette from her purse.

As Kyle had foreseen, they held each other as they smoked. The moment could have been their perfect purgatory, as far as the pair were concerned, and they would choose it over heaven with little consideration

Thoughts of the task at hand had been forgotten since the front door had closed behind them. So lost in the throes of need, neither one felt the fear that had led them into their naked embrace. Judith would not figure out if it was love, blindness, or over confidence in the many hours she would soon spend looking for the answer.

Fear was far from a missing person on a milk carton. It was a guest, having gone to the toilet for relief during a lull in the entertainment. As Judith and Kyle lay in the glow of their love, the loud knocking at the door ensured that fear had shaken twice and flushed.

Their nicotine riddled embrace lasted for a full minute until the explosive sound of fear's re-emergence marked the end of their seventh minute in heaven.

KNOCK.

The two jumped to their feet, the joy of the moment lost in a deluge of frantic panic. Both scrounged for clothes, but realized that their nakedness would be the least of their worries before long. The door shuddered from the force behind the knock. It wouldn't take many more for the big bad wolf to let himself in.

Kyle dug through Judith's purse for the can of high grade O.C. spray. It wasn't a gun, but it would due for a distraction. How Kyle wished he had found the guns hidden in the cavernous warehouse first! Though he doubted either of them would have been safe with a weapon close by, as the damage to the room could attest.

They had broken a coffee table, and two chairs.

KNOCK.

Kyle positioned himself in front of Judith, knowing that this time she might not be able to fight whatever came through the door. His heart would never forgive him should evil trespass into her soul. Not so soon after a moment so perfect! His story would not be a tragedy, ending with the loss of this love.

KNOCK.

Each knock drove the fact that no recent event would compare to what was about to happen home. It had been preparation. The watch, brighter than ever, had grown heavy and physically weighed his arm down. The weight came not from those six that lit the dark warehouse with red ambiance, but by the one that had yet to glow. The one that had yet to set him free.

The unrequited sin. Wrath.

Who or whatever wrath was, each knock brought him closer to his final puzzle piece.

KNOCK.

The one thing separating him from freedom. From completing his mission. Against the odds, and not without his fair share of fumbles, the clock was ticking. Either wrath would illuminate and break the chains of Lucifer's eternal bondage, or wrath would end luminescent comforts forever.

KNOCK.

Kyle stood tall and naked and waited. He was through running from his destiny. He had to quit using the unexpected nature of it as an excuse, because fate and destiny were always unexpected. To predict either was to play God, or to be God.

He'd read enough of the bible to know what the latter did to the former.

Judith wrapped her arms around Kyle's waist. His back moistened with her tears. He loved her. He would protect her. He had made a fucking promise! He could not forget that she loved him, too.

A familiar voice came through the thick wall. Barely audible, but recognizable.

"God dammit, Judith, it's your father! If you don't let me in, that demon is going to tear Molly and me new assholes with a fucking pitchfork!"

Kyle and Judith exchanged looks of disbelief. The knocking grew more and more frantic as they dressed with whatever clothes were closest.

"I'm not mad at you, dear Judy. You needed your freedom and after what I've seen these few days, I give it to you with blessing! And Kyle, you crazy fucker, I don't care that you kidnapped my daughter as long as she's happy. But I swear to God if you don't..."

Kyle unlatched the door. The demon lived. Even they had been running from Jonas longer than the demon, those words let Kyle know that Jonas had been running from something, too. He had to help. It was his mission.

Jonas fit the role of Wrath. If he could save him before the demon arrived? Would it be finished?

Would he win?

The look on Jonas' face matched the tenor of his voice. Blood covered his suit and face. Molly stood beside him, hands at her side, one of them clutching a gun.

Judith thought that odd. Molly never used a gun.

Kyle opened the door quick, rushing the two in as if the weather outside were frigid instead of blistering. Molly moved like a robot, slow and methodical. Jonas hustled her along with quick steps and pushes. Kyle gave the horizon a glance before closing the door again, the auto lock clicking.

Jonas and Judith shared a look. One of seething hate. One of hearts broken, mended, and broken again. One of complete understanding.

Jonas opened his arms for her, every apology he'd never spoken reaching out to her through the layers of blood and bad memories, and the two embraced. She cried, he whimpered, and Kyle marveled. Molly just stared ahead in silence.

"I thought I'd lost you forever, my dear," Jonas said, pulling away from his daughter.

"I wanted to be, dad. That was the point. But seeing you like this, knowing you've seen what we have, I can't turn my back on you now. Just like Kyle wouldn't turn his back on me. This isn't just human versus human. This is us versus evil. I'm happy you're here! Just don't cripple my new boyfriend, ok?"

Jonas turned towards Kyle, who was shaken at the prospect of disability.

"You broke my trust. You took my daughter. You robbed me blind, right under my own roof!"

Kyle, flabbergasted by Jonas' change in demeanor, said nothing. He opted to pinch the piece of skin at the top of nose to fend off an approaching headache. Jonas' face softened, and he chuckled.

"Or so I've thought this entire time, m'boy! I've wanted nothing but revenge for your lies and trickery, until that demon showed up to the bar you were so quick to run from. The horror of it woke me up to the truth in your salvation story, and my faith in you."

"Uhm, thank you?"

"No, thank you. For saving my daughter. For keeping her safe. And for giving this old fool the opportunity to see the wrong in his ways." Jonas turned to Judith. "Judith, my dear, I have kept you locked up for years, since your mother passed, because I was greedy for affections. I missed your mother's love so much that I expected the same from you. God, you're her spitting image!"

"But I'm not mom. I can't give you that!" Judith said.

"I know, I know, love. Now I know. Last night was an eye opening experience for me. The demon came in to the bar and it was a bloody massacre! Molly hasn't spoken since we high tailed. She just stares, remembering the screams and the blood and that red, winged bastard killing Ian! The only time she has any speck of life is when I try to take that gun from her."

"Ian! Shit, I'm so sorry, dad...and Molly," Judith said with sincerity.

"What's done is done. James wasn't so innocent. He was the one who talked me into the idea that Kyle had kidnapped you. Even planted evidence and stole one of my guns to assure the full extent of my wrath! James confessed to me his desire to take over my business, using the situation as a catalyst. The demon suffocated him with a pool ball. Envy of all I had, and all I took for granted. Those were his last words before 'I'm sorry.'"

Kyle looked down at the word Envy on his watch.
James had been Envy? He hadn't spoken a word to James. Hadn't done a thing to save the man. The rules had flexibility and he wasn't sure what to make of it.

"My own sins were brought to light as I sat there, bound to a chair, realizing I would die. I had taken you for granted, Judy. I had suffocated you with my greed, and this man, whom I will never be able to fully thank, saved you from that. I should have just let you go, but I just brought shame and destruction to my family..."

She held him again, concerned. Even in his worst business slumps, even after the loss of her mother, she had never seen him break down like this. He drank his problems to the abyss and carried on, overcoming what he could with mind, what was left over with force. What he had endured at the hands of the demon must have been tragic.

"Oh my Judy, I'm so sorry. I love you, Judy...so much," he cried.
"Dad, don't call me Judy...you know that!" Judith said, perturbed at his use of the nickname.

"Why not call you by your name? I'm relieved."

Judith put her father at shoulder's length, thinking that he had lost it. Though she saw fear and sorrow, she saw no madness in his features.

"Nobody called me Judy except for Mitch, Dad. Before you fucking paralyzed him! The only promise you 've ever kept was to never call me that"

"Oh, right, of course," Jonas said, seeming confused. "It must be the shock, dear. It was traumatic, my dear, what he did to us! I thought I'd lost you like I lost your mother."

Something in Jonas was amiss. Judith paid close attention to her father, studying him with speculation instead of relief. Though he was covered in blood, she saw no wound. Though he claimed terror, his eyes were too aware and full of thought. No way would he make a mistake like that. Not with eyes that aware. If his words were honest, why would he call her a name that would cause such heartache? Judith backed away from her father, towards Kyle, who reached out to her and pulled her close as soon as instinct informed him it would be best.

Kyle understood none of their exchange, but knew by her body language that something was not right.

"Dad, what's my full name? Middle and all? Why hurt me with that nickname that filled you with such hate?"

"It fills me with love, my dear Judy! Not with hate! I embrace it, now! A nickname, given in love, like the new love I've found for you!"

"What is my fucking name, Dad? NOW!" Judith screamed from Kyle's side.

Jonas' face went dark. There was no other way to describe it. There was no slow transformation. His features shadowed over into a dark hue, like the dried blood that had dried to his skin and clothes, and every expression except for hate drained from his eyes.

"All this planning, carrying this fucking bitch on my shoulders like I was Delta-Demon airlines, and I'm going to have to go fucking medieval. Bah. Sentimentality was never Jonas' strong point, was it? Guess flashing it through his head while I snapped him in two was his way of feeling remorse. No matter. I should have paid more attention to the priest, but amidst all the suffering and torture, I forgot the extended version, Judy. Why I should have to learn the name of something so far beneath me, I'll never understand. No use for the hassle of theatrics anymore, I suppose."

Judith and Kyle watched Jonas' skin turn red. Large, leathered flaps of skin burst from his back. Horns grew from his head.

They had let the enemy walk in to base camp without so much as a cautionary defense. He reached the height of a basketball hoop before the crunching of bones and mashing of muscles ceased. Absolute Horror stretched his body, arms spread, back tight, before relaxing and turning his gaze to the couple. Their chests grew tight in his presence. He was a Titan in their presence.

Good. Daddy's home, he thought.

"Pleased to meet you. I'm Absolute Horror, Mr. Thimall. It's nice to see that I can stomp out that pitiful emotion you call love, once again! Though my satisfaction must be brief, I'm sad to say. My lovely Judy...I assure you that this pathetic creature's weak thrusts and gyrations will be outdone tenfold once I remove him from your heart and his life. You are my prize, after all! I will ream you bloody for lubrication, and you will cease to scream only when you taste yourself go sour on my loins! As for you, Mr. Thimall…" Horror began. He pointed a long, red finger in Kyle's direction, smiling with threat and promise as the boy moved to shield him from his prize.

To protect Judith from inevitability.

"I've been sent here to destroy you."

WRATH

Wrath consumes me

Fury an eternal fire

Never to smother

k.o.

Kyle didn't know what the he was going to do. Absolute Horror had assured Judith as his prize, to own and rape and far worse, if desired. After killing Kyle, of course.

Kyle found no way around the situation. He couldn't fight this beast. He would be destroyed. Judith would be defenseless. He couldn't die until she was safe. He doubted Horror would leave him much room to remember how to piss outside of his pants, let alone plan her escape.

"Poor Jonas. Dying while asking the forgiveness of an ungrateful daughter while she was shacking up with the "savior" in this pathetic excuse for a fortress. Hell, I feel worse for Molly, here. If you want to know what's in store for you, dear Judy, just ask her. Or better yet, look into her eyes! Talk about a sex coma. Bitch hasn't talked in hours! I've found the perfect woman!"

Horror grinned and waited for a reaction. Neither had the energy to muster disgust, let alone a pitying smile.

"Tough fucking crowd. I do understand your dying sense of humor. You were so close Kyle. So close. One little flash of light on that watch and you'd be blowing God's trumpet for eternity! But you've let your guard down in the throes of passion with pitiful tramp you protect, and now we end this. Choose your weapon."

"My weapon?" Kyle asked.

"Sure. Murderer's get a last meal. Why shouldn't I get the last laugh? I want to see what pathetic tool of death you fuckers invented that will tickle me before I tear you to pieces."

Kyle thought long and hard under the gaze of the devil before him. Judith wrapped her arms around him again, not wanting to let him go, bruising his ribs in the process. Kyle felt no pain. He was using the decision he had been given to figure out what, if anything, would defeat Horror.

Wrath. What would kill wrath? He didn't know if Molly and her anger was last to be saved, or if the demon himself represented the missing light.

Could Kyle save a demon? He doubted it.

Wrath begot war. Punishment. Hatred. Any weapon Kyle chose to use would fuel the demon's sick humor.

Love? He doubted a kiss or any other affection would harm

him. The demon had been privy to their love making. But what could he use or sacrifice to defeat Horror and save Judith?

Sacrifice. If wrath begot war, the opposite could stop war, could it not? To lay no hand, but to offer himself as a peaceful sacrifice. To turn the other cheek. Either that or the bulls eye on his chest would bitch smack him before Horror did.

He had learned enough through passive exposition while saving souls. It wasn't always what was done on purpose, but what wasn't done due to lack of motive, that caused his watch to glow.

"I choose nothing as my weapon," Kyle stated, defiance lacing his voice.

"You've got to be kidding me, you stubborn fool. Are you so quick to want the grave? Shit, Judy, I should rethink you then, no? Not ten minutes after a fuck and the man would rather die than fight. You must be terrible!"

Kyle turned and kissed Judith. He knew he might not get the opportunity to do so again, and he wanted to assure her that the "fuck" had not been terrible, but meaningful and gratifying.

"Oh, stop the kissy shit. You had your time with her. You're mine now!"

Absolute Horror swiped an arm to the side. Judith flew from Kyle's arms, as if being pulled by an invisible lasso, and was hurled into a crate filled with blankets and bed sheets. She lay still upon impact.

"Damn! The next one over was sheet metal. Missed it by that much," Horror smirked, holding his thumb and forefinger a small distance apart.

"You bastard! I swear, I'll..."

"What? Go Tiananmen Square on me? If your weapon is inaction, then so be it. The greatest evils in this world were due to the inactions of good men. Isn't that a famous quote from one of you pathetic blood monkeys? All your passive death will do is deny me entertainment and haste violation of your little girlfriend over there. If you're so quick for..."

"This isn't inaction. It's sacrifice. Take this life! I'm right here, you big red bastard.. Take me in place of her. Take me so I may serve your master for all eternity, as promised. Let my screams tune his violin and my blood lubricate his bow. Through my sacrifice, my choice, you'll not touch the girl or hurt another again. Because without me, there is no fucking you!"

"Pathetic. You buy that bullshit?" Horror said, his eyes half closed with boredom.

"The question is, are you arrogant enough to test it. The look in your eyes tells me that not even you know what to expect."

Kyle was right. The idiot savant of dogma, he had become.

Horror was surprised by Kyle's growth of testicles and willingness to sacrifice. Sure, killing Kyle wasn't the plan, but it would not negate the deal. Kyle's destruction for the favors of the bitch, Judy, and a seat in the highest of thrones. Not much fine print in that contract.

"Fine. You don't even want to put up an effort to fight, I won't waste the sweat on your ass. Molly, raise the gun."

Molly, forgotten next to the goliath sized demon, moved. Her arm raised towards Kyle. Her eyes grew sullen, but not scared, as if she had expected what was happening and had prepared herself. She had come to her own peace, regardless of the demonic hypnosis.

"Molly, you don't have to..." Kyle began.

The sound of wood falling to the ground echoed throughout the room. Judith was stirring.

"She doesn't have a choice. She's under my control. Same as Christopher, my vigilant rookie sidekick who took out your dear compadre, Leon. You see what I did there, kiddies? Com-PADRE?"

The demon gave Kyle a wide eyed half-smile and waited for a reaction. Kyle gave him nothing. The demon sighed with false despair.

"Pity you don't enjoy puns, Kyle. They are the only jokes allowed in Hell. Hell will be your vacation destination once I help to your destiny. It looks to be an unworthy death for you, Kyle. Just like Leon. You should have chosen better weapons than blind faith and no sense of humor. Westboro Baptist Church should have proven that much. Have fun in Hell. It gets warm this time of year. Just because you didn't laugh at my joke, I'll make it hurt more than I had intended to."

"I'm so sorry," Molly whispered.

The pitter patter of footfalls let Kyle know that Judith was running towards him. He relaxed his arms and looked in her direction, realizing that he was, perhaps, that protagonist, after all.

"No! Not him, God dammit!" Judith screamed, running towards Kyle with a limp.

"Damning the wrong person, my sweet. Shoot through the

heart, Molly."

"I love..." Kyle said, with as much conviction as he could muster since being shocked by the knocking that had ruptured their cuddling time.

The bullet piercing his heart stopped him short by one word. Judith reached him in time to catch his body as it fell, a smile across his face, his eyes never leaving her own. The weight of his body knocked her to the ground. She cradled his head and cried onto his face, mouthing incoherencies and kissing him as much as she could.

"...you," Kyle said, though it was more a whispered death rattle than a coherent word.

"Oh, way to go sport!" clapped Horror. "Died like a pansy, but got your last words in to your lady fair."

Horror walked towards Judith, the ground vibrating with each step he took. Judith didn't looked away from the open eyes of Kyle. Her hand pressed into the bleeding gunshot wound over his heart.

Her heart.

Horror grabbed her by the wrist and yanked her to her feet. She sobbed with muted tears, but did not resist, lest Horror defile Kyle in a far more brutal fashion.

"Come, bitch. You're my play thing now! I hope you like 'em big and red. You can call me Clifford, if you like!"

Tears streamed down Molly's face. Her actions were not her own, and she hated the knowledge that the one time she did not want to kill, her choice had been taken away. She had always loved Judith like a daughter. She had killed someone very important to her, and possibly to the world.

'The devil made me do it' just didn't seem like a good enough excuse when she couldn't even offer the girl comfort. She thought of her Jonas, her Ian, and hoped Horror would give her peace. She would trade an eternity of torture at his hands to offer Judith a reprieve from that, even if it meant her death. She tried to move the gun towards Judith, but her arm wouldn't budge.

"Oh, so now you're willing to put up with my shit?" said Horror. "Well, now that you're willing to live for something you believe in, I don't much care for your presence. You give sloppy head, and I'll bet Judy here won't cry out so much when I puncture that puckered starfish of hers. Go to hell, bitch. Jonas can have the scraps."

Horror placed his baseball glove sized hand over Molly's face and squeezed. Her head burst into flames. Within seconds, her entire body was alight. The skin melted like wax. Her hair disappeared in a flash. Her screams were lost in the damaged tissue of her throat before she could find the voice to shout them.

Her eyes remained unscathed, avoiding their biological desire to bubble and burst. With horror, she was able to watch as bone melted from muscle, muscle from bone. The white of her hands charred black, but never turned to ash. Within seconds, her skeleton sat in a puddle of blood, guts, and melted layers of flesh and sinew.

Still, her eyes had not been touched. Horror wanted her to see and feel everything. It would be a long period of suffering before death gifted her with his scythe.

Judith continued to sob, but said nothing.

"And as for you," said Horror, looking to Kyle.

"No!" Judith screamed, finding her voice. "You got what you want, you bastard! He's fucking dead! And you get to burn my insides with your demon seed for eternity! Just leave him in peace. I beg of you!"

Judith broke free from Horror's grip and dropped to her knees, begging him in action as well as words, offering her subservience. Horror looked at her amused for a moment before producing his member from the torn shreds Jonas's clothing that still clung to his body. It hung to his knees, and was as thick as a flower vase. Judith, weeping in terror, shrieked as Horror turned his body to aim it towards Kyle.

"That's right, baby. Take it in. Later, daddy wants his sugar. Better you meet the rascal before he tears you apart, no? As for your boyfriend, here..."

Horror let loose a steady stream of red urine, which turned to flame as soon as it hit the ground.

Everything burned. The clothes lying on the ground. The broken splinters and debris. Judith's purse. Everything flammable except the body of Kyle Thimall. Horror looked confused, twisting his stream this way and that, covering Kyle with flaming urine.

Kyle lay there, unchanged by the flames. It was as if a bubble were wrapped around the boy, preventing him from catching fire. The devil cut his stream without tucking it away, a look of dissatisfaction crossing his face.

"Must be a God thing. But just because the vessel is fire proof doesn't mean the soul will be, you white bearded bastard!" Horror shouted, looking up towards the ceiling and beyond it towards the heavens.

"Thank God," Judith whispered, her hand reaching out towards Kyle's fallen body, unaware of the flames heat on her fingertips.

"Lady, you say that now, but in a few hours, you'll be cursing the day God ever decided to grow an apple tree and let some bitch eat her fill. I guaran-fucking-tee it."

Horror scooped Judith up and over his shoulder, not bothering to cause any more damage. Good had been vanquished. It was his bloody Sunday. Time for rape, rest, feast, and a good ole fashioned foot massage. He kicked open the door as if it were made of corkboard instead of reinforced steel before taking flight.

Inside, the flames licked at Kyle's body. His blood boiled as it spilled to the ground.
Still, his skin remained unscathed.

On Kyle's lifeless wrist, Wrath illuminated. The entire face of the watch glowed bright red. As the intensity of the glow increased, the fire spread farther from Kyle's body and exploded in a burst of blue and yellow. As soon as the explosion reached maximum capacity, licking at the walls of the warehouse, it reversed, sucking back down and inwards, towards Kyle's watch.

As it neared, the flames concentrated and sucked into Kyle's open wound. Kyle's back to arched, his eyes wide, a screaming conflagration escaping his chest.
There were echoes. Then Kyle was limp, no more than a cadaver.

All seven words illuminated, the watch stuttered like a strobe. The glow from the glass face slowed into stillness. The face cracked, the mechanics grew silent, and the illumination went dark.

Smoke and fire filled the room, encapsulating everything save for the tools of salvation, discarded with their purpose served, in darkness.

The nightmare had replaced the dream.
On the fifth day, Kyle Thimall died.

a cliche lazarus pit

A hero awoke with a shiver. A quilt covered him. His outside was warm, cozy even, but his core was cold.

What is this? the hero thought. *It's all wrong. Where are the chains? The brimstone? The screams of the damned?*

Kyle looked around. The mirror on the far wall was framed by a wreath of carved rose. The bookshelf was lined with unread encyclopedias, National Geographics, and books on Mythology. The green door, behind which was a Jacuzzi sized bath tub and a brand new black tiled floor. The sound of the air conditioning on full blast explained the chills.

This had been his home. When Sarah was alive. When life had been enjoyable.

"What kind of fucking hell is this?" Kyle screamed to nobody, shaking with anger as well as cold.

No answer. Only a rustling to his left, followed by a head of messy blonde hair rising, and blue eyes looking his direction.

"Dammit Kyle, what are you yelling about? I told you we'd get the air conditioner fixed later this afternoon! It's only..." the blonde cast her eyes to the alarm clock, "...five thirty in the morning."

"What is this?" Kyle stammered, wide eyed, as Sarah moved the hair from her face.

She was still as beautiful as he remembered.

More so.

"This is a warning from your wife to curl up next to her and fall back asleep for another before I give you something to shout about."

A devious smile crossed her lips, and her hand traced their way to Kyle's thigh, moving towards his naked crotch.

"Unless, of course, that's what you want me to do?"
Noticing the look in his eyes, she stopped her hand.
"Jesus, Kyle, what's wrong? Was the nightmare that bad?" Sarah asked, concerned.

"You're dead, Sarah!" Kyle said, his voice unquestioning.

But damn, was her hand warm. It was the only thing in the room that *was* warm, it seemed, and it was comforting. Exciting. Pleasurable, as his twitching member hinted.

"Whatever you were shouting about could wake the dead! Now do you want me now, stud, or do you need more rest before I leave you gasping?"

"I, uhm..."

She leaned over to him and kissed his lips with gentle love, reaching up and holding his head between her hands.

"Get your rest, hot stuff. I know you have vivid nightmares, but we do have a long day tomorrow. I don't want you falling asleep on me while we're celebrating our anniversary in the Jacuzzi-tub later."

"I'm going to get a glass of water," he said, still staring at her with wonder.

"Well, hurry back to bed," Sarah said, laying back with her arms over her head, her glorious breasts begging him not to leave. "I can't sleep without you next to me. You know that."

"You'll never know how hard it is for me to do the same," Kyle he said, sliding from beneath the quilt.

Without thinking, he leaned over and kissed her in the middle of her chest. She smiled and let out a sigh, tilting her head to the side and relaxing.

Kyle couldn't tear his eyes from her as he backed towards the door, but forced himself to turn around once he reached the hallway. He mumbled as he entered the living room.

"What is this? How? Who? What? The? Fuck?"

As he turned the corner that overlooked the main sitting area, Kyle saw a man sitting in what was once his La-Z-Boy. His first reaction was to jump back behind the wall and hide his nakedness, turning red with embarrassment.

Upon seeing the man's face, he did turn red, but with fury instead of shame.

"Lucifer! You sick fuck! What torment is this, huh? You going to tease me with happiness before you have me fucking molested by Hell's harpies and consoling the suicidal for all eternity? You already showed me your sick illusions, so why not just drop the pretenses?"

"Consoling the suicidal for eternity? That would be torment. Ever thought about becoming a guidance counselor for the damned?" Lucifer said, smiling.

"Just have your way with me and let me suffer in peace, Lucifer. Leave my heart be. You've already put a bullet in it! Hell, you ripped it out of my chest the day you proposed this deal to me in my cab, if you knew this would be the outcome."

"My child, not even God can foresee the outcome of everything. Even He is a slave to fate, and has been since He set fate into motion so that He could rest. Fate is the autopilot that God can't quite turn off."

"Oh, and you know this because Lucifer and God are so fucking chummy, right?"

"Your use of vulgarity has increased exponentially since our last report? And here I thought it was doing you good. Pity to fall into old habits, kid."

"Well, since you exist, so does He. And since you've put me in a right fucking pickle, I'll not demean him any more than I have by believing that you claim to know a thing about Him! I can give Him at least that much respect, even if he didn't send me a MacGuffin."

"Well at least you realize the point of this whole ordeal. He appreciates the gesture, Kyle."

"How the fuck would you know, ya flaming fucking flamer?"

"Because I am Him."

"Liar," Kyle thrust forth an accusing finger.

"It's true, Kyle. I am not, nor have I ever been Lucifer. I am God. The One and Only," God said. He spread his palms and offered Kyle a movie star smile.

"Charlatan!" Kyle thrust his finger again, twice for good measure.

Corny, yes, but he had committed. If slapstick was all he had for a defense he was going to run with it.

"Kyle, sit and have a listen. I have a lot to explain to you right now, and all I ask is that you save your judgments for the end of the lecture. So sit a spell? Maybe cover up with a blanket?"

Kyle, realizing again that he was naked, sat on a couch and covered himself with a throw pillow, too confused to be embarrassed, but not comfortable enough with being completely exposed.

"That's the same attitude Adam had when he first realized what breasts were,"

"And then what, huh? Cast out of Eden because of you?"

"Well, he had time to fit in a proper shagging or two, didn't he? The whole Garden of Eden thing was temporary, anyway. Kind of like a vacation resort, you know? He told them it was a place of perfection and eternal happiness and all, but really it was a place for them to rest while He finished Canada. Based on what I've seen, I still don't think He got it quite right."

"I guess they won, if they weren't banished *to* Canada," Kyle said, having heard enough bad music on the radio to know where true evil was spawned.

"There was no banishment. The serpent offered the perfect excuse to send them into the finished world without feeling like He was selling their Playstation for beer money. Eden was like His personal greenhouse, and He told them not to eat the fruit because He wanted to offer pomegranates up at a later time, when they would boost the economy and proper chefs were around who understood how to make a good sauce. It was supposed to be a surprise. Those two spoiled that for Him. Still, it was a planned eviction. They just never got the thirty days' notice. Their embarrassment was less about nudity and more about of the realization of "premature ejaculation."

"Poor Adam," Kyle said, understanding the shame.

"Poor Eve, Kyle. Poor fucking Eve," God replied.

Kyle nodded, also understanding the disappointment.

"If you are God, why are you talking about yourself in the third person? Why are you being so foul mouthed? Why the hell did you tell me you were the devil and smoke cigarettes with me, giving me even an inkling of hope that I wouldn't fail? That I wouldn't suffer?"

"Did you suffer waking up next to Sarah, Kyle?"

"Well, no, not exactly. If I did, it was only in knowing that it was a ploy to happy me up before feeding me despair."

"Why do you think that?"

"Because I failed. I failed God, I failed myself, and I failed... Judith." The words made him feel guilty as they escaped his lips, what with Sarah asleep in the other room. Even if she was an illusion.

"You didn't fail, Kyle. Sure, you were all but dead when your watch brought you here, but you are far from a failure."

"How could I have succeeded when I acted like a coward? I offered myself as sacrifice when I could have fought and the bastard couldn't even kill me himself, he was so disappointed!"

"Evil doesn't understand self-sacrifice, Kyle. They only understand sacrifice as a means for gain. Your sacrifice was not in vain. The demon wasn't meant for salvation, because it has no soul. You saved your own. A braver man would have resorted to violence or trickery and played right into the hand of his wrath.

Your own anger was put to rest when you gave your life peacefully to protect a loved one. Molly, too, was changed, even if only for a moment, by committing the demon's act of wrath and, after a life of bloodlust, feeling the weight of guilt because of it. Just as you thought, your sacrifice was necessary. Your death was paramount."

Kyle looked at God in stricken silence for a few moments before tossing the throw pillow across the room at Him, nakedness be damned!

"Why the FUCK couldn't you tell me that when I signed the deal, huh?"

God chuckled, and said "Would you have done it, had you known you had to? No. You were either going to fail, as Lucifer thought, or your cowardice would lead you through the obstacles without a scratch! Except for the bullet. Did not see that coming."

"So I was chosen because of cowardice?" Kyle couldn't think of anything else to say.

"Well, your carelessness. And innocence. Your life took a dark, dark turn when Sarah died, Kyle. But she was always the stronger one. She planted seeds of strength in you, but due to her death, they were never allowed to grow. Those seeds made you fall harder than you would have otherwise, because you knew you should have been better. But the coward remained, strangling them with acid rain. Still, your cowardice makes you careful. Your strength, ever growing, gives you bravery when needed. But your strongest asset was your love. You were made to love, Kyle. That is why Sarah was drawn to you. What Sarah planted in you blossomed because of what you had to go through. It was the reason that another loved you, and why you could love her in return."

"Judith," Kyle mused, longing overpowering the guilt.

"To answer your third person God question, well, that's a bit more controversial. God can adapt. God can learn and grow. But He can't interfere. Remember what I said of fate? As powerful as God is, when He set fate in motion, He had to create a force as strong as He was in order to help him guide the world while he rested. When He awoke, fate had grown too powerful to handle. God will always be powerful, but by his own hand, he will always be privy to the fate He set in motion. Truth be told, I am not the God who saw Adam and Eve from the Garden, though I retain those memories. I remember everything that has been, is, and some of what will be. Fate darkens portions of it, jealous of sharing those secrets. But what do I lack? What truly caused such turmoil for you, my chosen candidate? Experience."

"A few million years not enough for you, old man?"

"As I said, Kyle, I am not that God. God created Angels to do more than serve him. They exist to replace him once he has grown tired. Angels, such as I once was, are bred to become God. Even God is not immune from weariness. He created humans in his own image, and you all die don't you? He simply dies slower and in a much different way, though job related stress does expedite the process. Another thing humans have in common with him. Obviously there has to be balance, right?"

"I guess?"

"Well you guess right, my dear man! Angels serve God, but things have changed. God is a strong proponent of evolution. Did you know that the German military requires soldiers to report any breach of human rights to prevent anything like the Holocaust from happening again? They are given permission to defy their leaders, when it is called for. So are Angels. They once served God without question. After Lucifer jumped ship, there was much death. That God, on his death bed, gave Angel's free will."

"Every once in a while, once God has been drained by fate and faith, the God who was passes his memories, his very essence, and his abilities into an Angel, re-energizing the position.

There can only be one God in the High Land, but he is ever changing. Retaining memories. But memories are not experience, and all of Us start with a learning curve. Last time we had a change of office, an entire race of red-skinned humans were decimated because the new God thought, for some reason, that small pox sounded like a European delicacy and wanted to make sure that the pilgrims had something to share at the first Thanksgiving. He must have fallen asleep at indoctrination."

"Why do I need to know all this?"

God sighed. "To understand that even God can make mistakes, Kyle. Even God sins at times. Like Nixon once said of presidents, that when they commit crimes they are not illegal? When God fucks up, it isn't technically a sin. God can bend the rules. That's how I could lie to you in that cab about who I was and leave out the nastier details. That's why I can partake cursing. Though, in good faith, that's as far as I go, and only with good intentions."

"That's an asshole move,"

"Well, I'd say sue me, but we're far away from the souls of lawyers, are we not?" God laughed at his own wit, smacking his leg.

"This is Heaven?" Kyle said, genuinely surprised.

"I told you, Kyle. You succeeded. Your contract has been satisfied. You may have eternity in Heaven with your lost beloved, if you wish, because you have earned it! I came to congratulate you!"

"It sounds like you came with a proposal, with that "if you wish" line, your Holiness. If I succeeded, why even show up at all to congratulate me? Don't you have a universe to run, not to mention an afterlife?"

For the first time since the conversation began, God's smile waned.

"Yes, Kyle. What I'm about to ask of you may be unfair. Dastardly. I owe you transparency, at the very least, so that you may have a full scope of your choice. The reason you had to be chosen in the first place was because, well, though God may have to go through changes of office, Lucifer...Satan...whatever you call him, is timeless. He doesn't transfer power to a demon. He consumes them for nourishment. God takes by charity, Satan by force. The good that fuels God is ever depleting by doubt, overpopulation, and hatred; it is consumned by anything evil. The little experiment God started is what struck him with a means to become weak. Lucifer, however, is fueled by evil. Evil exists, period. As long as evil exists, he remains. It's like God runs on fossil fuels and the devil runs on sand."

"Lucifer wanted a rematch for Job, as I explained, but as bad as he can be, he had a good reason for it. We exist in spite of and for each other, after all. He claimed that, with so many faithless running around, nobody could be sure who would choose what side if they knew the honest answer. The real purpose behind the entire deal was to see if people who had gone astray from faith or goodness were inherently good or inherently bad. Your mission put people face to face with the simple truth that the devil existed. James was the only one who captured the notion of the situation with such clarity. If a person, whatever their place in life, was given proof that the Devil was real, which in turns meant that God was real, what side would their true self lead them to out of reaction? What would their true colors be? White, or Red?"

"I've been used!" Kyle screamed without conviction. He was drawn in to the story.

God ignored him.

"I made the deal. I picked the person, only he put him through hell. He could not directly do anything, as he would have just outright killed you, but he could send a minion to do so. The minion could do nothing physically to harm the holy, either. And he would know all except for good intentions and names, because to a demon, a name is a cherished thing. He had to earn his, and he had to learn yours. That included you, Kyle. He could only keep you from succeeding. If, in a week, those who you "saved" strayed towards the side that would be considered primarily good, your watch would light, proving that humans were still able to have faith in God, and in turn, God could have faith in them. If they had strayed into chaos, a place of pure evil, than, as the Devil put it "The entire point of your office has become slow suicide. There are only so many angels." He was right. If that had turned out to be the case, Lucifer would have taken control of the reigns, still guided by fate, mind you, but with a hunger for chaos, because God would have needed to rest again. There would have to be much pain and evil for the good to re-awaken, morbid as that sounds. So I agreed to the deal, not realizing that I had overlooked something as it pertained to you."

"Physically, the demon didn't kill me..."

God smiled at Kyle, glad he had picked up, and knowing full well he had chosen the right, albeit awkward and quirky, man for the job.

"Correct. His lack of interest in killing you had nothing to do with your choices, Kyle. He couldn't do a thing to harm you, bound by fate as he was. Molly was not bound by that decree, so he used her to kill you in a way he couldn't. If he had tried to do so, he would have been destroyed. It was for that same reason he used Christopher to kill Leon, who has earned himself a wonderful job as my assistant for his desire to help people, even through his faithlessness."

"Well, that's worth something at least."

"He's really quite good. Funny, to boot! Remind me to tell you the one about the priest and..."

"God?"

"Right, right, sorry. You were chosen. If you would have rejected the deal, there were others in mind, but I had no reason to believe you weren't the perfect choice. Though the deal could have, literally, ended with Hell on Earth, the point was to understand where the balance was, and overcompensate the winning side to the point that the scale equalized, if it was needed. The Devil and I aren't the same kind of boss, Kyle, but we're both in the same business. Once, Lucifer was an Angel. He finally had the chance to get the one thing he'd always coveted, and would never attain because of his fall from grace. The chance to become God."

"Jesus Christ, that's a lot of faith to put in one man,"

"Well, he thought so to, but even Jesus agreed that you were the only viable choice after looking into your soul. Strong, however fucked up your body was."

"I feel so violated..."

"We only poked around for a bit, I promise. If I had won the wager, Satan would retreat to Hell for my tenure and we would have a semblance of peace on earth. Humans might still be do bad things, but only of their own accord. At least for three hundred years."

"So you won. That means peace and hippies and a whole lotta pot, right?"

"Well, that may have been. Lucifer didn't send the demon he did without purpose. He was a Plan B. Nothing human can kill that demon, Kyle. That demon was not a minion brewed from the souls of the damned and forged in Hell's fires. He was born long before man, one of the original tenants of the Hell that Lucifer took up residence in. Normally, a demon must earn a name, but can never have a soul. Until they have a name, they are lower than even the souls they torture. Those are the rules of the original demons. But remember all those lawyers you don't see up here? They found a loophole. That demon gave up his name in trade for a soul. And now, thanks to a dead police man, he has both."

"Why does it matter if he has a soul?" Kyle asked.

"Souls are like filters, Kyle. The purpose of a soul is to absorb the evil and good in a person and separate the portions to their proper place. Heaven and Hell host consciousness more they host souls. The place where dreams and nightmares are born is where eternity is spent, and fate makes that decision. The soul is the power source for the balance, which is why God has less power to draw from and must turnover often to stay ahead. The demon, with his knowledge, has found a way to pervert the soul and use the full potential of its power. He has filled it to capacity with evil, but he has also found a way to tap into the unfiltered power of the soul. The power that should have carried to one of us. You couldn't imagine what he's capable of. He hardly can. I prefer Lucifer. At least he gets tied up with paperwork. This demon, Absolute Horror as he has been named, will remain earthbound until he dies because of that soul. The power of both a soul and a name will make it difficult task to kill him. At his full potential, it will become impossible."

"I'm so confused right now, God," Kyle said.

"Superman is now immune to Kryptonite," said God.

"Oh shit."

"Indeed."

"If no human can kill it…" Kyle started.

"Then humans are without hope. Except for you, of course."

"How did I see that coming?"

"Foreshadowing? Who knows? Now, on to the deal I am so reluctant to make, but must for the sake of good. I am not a beast, Kyle. I do not take without reward. New policy, I swear to Me. I'm basically asking you to hop the fence at Guantanamo Bay, naked, with toilet paper rolls strapped to your chest."

"Had to go with that one while I'm not wearing pants, didn't ya, Big Guy?" said Kyle, reaching down to protect himself from invisible razor wire.

"I hate that name," God grumbled.

"I know," Kyle responded. "Lay it on me, though, so I can decide rather or not to get comfortable."

God gave Kyle a look that said he would do nothing if Kyle refused, though what he could do was plenty. Adventure had made him curious for details.

"You may stay here, Kyle, for eternity, as promised. I'm not going to bullshit and say that the Sarah in that room is the real Sarah. Her soul has filtered and become part of the good. It is her consciousness. Little more than a ghost who, in this place, feels real and acts as Sarah did, though without a soul she will never be the same. Your soul is your own, earned true by success. With that soul, you will never feel the same tranquility and love you once did. The evil that was once a part of her has long been forgotten, you will always remember and retain your own evils. You will have your own Garden, my son. She will be your Eve, though you will always remember the other you loved. Your Lilith, as it were."

"That sounds great and all, but there's a problem with your logic," Kyle said.

"What is that, Kyle?"

"I didn't love a part of Sarah. I loved all of her. I've found that same love in another. The prize doesn't have the same appeal, especially an incomplete prize. I'd be safe and content. Happy, even. But in the end, if I remember everything, then I'll never forget Judith. She'll always be a part of me, and I can't trade her an incomplete clone of my dead wife."

"The point was being with Sarah, was it not?"

"Yes. And you didn't bullshit me, God. That is not the real Sarah."

"This may sound callous, but I'm relieved to hear that. The other choice carries far more risk and chance for pain. Guaranteed happiness may be better than a fifty-fifty chance at nirvana, and for that reason I implore you to think on my proposition. Success will bring you more satisfaction than anything I can contrive."

"He has Judith," Kyle said, knowing it was the truth.

"Yes. Judith remembers you and loves you well. That beast wishes to sodomize her before pillaging the earth with its evils, Kyle. He wants to make her his queen by force, for her heart can never be his. It belongs to you."

"Tell me two things. Can I stop it, and how?" Kyle asked with humorless confidence.

"I will return you to life. Not only to save what I cannot, due to fucking contractual constraints that Zeus would have spit at, but for the opportunity to save what now matters most to you. This experience eased your pain. You found two people you never would have found, had you not let that burden go. The person you were meant to become, and the person you were meant to love. And..."

"God?"

"Yes, Kyle?"

"Shut up and tell me how to kill the fucker," Kyle said.

"I cannot guarantee success, but I can offer you celestial leeway. The rest is up to you. If you fail, your soul will split as intended, and you will be left to whatever fate wills."

"I can only imagine the possibilities."

"I have faith in you, big guy," God said, lightly bumping His fist against Kyle's chin for maximum ridiculousness.

"Wow, that is annoying," Kyle said.

"Told you so. Shall I leave you to think on it?"

"Haven't thought about much in the past week, God, so if the instinct I'm feeling is still my own, there's no reason to stretch this out. It already feels like someone is writing my life story with more complication, cliché, and third act monologues than are probably necessary, but I have to save Judith or I will never find peace."

"Yeah, fate isn't overly original. Plagiarizes Shakespeare more than he plagiarized everybody else, but that might also be the muses fault. They go on strike a lot. Guess it's time to see find out if your story is a comedy or a tragedy then?"

"Yes.

"Your service will be duly noted. The power of the souls you saved is yours to use until either you or Horror succeed. At least you won't be terribly outmatched, though I'm fresh out of instruction manuals. Use it wisely, for I have chosen wisely. I offer you this small gift. A token of my eternal debt to you," God said. He spread his hands before him.

"Is it a light saber? Because this is where a just God would offer me a light saber," Kyle said.

There was a rich sound of laughter. As Kyle watched, God faded into nothingness, the sound of his laugh fading in volume the more evanescent he became, until all that was left in his place was a bright blur. An out of focus light. One that was moving towards Kyle with haste.

"Kyyyyyyyyyllllllleeeeeee..." said a voice, elongating his name in a way that, he figured, was supposed to remind him of a cartoon ghost. Kyle recognized the voice, and the goofy sense of humor, at once.

"S...Sarah?"

"Yes, my love," said Sarah.

"The *real* Sarah?"

"Can I at least solidify before the sass starts, so I smack you one," Sarah said. She came into focus clothed, unlike her sleeping clone.

"Sarah. It is you." He smiled and embraced her.

Sarah's embrace felt strange, but warmed his soul. It was happiness, but not a happiness infected by the blindness of lost love and despair. It was good to be in her presence again, nothing more, nothing less.

Kyle's heart had truly moved on. He shifted from foot to foot, anxious to save Judith despite a true depiction of Sarah standing in front of him, without noticing. Sarah noticed, but said nothing.

She was happy for him.

"We don't have much time, Kyle. It's normally a bad idea to put dead people back together again, but there are always exceptions. I want you to know that I will never stop loving you. It sucks finding out that my memory has brought you such pain while yours has brought me such joy, but I am a part of something so pure now, Kyle. I don't want you to be burdened by me anymore."

"Your memory never pained me. Codependence did. Loving you so much I'd never planned on doing anything else did. I did this to myself, Sarah."

"You have to understand that I was meant to find you, just as I was meant to hit my head on that damned board. Fate willed it so. You were always destined to complete my life as I was always meant to complete only a piece of yours. You were always going to end up with Judith, Kyle. I know this because fate knows it. I'm glad the pain my death caused you has been dulled enough for you to realize it, too."

"She can never replace you, Sarah."

"She can and she will, Kyle. She already has. Look back on me fondly, and never forget me, but give yourself to her completely, Kyle. As you did to me. Anything less would be unfair. I won't be offended."

"Sarah..."

"Love her, Kyle. As she loves you. As you loved me. And give that big red fuck a kick in the groin for trying to piss in the cereal, will you?"

"Sure thing," Kyle smiled.

"Goodbye, my love," Sarah said.

"I never will forget you, Sarah."

"You'd better not," she said, smiling in a way that blinded him as the glow intensified.

Sarah kissed Kyle's forehead, leaving a pieced of that glow behind with the moisture. The glow seemed to stretch between her lips and his forehead as she pulled back.

"What was that?" Kyle asked. He felt the same warmth he had felt when God laughed, only more focused.

"Your weapon, from God. A gift, from fate. Now wake up..." she whispered. Her form grew blurry again. The glow whited out his vision.

"My weapon? What?" Kyle said, trying to shield his eyes from the light.

"Wake up, Kyle..." she repeated, her voice taking on a fuzzy tone, like a radio station slightly off of the frequency.

"Wait, did you turn me into a freakin'..."

"Wake the fuck UP!" Sarah's voice screamed.

The white light turned orange, and the blur began to focus again.

The warmth he had been felt had consolidated into his wrist. Even though his eyesight had not fully recovered, he could see the face of the watch glowing white.

And so it was, on the sixth day, that Kyle Thimall was resurrected.

worst hangover ever

The bunker smelled of burned meat and scorched cotton. Smoke filled the room, but it was transparent, as if the fire had been venting for hours, which unbeknownst to Kyle, it had been. The source of the burned meat smell was visible. The pile of Molly's remains resembling a deflated member of the Hutt family. The cotton was positioned closer.

"Fuck! My clothes burned off!" Kyle shouted into the empty room.

Kyle had been protected from injury, thanks to the secret powers of the watch. Horror's fire had not spared Kyle's drawers.

Kyle searched through the salvage in hope that he could find something suitable to wear. The longer he stayed away from Judith, the closer she came to a carnal knowledge that would destroy her. After searching through a few of the unscathed boxes, Kyle managed a pair of jeans, a too large pair of worn in boots with socks, and a bright pink polo shirt.

"Two out of three ain't bad," he reminded himself, dressing quick.

Kyle rushed to the door of the bunker. He took two steps before he was halted. In front of the bunker, a shiny new sports car was parked, white in color and interior. It looked expensive. Kyle approached the driver side and bent down to check the ignition. There was a key. From his bent over vantage point, Kyle also saw a note on the seat. He opened the door and sat, grabbing the note as he slid into the seat.

> *My love,*
>
> *Take this gift to save her. I know she means the world to you. Treat her with the same love and care as you did me. She will return the favor.*
>
> *Forever,*
>
> *Sarah*
>
> *p.s. This is the car I meant when you asked what I wanted for Christmas four years ago. Not a Geo Metro.*

Asshat.

xoxo

On the back side were directions and an address. There was a GPS system on the dash, powered on and awaiting his input. Kyle thanked Sarah as he entered the address into the GPS. Once the robot voice told him to travel half a mile and take a right, he turned the key.

Without buckling in, Kyle stepped on the ignition and didn't let up, enjoying the feel of being behind the wheel and knowing that, for once, he was chasing the battle, not running from it. After a mile of unrestrained speed, he buckled the safety belt as he drive, realizing that there was no reason to take unneeded risk, even if demonic torture for all eternity did rank higher on the scale of painful ways to die than a car crash.

For that matter, he'd died once and it hadn't hurt one bit, though he some sort of divinity had been at play.

Traveling far past the speed limit, Kyle drove on fate's highway with unrivaled focus.

Whether it led to Heaven or Hell, he would soon find out.

wait for it

Even bundled up in heavy layers of clothing, the wind whipped at Judith without mercy. After being chased for days by the promise of fire, the shock of displacement was numbing.

The bright moon signified night time, but light surrounded her. Colors of so many hues and intensities that Judith wondered if Horror had drugged her. Or taken her to a carnival, which was a dreadful prospect. If he was going to torture her, he preferred it be done away from the prying cell phones of clowns, jugglers, and acne riddled pre-teens. The demon seemed like the type who would leave the evil facets of social media intact throughout the Armageddon.

She sat up, unsure if she should expect pain or injury, but cautious as to not exacerbate them if they did exist. Her arms, legs, and chest were free of injury. Her neck hurt from being hurled across the bunker.

The memory of flying across the bunker and into a pile of crates woke the rest of memories from their slumber.

Kyle. Shot through the heart and dead. She remembered kissing his face and crying painful tears. More tears were falling as she remembered what they represented.

Horror took Judith after the black out, but she remained conscious long enough to see what became of Kyle.

His final moments were not spent alone. She would live with her pain knowing that he had died with her easing his. She praised him for not committing suicide on the day Sarah died.

The sorrow was unbearable.

Life ceased to matter. The freedom Kyle gifted her didn't mean a thing without him there to share it. It was so much worse than what her father had done to Mitch. If she had been a little faster, a little stronger, she could have stopped the bullet and saved him, like he had saved her. After the life she'd lived, even with the threat of Hell looming over her, she would have died for him. She had tried. She could think of no virtue greater than the complete, selfless sacrifice. She would have waited at the very gates of Heaven for him, if she could have kept him safe.

But it was Kyle, always Kyle, who sacrificed.

Judith failed him. She was impatient for the pain Horror

promised if there was even a chance it would cloud the pain she felt in her heart.

So much loss.

She pushed herself to a vertical base. Vents rose from the ground. Small misshapen skyscrapers surrounded her. Satellite dishes. Pipes and boxes she couldn't begin to think of uses for.

She was on a rooftop. She swiveled her head to the right and found a ledge. She walked towards it, the lights intensifying in both color and brightness. The carnival it was not, but it was close.

The bright lights kept her from knowing where she was until she peered over the ledge.

A sphinx.

A pyramid.

The Eiffel tower.

A stream of cars and people. Flashing lights. Smells of food and steam and stale air. How had she missed the horns? The aromas? She must have been more disoriented than she thought. Direct contact woke up every sense. She marveled at the city below her long enough to hate that she allowed herself to marvel at all.

Horror promised everything but a sightseeing tour. Why he left her on the roof, she didn't understand, but there was no satisfaction in her solace. Only a deep unease, worsened by the fact that Kyle wasn't with her.

Fresh tears fell, gliding along the backs of those before them.

She missed him.

Needed him.

Wanted him.

"Marveling at my city of sin, are you?" a voice behind her said.

The voice of Absolute Horror.

The world stopped. The chill, which had started to calm, intensified. Her senses numbed. The sensory deprivation was overwhelming. His voice drowned out all other sound.

Judith turned to face Horror. To face the beast, as Kyle had done for her. He could maim her. Rip her apart. Destroy her body and essence. She would keep her dignity. Her strength was her only friend.

The enemy had grown.

Horror spoke, gesturing at the city beyond the ledge.

"Only place left in America where cheap and easy doesn't mean fast food burgers and immigrants, am I right? Sinners feed on greed. They work for nothing to lose everything. This city will be my throne. Fear and loathing, my dear. No reason to build a kingdom when it already exists. The streets will turn into rivers of blood. Money will be the only foliage. The bodies of the righteous and undeserving will sustain my children. I wish Siegfried and Roy were around to jester my court. There are plenty of magicians left to choose from. They will be the first to suffer."

Horror took a step toward her. He covered a distance with that step that would have taken her ten.

"You don't like magicians, do you?" Judith said.

"You have no idea. From Jesus Christ to Jay Sankey, I would erase them from history were it my choice."

"Now that I can mark casual conversation with a demon off of my bucket list, can you tell me what kind of Hell is this cold?" Judith chattered, her teeth clicking through every word.

"Soon you will never want for fire again, my queen. You will soak yourself with the ferocity of my flames. The seed I plant in you will keep you warm forever. Consider this your epidural. The cold will numb you. I assure you, I'm thinking of your comfort."

She let loose one dry giggle at his display of comfort, fallacy that it was. She wanted to give into the numbness and knew he wouldn't let her. She wasn't the naive damsel in distress waiting for her hero to rescue her. Her hero had died. She knew what giving into that numbness would entail, and she knew what the demon meant when he said he would make her hot.

An incurable burn. An indescribable pain. She would be his mistress. His harlot. His whore. Bearer of ill-consummations. She would be his queen bee. Taking what he gave, giving back what he craved, and dying when his needs were met.

Judith looked over her shoulder towards the street. It was a long drop. She could just make out the short pink dress on a blonde woman walking into an all-night diner. The entertainers littered the street corners. They might as well have been mimes. The tops of the cars danced about each other. A silver hummer. A yellow and black stretch limo. A white Ferrari pulled up in front of the very building she was atop.

The lights, the sounds, the luster were luxuries she would

never enjoy. Height separated her from the world. The vantage made everything seem alien. Judith had been infected by the numbness of Absolute Horror!

She didn't have time to ponder the only real choice she had.

"Which Hell do I choose?" Judith said.

"Sweetheart, you don't have much say in the matter," Horror replied.

Judith took a single step backwards. Nothing startling. Absolute Horror smiled. She was playing hard to get. He was pleased. What was the point of a new toy stopped working the second you touched it?

"Choices are a figment. Nothing more than a tool. A tool of fate to keep you pathetic creatures on a linear path without interrupting their woven quilt beyond repair. This has always been, and will always be, your destiny my dear."

Horror sent a lazy arm out to grab her, knowing he was giving her incentive to back away further. He was calling her bluff. The ball of one foot pressed beyond where the ground should have been and rested just below the edge. She had nowhere left to run. Soon, the demon's terrible work would begin.

"I don't believe that," Judith said.

"To call that your choice would be contradictory. Your words and your decisions, even while you rebel against the theory of Fate, are not yours. You humans think that you matter because Fate made you the stars of your own destiny. You all read from the script Fate hand delivered the day you were born. I am my own creature. I *matter*. I will rule over the dust and rubble, picking you off one by one to feed my brothers. I am beyond the quill of Fate! I am eternal. While evil exists, I exist! Evil exists in you, Judy dear. Evil exists in all of you, but your importance ends on that fact. You are fodder. You are food. You simply…exist."

Horror was inches from her now.

Relaxed.

Confident.

Judith's opportunity was fast approaching.

The building would be ripped from its foundations with the intensity of his claim, and his throne would rise from the bones of those within it. This moment was his fate. Hell's fate. And the end of that morphine drip called hope for humans.

"Kiss me now, Judy dear. Do it by choice and accept your destiny. You will stand by my side I'll swear to be gentle. If I have to force you, there will be no pleasantries. You will be the first human to avoid living through the extinction of your kind."

Judith looked at him, so cocky in his position that he couldn't see the honesty in her intentions, and realized he was right. Her choice had been made for her. The second the bullet ended Kyle's life, the choice had been made. If it had been fate who had written that choice, then it was fate who had written hers. Horror had said fate could not be denied, and she wasn't about to prove him a liar.

Judith was ready for her life's play to end. She leaned towards Horror until she could smell the heat on his breath.

The decay.

The death.

"Fuck you," she whispered.

The fraction of a second hesitation while his eyes adjusted from the panorama scope of his kingdom and focused on her was enough. He made a small movement backwards, perhaps to hit her, or force her into a kiss as promised, and she flung herself back from the flat ledge of the rooftop.

Away from the demon, her senses returned, heightened in acceptance that she would feel them for a short time longer.

The further she fell from his presence, the less numb she felt.

She felt the wind against her skin.

She smelled the steam of the street cards and car exhaust.

She heard the honks and the screams begin to react to her decent.

She saw Horror's face, distorted with surprised fury, disappear into the glow of the lights speeding by her.

She tasted freedom.

The whole way down, accenting the physical feelings, she thought of Kyle. Even as her body twisted and turned, the asphalt and cement rushing up to break her final fall, she forced her every last thought to be of him. So overwhelmed was she by the recycling thoughts of his face, she swore she saw that face somewhere amongst the crowd of wide eyes and screaming mouths.

Few stories remained between her and Fate's finale. Judith

vowed that she would find Kyle again. Impractical and unrealistic as it seemed, who was she to quell the last thoughts of a dying woman?

Especially since she *was* that woman.

Judith closed her eyes and smiled.

Soon, Kyle. Soon...

Moments before she would have painted Vegas red, nothing left of her but a beautiful cadaver, the numbness returned. Everything went black. The numbness was not the sweet release of death she wanted. Her awareness of it was in not purgatory.

Judith parted her eyes, both knowing and hating what she would see.

As she opened them, the numb disappeared again, filling her with senses far beyond the spectrum of terror.

She saw red leather floating, turning the lights of the city into macabre strobe lights across her face, as acid sweat flicked into her eye.

She smelled dead flesh, dried blood, and smoke from a pyre of disease that would never extinguish.

She felt fire hot muscles squeezing into her, bruising and breaking, knowing that she would never be free of them.

She heard screams, the surprise in them replaced with primal fear.

She tasted death, and knew it was a meal Horror would serve her long after appetite had devoured every last drop of her goodness.

Every beat of his wings coupled with an exhale, laced with a chuckle.

Judith would have begged the fate, knees on broken glass or molten lava, for cowardice. To turn back time, give in, kiss the demon, and take the easy way out. Anything to get her away from the pain pulling her further from the comforting numbness she had forsaken with her decision.

Judith leapt from that choice, and though she lived, the numb had taken her place, lying dead somewhere on the street, beneath the screaming faces of strangers.

So it was written by Fate.

Absolute Horror may have been beyond the reaches of Fate, but he knew a blockbuster script when he saw one.

Pain would be her new reality.

Horror was going to make sure she gave the performance of her life.

CHAPTER 41

you're going to need that adrenaline

Kyle had always wanted to visit Las Vegas. He could appreciate the irony in his quest against sin culminating in the city of sin, but wished the circumstances were different. His resurrection, if he had ever *been* dead, and the subsequent power filled his senses. Every dust particle shone with brilliant, albeit manufactured, beauty. He wanted the time to appreciate it. The clarity of new life filled him. A second chance. He understood why people appreciated the small things in life after cheating, or beating, death.

His years of drowning his sorrow in drugs and apathy had been just that. Dying in a self-imposed coma and never finding the final breath. He treated life with indifference and hate, as if he died with Sarah. Though a piece of him died, the part that lived wanted to heal. His bleak prescription had been pity for guidance and chemicals for direction. Both bob just under the surface of reality, muffled from the world, yet unable to reach the hook that would send him to the abyss.

As directed by the GPS, he stopped the car in front of an impressive, and tall, hotel. Sleek, with just enough brick visible in the design to not look pretentious. The building, flying a "Grand Opening" banner on its marquee, would be where he would find Judith. If the two of them survived (the thought that she had been killed by the demon crossed his mind, but he ignored it in the throes of purpose), they would buy the largest, most comfortable suite in the building and enjoy the brilliance together.

The beauty of the city was in the architecture. The glow and hum of electricity. The air of possibility. The sin of the city rested in the souls and pocketbooks of man. Even his experience as a cabby had educated him in the ways of big shots. The number of those who leapt the line between business and evil was small compared to the number of cowards who pretended the line didn't exist.

Kyle shook his head to, clearing it of irony and awe of brought on by his new found perceptions.

Judith was the priority. The rest would be the epilogue.

Kyle opened the door and heard gasps. He tried on a shy smile, ready to act humble about a vehicle he knew he looked out of place in, because that's how rich people acted in public. The smile was unnecessary. Nobody was paying attention to the unshaven man in the fancy car waiting for valet parking. Vegas saw men of every shape, size, and personality through its city on a daily basis. Not a damn thing about him was new to them, even if it was new to him.

What was new to the desensitized citizens of Sin City was the attempted suicide being halted by a flying red devil-beast.

Kyle followed the scared eyes upward, both scared and pissed off by what he saw.

Judith, falling. Smiling. Moments away from sending Kyle back into an abyss from which he would never recover.

Absolute Horror, the demon who had signed his voided death sentence, scooped her out of the sky and flipping a mid-air turn towards the top of the building.

Emotions that had danced through him since the day God approached him in the cab surfaced. Through his new focus he felt each one as an individual entity, even as they tried to overwhelm him.

Fear.

Lust.

Relief.

Terror.

Love.

Until that moment, true, unbridled fury had not been among them. Until that moment, unfocused anger hadn't been an option. It would have gotten him killed, or worse.

Kyle was a week removed and a universe different from who that man had been. He wasn't afraid of the bastard carrying his girl to the roof of Vegas' newest sin den. He was angry that he wasn't the one doing it. The whole trying to *kill him in a bunker* thing didn't help Kyle's opinion, but that the demon was trying to make an example of Judith infuriated him.

Kyle, remembering Ken, threw the keys to a homeless teenage girl. She held a sign that read *I Lost Everything on America's Got Talent.*

"Keep it," he said to the girl. He didn't need it anymore. If his life was a movie, Kyle knew such a cliché line meant the climax was close.

He ran towards the hotel's revolving doors, following the hard path. The unrealistic path. The path that could end in a fall no demon or angel would save him from.

The path that led to Judith.

Kyle slid into an empty elevator, bumping into the faceless

somebody who exited it and unaware of their protesting cry. They would have plenty to yell about once they found the exit. His hand found the top button and pressed hard enough to crack the new glass covering. Kyle flexed his hands, trying to draw upon whatever strange strength he had been granted, and looked at the ceiling of the elevator.

It was one minute after midnight.

Kyle looked upward and through the elevator, towards his unknown destiny, sure and prepared.

Absolute Horror laid Judith on the roof, her eyes fluttering. He stroked her with deceptive care, ready to take his queen.

The seventh day had begun.

final battle - las vegas

Focus overwhelmed Kyle as he burst through the roof access door of the hotel. He had a vague awareness of the clicking noise the door made as it locked behind. His decent from the rooftop would involve more complicated means of travel than stairs and elevator.

The roof was unremarkable when compared to the lavish interior of the hotel. No blinking signs or lights shooting towards the heavens. Just air conditioning units and satellite dishes, laid out in a maze. Not knowing where to begin, he let his feet carry him. He had entered the state of an infantryman, head on a constant swivel, ready to react at a moment's notice.

Kyle found Horror, back exposed and bent over Judith, within his first minute of searching. Her body was hidden from him, but he could see her legs and the spread of her hair from either side of the crouched red beast.

The scene was still enough to be a painting. A painting anybody but Kyle might have found artful and full of deep, intricate, emotional complexities.

Fucking idiots.

Kyle wondered how many disturbing paintings would disturb the highbrow people they enlightened if they understood the true basis of their messages.

Kyle discarded stealth. He wouldn't make the mistake of assuming Horror was ignorant to his presence. Surprise did Kyle no good if he had no way to use it. Kyle hoped his presence would be enough of a surprise to move the situation to culmination.

"Hey, fuckface. Forget something?" Kyle said.

Horror stiffened for the briefest of moments, the surprise in the gesture telling Kyle that Horror had not been privy to his presence. Kyle approached the demon, not wasting time mulling over lost opportunity.

Horror stood and turned to face Kyle. He had grown larger. Redder. Even the smile that decorated the demon's face as he turned around looked larger. That cocky, arrogant, evil smile. The smile that had met every person sacrificed from the day Wilkins' uniform was left as a shredded sacrifice to his newfound purpose.

"Well I'll be a dickless cherub; I don't remember ordering a gay escort. Looks like you have more tricks up your sleeve than I gave you credit for, boy. More balls than I ever would have given you credit for, considering you're in front of me instead of begging a psychiatrist for a jacket and a room."

"I don't need tricks. I'm a tool of the opposition, remember? You think, after all that stock God put into me, that you'd take me out with a bullet you didn't even fire?"

"A bullet. A baton. A bumble bee. God couldn't have saved you from a thing if you failed, Kyle, and I made sure your failure was a surety. No, you played dead in the face of the bear who was ready for heavy sex and light hibernation after a heavy meal. And you were stupid enough to intrude before he'd gotten a chance to enjoy either. But hey, free appetizer," Horror said, stepping towards him.

"Your metaphors are losing their punching complexity, you know that? Ask yourself something before you attack, Mr. Grump Bear. How sure are you that you guaranteed failure?"

Kyle held his ground, reveling in every step Horror took away from Judith. Banter wouldn't last forever, but it would cause distance between Judith and the demon.

"It's sweet. The dishonest confidence you spew forth just to pull me farther away from her. What do you expect to happen, Kyle? The very hand of God to smite me from the top of this building, giving you and that bitch a happy ending? That's just plain uncreative, Kyle. There's been too much destruction for this movie of ours to end like a fairy tale."

"Avoiding the question? Facts are facts. You know as well as I do that I wouldn't be here if I'd failed. I'd be ball gagged and in agony right now, leaving you free to rape civilization to dust. But here I am. Despite the blood loss, there's not a scratch on me," Kyle said, lifting his shirt to prove his words.

"You are failing to connect very important puzzle pieces, you big red fuck. What do you think my resurrection means? What would have the power to bring me back if I had failed? How would a dickless cherub find a loophole in the most omnipotent of contracts?"

Something in Horror's smile faltered. Perhaps it was the knowledge that he had succeeded in killing Kyle back in that warehouse, and that he shouldn't be breathing at all had his plan been a success. Kyle spoke the truth; he never would have escaped Lucifer. He didn't understand his failure. He was far from dead. His red wings beat as strong as his heart. Wrath was alive and well. Kyle could not succeed while he lived.

Or so he had believed.

The smile returned, but his eyes were unable to shake off the contemplative, unsure gaze. A twinge of hope filled Kyle with every contortion of the demon's face. Behind the demon, Kyle saw Judith stir. He hoped that she would hide before the demon realized he wasn't going to be able to finish what he had started.
Kyle wouldn't allow it.

"You're bluffing me. Your facts don't add up, Kyle. It doesn't matter that I can't see what's going on in that head of yours, because you speak the impossible. Whatever crafty Clint Eastwood shit you pulled to trick me, bravo. Well done. But the invisible chains that stayed my hand have been unlocked. I can hurt you now. Hurt you real good. I'm sorry to say that you've done nothing but delay the inevitable."

Horror raised a pointed finger up and pointed it at Kyle's chest, repeating his threatening stance from the bunker.
Kyle remained still. Self-sacrifice was hard the first time, but as Horror knew he had the ability to hurt Kyle, Kyle knew that the demon would fail. He wasn't scared or full of adrenaline; he was bored, as if he knew the outcome and wished the talking would stop and the demon would just finish the job. He supposed most martyrs didn't get a second chance. On top of it all, he had accomplished nothing.

Death part two was likely, but they were meant to battle, not debate.

"You're lucky you got me on a day when I have more on my mind then your demise, boy. This is mercy. Oh, it's going hurt something fierce, but it'll be quick. Master must be impatient. Consider it a taste of the eternal burn to come..."

A large jet of fire shot from the demon's fingers, as if on a zip line leading towards Kyle's chest.

Kyle's eyes remained open, his feet remained planted, and he felt nothing.

Nothing had changed. His skin was still wet with the perspiration of running that last few flights of stairs. Judith was still finding her feet. If he was experiencing the death that Absolute Horror promised, death felt like standing on a Las Vegas rooftop in the middle of the night. He wondered if that was sincerely poetic in its simplicity, or insanely bleak in its connotations.

Orange and yellow fire surrounded him, but there was no heat. His skin hadn't so much as tanned, let alone burned. The cocky grin that the demon wore like a badge had faded into a hateful grimace. Fire billowed from his hand, and not a lick of flame was affecting Kyle.

Kyle offered his own cocky smile, knowing it would cause further structural damage to that of the demon, and took a step towards Horror.

The demon doubled his efforts, using both hands, palms facing Kyle. The flame was catching debris and the air conditioning units on fire. The oxygen around them thinned due to the intensity of the flame.

Kyle took another step forward, and any pretenses of confidence in the demon broke.

"What the fuck are you?" the demon screamed, nothing but hate deepening his rasp,

"You ever watch baseball, Big Red?" Kyle smirked.

Horror ignored Kyle and opened his mouth, breathing blue flame to mingle with the orange and yellow from his hands. The whining sound of fire and the roar of his gut approached the volume of a jet engine. The natural glow in Horror's eyes intensified.

"Ten points ahead, bottom of the ninth, and your arrogance made you sloppy."

Kyle, so surrounded by flame he was little more than a bright silhouette, had stepped close enough to touch Horror, but was beaten to the punch. The demon slammed his hands onto Kyle's shoulders, gripping them tight, trying to shoot flame into the very depths of his soul.

To burn him up from the inside.

To Kyle, Horror's failure felt like a light shoulder rub.

Kyle looked at one of the demon's hands with bored passivity, staring into the fierce red eyes while his own shone a bright white color. A welcome change of pace, though Kyle felt cool as a penguin's pillow, he saw a lick of sweat break on Horror's forehead.

"Would you look at that? Your own fire is too hot for you, and to me it feels like breath of a newborn kitten," Kyle said, laughing in Horror's face.

Absolute Horror grunted. The flames were losing potency. Even though his eyes were glowing orbs without definition, Kyle saw something in them he was sure the demon had never known before that moment.

Fear.

"Back to baseball. Rule number one, and pay close attention! Never, and I mean never, take your eye off of the runner on first."

Kyle held his own hands, palms up, to chest level, eying them

"Rule number two, confidence is everything."

Kyle held his hands with the palms facing Horror's midsection.

"Rule number three, and I can't stress this one enough. Sometimes, deep in the ninth and close to losing, all it takes is one stolen base to change everything."

Kyle thrust his palms forward with little effort. The flames extinguished with a whoomph. Absolute Horror flew twenty feet through the air, a satellite dish stopping his trajectory with a crash.

Kyle wondered amongst the cheering voices in his own head if anybody would be missing one of the fights on pay-per-view tonight due to the damaged dish. Poor bastards would complain to the desk for hours about their lack of reception, not realizing a quick elevator ride and a couple flights of stairs would give them more entertainment than two barefoot men in a cage could ever offer.

Judith had gained both her footing and her bearing as Horror flew over her body. Her eyes grew wide, but did not follow the trajectory thatAbsolute Horror's body took. Her focus was on Kyle.

Healthy.

Grinning.

Alive.

Glowing? she thought

Judith wasted no time running towards him, ignoring disorientation and willing herself not to turn to jelly. She'd deal with the pain another day. All that mattered was that Kyle lived. She could smell him. Feel him. Taste him on the air. He pulled her in as fast as she ran to him. The Numb had returned, but it only numbed the pain. Her heart beat hard, making up for the beats it had missed while she thought he was dead. She smiled against his neck.

Kyle kissed the top of her head, knowing the honeymoon would have to wait.

The crashing sound of the satellite dish being thrown into a wall signaled the end of the time-out. Kyle would do everything in his power to explain and explore after he had taken care of business. There was still a monster to kill.

Kyle kissed her, quick and soft, on the lips.

"You're glowing, Kyle. Glowing!" Judith said. She wanted to tell him she loved him, but she was too surprised to say anything else.

Kyle pulled towards the charred units to their left for cover.

Again, Kyle stepped toward Absolute Horror. Each silent step was met by the infuriating stomp of the demon's foot.

The time for playing patient gunslinger was through. Whatever holy power Kyle's part in this fucked up wager offered him against flames, he was ready to explore the extent of it using Horror as a punching bag. He had a moment to wonder if that power would protect him from a punch before Horror, with blinding speed, rushed forward and threw a hard fist to the underside of Kyle's jaw, sending him through the air.

The crunch that echoed through Kyle's head answered his question.

Punches still hurt.

Kyle flew farther than Horror had. Over Judith's head and the units she hid behind, over the side of the roof into the open air beyond, with nowhere to go but down.

Horror pushed off after him and took flight, ready for war. His goal was no longer to save the one who fell, but to speed the ascent. To drive Kyle's body into the ground with enough force powder his bones. To give Vegas a show worth watching.

In short, Absolute Horror's goal was to send Kyle Thimall straight to hell.

crossfire

Vegas' streets had become crowded with onlookers. Phone calls had been made to the local police about a giant winged monster and somebody attempting suicide. Though most of the police were used to suicide calls in a city where people lost their lifes savings and meaning, the former complaint was a first for most of them. Upon arriving to the scene, many of the police had seen flashes from the roof, followed by crashing noises and what sounded like sounded like a jungle cat roaring in pain.

Fearing terrorism, the fire department and SWAT team had been dispatched. Surely the crowd had just been seeing things when they mentioned a flying person of any kind, but they had seen something. And whatever that something was, they would detain first and ask questions later.

Fifteen cars had pulled up, along with multiple fire engines and an ambulance, before a loud popping sound drew their attention skyward. Over the side of the roof, something luminescent began to fall. It looked like someone had covered a mannequin or a crash dummy in the liquid from a broken glow stick, the kind that the performers used to give their street shows extra oomph, but it was uniform, not splotchy. Too well covered. As far as any of them knew, mannequins didn't flail their limbs as if they were trying to flap invisible wings, either.

It was nothing but a jumper, over exaggerated by the lights and glamour of the strip. Every man and women in a uniform believed that very thing until the red beast reported by the scared faces in the crowd followed the figure over the side and swooped after the glowing figure with like a bird of prey.

Nobody screamed. Nobody breathed. The spotlights pointed upward, and cell phones were ready to film what would be remembered as the most amazing proof of alternate existence ever to be systematically criticized by the YouTube community.

They were transfixed, and could only look skyward as this glowing man and a red demon plummeted towards them. Finally, breaking himself from the trance, a lieutenant grabbed one of the megaphones from the passenger seat.

"Everybody, get back as far as you can! Be orderly, but be quick! This is a highly..."

The officer didn't get a chance to finish his warning of danger before the flying creature reached the velocity of the falling man, grabbed the man by the waist, picked up speed at an unfathomable rate, and drove the man downward and into the gravel, spraying chunks of asphalt and debris at everyone who surrounded the point of impact.

finality

Resolution, rather that meant rapture or respite, was at hand.

There was no more time to contemplate, muse, or analyze; none of it mattered to Kyle while he was lying in a crater of black top. The creature next to him was twice his size and ready to tear his head off and send it express to the Lord of fucking Evil.

The terrified faces surrounding the hole watched Kyle and his foe spitting up dirt like a frost bitten frozen dinner. They looked down on the two with the quiet, awe filled fear that Roman citizens once used looked down at their gladiators. It may have excited combatants in those ancient times long gone, but it didn't help Kyle.

They expected something phenomenal from him, hoping for the Vegas show to end all shows. They were desensitized to spectacle. Curiosity overpowered fear. Nobody realized how lucky they would be to survive the evening.

It depended on that fragile word.

Resolution.

Kyle would have to be careful not to injure anybody with his new power. Horror wouldn't be so merciful. He was amazed at how people would put their life on the line if it gave them a chance at more Twitter followers.

Horror was the first to stand, but Kyle knew that he wouldn't win this fight with strength or force. He'd have to use intuition and guile to his advantage. He kicked the demon above his saucer-like knee, amazed at the strength in his leg.

Horror roared, flame spewing skyward from his throat. All traces of peering eyes disappeared behind the lip of the hole, safety pushing curiosity off of its own metaphorical hotel ledge.

Kyle jumped to his feet and ran up the incline of the hole. When he was close enough, he jumped, grabbing on to a chunk of solid asphalt and hoisting himself up and out. No sooner was he vertical than Horror appeared in front of him, levitating as rage peppered his body language. Smoke poured from his nostrils.

Most of the crowd had realized the extent of the situation and had run for cover, but a few stood too close to avoid damage, as if they were directing an awesome action sequence. To remedy this, Horror swiped a large claw sideways, splitting a young man with a video phone in half without even touching him. The sight of the man's innards spilling from the halves and slithering down the crater was enough to deter the rest of the brave.

"You can't hurt me, demon. You didn't have the guts to kill me yourself in that warehouse, and now I understand why. I'm the Alan Rickman to your Bruce Willis! I have diplomatic immunity in the face of your hell fire!"

Kyle would have regretted it if he had never shown his pointless pop culture knowledge to a large group of people while evil stood inches away. He was VH1's holy savior, personified.

"You think because you're safe from fire that I can't find a way to tear you apart, boy? If what you say is true, than I have failed my master. Though I may suffer for that failure, that day won't be today! You won't stop me from delivering you as a consolation prize. I have more tricks up my sleeve than a rabbit in a trench coat."

To prove his point, the demon thrust his arms upward. A taxi cab behind him, the driver still asleep behind the wheel despite the commotion, jerked upward. Horror pointed his hands towards Kyle, and the cab hurtled in his direction. Kyle was able to duck and roll out of the way as the vehicle passed inches above his body, slamming into a row of newspaper machines and coming to a rest sideways against a wedding cake shop behind him. The driver was still asleep. He had obviously had a much better dealer in Sin City than Kyle had ever found.

But that was a different man, and a different life.

Horror used Kyle's distraction to fly at him. His feet inches above the ground, he glided at Kyle, grabbing him by the shirt collar and slamming his back into and through a telephone pole. The pole fell against the building next to the hotel, further spreading the crowd apart and destroying cars that cost more money than the people on the street had in their collective bank accounts.

Still holding Kyle by the shirt, the demon threw him upwards. Kyle flew half the height of the hotel before gravity began to slow him. He reached out for a handhold, but his hands only grazed the rails of a balcony. Horror had followed Kyle upwards, and as Kyle's ascent was close to reversing direction, he slammed into the back of Kyle's body at an angle and putting him through the rails, the window, and the very wall, coming to rest in a carpeted room devoid of furniture or occupants.

Kyle experienced no pain or injury. Since the demon was causing him little more than annoyance, and since he was basically invincible, he took a chance. It was the only way he would be able to end the fight.

Kyle was the first to his feet, and he sprinted towards the gaping hole in the wall they had just made. Before he reached the edge of the hole, he jumped, launching himself hard out of the opening and towards the opposite building. He sped through the air, turning his body as he flew and planted his feet into the wall of the opposite building.

Bricks and powder fell from the impact. Kyle bent at the knees and, using his unfathomable but handy new powers to defy physics, launched himself hard in the direction he had come, flying through the open hole and smashing into the midsection of Horror with a force that shook the building.

The impact drove the demon backwards and off of his feet. The pair crashed through three opposing walls before meeting fresh air. They separated as they fell, landing in a vacant alley. Kyle was able to land on his feet as Horror hit the ground, twisted, and bent in half under his weight. Kyle stood upright, looking at Horror with confident pity. He licked his finger and placed it on an imaginary burner, making a hissing sound between his tongue and teeth.

"You cocky son of a bitch," Horror said, spitting small pellets of flame out of his mouth as he stood. "You do realize that whatever is protecting you protects me from the very same. We're going to go to a stale mate, you and I. One that breeds legends and spreads destruction like California wildfire."

"So be it, if that's what it takes to keep Judith safe."

Horror laughed.

"You think her or anybody else will be safe? Where have you been the past few minutes, boy? Wherever we fight, destruction will follow. Humans aren't so lucky as to avoid destruction's wake for very long. People will die. Lives and livelihoods will be destroyed. My fires will burn, and even if you don't feel them, others will. Innocent and guilty alike will suffer. Including your dear Judith. Our stale mate will destroy the world, Kyle. We can do this forever, and no matter how many times you put me on my back, evil still wins in the end," Horror said, cutting his hands through the air and cutting a power line so that it swung towards Kyle to punctuate the statement.

A large section of the alley grew dark as the lights in the buildings lost power. The darkness was coupled by screaming and crying. Kyle grabbed the power line as it arced around his body and punched the sparking end through the ground, hoping he wasn't being too literal in grounding the live wire.

Kyle and Horror were left in the dark, the glow emitting from their respective bodies their only illumination.

Kyle realized Horror was right. How many people would need to die before he could defeat the monster? It didn't seem fair, but what about the week, or life, had been fair?

"Why don't you crawl back home to your master like a good little pup then, huh? You can't kill me. You have failed. You think he'll let you off that easy just because you took out a couple of gambling addicts and a phone pole? I'm worth jack shit if he doesn't get the power my failure represented!"

Kyle flung a fist forward, sending a white ball of energy at Horror. The ball clipped the demon's shoulder, ricocheting into the wall to his right and destroying an alley wall covered in amateur graffiti.

"Silly man. You'll follow me anywhere and everywhere to stop me, but I won't be stopped. If he can't have your head on a platter, then I'll give him the rest if the world in your stead. You can live alone amongst the dead that your decisions have wrought. You should have stayed dead, Kyle. With Sarah. Judith wouldn't have suffered. She would have been my fuck queen. I just wanted to run the place, Kyle. Upper management with all the perks! Instead? I'm going to burn the whole fucking place to the ground!"

"Over my dead body," Kyle said, the words echoing conviction in the ruins of the alley as he began to run at the demon, knowing he was the one who could end it, and knowing he would have to fight until he figured out how.

"That's what I'm hoping for," Horror said in a whisper, closing his eyes and clenching his fists.

The earth started to shake in rough fits and gasps. Kyle dropped to a knee as car alarms at the far end of the alley echoed to meet them. Something trickled onto the back of Kyle's neck, hard like hail. Brick and glass from the building tops took the place of small rubble and dust, slamming around Kyle and smashing to the alley floor. The fire escapes bent off of their bolts and crashed into the buildings across from them as jagged pieces of metal fell from them and joined the rest of the rubble on the ground. Twisted metal and broken rock surrounded them. The screams of the cars and the scared people of Vegas were creating an eerie soundtrack to their battle. Kyle knew the demon wouldn't stop destroying until one of them was dead.

Hating what he knew he had to do, and cursing fate and God and Lucifer and the rest of them in spite of knowing that he was on borrowed time, Kyle realized that he would have to die a second time, after all.

He was prepared. And he would accept it with a smile.

Kyle sent Judith a silent apology, wondering if he was to be the first man in history to earn the achievement for double martyrdom.

"Fine. What the hell do you want? If it's my unimportant fucking head you want, than take it. You won't have me at the expense of the world. The expense of Judith. Take me and go to hell, demon. I'll see you there, and we can continue this little tiff until fucking Revelations. Bet your ass that when nobody else is around to get hurt but you, there will be pain."

Kyle turned over the arm that bore the watch and noticed that a clasp had formed on the underside where once there was nothing. Kyle pinched the clasp and flung his arm to the side, letting the watch fly off of his wrist and hit a wall.

The glow that protected Kyle extinguished. The power was gone.

Kyle extended his hand to Horror.

"Shake on it, you big red bastard," Kyle said.

"You want to shake the hand of your destroyer? How very noble. But handshakes are unimportant and irrelevant. Your words are plenty, you little worm."

The quaking stopped. Absolute Horror ran towards Kyle. Something warm and salty flowed from his nose, breached his lips, and flavored his tongue.

Blood.

He was no longer wearing a holy suit of armor. He was just Kyle. Junkie. Cab Driver. Everything he had been except for scared. Not even as the demon stood inches away, enveloping Kyle with his dark shadow, his face a return to arrogance.

"If you ever break this deal, I will…" Kyle started.

"You won't do a damn thing. She'll be my queen and your sacrifice will go as unnoticed as an introvert holding open a door for an old lady. Pity you gave up. I was just getting started."

"You want so much to destroy. To maim. To rule. You know what the sad part is? You still have no free will. You're a slave, more than any of the people you killed on your path to finding me. You still answer to your master. You still answer to fate. That you deny both makes you weak. Whether your vacation lasts a millisecond or a millennia, you'll have to go home to daddy one day. And when you do? He's going to take off his belt and spank the fuck out of you. I wonder, what color does a red ass turns when it's beaten? Even if you kill me, you've still proven yourself the failure."

Kyle spat in his face. Horror wiped it away and growled.

"Your priest friend did the same thing before I killed him, Kyle. I burned him like I burned you, but he won't be coming back. He suffered, Kyle. Suffered plenty. As for you, I'm going to make you one promise that won't be broken. Trust me when I tell you that this is going to hurt. Really fucking bad..."

Absolute reared both of his fists up and above his head. Kyle leaned his own head forward, waiting for the inevitable. He was free of thoughts. Free of worry. Free of anything. He would take what the beast had to give and accept Fate's plan. He would haunt Judith until she could join him and do the same. She would want it that way.

Horror's hands smashed into Kyle's shoulders. Kyle's legs buckled underneath him, and he was driven to his knees. Something broke, but the cracking noise he heard wasn't his shoulder blades. It was the demon's hands.

Kyle looked up to see the demons hands, bent at awkward angles and useless. Horror howled in pain, causing more debris to fall from the sky, before coming at Kyle again. Horror reared back and kicked, as hard as he could muster, at Kyle's face. Kyle felt the pressure, and was shoved backwards by the force, but the demon's inverting knee cap was the only thing that broke.

Red bone splintered from the back of Horror's leg. The demon stumbled, pain radiating through his body. The demon had never known pain, and he used it as most powered by wrath do; as adrenaline. He popped his leg back into place, the bone and kneecap slicing through his thick red skin. He half-ran/half-hobbled at Kyle, his head bent downward like a bull, horns ready to gore him through.

The horns hit Kyle square in the chest. Kyle grasped his hands around them as they lifted him up and drove him back and against a wall. Once Kyle's body offered resistance with a wall at his back, the horns snapped off in his hands. Horror grabbed his head and screamed, thick red smoke bellowing from his throat.

"Why can't I kill you?" Horror screamed, dropping to his own knees as his skin began to blacken.

"Because I would let you," Kyle replied.

Kyle dropped the horns and bent towards Absolute Horror. He finished off the demon not with a punch or a kick, but with a kiss to the forehead. Gandhi would have been proud.

Horror's skin began to crack and peel from his body. The skin pieces floated in the red smoke, like debris in a twister, before turning to ash. In his last moments, the demon beat his broken fists into Kyle's chest without strength. Muscle pushed its way out from the cracking skin, a viscous liquid the color of lava flowing in place of blood, causing the ground to sizzle and burn as it dropped. His wings flapped behind him, trying to leave his body before they too were destroyed. The webbing had fallen away in thin clumps. All that remained of them were the hollowed bones, splintering apart with each flap.

As the last of the skin peeled away, the demon burst into flames. The flames worked quick, burning through muscle and bone, drowning out the roar of screams with the roar of flames. Within seconds, all that remained was a pile of ash at Kyle's feet.

For a moment, everything was still.

He had won.

As her voice called his name, the pain hit him all at once.

"Kyle!"

He turned his head to look, his vision blurry and his body screaming in new found agony with every movement. The voice moved towards him, the few emergency lights that were able to glow leading the way, but Kyle was too busy losing his grip on reality to care.

Was it an angel? Another demon? Was the only reward for his sacrifice to be living long enough to see the demon die?

He realized he could accept that.

The shape grew more focused, calling his name all the while. When it reached him, he saw that it was no angel to take him through the gates. Nor a demon to lead him to the throne.

"Kyle, baby, are you ok? Where is that big red fuck? I'm going to kill him for hurting you!"

"Judith," Kyle said with a whisper and a smile, before collapsing into the wall.

Judith caught him as he slumped down, guiding him along into a sitting position and joining him there. Cradling his head. Kissing his hair. Making sure that he didn't stop breathing even for a second.

As she looked absently at the damage around the alley way, hating that Kyle had been a part of the post-apocalyptic scene while she had spent the whole time fighting through crowds and darkness to find him, her eyes grazed across the pile of ash near their sprawled out feet. A piece of yellow paper stuck out from the top.

Judith took one arm from around Kyle for the briefest moment to pick it out of the ashes.

It was an envelope addressed to Kyle and Judith. She opened the envelope and pulled out a small piece of parchment.

Blank.

She turned it over to find a message that covered her skin in goose bumps.

Kyle and Judith,
Evil begets evil. Wrath destroys wrath. Love conquers all.
        -The "G" Man

Judith tucked the note into Kyle's breast pocket and put her arm back around him. He snored softly. She kissed his hair and his face, creating a path to his lips as she would do for the rest of their lives.

"I love you, Kyle. You rest for a moment, and then we'll go home. Wherever that is," she whispered into his ear.

Amongst the sirens and the car alarms, the screams and destruction, the darkness and the rapture, she fell asleep holding her savior.

Her lover.

Her home.

Her forever.

Evil had been vanquished.

On the seventh day, Kyle Thimall saved the world.

from the journal of leon grebowski

All of these musings. Writings to myself and nobody in particular. Was it God I hoped to read over my shoulder? To answer my questions, as if I was deserving of such an honor, and lead me down the path I had strayed from? A path so many had been far worse removed from, and that some never found at all? Yes. That is exactly what I wanted. As a servant, I demanded face time with He I serviced. And when I received none, I strove to be for others what he had never been for me. At least not in a capacity that I could accept and digest.

My blindness was cured through Him. I saw a hilarious movie a few nights ago. I feel shame in how filthy it turned out to be, but I couldn't look away. In it, a character said "Sometimes we just need someone to show us what we can't see for ourselves. Then, we're changed forever."

The blindfold was ripped away because of a shotgun and two strangers, and I am forever changed and humbled by my encounter with them. And guilty. Shamed far more for my transgressions than because of watching a movie with cursing and breasts.

Two who had no real interest in the path I was supposed to lead others down were facing things that I had imagined long ago to be myth and scare tactic. Facing them without hesitation. Walking blindly into the very presence of possible evil and demise for what? Not out of faith. Nor for any real repentance. One did it following another, to escape from a life she knew to be wrong in exchange for hope. The hope that exuded from the other, however subconsciously. And the other? He did it because he felt he had no other option. His entire being and soul had been ripped out, and he accepted an offer than was never really a choice with the full intention of seeing it through. Not for God or the Devil, but out of love. The very love that caused him so much pain.

I say they walked in blind, but not blinded by a strip of self-imposed cloth. They were blinded by the very bonds that bind us together, faith or no faith. Hope. Love. These two things, so overlooked and cheapened by the world today, are what drive us. What make us human. What make us serve a higher purpose, whatever or whomever that might be. Though my life has been aimed at helping, belief or no, and they have spent portions of their lives sinning in ways that I couldn't begin to explain, I feel they will meet Him long before I ever do.

They had nothing at all, have nothing still, and they still fight forward. I am a privileged man who turned tail on his very soul. The devil need not bring me a contract, for I fear my very pride signed that blood clause for me.

Did Kyle save me? Only God can tell. I will use all of the energy my body possesses to ensure that I can ask him one day.

Forgive me Father, for I was wrong.

Dead wrong.

L.G.

CHAPTER 46

a celestial sense of humor

A little more than nine months later…

The last brick sat, dusty and welcoming, next a bucket of mortar. The last brick that mattered to the protagonist, anyway. St. Christopher's church stood before Judith and Kyle, sunlight turning the stained glass into glistening stills of lives being lived and adventures long over.

They decided to rebuild in a better town. They found a priest who reminded them of Leon to run the church. Jonas' inheritance funded the construction. After learning the truth of Jonas' sacrifice, all had been forgiven.

St. Christopher's was destroyed by an evil that the world had avoided. Kyle hoped the church would help keep it from becoming a repetitive occurrence.

"This is it," Judith said.

Judith cradled baby Samuel in her arms, consummated the night that Kyle had won his own personal war.

Kyle was with his family, where he belonged.

God had kept His promise.

"After so much work, I'm not sure how to finish this. What's next?"

"I'm voting on moving somewhere nice. Our little Sammy needs to grow up strong, healthy, and far away from the influence of the damned. The usual parental concerns."

"I have a better idea," the man in the glasses said.

Kyle turned to see God leaning against a tree in the courtyard.

"Oh, not again," Kyle exhaled.

"I'm not here to take you from the gift you were promised. Not this second, anyway. This entire ordeal was my doing, I wanted to give you my sincere gratitude. It's hard being the new guy and you made the transition worth the trouble."

God reached his hand to Kyle. Kyle shook it tentatively.

"I appreciate all you've done."

"What do you mean, not this second?" Judith said.

"Well, you never know. You've been an excellent crusader! I might need help smiting a demon or two. Smacking down an evil doer.

Preventing the end of the world. Plenty of unfulfilled prophecies of disaster left on the books! If nothing else, you have become lifelong consultants for how to save the world. You are the world's first super hero, my boy."

"Har-dee-har," Kyle said.

"Really though, thank you. Great job on the church. Leon would be proud. So would Jonas. Now how does happily ever after sound?"

"Thanks Big guy."

God laughed.

"I'll let it slide this once."

God bent down and kissed Judith's forehead, then Samuel's. The baby's head glowed and he cooed.

"What was that?" Judith asked.

"A gift, my dear. Nothing more. Kyle?"

"Yes God?"

"I'll be seeing you," He said. He turned and walked away, whistling out loud. With each step he became more evanescent until he had disappeared completely.

"I was afraid of that."

St. Christopher's was rebuilt.

Balance had been restored.

Kyle and Judith lived in complacent happiness until their story reached finality.

Baby Samuel's story, as yet untainted by pendulum of emotions or consciousness, began on day number eight.

SIN

I am a sinner

I couldn't be happier

I am my own God

to be continued...

Captain Franklin Fogg was trying to get the webcam on his computer to work when the video chat program rang like a telephone. The clock on the bottom corner of his computer screen read ten-thirty. The doctor was punctual, if nothing else.

Doctor Lynn Erickson had called earlier in the evening. He had been on his way to see The Capitals, a game he had been looking forward to for weeks. The politics of being a police captain were complicated and fragile and did little to cure his fits of nostalgia. The Caps, on the other hand, always made him smile.

Doctor Erickson spent more time trying to determine whether or not he was a real cop than she did explaining what she needed. Frank was patient, knowing his alliterative name made him sound more like a magician more than a police captain. The call must have been important, as there were only two ways to get his personal cell number: she was the beautiful stalker he had been wishing for every birthday since he was fifteen, or whatever she was calling about was important enough for someone at the station to give it to her.

Frank knew it would always be the latter, but he would never grow up to the point where he lost hope. She sounded cute. Stranger things had happened.

Doctor Erickson explained that she had found a flash drive and a note on one of her examination tables when she had arrived at work. The note contained his name and phone number. The flash drive contained security footage. The second she stuttered over the word footage, Frank was prepared to give up hockey night and head back to the station.

Instead, she told him that the best way to explain to him why she had tried the number on the note was to show him. Since she lived in Las Vegas, it was impossible to do so in person.

Frank had to stifle the small feeling of disappointment that tried to sneak in.

"Best to do it when it slows down," Doctor Erickson had said. "I know neither of us work in professions with set hours of operation, but I get off of work at ten and I'm not on call tonight. Would ten-thirty work?"

Frank had agreed, happy that he wouldn't miss the game and frustrated that curiosity would keep him from giving it his full attention.

Frank clicked the button to accept the call, and a young, stern face filled his screen. Pity she hadn't been a stalker. She was beautiful.

"Evening, Doctor," he said.

"Evening, Captain. Shame that I can't see you. Feels a little like I'm being catfished, you know?" she said, sounding impatient and looking apprehensive.

"The video isn't playing. Not sure why," he replied.

"Can you see the red light?"

"What red light?"

"It isn't plugged in, Captain," she replied in lieu of an answer.

Pulling on the cord of his computer, he realized she was right and smacked himself on the forehead before plugging it in. No reason for the pretty doctor to see his embarrassment.

The red light on the camera came on and he saw his own face fill a tiny box in the lower corner of the screen. The look of relief on her face made his spine icy. It was too transformative to just express finding out he was, for sure, a cop. It looked more like she was relieved that he wasn't the monster under the bed. It made Frank question rather or not he wanted to see what she had to show him.

"In a few moments, I am going to let the video play on share mode so that we both can watch," she began. "If you can tell me that you believe this video is a hoax with complete honesty, I may be able to sleep this month. I know technology has come a long way, but I work around dead bodies for a living and this made me want to hide underneath a blanket in a locked, padded room."

"What is it that has you so frightened, Doc?" he asked, more than a little concerned for the both of them.

Her face disappeared, replaced by a black screen, as she gave her answer.

"You know how people say that the greatest trick the devil ever did was to convince the world he didn't exist?"

"I've heard that a time or two before, sure," Frank replied.

For a moment, she didn't say anything. With the screen black, he was worried the connection had dropped. When she did reply, her voice was so quiet that he had to lean in close to the speaker to hear it.

"After watching this video, I'm sure that whoever or whatever was able to pull off that kind of lie was the opening act."

She hit play.

There was a man in a white coat walking around three morgue tables. To the side, another man stood. He was tall, thin, and so pale the white of the wall would have camouflaged him had the image not been in a high definition.

"The doctor in the coat is Steve Jenkins," Doctor Erickson said.

"And the slender guy?" Frank asked.

She said nothing.

Three corpses lay on the three steel tables. Below the cold clavicles and white fabric of each hood they wore naught but rigor mortis and toe tags.

The slender man watched as the nervous coroner paced around the tables, stopping to make a slight adjustment to a corpse. A finger nudged an inch to the left. A foot rotated a few degrees inward. Not once did he blemish the skin. He stilled his hands before each adjustment as a painter would before a brush stroke, though his nerves never remained still for long.

"Is it cold or nerves?" Frank asked, referring to the twitchiness of the doctor on screen.

"He has a condition of the nerves, but his mental aptitude is off of the charts. He is one the rare few who is accepted despite the handicaps," she replied.

The bottom left of the screen turned black for a moment, and a deep, guttural noise that sounded like an air compressor grew in volume from just off camera.

Up until this point on the recording, I thought it was a hidden camera prank or an odd test being proctored by the skinny one.

The sounds of the air compressor grew louder, and Frank noticed that little red dots were appearing on the floor and wall. When the red, horned beast walked into frame, blood spraying outward with each wounded breath, Dr. Erickson's nervous and cryptic warnings hit him like an adrenaline shot to the chest.

"What the hell is that?"

"Keep watching," she said.

****

The beast gave wide birth to the work of the slender man and the doctor. Patience lined his face. His breathing and coughing, while audible, did nothing to distract the doctor, even while spraying the white room with fresh droplets of blood. The drops produced by the coughing were the size of marbles.

When the large red beast walked into the room, charred flesh smelling of burning trash and old infection, neither of them paid him any mind. The beast let out deep, heavy breaths, blood spraying the clean linoleum with each exhale, but he dared not interrupt. Everything had to be perfect. If he died before he could speak, he would have to wait a little longer. He'd died before. Monsters never stayed dead.

Patient and quiet, the beast joined the observation. For a time, the air filled with the bored tension of the immortal.

The slender man watched.

The doctor of death worked.

Absolute Horror breathed.

After a time, the doctor broke the silence. His weary voice expressed no hint of worry or excitement. Only finality.

"We are ready," he said.

The slender man raised a lazy finger towards the coroner. His eyes flashed pity. It was no matter to the coroner, who had closed his own eyes. The slender man moved across the morgue floor without taking a step.

As the slender man closed in on the coroner, the pointed finger was joined by its siblings. When the slender man's hand reached the coroner's chest, it was no longer a lazy finger, but a vicious claw pushing through flesh and bone. The coroner did not scream. Not once.

Even as the slender man withdrew the still beating heart from the dying doctor's chest, no blood spilled.

The slender man let the coroner slump to the ground as he moved towards the head of the three tables. Over each masked face, he squeezed blood from the beating heart over the covered mouths of the dead. The blood did not splatter or drip as the masked faces absorbed the liquid like paper towels. Once the three corpses had fed, the slender man tossed the heart, smaller but still beating, to the red beast with a lazy flick of the wrist.

Absolute Horror caught the heart and pushed the entire thing into his mouth in one swift motion. He worried it with slow, careful chewing. Every so often, the heart would beat and his cheek would move in response. With every stolen beat of the heart, his breathing eased. Still, it was not time to interrupt.

Without ceremony or grandeur, the slender man clasped his hands together and said "Wake up". The corpses rose to right angles with synchronicity that made the red beast uncomfortable. Recent events had instilled a permanent sense of dread towards dead human's who came back to life.

The slender man, aware and uncaring of Absolute Horror's awe, made his way to the foot of the tables. Though his movement did not break the silence, the wet smacking of the cloth against skin, caused by the corpse's newfound breath, joined the beast's own breathing in what sounded like a chorus of iron lungs.

The doctor lay dying, his body still for the first time in his life. It was forty-two seconds before darkness stole him, but they were the happiest forty-two seconds of his life.

"Good morning, class. Or should I say good mourning?" the slender man paused. He looked towards the doctor for a moment without of ounce of empathy present in his features.

The corpse's heads followed the slender man's own, separate pieces of the same monster.

"Our doctor has given much to bring you three to me. You perfect, tortured three. The children of the most hypocritical of charlatans cast aside and sacrificed so that the ignorant and rotten would have a few more precious moments of breath. You were cast aside, but I will fulfill the broken promises you were denied."

Absolute Horror lurched towards the three tables with drunk, heavy steps, knocking over formaldehyde bottles and medical instruments with no apology. The slender man and his mirrors watched, knowing Horror was punctuating what was to be said, not interrupting what had been.

With a whimpering roar that sang of finality, the beast fell forward. His head rested inches from the splayed legs of the dead doctor. The slender man reached towards Horror and began to close his fingers into a tight fist. For the first time, there was emotion in the eyes of the slender man.

Excitement.

Horror's body began to tremble, the lines and shadows of his form losing and returning to focus in bursts. The slender man's fist closed so tight that his hand should have been reddening. Instead, it grew more pale with the pressure.

The corpses, still watching through bloody hoods, began a whisper. Fast words flew from their lips, muffled by the bags. Horror's body began to hover above the floor as the slender man began to open his fist again. Once his palm was flat, Horror opened his eyes and sucked in his final breath and spoke his final words.

"Do it now," Absolute Horror said.

The slender man snapped his fingers, and it was done.

There was a loud, echoing pop. For a moment, where Horror's body had hovered, the shape of him remained in blood. It was the most beautiful thing the slender man had ever seen, and he had existed for longer than time had a name.

When the blood fell, it covered both the dead doctor and the floor. The doctor looked to be wearing a suit of thick red latex. Though the room was large, the floor was covered within seconds. The contrast of red and white was royal in its cleanliness.

Once the deluge of blood calmed, the only piece of Horror that remained was his large black heart. Even without a host, it pumped. With each pump, the blood level in the room rose. The slender man stood atop the little red sea, the white and red kissing but never embracing, rising higher with the each pump.

"Wake up," said the slender man.

The doctor's eyes opened. His eyes, as white as the slender man's skin and without iris and pupil, were nonetheless aware. Without moving his head, the doctor grabbed the black demon's heart and shoved it into the hole where his own had once been.

A sucking sound, like a child trying to taste the last of the liquid at the bottom of a cup of chocolate milk, filled the room. The blood began to flow downward from the top of the doctor's head and away from the white walls. The clean hair underneath showed not a drop of leftover blood, nor did any of the exposed linoleum. The sucking sound grew louder, and the blood moved faster, every drop in the room attempting to reunite with the familiar heart in the new body.

Once the sucking became a slurp, and the blood was flowing through the resurrected doctor's veins, there was no evidence left in the room or on his body save for the hole in his shirt. The skin underneath was unscarred and porcelain white. Just like the slender man.

The sheets over the corpses were damp and red with what remained of Absolute Horror's blood. The cloth in front of their mouths moved in tandem as they whispered words that had gained clarity.

…klthml…klthml…klthml…

"Oh, look. You've woken up the children," said the slender man.

The doctor got to his feet. He examined his body, pleased with the gift the slender man had given him.

"I failed to destroy the vessel of the uncertain child," the doctor said.

"That's why true evil believes in contingency. The poor idiot thinks he took you out with a kiss to the forehead. Mel Brooks is the only human worth half of a damn. Good truly is dumb."

…klthml…klthml…klthml…

"True, but we were arrogant. He was strong. We underestimated the deal," the doctor said.

"Well, we make mistakes to find our weaknesses. Now that this farce of a deal has concluded we can come out to play. Are you strong enough to lead?"

"I will be. Did you find three worthy of the reigns?"

"You have no idea," the slender man said. His smile was so wide that the corners of his mouth touched his ears, though his skin did not wrinkle or bulge. His teeth were as white as his skin and sharper than his wit.

"Shall I take my sword, then?"

"Not this time. You will take back your true name, Moloch. With it comes a promotion. We are done hiding."

The slender man reached to his left and plucked a hand scythe, black as ebony, from the air. He handed it to the doctor. As soon as the weapon touched his hand, Moloch's skin turned a shade of pale, parchment yellow. Black markings covered his skin giving the faint impression of the bones beneath them. A splotchy birthmark-like stain appeared on his face in the likeness of a skull.

"Moloch, you have been chosen for the mantel of Death. You gave up your demonic namesake to plant the seeds of victory. Your time as Absolute Horror has come to an end. You will carry the scythe and reap the souls of men, pious and wicked alike. Do you accept your charge?" the slender man asked.

"I do," Moloch replied

"Have fun with it, Moloch! This will be a war for the ages. They don't even know we're coming! Are you ready to meet the team?"

"Abso-fucking-lutely," Moloch said. The voice of the doctor was gone, replaced by a deep, feral baritone.

..kilthimal…kilthimal…kilthimal…

The slender man motioned his hand towards the corpse farthest from him. The crimson sheet shriveled and lost color and weight. It turned thin as a sheet of dark tracing paper, before disappearing into the skin of the corpse. The skin of the corpse was left as black as ebony. His skin pulled tight against the bones. His eyes were the off-milk color of cataracts.

"You have been chosen for the mantel of Famine. In life, you starved those close to you of love and caused suffering with judgments. You will carry the gavel and pass judgment upon those who are unworthy. Do you accept your charge?"

His whispering stopped. His voice was raspy and choked.

"I do," said Famine, the man once known as Jonas McMillan.

A large wooden gavel, like those used in carnival games and made of a black wood stained by blood and decay, appeared in the hands of Famine.

The whispering was carried on by two dead voices.

…klethimal…klethimal…

The slender man motioned towards the middle corpse. The crimson sheet melted over the corpse beneath it, taking on the color and consistency of thick, fresh blood. The corpse beneath was female. The blood clung to it, a second skin made of wet crimson. Her black eyes were the only parts of her not touched by blood.

"You have been chosen for the mantel of War. In life, maimed and tortured without question. You will carry the sword to strategize and bring suffering without mercy upon our enemies. Do you accept your charge?"

Her whispering stopped. Her voice was muffled and gargled, but no blood spat from her lips as she spoke.

"I do," said War, the woman once known as Molly Levesque.

A large sword flowed from within the bloody liquid of her left hand and turned solid once her hand wrapped around the hilt. The blood flowed back to her body, leaving behind a sword that appeared to be made of red glass. A light red flame shimmered over the surface of the blade.

One whisper remained.

…kylethimall…

"Why is it saying his name?" asked Moloch.

"Quiet now, or you will ruin the surprise," replied the slender man.

The final corpse, close enough for the slender man to touch, received special care. The slender man reached out and pulled the sheet off of the corpse himself. What remained of the corpse was bone, rotting flesh, and tufts of dry, dirty hair.

The slender man brought the head of the corpse to his lips.

"With a kiss, we feigned defeat. With another, we guarantee victory," the slender man said. He kissed the head of the corpse and the whispering began to gain clarity.

"My special girl," said the slender man. He stroked the skull of the corpse as fresh flesh and blond hair overtook the decay.

"Why is Pestilence growing healthier?" Moloch asked.

"This world has poisoned itself, Moloch. We have no use for a rider of Pestilence."

The corpse had become a beautiful young women.

"Kill them all. Kill them all." She repeated.

"Yes, my dear. My horsemen. You will kill them all. But your job is special."

The slender man pulled a white bow and quiver from beneath his own robes and handed them to the woman. Her body back to health, she was perfect.

"You will carry the bow to destroy our greatest of threats. Without you, none of this is possible."

"Kill them all. Kill them all."

"Yes, but who will you kill first my dear?" the slender man asked.

With a slight change of inflection and an extra syllable, her whispering changed.

"Kill thim all. Kill Thimall. Kill Kyle Thimall. Kyle Thimall."

A new whispering chant began.

Kyle Thimall...Kill Them All...Kyle Thimall...Kill Them All...

"Oh, fantastic," proclaimed Moloch. The realization of the moment washing over him.

"Horsemen must choose to take the mantel willingly, as you know." The slender man spoke to Moloch, but never took his eyes off of the woman before him. "Our precious Conquest has made her choice. I can see it in those brand new baby blues of hers. Do you know why she would do that, Moloch?"

"Same as the rest of them, I guess. To get out of hell."

"You are half right. She belongs in heaven. Her hell didn't start until the day you killed Kyle Thimall. On that day, Kyle Thimall met God and was given a choice."

At the mention of Kyle's name, the woman's whispering grew softer. Her face took on an expression of sorrow. She dropped her gaze away from the slender man, who tilted her chin back up so that she looked him in the eye.

"God paraded a visage, a poor imitation, in front of Kyle and he barely knew the difference. The promises he made in life were forgotten because he heard the words he wanted to hear. A glorified mannequin with a pulse took away his guilt and he was grateful for it. A long time ago, he promised you forever, my dear. He promised you the world. Yet when given the choice, he let a parlor trick break his promises! When given the choice, he chose her!"

Tears fell from the woman's eyes, but there was no sorrow left in them. All that remained was hatred, anger, and hurt. The slender man dropped his hand from her chin and backed away. Her whispering had turned vicious, each syllable dripping with pain.

"You have been chosen for the mantel of Conquest. In life, you were pure. You were loved by prideful charlatan. You were the tragic victim of sloth. You were forgotten thanks to lust. You were replaced by a harlot, a glutton for attention and chaos, before you had been dead a decade. Your vows were shit on with greed. You are to be the envy of heaven and hell alike. I offer you the promise of wrath, and I do not break my promises. You will kill them all. You will bring victory to our conquest. Do you accept?"

Her whispering stopped. Her voice was clear, beautiful and strong.

"I do," said Conquest, the woman once known as Sarah Thimall.